ENLIGHTENMENT AND
THE DEATH OF MICHAEL MOUSE

enlightenment and the death of michael mouse

HOWARD BAKER

MAINSTREAM
PUBLISHING

EDINBURGH AND LONDON

First published in Great Britain in 2001 by
MAINSTREAM PUBLISHING COMPANY (EDINBURGH) LTD
7 Albany Street
Edinburgh EH1 3UG

ISBN 1 84018 460 4

A catalogue record for this book is available from the British Library

Typeset in Garamond
Printed and bound in Great Britain by Cox & Wyman Ltd

Who knoweth it exhaustless, self-sustained
Immortal, indestructible – shall such
Say, 'I have killed a man, or caused to kill'?
Bhagavadgita

PART I

ONE

I remember well the shoes I wore that night in the Crown and Anchor: bleu d'azur suede loafers with tassels, fringe and leather soles; expensive but relegated to second-best now that the novelty had worn off. Bleu d'azur, I ask you, but that's what it said on the box – the sort of shoes you'd wear for a Sunday lunch drink rather than a pulling night.

And the jeans, battered 501s, only ever worn during the day, never at night when you had to get out there and strut your stuff, let the world know that you weren't to be taken too lightly. The shirt I don't remember (a black knitted-silk polo shirt from Cecil Gee?) but that's because the blood of Michael Mouse had only splashed up as far as my thigh.

I was talking to Waller at the bar where we'd been sitting since opening-time waiting for the boys to come in, but it was one of those nights when for some reason or other everyone failed to make it. I knew that Stillson wouldn't be there because he was seeing a girl, and Frankie was keeping low because the police wanted to question him about something – but the others? As I say, it was one of those nights.

Waller was dangerously bored, in that trouble-making mood that usually meant someone was going to get hurt. 'It's nearly ten, let's get out of here before I set light to the place – how about the Bali Hai? That bird from Fulham might be there.'

Which meant travelling to the other side of London, and I couldn't be bothered. And London was beginning to get on my nerves. I suggested the Flamingo.

Waller grimaced. 'All that black stuff? No, I fancy something smooth, something nice and easy-going with plenty of women.'

'What, dressed like this?' I looked down.

'Go home and change. It'll only take five minutes. I'll borrow Billy's car.'

But I wasn't in the mood for pressing suit trousers, polishing shoes, ironing shirts, bathing, shaving, finding pairs of socks – it'd be eleven before I was ready. 'No, I'm just going to sit here and get pissed. Anyway, little Sandy and her mate might come in.'

Waller laughed. 'Yeh – what's her name – Shirley. I got real bad blanket burns the last time I gave her a seeing-to, both my knees had the skin burnt off 'em.'

'You lying toe-rag – if anyone's a virgin she is.' I couldn't see it somehow – I'd tried for weeks, but hadn't got anywhere.

'Virgin! Are you kidding? She's a right little goer. You should have seen her: I had her on the end of my dick while I was dancing around the bedroom wearing her old lady's pink dressing gown and fluffy slippers for a laugh – and her hairnet.' He chuckled into his beer.

'You're a lying bastard, Waller.'

He laughed again. 'Straight up. I have definitely given that one. Ask her. If she comes in ask her about the champagne cork.'

There's something disturbing about someone else getting there first, especially when you think that butter wouldn't melt in the girl's mouth. And Waller was depraved, a sex monster without a conscience, the proud owner of a performing dick renowned for its after-hours antics in the pub. Even the Christmas turkey wasn't safe. Neither was he averse to poking the thing in your ear for a laugh when you weren't looking, or dipping it in your beer, which was why we always stood at the bar when he was around rather than sit down at a table, but even then he'd act the queen and rub up against your leg just to provoke anyone who didn't know the score.

To think that he'd shagged Shirley Brown, quiet little Shirley. No, I can't believe it – he's lying.

As I was trying to work out the implications of the champagne cork a stranger walked unaccompanied into the pub. Nobody minded too much during the day, it was open house, but at night strangers were expected to be escorted by someone known to the regulars – and this one was alone and flash.

'Light and bitter, guvnor,' he said, looking confidently around. I could see Harry the landlord looking down his nose as he pumped bitter into the glass.

Waller gave me a nudge. 'Clock Michael Mouse.' The stranger had large, round protruding ears. 'He's a bit too flash for ears like that.'

'Ask him if he wants any cheese.'

Waller caught Harry's eye. 'You'd better put your cheese biscuits under lock and key Harry.'

Harry cottoned on and looked down, trying to hide a smile.

Ignoring everybody Michael Mouse paid for the drink and took a sip; then he turned to face us. 'I know you, don't I?' he asked, looking at me. He took another sip from his glass.

Cheeky bastard – he was either stupid or really hard. 'I don't think so,' I said, waiting for him to say otherwise.

'You know fuck all,' said Waller.

He must have been about the same age or maybe a bit older than us, in his early twenties I guess, and was well dressed in an understated sort of way – basket-weave shoes, maroon mohair strides and a cream fine-knit wool shirt with a maroon-edged collar and bone buttons – but he wasn't the real McCoy. Anyone could see he was out of his class, the sort of poser who waited until a fashion was well-established and safe before kitting himself out with the best he could afford. Then it was all down to parading about and saying 'Look at me.'

'No, no, I mean I've seen you about. Don't you go to Mister Smith's?' He'd realised the gravity of his mistake and was beginning to look slightly unnerved.

'He's a nosy fucker, ain't he?' Waller was trying to wind me up. I knew that, so I tried to defuse it, or should I say, give the fellow a chance, after all, he was no threat. For a start he was skinny, definitely wasn't Old Bill – you can tell them a mile away – and had probably strayed into the pub by mistake. Maybe he'd had a row with his girl, or had just got off the bus and wanted a drink. Thirsty and innocent. The problem was, Waller was feeling mean, and so was I.

'D'you live round here, Michael?' I asked.

He ignored the nickname. 'Yeh, on the other side of the estate, Buckingham Drive.'

'So what are you doing in here? You're trespassing. You should be in the George or the Wellington.'

He laughed nervously and looked to Harry for support. 'It's a free world. Why shouldn't I come in here?'

But Harry winced and walked away.

If ever I'd heard a question that demanded a violent response, it was that, but his little-boy-lost face stalled an immediate reaction. Waller looked at me. 'He's a flash git, ain't he? What do you reckon?'

'So what's your game, then?' I asked.

'What do you mean?'

Waller stared at him. 'I reckon he's an earwig and needs a spank.'

'Look, you've got it all wrong . . .' He suddenly looked alarmed, took a gulp of beer, said he wasn't looking for trouble, and turned to go. But Waller wasn't satisfied and shouted a warning to him as he reached the door. 'And stay away. If I see you in here again I'll cut your ears off.'

And that might have been the end of it, but Michael Mouse had to murmur 'Bollocks' as he left, as a sort of face-saver I suppose. Whatever, Waller was after him, and I followed.

He'd already covered a hundred yards in the darkness by the time we were outside, trying to walk fast without looking scared. Following silently until he crossed the road into a side turning leading to an estate of houses, we broke into a trot and caught up with him.

'Something to say?' I asked, stepping in front.

He was frightened now. Eyes wide, he kept glancing about, hoping someone would happen along, but the street stayed empty. Not even a car passed.

'No, look, I'm sorry, but . . .'

He never had time to finish. Waller caught him with a glancing blow to the side of the face. 'Leave me alone!' he yelled, and made a dash down the garden path of the nearest house, but as he reached the door we were on him, kicking and punching as he hammered on the knocker screaming for help. From the corner of my eye I saw a curtain twitch, but no one came out.

Back outside the Crown and Anchor it was Waller who first noticed the blood. 'Look at this,' he whined indignantly. 'He's bled all over me.'

The front door went.

I was hanging a favourite mohair suit, an oyster Tonik, in the wardrobe as Mother came home from the factory where she'd once, quite innocently and with my best interests at heart, tried to get me a job on the grounds that the pay could be worse. I'd laughed in her face.

Now what sort of welcome would I get? More than a year had passed since I'd last stepped inside the neat little house where she lived with the old man.

Hearing nothing, I coughed and shuffled about on the beige carpet tiles to let her know the house wasn't empty, but surely she'd noticed the heavy rucksack leaning up against her new bamboo wallpaper in the hall?

A hesitation, then movement from below.

'Tommy! Is that you?'

'Yeh,' I replied, as casually as possible.

'What are *you* doing home?' As if it could be anyone else.

'Putting some of my gear in the wardrobe.' I could hear her coming up the stairs.

She appeared in the doorway, pleased to see me but ready for a fight. 'What do you mean "putting your gear in the wardrobe"? You can't just walk in and out as it pleases you, you know. I've told you before.'

Where I'm concerned, my parents have little room for diplomacy or discretion; any attempt at tact would be taken as a sign of weakness. And as for twelve months – it might just as well have been twelve minutes. Or seconds.

'Don't start.' I could feel the same anger rising as if it had been biding its time all year since our last encounter, and it made me mad to think I was already rising to the bait. Why always the inquisition and distrust, the need to control? I know it was their house, but I was family after all.

'Don't you tell me not to start,' she said, pouting her lips and frowning, thrusting her carefully made-up face towards mine. Why she went to so much trouble to exaggerate her appearance was beyond me and that's the way I wanted it to stay – but it seemed absurd under the circumstances, absurd as an assembler of someone else's electrical appliances. There were appearances to maintain, and the social requirements of her workmates to stick to, I knew that, but we were still a generation and a million miles apart.

'Well . . .' I looked down my nose, 'I'm home five minutes and you're on my back.' I shifted another suit about on the rail – a two-piece midnight blue kid mohair – rather than provoke any more unwanted attention. She had me cornered and knew it, and I needed a favour and she didn't owe me one.

'Well, that's rich! My own bloody son, who doesn't bother to come and see me for more than a year – thirteen months come June 8th – and he's wondering why I'm on at him.' She breathed heavily through her nose like her father did, but I could see behind the anger that she was but one soft glance away from tears. The trouble was she loved me unconditionally, like most mothers do their sons, and I knew just how to manipulate this weakness to get from her exactly what I wanted. 'You didn't even come home for your birthday,' she went on. 'You could at least have phoned to let your father and me know you were all right. Twenty years of age and still no respect for your parents.'

'Well, there you go. Less said about that the better.' I couldn't resist it, although I didn't really mean it. Despite everything I thought, they were good people, if society's rules were anything to go by.

She shifted weight onto her back foot and folded her arms. 'Just what do you mean by that?'

I rearranged a shirt. 'Oh, come on. You get everything you deserve in this life. Including respect.'

She thought about it for a few seconds then responded with a note of disgust. 'You saucy sod! Your father and I have done everything we could for you, but you've thrown it all up in the air because you think you know better. Everything. And don't think I don't know what you've been up to.'

What I've been up to . . . Michael Mouse? Did she know about my job collecting protection money for a firm in the West End? Or was it Beryl she'd heard about, who was almost old enough to be my mother? Heat was creeping up both sides of my neck, and if I didn't change the subject rapidly she'd notice it. It was time for a truce, not confrontation, and if I wasn't careful she'd tell me to clear off again and I'd have nowhere to leave everything . . . because tomorrow I was going to Paris but she didn't know it.

I hung my head. 'I'm sorry I haven't been in touch, mum, but I've been so busy trying to get things sorted out, finding a real job and all that . . .'

'Did you find one?'

'Well, no. I tried a couple but things didn't work out so I thought I'd try something else.'

'Like what?' She looked as if she didn't believe me.

'Frankie says there's plenty of work in Germany, so I thought I'd give it a try.' Which was a lie – there was indeed plenty of work in Germany, but all I wanted was a long holiday with the money I'd siphoned off from the job in the West End, the job where Beryl was the boss's wife. By rights I should have been dead by now, but I couldn't resist her.

'Germany! And what does Frankie know about anything? I can't understand why you still knock about with him – you know he's trouble.' She stared hard at me, then made up her mind that I was mad and walked away, out of the room, muttering 'Bleedin' Germany! Whatever next . . .?'

That night, the last night, I went for a last beer. Granger and his brother Billy were there, along with Frankie, Micky, Waller, Baz and Jacko. As usual, the regulars were there, in their same places, their same parts of the bar, trying to look or sound clever, and Harry the publican was providing the encouragement, joining in with one conversation while listening to at least two others so that he could pass the information on at a later date to the highest bidder.

Granger wanted to know where we were going and what countries we planned to visit, but he was only looking for something to ridicule, something to give him a reason to take the piss. Coincidentally, Frankie had also made up his mind to get out and see a bit more of the world, and when one night over a pint we'd discovered each other's plans we'd agreed to try travelling together for a bit, hitchhiking, or whatever took our fancy, until we felt like going our different ways. 'We're going to see Mistah Odinga Odinga in Africah, den up de great ribba to Babylon . . .' said Frankie, almost absentmindedly.

15

'To de coast of Coromandel where de early Bong tree grows
. . .' I added.

Granger gave up.

So his brother Bobby started. 'No, seriously. Are you going
across to France on the ferry, or what?'

Frankie screwed up his face: 'I don't tink so. Mebbe ah take de
boat to Madahgascah to see Doctor Canaan Banana . . .'

Neither of us wanted to pass on information, especially
information that we knew would immediately be attacked or
ridiculed, albeit light-heartedly. There was bound to be resistance
because we were effectively breaking up the gang.

'I don't know why I bother trying to talk to you two – you're
both silly in the head.' He sipped his beer. 'But I tell you what
– I bet you're back within the month. You mark my words . . .'
He liked talking like an old man – he must have been all of 24.

TWO

The last door slammed shut as the train began rolling. The cord
was severed and a new life began as London flashed by and finally
receded. First the blackened brick and shattered factory windows,
then the dreary little streets, council estates and flats, neat
suburban semis and the nightmare order of small lives. Croydon
. . . Coulsdon . . . over the Brighton road, down which I'd been
many times – hitching, by scooter, in the back of an open-top
Mercedes . . . then damp green fields dotted with motionless
black and white cows and every few miles the roaring blur of a
nameless station that tore at the eyes.

The chattering of two French girls opposite shattered my
preoccupation with escape and I turned to find Frankie sharing
his cigarettes with them.

'D'you want one?' he asked, pushing the packet across the table.

I took a Piccadilly filter and stuck it in my mouth. Both were about our age, blonde and good looking; nothing like the French girls I'd been used to in Soho, who tended to be dark. These were more like Swedes, wholesome, raised on fresh air and privilege.

Searching for come-on signs in their faces as our eyes met through the smoke, I found little but shallow friendliness, the courtesy usually shown by foreigners to a native. Soon would come the time to reverse roles – when they were back on home soil, back on mainland Europe, on the edge of that piece of land that stretched all the way to China – when we'd become the foreigners and have to adjust, I guess like crossing the Thames from north to south, or wandering into Mile End from Bethnal Green.

But the difference here was that being English, we were superior. This wasn't a local tribal affair, but an international tribal affair, and everyone knew that we were top of the pile – and that Germans were warlike, the French untrustworthy, Italians cowards, Turks bloodthirsty, Indians weird, Chinese clever but inscrutable . . .

And French girls were good in bed. So the scene was already set in my mind for a few beers on the boat followed by ingenious French lovemaking in some dark and remote corner of the boat. After which there might be a chance shacking up with them for a few weeks in Paris until we felt like moving on. Do the bohemian thing.

'Where do you come from?' I asked in English.

'Nantes,' they chimed.

'Where?'

'Nantes – it is to the west of Paris, towards Brittany.'

I looked at Frankie. 'That's a shame.'

'Have you got any mates in Paris we can stay with?' he asked. 'Any . . .'

'Mates – friends, we can stay with in Paris.'

'Only my grandmother, but I don't think she will like it,' laughed one.

'What's your names?' I asked. What was it in French? Comment vous appellez?

'I am Lucy and this is . . .'

'Pascale.'

'Lucy and Pascale, Frankie and Tommy, pleased to meet you, how do you do and all that.' I shook their hands.

'You all right for a tiny piece of the other?' asked Frankie with a pleasant smile on his face, knowing they wouldn't understand.

'Yeh, a little bit when we get on the boat, know what I mean?'

Politely they stared back, their sweet faces radiating innocence as they failed to take in what we were saying.

Frankie gazed at Lucy, who sat opposite. 'In fact I could definitely give you the most severe seeing-to,' he added. He looked at me. 'Ain't she lovely?'

'Five pounds says I get legover first.' Pascale had stared at me a second longer than was necessary when I'd given her a light for her cigarette.

'I don't know. She's giving you the eye already.' Frankie never missed a trick.

The two girls conferred in French, then Pascale said, 'Sorry, we do not understand what you are saying.'

'We were saying that it's a shame you don't live in Paris because we could do with somewhere to kip for a few nights – you could show us the sights, we could give you both a seeing-to up the Eiffel Tower, and there you go,' I said, more for Frankie's amusement than anything else.

They began giggling.

'We – want – sleep – somewhere,' said Frankie slowly, 'in Paris.'

'With you,' I added, 'We want to sleep with you. In Paris.'

'Here'll do me. How about the karsie? Fancy a knee-trembler in the bog, darling?'

Lucy pulled out a pack of tissues to wipe her eyes. 'I am sorry, what language you are speaking? You want to sleep?' she asked.

I shrugged and sighed. 'It's because we come from London. It's cockney. Difficult to understand. Comprenez vous?' School French was surfacing now like weedy flotsam freed suddenly from an ancient sunken galleon.

'Oh, cockney. I have heard of this. Can you speak proper English please? I do not know cockney.'

'Cock . . . knee,' explained Frankie, 'You prefer cock or knee?'

Lucy whispered something to Pascale.

'What're they going on about?' asked Frankie suspiciously.

I didn't understand, but I thought I recognised 'nez' and 'cacahuètes'. 'They're talking about your nose. They said you're an ugly bastard.'

'It's not my nose you want to be looking at, darling,' said Frankie defensively. They were laughing at us now.

The door opened and in came the ticket inspector. I watched as Frankie searched through his white Levi jacket pockets for a ticket – he'd had his hair cut too, like mine, down to a short crop. I thought back to what I looked like just a few weeks ago: white Aquascutum trench coat, tailored mohair suit, pony skin shoes and slubbed silk tie. Hand-made shirts. Now it was travelling gear and a change of style: Levi jeans, green suede mosquito boots, T-shirt and US Airforce bomber jacket. And hidden deep within our rucksacks were large new Bowie knives waiting to be hung on our belts the moment we were beyond reach of British law: symbols of survival and manliness.

Not that we needed to worry about the knives – once past Passport Control, Customs seemed glad to get shot of us, scarcely bothering to check anything, and within minutes we were on board the ship looking for a bar.

By this time we'd more or less paired off, and as well as my rucksack I was carrying one of Pascale's suitcases as some sort of territorial claim. Shame she was going to Nantes. We'd briefly considered going to Nantes with them but had checked the map and come to the conclusion that it was too far out of the way and likely to be an expensive diversion – besides which both lived with their parents. But to liven things up Frankie had accepted the £5 challenge, feeling that his chances with Lucy had improved since she'd accidentally touched his knee while making her way to the WC.

Finding a table a few paces from the bar we began the race for seduction by taking it in turns to buy drinks, and for a while all went well, but as darkness fell the wind rose to screaming pitch and the ship began to roll about until it was all we could do to hang on to our seats. Around us, glasses shattered as they slid from table to deck, and panic began to spread as we were battered sideways by a storm blowing in from the Atlantic. When Lucy finally vomited across the table and collapsed groaning into Pascale's arms we knew the bet was off and made our way through the debris to the bar to stand braced against the woodwork for the next three hours sinking pints served by a pudgy-faced sadist from Manchester who thought rough crossings were the business. 'Oh, I love it when it gets choppy,' he said with a sly grin. 'Normally they come in here half-pissed and showing off, so when it gets a bit lively I feel like I'm getting my own back on them. I love watching them spew their guts up, the bastards. But the best is when someone has a fit – I like that – when they scream and go all rigid. I try and get to them first so I can slap 'em.'

By the time the ship reached Dieppe we were the last two passengers standing. Bodies lay everywhere. Abandoning Lucy and Pascale, we strode down onto a dark and rain-glistening quayside and passed through Customs without a problem, despite the knives being discovered which they said had to remain safely tucked away in our bags. Once aboard the Paris train we slipped them onto our belts and stretched out on the seats to wait for the train to pull away.

When the train eventually moved, hours had passed, the sun was up and the alcohol had worn off leaving us tired, short-tempered and hung over. Other passengers looking for a seat were discouraged with hostile stares and a silent refusal to move. Soon, lulled by the movement of the speeding train, I was dreaming of a submissive Pascale and what might have been. Lovingly staring into my eyes, she gasped, 'Now, now, now', or should I say, 'Maintenant, maintenant, maintenant' – and I was agonising over whether I knew her well enough to whisper 'Je t'aime', or whether I should be more formal with a 'Je vous aime', in which case, would she think I was speaking in the plural? 'Est-ce-qu'il y a quelqu'un autre mon cher?'

Everything shuddered to a halt as we pulled into the Gare du Nord, and Pascale was gone forever. But outside was Paris. The freshly washed cobblestones glittered with morning sunlight, and the air was permeated with coffee and Gauloises and stale wine and garlic and bread and petrol fumes, and Charles Aznavour and accordions competed with the scrape of iron chairs being pulled into place outside cafés. 'I could get used to this,' said Frankie, looking about in wonder.

To avoid a long march through the city centre we grabbed one of the taxis parked outside and asked the driver to take us to the Porte d'Italie, a starting point we'd discovered on the Metro map.

Some way into the ride I pointed out that the meter hadn't been switched on, but all the driver said was 'kaput' and carried on with his foot to the floor, a Gitanes non-filter dangling from his moustache. I reminded myself to buy some, to look and smell the part. At the Porte d'Italie I gave him half the fare he demanded and walked away, leaving him cursing us roundly across the cobbles. 'Ta gueule!' I shouted back.

'How come you know all this French?' asked Frankie.

I'd been waiting for it, wondering how long it would be before he pulled me on my language, because the ability to do anything beyond the street norm was seen as treachery, as selling out to the other side.

'I did French at school – you can't help picking some up.'

'You're a bit of a bookworm on the quiet,' he jeered. 'I'm going to have to watch you.'

After an espresso coffee in a nearby bar which got both of us talking earnestly for fifteen minutes about the advantages of being French, we stopped our first lift, a mobile corrugated-iron shed, and were dropped south of Paris on the road to Lyons. Already the temperature was rising, well into the eighties I guessed, and we began to suffer as we marched silently along the roadside looking for a shady spot from which to hitch. But a couple of 20-year-old males isn't the ideal pick-up and by midday we'd covered only a hundred kilometres and were stranded in a small village, just as France came to a standstill for lunch. Across the street an *épicerie* was about to shut so we bought bread, a kilo of cheese and two large bottles of red wine, and sat down by the war memorial to eat. Behind us a bronze plaque listed forty-seven local men killed in the First World War.

But as soon as the bread was divided and the cheese laid out, a faded old Peugeot saloon stopped and we had to bundle everything together again and jump in – only to be dumped just ten minutes later several miles away from the main road, in the middle of the shimmering countryside.

Nearby stood a copse, inside which was a pond. Giving up for the day, we made camp, ate bread and cheese, drank the wine and passed out in the cool shade of a fat beech tree which whispered softly overhead. In the middle of a jet black night I awoke to a new world: crickets were chirping in the bushes and Frankie, deep inside his sleeping bag, was snoring like a pig. But despite a hangover I felt wildly happy and free, and understood for the first time what it was to be without a care in the world.

It took another three days to reach Trieste – three days of tramping, waiting for lifts, and sleeping by the roadside. By the time we'd set eyes on the Adriatic Sea we knew that we'd have to travel alone. Several cars and lorries had stopped and offered lifts to just one of us, but we'd refused, sticking to our agreement to remain together at least until Trieste, and now we'd arrived I for one was relieved. Friends that we were, we were also gifted with very independent characters, and a touch of edge had already crept in: if I wanted to stop and eat somewhere, Frankie would object and say we didn't have the time; if he wanted to take a break, I'd ignore him and carry on walking, not caring whether he came along or not. A power struggle had begun. What it boiled down to was that each of us was setting out on his own journey – this wasn't a two-man thing at all. Sooner or later Frankie would go his way and I mine, and as far as I was concerned, the sooner the better because I had a lot of being alone to do. Together, we were still living in the past – he was Frankie and I was Tommy, two young London geezers out for the crack – and we continued to act our part in what seemed to be at times little more than an overseas extension of a holiday weekend. But for me this trip was about self-discovery and the future – and constant reminders of the past were a bummer. I never wanted to go back. Ever. Something wonderful was happening, something that was giving me a buzz like I'd never felt before. Since leaving, since crossing that 22 miles of cold seawater, I'd felt a powerful sense of liberation, a release, an emergence into another world, and I wanted to savour it at leisure and soak it up alone.

Increasingly, at times I felt torn between the old me and the new, the one that was struggling through the murk towards the light. One minute I'd be euphoric, marvelling at the sights, the scenery and the architecture; the next I'd be acting the evil-minded adolescent. An attractive woman had given us a lift for the last few miles into Trieste, and far from being appreciative of her brave gesture – she explained that her son was also travelling around Europe and that she felt it auspicious to help us – all I could think about was her breasts, the wispy dark hair of her armpits, and whether she was a secret nympho driving about looking for young men.

Having overcome our reticence about staying in a youth hostel, we finally found one a couple of miles west of town on the seafront with its own private beach. The place was empty except for a couple of aloof Swiss blokes, but on the second day, while we were sunbathing on the beach, two English girls arrived.

Frankie saw them first. 'Tom! Look! Over there. Women.'

I looked up. Blondes again – two of them. They'd just crossed the road from the hostel and were walking towards us. Straight towards us. Aiming for us. We waited, pretending not to be too bothered. 'Hello,' said one, 'are you English?'

'Yeh. Is it that obvious?' I asked.

'Oh, great.' They seemed genuinely pleased. 'Can we join you? The manager said you were English.'

What a silly question. If they hadn't come over we'd have been chasing them up the road. 'Make yourself at home,' I said lazily. 'This is Frankie. I'm Tommy.'

To look at they weren't unlike Lucy and Pascale, but were somehow less confident, more British I suppose, despite their forward approach. They called themselves Jenny and Mary and began by fervently describing the difficulties they'd had hitching from Calais as if they needed to exorcise the experience from their minds. 'Every bloody driver we met was all over us,' declared Jenny. 'Outside Lyon we had to fight off a gang of blokes and go to the police for protection – and they were just as bad. And in

Milan some bloke tried to drive away with Mary in the car, but she managed to throw herself out at the traffic lights.'

Mary showed her grazed knees and elbows.

Out of the frying pan and into the fire with us two then.

But what did they expect? English males were bad enough. I mean, we're talking foreigners here – all the women between Calais and Shanghai have to be chaperoned or covered from head to toe to avoid causing riots.

'Don't worry, girls, we'll look after you,' said Frankie through a cheesy grin.

That evening we went for a pizza, then sat together on the beach watching the pale moon shimmering in the waves as we smoked and talked and swigged wine in the warm night air. It was then that they asked if they could hitch with us to Istanbul. I looked at Frankie and smiled. We'd pulled. And his tan was coming along fine, so mine had to be as well. 'What do you reckon?' I asked, feeling suddenly golden brown and worldly wise as I stared into Mary's blue eyes, 'Should we go with them?'

'No, leave them to the Turks.'

A day later I was on the road with Mary, heading for Istanbul via Bulgaria; Frankie and Jenny were on the road to Istanbul via Greece.

Mary. I considered her as we walked silently side by side. I'd never been out with a Mary before, probably because the name was alien – there were no Marys in the family, no cousins or aunt Marys. And the name itself had been tainted by my grandmother who'd long ago referred to a neighbour's daughter as a 'mare' – every Mary since had been tarnished in my mind by the image of the girl who'd put me in hospital with a brick dropped from an elm tree.

This one had long blonde hair and a neat body, but a slightly Slavic look which I didn't find attractive, although others might, and once alone together, her real shyness came out like a fog. In fact the only time she spoke with any feeling that first day was when she spotted a large unicorn beetle clambering through the dry grass in a roadside ditch. 'Oh, look! Look!' she squealed, dancing up and down, so I rushed over to do my male bit, but like a delicate sea anemone she shrank back inside herself the moment I touched her. Later she timidly asked where we were going to sleep for the night, and I fantasised that maybe she was getting a bit horny, but in fact she was worried about insects getting into her sleeping bag.

Differences aside, at least it was easy getting lifts with her standing there. Car after car after lorry after bus after farm cart stopped to take us a bit further down the pitted track described as a motorway on the map, and by nightfall we'd reached Belgrade and were congratulating ourselves on our progress. But we then had to walk through town and run the gauntlet with males who seemed to find us *both* irresistible. Italian blokes had been a pushover, but these guys were different, they didn't seem to care what they stuck in you. Leaving the town centre, and followed at a distance by a growing gang, we marched on up a long hill lined by weird shops run by creepy owners who crept out to stare suspiciously after us as we trespassed through the yellow light of their windows. With perfect timing an old truck driven by a stinking, hay-strewn peasant stopped to pick us up, and dropped us ten kilometres later, well away from town where, exhausted, we gave up and decided to bed down for the night. As far as I could see, providing we got off the road and out of view, there'd be no problem with marauders or rapists. Scrambling up a high bank we found a clearing in the darkness and made camp, where at least we'd have the advantage of high ground should an unfriendly approach be made from the road.

The approach came from an altogether unexpected quarter. After unrolling our sleeping bags and going through a distance thing about how close together we should be (no closer than two yards), we finally crawled fully clothed into our bags and tried to sleep. I'd suggested we zip the two together for warmth and safety, but this had thrown Mary into a state of defence and jolted our struggling relationship back to square one.

Strange noises disturbed the silence – strange unearthly whistling sounds and muffled thuds – and I wondered if we'd camped on an old battlefield or some other place of slaughter inhabited by ghosts, but after a while I became too tired to worry any more and dropped off, despite believing I was still awake and strolling down Whitechapel High Road. Some time later, as I was trying to make up my mind whether to buy a plate of cockles or a plate of whelks at Tubby Isaacs seafood stall, Mary's voice came hissing urgently through the darkness, 'Tommy! Tommy! Wake up!'

'What?' I grumbled. Then I thought that perhaps she'd relented, maybe she was feeling lonely, wanted company and couldn't resist me after all. (I'd have to get some johnnies somewhere – you could catch a dose from the most innocent-looking bird, you know, and these middle-class ones were the worst according to my mother; I mean, look at Christine Keeler. Not that I'd mind giving her . . .)

'Listen! I can hear something.'

I held my breath. Sure enough, something was in the bushes nearby. But the odd thing was that whatever it was, it was all around us. Slowly I sat up and began to get out of my sleeping bag while groping around in the rucksack for the knife I'd removed from my belt that very morning. I'd felt silly wearing it. Then a deep growl, and another, and another, came from the darkness and I came to the conclusion we were about to be attacked by a pack of wolves. Finding a box of matches, I struck one, and there in the flare could see that we were surrounded by a pack of wild dogs.

'Pick everything up and get onto the road,' I shouted, striking matches to flick at the dogs. From the side, one rushed forward but I managed to kick it off, then another came in snapping which I fended off with the rucksack. Two meanwhile had clamped their teeth into Mary's sleeping bag and were trying to drag it away, but she kicked and fought back with an indignant middle-class ferocity until between us we were able to drive them off.

We had a firm footing once back on the road but the matches were running out fast, and the dogs who were now following along the top of the embankment seemed to sense it and began to venture down onto the road to harry us from behind.

But again luck was with us: as the last match died headlights appeared in the distance and the dogs disappeared soundlessly into the night. Flagging down the car, an old Fiat, we ran to the driver shouting for help, and although confused by our attempts to describe what had happened, and full of booze after a night out, he eyed Mary up and down and told us to jump in.

When he dropped us off several kilometres, gropes and outrageous suggestions further on, we again made camp – this time beneath a road bridge in case it rained – and finally got to sleep only to discover in the first light of morning that we'd spread out our sleeping bags in the middle of a sea of human turds left by passing travellers. Somehow we'd managed to miss every one.

At Nis we took an hour off to check out the sign-posted Tower of Skulls built by the Turks as a reminder to the inhabitants not to resist their occupation – and as a reminder to us not to be too complacent about the inhabitants when we got to Turkey – then marched on again into Bulgaria, passing the single strand of rusty barbed wire and sentry-box that represented the border checkpoint. Keen to get our passports stamped, we had to wake the guard and insist he did his job.

'From what I've seen of communism so far, they can keep it,' Mary observed airily.

Amazing – she'd spoken voluntarily. All I had to do now was keep her going. 'What d'you mean?' I asked, trying to look intelligent. Politics was never a strong point with me.

She stared back. 'It's obvious, isn't it?'

'It might be to you, but I don't see what you're getting at.'

She sighed, and jutted her tits out. 'I suppose I'll have to enlighten you. They tell us that communism is the panacea for mankind, the answer to all our problems – you know, share everything so that nobody suffers – and all I've seen is suffering everywhere we've been.'

Enlighten. I liked that word. An easy one to remember and use. And *panacea.* I was about to ask if Yugoslavia and Bulgaria were communist, but suddenly I saw the light, or should I say, I was *enlightened* – she thought I was thick. All this time and I thought she was shy – but she won't talk to me because I'm working class and therefore intellectually substandard.

'What do you know about suffering?' I asked scornfully. I'd heard three generations of my family use that argument on these occasions, and it always seemed to work, stopped them in their tracks.

She stared at me as if I'd cheated by being personal about such a touchy subject. 'Well, you've only got to look around you.'

'I've *been* looking around ever since I left London, and Biafra still seems a long way off to me.'

'Oh, come on! Biafra's different, that's a civil war. I'm just comparing communism with capitalism; I'm not talking about genocide.'

'I just thought "suffering" was a bit strong, that's all.'

'Okay. They're backward.'

'And we're forward, are we?'

'Comparatively . . .'

'Depends which way you're going, I suppose.'

'Can't you see? It's all about standards of living, freedom, healthcare. Democracy.'

'Don't tell me – your old man's a Tory politician.'

At last she smiled. 'My mother actually. A councillor.'

'Don't believe anything she says,' I said, raising an eyebrow. My grandfather used to say all politicians were liars and hypocrites – I wasn't sure of his logic, but he said it with such an air of wisdom that people were always impressed.

'Don't worry, I can think for myself,' she said with a real smile.

We began walking along the road into Bulgaria, and I felt our relationship had turned a corner. Now she walked alongside me, not ten paces in front or behind, and her arm occasionally touched mine as we strode on.

The night found us in Sofia, in the tourist agency where travellers have to report for registration if they wish to sleep within the city limits. A nice girl called Krassi arranged a bed and breakfast room and jotted down her own address on the back of the directions she gave us, which I was pleased to note irritated Mary. She didn't speak again for half an hour until we found our lodgings, an old terraced house in the artisan quarter close to the city centre. An couple answered the door ceremoniously and directed us into the front parlour where they immediately began a friendly but persistent interrogation in Bulgarian. Seeing our confusion the old lady seized my left hand and began tugging at my third finger. Mary by now had caught on and was shaking her head vigorously and crying, 'Nay, nay'. This had the desired effect and immediately calmed them. Beaming, they led us upstairs to a fair-sized double room with an adjoining bathroom and, to Mary's dismay, showed us in. Defeated, she dumped her rucksack on the floor and sat on the edge of the bed with a sickly grin on her face. After they'd gone I sat next to her and asked what the questioning had been about. Devastated, she explained that they'd been asking if we were married.

'But when I said "no" – you saw me shaking my head – they showed us up here. I don't believe it.' What neither of us knew at the time was that shaking your head in Bulgaria meant 'yes', as does 'neh'.

Looking as sincere as was possible under the circumstances I suggested we go back to the tourist agency to request alternative lodgings, but after a few moments of nail-chewing anguish she decided it would be unfair to the old couple. Yeh, sure, and the last thing she needed right now was a long walk back to find the tourist agency closed and the prospect before her of another night on the road. Alone. A night without the backup of a strong working-class male. Did I not after all have the address of Krassi, the nice little Bulgarian girl, to fall back on?

'I'm going to take a bath, d'you mind?' she asked wearily.

'No, you go ahead. I'll have one after.'

I pulled off my boots and stretched out on the bed. Yes, things were definitely looking up. It was all just a matter of time now. Girls always said 'no' when they meant 'yes', it was part of the ritual.

Sheets nice and clean. Get up and draw the curtains. Have a quick look about for spy-holes and microphones – got to watch these commies – then unpack the rucksack. Change of socks and underpants due – can wash the dirty ones in the bath. Don't forget the toothbrush and toothpaste.

The door opened and in walked a damp Mary, clutching a bath towel around her. 'Your turn,' she said.

Taking special care with the important bits, I was in and out of the bath inside a few minutes and tiptoeing back into the bedroom, but she was already hidden beneath the covers, and down the entire length of the middle of the bed she'd placed the bolster and some cushions.

'What's this about?' I asked, not believing my eyes. She was facing the other way.

'Just so you don't get any ideas,' she said to the wall.

'Oh, come on! We're big girls and boys now.'

'That's what I'm afraid of.'

At first light I went over the top and pinned her to the bed, smothering her mouth with mine, and she responded by opening her mouth. For a moment, I thought she was going to try shouting, but she was responding . . .

And when she asked timidly if I'd got anything to put on and I said, 'no,' and she said, 'You'd better pull out,' and I said, 'yeh, sure', I didn't.

That day we reached Istanbul and checked into the Gulhane Hotel, a seedy three-storey tenement where we'd agreed to meet Frankie and Jenny, after seeing the place recommended on the notice board back in Trieste Youth Hostel. We'd won the race and Mary was jubilant, like the jolly-hockey-sticks sort of person she was.

The foyer appeared to be some sort of international waiting room for travellers and I felt conspicuous in my casual London street gear. On one seat reclined a long-haired man dressed in a charcoal grey worsted suit and sandals, looking for all the world like Jesus attempting incognito time travel. As we walked in he looked up, half nodded, and called out for the boy to carry our rucksacks to our rooms. 'You wouldn't happen to have a cigarette on you?' he asked with a cool smile. He was English.

Mary booked herself into a separate room with a vacant bed she was saving for Jenny, and threatened me with death if I opened my mouth about what had happened between us. Then she became distant and rowed me out of her life by reverting to the Mary I'd known in Yugoslavia.

And women can be hard. Despite everything, I think I'd fallen in love – just a little bit.

Two days later, Frankie turned up without Jenny, and went straight to Mary's room to ask if there was any news from her. Apparently she'd met an Australian in Thessaloniki and gone off with him to check out some remote monasteries, but Frankie was cool about it. 'Didn't fancy her anyway,' he said laughing.

Then one day Mary went too, leaving a note on the board at reception. 'Jenny,' it read, 'Am staying at Youth Hostel. Mary.'

And that was that.

Istanbul was like all the dodgy areas of London rolled into one, and we slotted straight in, soaking up the atmosphere and the sunshine and getting a feel for the place. High on amphetamines bought over the counter, we spent our days strolling around the bazaar, exploring the tourist haunts looking for suckers to have over, and making friends with Turkish villains who seemed keen to recruit Western kids into their gangs. Within a couple of weeks we were making enough spare cash changing tourist money on the black market to rent a room on Sultanahmet Square with views of the Blue Mosque and Aya Sofia.

Now that Frankie was occupied the pressure was off, and I could start thinking about getting on the road again. My plans were to head south, find a remote beach somewhere, and turn my brain off, but I wanted to leave on good terms.

One of his contacts, Mustafa, was coming to speak to us about 'special business' which, he said, would give us the chance to earn a lot more. I could tell Frankie was already well into the scheme, whatever it was, but he refused to discuss it until Mustafa was present as, he explained, he would be the best man to get the idea across. I knew Mustafa – a trendy young Turk about our age from the Pudding Shop, a local café – and I also recognised his kind well enough to know that he'd put his mother on the game if he could see a lira or two in it. I also knew from what I'd seen in just two weeks that the Turkish police were best avoided – in the bazaar I saw one knock a man's eye out with a gun barrel for thieving – and any dealings with Mustafa meant that we automatically moved closer to them. I knew we were surviving for the sole reason that we were new to the scene, and foreign, and very low key, but I also knew that as soon as we stepped up into the Turkish league it would only be a matter of time before the police became involved.

'Don't worry about it, he's reliable,' shouted Frankie from the bathroom. 'Anyway, once you hear him out you'll be right there. You'll love it.'

Despite the change of scenery, the sunshine and the beauty, and the chance of changing the old way of life, despite everything he'd said about getting away from it all, Frankie's criminal mind had hitched a lift with him. No matter what I said he couldn't see the dangers of playing away and I was beginning to wonder if he'd lost his touch.

'You know Mustafa's only going to use you, don't you?'

'He's sound. Believe me. Anyway, if he tries to have me over, he'll get a bit of English revenge.'

'Yeh. And before you know what's happened you'll have one of Ataturk's truncheons up your arse – and that'll just be for starters.'

'What's the matter with you? A chance to make a bit of wedge and you're bleating like a fucking nanny goat.'

Frankie was pushing his luck and was relying on the impending arrival of Mustafa to stop me from making anything of it. 'Listen, you wanker,' I shouted, 'if you want to spend the rest of your life inside a Turkish nick that's all right by me, but do it on your own – keep me out of it. Anyway, I thought you said you wanted to get away from all that sort of stuff.' There was a knock at the door.

'Yeh!' I shouted.

Ali the room boy came in, followed by Mustafa who, without as much as a by-your-leave, dismissed him. Already Mustafa was lording it over us. 'Ali!' I shouted after him. The boy returned. 'Get me Yeni Harman.' I gave him some money for the cigarettes.

'I have cigarettes,' said Mustafa smoothly, looking around at the room after the boy had left.

Then Frankie came out of the bathroom in a new mauve silk shirt looking like a pimp and smelling of carnations. 'Mustafa! Nice to see you. Sit down. I'll order some tea.'

'It's okay. I must go in five minutes.'

'Mustafa,' Frankie sat next to him, 'tell Tommy about this idea you have.'

Mustafa looked me in the eyes. I knew it wasn't a strong reliable look, but sheer animal observation – to see my reaction when he came out with the plan. 'Okay,' he said, 'is simple. I want girls.'

A mosque loudspeaker began calling over the rooftops for the faithful to get praying – I loved the moodiness of the sound and the way it made me feel like I was a long way from home.

'What do you mean you want girls?' I asked.

'You bring me girls. If they good – nice girls – I give you £3,000 each one.'

Three grand! Mustafa didn't need to pay three grand for a girl. Something wasn't right. 'Then what?'

'Then you bring me more and I pay you more.'

I looked out through the window at the crowds. A man in gypsy clothing was forcing a miserable-looking bear to dance by yanking on its chain. 'What happens to the girls?'

Mustafa looked at Frankie then back at me. 'They go far away. I have very big client who wants nice European girls, especially English, you know, clean English girls, no bad girls.'

'Where?'

'Long way from here. Girls disappear, no problem. You never see again.'

Frankie looked keen. 'We could pull a couple a week easy without any comeback – you know how fast the turnover is in backpackers around here.'

'Where do we deliver them to?' I was looking for flaws now – that so I could get out without losing face.

Mustafa jumped in. 'You find girl. I tell you. Different places.'

'And the money?'

'We pay you one day after.' Suddenly Mustafa had become a 'we'. Discuss payment of money and immediately the responsibility gets spread around a bit.

'No, it has to be the same day – you pay on same day.'

'Oh, come on, Tommy,' interrupted Frankie, looking hard done by, 'we can't just hand her over and expect payment there and then – she'd know something was up.'

'So what? It'd be too late by then for them to start suspecting anything. We take the money and the rest is up to Mustafa and his crew. Or they can pay us up front – what's wrong with that?'

Both Mustafa and Frankie made a good show of sounding astonished by this absurd demand, and Mustafa suggested that I needed to learn a little bit about business: 'Maybe you find another partner, eh, Frankie?'

I laughed. I didn't want any part of this business anyway. 'But it's all right for *us* to pay up front. We give you the goods and you pay later – maybe.'

Mustafa stood up to leave. 'Frankie, I go now.' He looked suspiciously at me. 'Let me know what you do.'

'Yeh, yeh, okay, Mustafa, I'll see you tomorrow. Don't worry about Tommy – he's a good bloke. Just a bit careful.'

'No, don't worry about me, Mustafa . . .' I shouted after him as he left, 'forget we ever had this conversation.'

After he'd gone Frankie tried to change my mind, but I was having none of it and tried to explain that I'd come away to escape from the sort of rubbish he was trying to embroil me in. Already, I felt lighter and freer, and all this talk of selling girls took me straight back to Soho. A bit of mischief to survive was one thing, but selling people . . .

Frankie sucked on his Birinçi cigarette. I was still waiting for Ali to return with my Yeni Harman.

After a while he spoke. 'I tell you what – how about if we only capture the evil ones, the flash cows and rich cunts who deserve it? Then you'd feel as if you were doing the world a favour every time we got rid of one.'

Ali returned with the cigarettes.

'Ali,' I asked, 'is Mustafa a good man?'

Faultlessly, he replied, 'Not for me to say,' and left the room.

I thought about it. Bad girls only. Almost interesting. If nothing else it would be major entertainment trying to snare one. But I couldn't see how it might be done. 'The problem is, the only types gullible enough are going to be nice sweet trusting types who don't deserve it,' I said, lighting one of the oval cigarettes. 'Who's the client, anyway? D'you know?'

'Some Arab. They go out by private plane. We pull 'em, spike their drinks, hand them over to Mustafa and they go out in a private air ambulance. There's no risk because everyone's in on it – even the customs geezers are getting paid off.' He fished around inside a drawer in the bedside table and produced a small bottle of pale yellow liquid. 'Knockout drops. A couple of drops of this and they're out cold.'

'No risk! Are you joking? Once we get involved that'll be it.

How could they let us leave? Frankie, I can't believe you can't see it.'

''Course there's risks. Life's risks ain't it? And there's you mixing with the likes of Vince Bell back in London.' Vincent Bell was an old friend who'd turned out to be a mass murderer. We can all make mistakes.

Frankie went on and on about it and I could see there was no point arguing with him. Maybe going it alone would help him see things in a different light, unclutter his vision for a bit so that he could see that all he was doing was dragging his rubbish around with him. Was I going soft? Nah. I just wanted a different take on life. 'Anyway,' I said, 'I guarantee you, you'd never get any further than the first one; they'd take the girl and burn you. If this is the way you want to go then you go ahead, but I'm off. In fact all this has cleared up a few things in my head. Another week and I'm splitting off for Athens.' I couldn't see the point in letting him know where I was really going because he probably wouldn't be listening anyway.

'Let's go and get a coffee,' he said, as if nothing had changed.

We walked along in silence for a bit, dodging traffic as we crossed the streets taking a roundabout route back towards the Pudding Shop.

'I've been thinking. In fact, I've been thinking a lot since I got here,' I began.

'It's okay. I know what you're going to say. If you want to split off, please yourself. You don't have to explain yourself to me – I mean, we're still friends ain't we?'

'It's just that our paths are taking different directions, that's all. I left England to leave all this stuff behind. I've done my fair share, know what I mean?'

'Can't say I do. I thought you came out here for the crack, like I did.'

'Yeh, but a different sort of crack. All this is just leading down the same old road, and I feel like it's time to do something else. I don't want to keep scratching about on the edge looking for someone to have over – there's got to be more to life than that.'

'Horses for courses. You go and do your exploring and I'll meet you back here in a year's time. How about that?'

'Yeh, maybe,' I said, and we walked off in different directions.

Frankie didn't come back to the room that night, and I set out first thing in the morning, full of energy and free, to catch a bus for Antalya on the south coast, and I forgot about him and Mary and Jenny and Mustafa the moment I walked out into the warm early sunshine.

THREE

I could have stayed longer in bed. Ten minutes after midday, a plate of rancid meatballs, a box of rose-flavour Turkish Delight and half a dozen glasses of tea later, the packed bus shudders and roars into life and pulls away through the gathered crowds of dusty peasants who seem to be forever on the move in this part of the world. Out into the crazy Istanbul traffic and the old beast makes its way through the streets, across the Galata Bridge and onto the ferry to Asia. Once there it speeds south towards Antalya without regard for anything else on the road.

In agony with stomach ache, I go on to spend most of the night pacing the gangway clutching my guts, watched by expressionless parcel-carrying Anatolians who offer about as much sympathy as bystanders at a stranger's funeral, and each halt I spend crouched in some dark corner of the landscape trying to rid myself of meatballs, Turkish Delight and tea. And I'm cursing myself for being such a spineless fool: the moment I'd smelt the meatballs I knew they were off – I just didn't want to upset the café owner by sending them back or leaving them.

Antalya mid-morning and I descend with great joy from the coach, only to step on the result of a union between Humpty Dumpty and Cyclops begging propped up against a wall. A huge hand clutches at my jeans but I pull away sharply and continue along the road and out of town in search of a quiet beach.

As the town dwindles into nothing and the hot dust and scrub landscape of southern Turkey takes over, I turn the image over and over in my mind – the single large eye in the forehead, the single powerful arm. And no legs. Just two very large feet.

After the initial shock there is disbelief, then wonder (just wait until I can tell someone about it), then sadness for his lot.

I'm pretty sure it was male.

I feel even deeper sadness for his mother – I must be getting homesick.

But how does he get there to beg? Someone must carry and put him into position each day. Probably in a wheelbarrow.

Never for him the soft caress of a beautiful woman, the flirtatious smile of an admirer.

What a miserable existence. Why didn't someone kill him at birth? Somewhere inside that monstrous shell resides a human, a human I couldn't bear to look at, a human who watched me reel away in horror.

Please God, please forgive me for being weak. If only I'd been able to stop and smile, say cheerily, 'How you going, pal?', share a moment with someone who is unloved, has never seen his mother gaze adoringly into his . . .

Maybe he was dangerous. The one arm looked capable of strangling a donkey. And did he have sexual organs? Where does he go every night? Probably back to some hovel to be propped up in the corner or, worse, put in with the beasts in a shed.

When I was a kid, we picked on Raymond, a big 17-year-old boy with the mind of a two-year-old. His family had just moved up from the country, and at first he was let out to play, but although his comical behaviour and wailing had initially amused us, we soon tired of that and began destroying what little confidence he did have by bullying him at every opportunity. Soon his freedom became hell and he was forced to remain indoors where, with his impossible demands he went on to torment his mother to the point of suicide.

Yet only now after all these years, as I tramp alone along this hot and dusty road do I feel anything about it at all, because suddenly I sense Raymond's presence all around, watching me silently as I come face to face with my conscience.

Way over to the left is the bright blue Mediterranean; to the right, hot dry Anatolia; straight ahead is an unmetalled road, a track, and a flock of fat-tailed sheep, shepherded by a lone, large, brown and white dog that has noticed my presence. They are crossing the track and moving north. 'Keep away', he barks deeply, sniffing in my direction, so I sit on a boulder and wait for them to get smaller as the sun beats down, shadows at minimum. There's a solitary unidentifiable bone in the dry prickly ditch, white and clean, and a large black millipede moves about below it. Without thinking I touch the handle of the knife now back on my belt, for reassurance, and wish I hadn't because it reminds me of my weakness. But the dog keeps looking back.

And what will I do about drinking water on the beach? No problem. I'll find a stream, a gushing stream of cold water running down from the mountains where I can wash and drink, and maybe discover a pool to bathe in and wash off the salt from the sea.

But first I'll have to build a shelter from branches and grass and make a fire. Then, once I'm settled in, I'll get down to being me, and try to discover what makes me tick. I'll read myself like a book then bury it in the sand or let it float away in the sea, be a new person, instead of being this thing assembled by others from second-hand material. Already they've ripped out my appendix, chopped off my foreskin, torn out my tonsils and various teeth. And my old man used to smack me in the face for chewing my nails.

The dog's disappeared round the far side of the sheep, and I can carry on.

Veering off towards the sea the track then rises slowly upwards until it skirts a line of brown cliffs high above the water and I trudge on feeling good, rucksack sitting squarely on my back. Disturbed by my arrival a zig-zag viper leaps from a rock and disappears into a hole, and I remember that somebody said they were good to eat. Overhead, a large vulture-like bird glides and observes, hidden by the glaring sun.

After a while the cliff road dips into a pine-wooded valley which extends from the mountains at the back down to a long curved beach of white sand and incredibly blue sea. Millions of invisible insects rasp loud courting signals from the trees, rrrr, rrrr, rrrr, rrrr, rrrr, rrrr, rrrr, synchronising every so often to play in harmony for a few seconds before drifting back into the mad cacophony which drowns all other sounds and shatters thought. The track, now carpetted with soft brown pine needles and patrolled by large wood ants, leads on beneath the fir trees and divides a hundred yards further on – one of the forks, almost overgrown, leading towards the sea. I follow this and find a freshwater stream gurgling down from the hills, and a little further on the beach begins, a long curved untouched beach of burning hot white sand.

Now it really begins, my solitude, away from the road. I hang the rucksack on the stub of a broken branch away from ants and other insects and remove first my boots and socks, then T-shirt and jeans, and looking quickly about to make sure no one's watching, my underpants – witness to the coach journey and the passage of suspect meatballs. The leisurely but self-conscious stroll to the water's edge with underpants in hand becomes a mad dash as hot sand begins to bite into the soles of my feet and I plunge, yelling softly – for fear of drawing attention to myself – into the cool, clear, silent depths.

Laundry over I swim parallel to the beach to a spit of rocks and find the sea around seething with shoals of tame fish. Masses of shellfish cluster in among the rocks, and crabs are scrabbling everywhere. Here is food.

And more. Inland is a jungle of fig trees dripping with fruit, one or two lemon trees, and an ancient mulberry with a nest of bees inside the cracked trunk. Leaving the mulberry well alone I gorge instead on figs. The lemons are a bit small and dry but will make good tea if I can find something in which to boil water.

Later, as the sun dips behind a headland beyond the bay the cicadas become silent and I light a fire on the beach and roast shellfish, digging out the hot little bodies with my knife – at last a use for it – and discarding the least palatable types as I go. A baked crab with long thin legs is very tasty, but I'm afraid to eat the meat from inside the shell because my grandmother once said that some crab meat is poisonous, so I pick at it and hope for the best, playing a game of trial and error. As long as the poison isn't lethal, vomiting and diarrhoea will guide me away from the danger areas, so the rule here is easy does it, eat a little bit, then no more for a day or so to await the outcome. So far so good. The figs and mulberries will keep me alive if nothing else does.

Darkness comes. And with the darkness mosquitoes, whining mosquitoes, attacking from all angles. Building up the fire does little to deter them, and I have no choice in the end but to let them feed and risk malaria, either that or go crazy. And there are noises behind in the bushes, noises of animals, creeping things coming to take a look. Humans would be quieter. And an owl with a strange short hoot like a time pip at school – at least I think it's an owl – and suddenly overhead the stars are unbelievable, just masses and masses from one side of the sky to the other, impossibly close. A rogue wave slaps the sand nearby.

Light a cigarette and indulge its comfort before laying out the sleeping bag as a mattress.

As soon as the sun comes up in the morning it is hot, and another day begins, another day of figs and shellfish, and swimming and laying about, and exploring, and later in the day I manage to seize a largish silver and blue fish, two or three pounds in weight, and throw it onto the sand. Cooked in the embers of the fire it is delicious and I am very pleased indeed – I am the great survivor, the wild boy; and even my dick is getting sunburned – but if I'm honest, despite these victories, I'm already beginning to miss company, and not being able to share this fantastic fish with someone hurts just a little bit.

Two weeks later. By now each day has its own similar routine: wake up with the sun and flies, plunge into the cool morning sea, eat, explore further, collect fruit, hunt fish or crabs, eat and sleep. Sometimes I sing aloud, hymns or bad old pop tunes – 'I just don't know what to do with myself' – in competition with the insects and at all times I remain naked, so certain now am I that no one will ever come this way. Also I've lost that feeling of nudity which accompanies the removal of clothes: now it feels odd and uncomfortable to put them on.

One night on the beach I made love to the universe.

40

A naked, hymn-singing boy.
The thing that bothers me is the hymn singing . . .
He who would valiant be 'gainst all disaster
Let him in constancy follow the master.
There's no discouragement will make him once relent
His first avowed intent, to be a pilgrim.
They brainwashed me. Now I'm un-brainwashing me.

'Fight the Good Fight', 'Jerusalem', 'There is a Green Hill Far Away', 'All Things Bright and Beautiful', 'Dear Lord and Father of Mankind', and the rest, flood back to give me daily bread in the wilderness, but I don't want bread disfigured with someone else's trademark. The singing of school hymns has resurrected itself like a habit from the dark past, and for a moment a touch of grey, a coldness, an underlying fear which has returned to taint the beauty around. The misery of schooldays and the threat of schoolmasters, pain and ridicule, flood back to spoil my day. And suddenly the world is no longer a nice place; it is a world tainted by enduring images of wet pavements, dog shit, and street lamps beaming false hope through salty tears.

I have to remind myself, drag myself away from all this nonsense: this isn't a legacy I *have* to live with, not some sort of punishment I have to endure for the sake of mankind's future. I can kick that rubbish into touch because here it is hot and light and free of torment.

Yes, this is Paradise, albeit without Eve. And I'm safe to dig into my head, because nobody's going to come along and accuse me of being mad or deranged because I'm acting a bit odd while my brain cells adjust to this new lack of restriction. As I see it, the trick is to know what you want to be then remove the old you which doesn't fit into the new scheme of things.

But what do I want to be? That's the real problem. I can only view the possibilities through these biased eyes. I can only conjure up the things that are already inside this brain, so I'll just end up another version of the same thing.

This latest crab I've caught is an ugly creature with a fat green bristly body and long legs and it has managed to crush the edge of my left thumb, which is now very painful. For this reason I'm not feeling the usual squeamishness when holding it down at knife-point in the red-hot embers while it struggles and bubbles and screams. I've tried stabbing and bludgeoning the creatures, but nothing seems to kill them outright.

So how am I going to bring about any real change in me that isn't just another version of the same equation? Yeh, okay, I can change on the surface, I can change my personality and my style, but can I change me? And what's happened to make me want to change anyway? It's not as if I'm coming back into the fold, or doing a prodigal son thing or anything like that. No. The point is that I am — my past is — a product of the very thing I despise: aggression, violence and hatred all come from that source, and I don't want to be aggressive, violent and hateful. Don't get me wrong, I've had a good time, but . . .

The crab's stopped screaming now, and has just popped. Juice is bubbling out from the edges and sizzles in the ashes.

Hoick it out quick and leave it to cool down. I'm really missing bread now — maybe I'll go into Antalya tomorrow and buy some. Unless there's a village or something in the other direction. He who would valiant be, 'gainst all disaster, let him in constancy . . .

And another thing: compared to the one-eyed mutant back in Antalya I'm in heaven. Compared to *Frankie* I am. Well, I think so, anyway. And millions of other people. Am I just being silly and immature in wanting to change, or should I brazen it out, see myself through to the grim end?

The crab's leg meat is all but non-existent, so hunger forces me to delve into its back. Light is fading fast and it is difficult to see exactly what I am eating. More pine branches on the fire, cracking and spitting and shadows in the orange glare. Acrid smoke in the eyes. What's the point in worrying about poison? If I'm gonna die I'm gonna die. Me wild boy.

Urrgh! A really bitter piece of something slimy is in among the chewy meat and I spit the mouthful onto the sand. Quickly I make for the stream in the dark along my well-worn track and swallow large gulps of cool water. The air is strangely cool tonight; maybe bad weather's coming. God, now I feel sick. Vomit into the pine needles; splashes on my trembling suddenly very weak legs. Hands shaky. Whatever was in that crab was nasty. Best lie down and sleep. Surely it couldn't have affected me that quickly? Dear Lord and father of Mankind forgive my foolish ways, reclothe me in my rightful mind, in purer life my service find . . .

Uncontrollable shaking now, sweating and freezing, gut-ache, pounding head, more vomiting, but I can't get up.

Lapping seadogs from an earthenware bowl and mother says it's time to get up. The strange owl bleeps to signal the hour. Sweet porridge and the smell of toast. Aching bones and a hint of tea-rose and carnation in a summer garden. Candy-twist earthenware edging to the flower beds. An aromatic tree. Pink and blue flowers on large-leafed shrubs. A verandah. Someone calling, 'Tommy, Tommy'. A female voice – mother's voice. Tender care and unconditional love.

But in the cellar lurks a monster. Something moving in the dark.

> He who would valiant be
> 'Gainst all disaster
> Let him in constancy
> Follow the Master

Cicadas return to my mind with the new day's heat, rrr, rrr, rrr, rrr, on and on and on. I sit up, empty, and look about. There is barely a breeze and a new sun is peering round the pines, radiating into my body, warming the bones. And the sea is still blue, the sand still white. My sickness has passed, and with it the confusion that was my old life.

The fog has cleared and I'm sitting staring wonderful, wonderful life in the face. I run and plunge into the sea and swim, out away from the shore until the colder waters of the deeper sea tell me to stop and take a look back at Paradise – the blue water, the beach, the green trees, the mountains beyond, and the blue sky.

Arms held high I sink into the cool depths and see the glittering surface above, beckoning. And I rise again to the day and the sun's heat.

Suddenly my mind is made up: I have to go back, back to civilisation and people, because without them I am nothing.

FOUR

Clothed again and feeling uncomfortable for it, rucksack heavy on my back, I set off west along the coast track hoping to meet with a main road somewhere. Good to be on the road again, going somewhere. You don't move, you die.

According to the map, Denizli was the town to head for as the coast road was almost non-existent. From there I could get on up to Izmir and Istanbul, get some money out of Frankie, then hitch back into Europe and Germany and work.

Short steps. Long roads. Long stretches of shade followed by longer stretches of hot sunshine; pine trees, turquoise sea, ants, butterflies, flying beetles, lizards, but no traffic for what seemed like hours, then an old pick-up stopped and I said 'Istanbul', which was more than five hundred miles and a universe away to the three men sitting in the cab.

There were three men in the front, and the driver laughed and said something unintelligible indicating to the back, so I clambered in and off we drove. Ten minutes later we were sitting beneath a tree in the middle of an ancient village drinking tea while everyone stood and stared in amazement – there must have been fifty men and children there. The women meanwhile remained unpolluted by this contact with a foreign male by watching instead from the doorways and windows of the houses.

A teenage boy was pushed forward. After discussion with the others, some of whom appeared to be getting heated, he turned to me and said, 'You boy, you girl,' and touched my hair, which by now covered my ears and was bleached almost white by the sun and the sea. If only I hadn't shaved that morning – not that my beard grew so vigorously – at least we'd have avoided this particular problem. There was no doubt I was male, I mean, come on, why were the women standing off, watching from a distance? The men were just having a bit of fun at my expense. The important thing was that I needed to continue my journey in one piece, and getting my dick out to prove a point would probably be a bad move, so I fell into a long and animated monologue, smiling all the while knowing that none of them could understand a word. 'Funny you should say that,' I said loudly, 'because the last time someone did I decked 'em with a single blow, know what I mean? And it's only because I'm here in a foreign land surrounded by you lot who look as if you'd eat me given half the chance that I've decided to let you off. But in answer to your query, if you'd like to leave me alone with one of your better-looking young ladies for a little while I'm sure she'd let you know, what do you reckon? Anyway, would anyone care for a fig?' I took a couple from my rucksack and offered them about.

The crowd conferred among themselves, questioning the young translator while a group of boys no older than eight or nine danced about taking it in turns to pretend to roger each other from behind while casting lewd glances in my direction. I finished the tea, put the little glass back on the tray which the truck driver was still holding, and said, 'Teşekkür ederim. Thank you very much'. As expected, the crowd was disarmed by this attempt to master their language. Nodding and murmuring agreement on the soundness of their foreign guest one of the men underlined the decision to give me the benefit of the doubt by soundly slapping the nearest dancing boy across the face. The boy didn't cry out or appear to object in any way but instead wandered away looking confused and betrayed. A few seconds later, his shattered thoughts regrouped, he set about one of his smaller friends who'd found the slapping funny.

Suddenly the decision was made to take me somewhere and I was escorted by the entire village back to the pick-up and loaded in clutching a hot loaf which one of the women had given me.

As we drove away, they all stood there staring after the truck, getting as much value for money as they could from the encounter, and as they disappeared behind the thick cloud of dust thrown up by the truck I felt a strange sense of isolation, aloneness, a sense of being I'd never experienced before. I grabbed the metal tailgate of the truck as it bounced over a rut. I mean, why? Why should I feel this aloneness so strongly right now? Was it just that I'd realised what I was missing – other people – or something else? I'd been on the road for six weeks, with plenty of opportunity to feel alone and far from home. No, this was something different from the need for company I'd felt on the beach – as if the realisation of something essential had tiptoed in through the back door and caught me out, the sudden awareness, a real awareness of a being alone in a strange land among strange people. Really alone.

Was this what they called enlightenment? If it was it didn't last very long. Before leaving England I was reading a book I found on the train written by some Indian bloke, Sri something or the other, who kept going on about enlightenment but I couldn't understand what he meant. It wasn't the sort of everyday enlightenment Mary had been talking about, but was something to do with how you saw the world and your place in it. And if you managed to achieve it, this enlightenment, you could be godlike and live in bliss – I suppose believing it could add a little something to your life if you were short on things to believe, but he said it was all about being and nothing to do with believing. You couldn't have your cake and eat it.

And if I had the book with me I could practise getting enlightened between lifts – there are several methods or paths apparently – then I could impress people by performing miracles and never have to worry about getting a job again. Pulling birds would probably be easier too.

The truck stopped at a junction with a larger deserted road and I got out and shook hands with the driver and his mates. After the initial baiting they were all now sad to see me go and offered impossible advice on the best route to take, gesticulating up and down the road, this way and that, so to avoid wasting time I did a few 'Tesekkür ederims', shook their hands and marched off.

The new route was obviously a main road compared to the track along which I'd just been driven so I strode vigorously down the middle of it in the burning sunshine repeating 'Om' to myself which, according to the Indian guy in the book, was a reliable method of reaching perfection. Om . . . Om . . . Om . . . Om . . .

Some time later an old lorry full of bright green melons stopped in a cloud of choking brown dust. It was the first vehicle to pass in either direction since the last lift. Exhausted with the heat, dehydrated, and delirious with the promise of divine revelation, I'd lost all sense of reason and time, but was aware that the sun had moved some way ahead and that it therefore had to be early afternoon and I was walking west. The driver, a bandit hiding behind a big black moustache, shouted something as he stared wild-eyed into his rear-view mirror as if expecting to see the devil himself appear over the horizon.

'Denizli?' I croaked.

'Hay! Hay! Çabuk!' He looked in the mirror again. I scrambled in and sat on my rucksack in the dusty gap where the passenger seat should have been.

Off he roared, just as another lorry tried to overtake, and we bounced along for a while side by side leaving behind us a billowing cloud of impenetrable dust. Clearly the aim was to get in front and stay there. Behind, you drove blind and if you didn't choke on the dust your engine almost certainly would.

A sudden pothole in the road threw me into the air and onto the driver but far from being put out he just carried on leering into his wing mirror with a mad grin on his face. At last we were gaining ground and were able to dominate the centre of the road, a fortunate thing for the long line of camels I could see in the distance coming towards us. But I didn't get the chance to enjoy the spectacle because seconds later we had engulfed them in our dust storm, blasted them with gravel and roared by. Inside the cab I hung on for life, one hand on the dashboard the other on the door, as we crashed over pothole after pothole, at speed, to ensure that our invisible rival didn't get the chance to overtake.

Ahmet, or whatever his name was, thought that this was the right time to fumble in his pockets for cigarettes. Finding a packet, he extracted one, and poked it into his moustache. Next came the lighter which he retrieved from his trouser pocket. Lighting the cigarette by cupping both hands as a windshield he then stuffed the packet and lighter back in his shirt pocket.

Behind, I could see in the tiny remaining piece of broken nearside mirror that we'd somehow lost the second lorry – either he'd slowed down to get out of the dust cloud or piled into the camel train.

'Er excusi . . .' I shouted, raising myself off the rucksack, using my legs as shock absorbers and allowing my voice to sound more normal, 'can I have a cigarette? Zigaretti?' I touched my lips with the first two fingers of my right hand. Without a word he retrieved packet and lighter from his shirt pocket and passed them to me.

'Tesekkür ederim.'

He grinned then got back to concentrating on the road behind while I went dizzy on the first tobacco fix for two weeks. Scrounged cigarettes always tasted best, and Turkish ones were excellent anyway.

I thought about it: a beachbum-type begging career maybe. And I remembered the long-haired beat in the Gulhane Hotel and suddenly wanted to be like him.

Denizli was a town I wanted to leave immediately. The moment I stepped down from the lorry I was surrounded by another untidy mob of stray males who kept prodding and poking and yanking my hair, and for a moment I had the feeling they were sizing me up for kebabs. A couple of young blokes, about my age, were trying to get their hands inside my pockets as well as the rucksack and, getting madder by the minute, I lashed out and caught one of them a glancing kick, but all this did was further excite the crowd who saw me as some sort of performing animal there to liven their day – the only difference being that they didn't have to pay to watch this one.

'Okay!' I shouted, raising my arms in the air, 'you want a performance? Yeh?' I dumped the rucksack on the ground. 'Right! How about this one then!' And I gave them three verses of 'To be a Pilgrim' followed by a few lines from 'The House of the Rising Sun', before being rescued by two soldiers who looked like inmates from a psychiatric ward. Their arrival cleared the crowd and they hauled me off to a tea-house for English practice. 'Be-at-lees good, we love you, yeh, yeh, yeh, Bobby Charlton good', and 'Russia no good, America no good', followed by 'You have dollars please? American cigarette?' and 'You, me, arkadesh, fren' with much rubbing together of the two index fingers and saucy looks. 'You, me, fren' heh heh heh.'

'No. Me Istanbul,' I said pointing to my chest. 'Istanbul. I go.'

Stupid grins and repetition of 'Istanbul'. After half an hour or so I picked up my rucksack and left the fly-blown café, shaking hands all round before walking back out into the afternoon heat.

A short walk along Denizli High Street would bring me back out onto the main road to Izmir which was just over 100 miles on, and I reckoned that with a bit of luck I could make it before nightfall. From there I'd grab a bus which would get me into the capital sometime early in the morning.

Caught a glimpse of a brown-skinned blond Adonis in the mirror outside a barber shop, but had to admit hair was not cool for hot weather. It kept the sun off the neck and crown but that was more than outweighed by the nuisance, sweat and dirt. Sensing a customer the barber came out and gesticulated, making cutting signs with his fingers, so I gave up and walked in, hoping that at least it might stop every male I met wanting to marry me.

Ten minutes later I was striding along the road feeling light and airy, washed, shorn to half an inch, and minus cash to the equivalent of an ice-cream. A glass of tea was thrown in too. And a cigarette.

There'd be plenty of time to grow my hair again.

Frankie was as expected still in bed when I hammered on the door at 6.30. He looked tired and thinner than usual, and hadn't picked up a tan, but I put that down to candle burning in dark places rather than some terminal illness.

'What are you doing back?' he asked, beaming across his face. You could fall out with Frankie but he never held a grudge. That's why I liked him.

'I'm on the tap. Can I come in or do I have to stand out here on the landing all day?'

'Yeh, yeh. What time is it?'

'About half six.'

'Stroll on. Where've you been anyway? Look at the state of you

– you look like a nigger.' He laughed aloud. 'I'll get dressed and we'll go down the Pudding Shop for breakfast.'

I began to tell him about my stay on the beach when I noticed that someone else was in his bed. Eyebrows raised I pointed silently to the huddled lump under the sheet.

'Don't worry about her – it's just some tart I shag occasionally.'

'Does she speak English?'

'Just things like "jig-a-jig" and "I love you". What's up, you been celibate for a while? Get in there. Go on – she's paid for . . . she won't mind . . .'

'What, after you've been there giving it one all night? You must be joking.'

He walked over to the sleeping form and pulled back the cover. Beneath was a pretty girl with long black hair and pale skin. 'Nilüfer!' He shook the girl. 'Nilüfer! Get up! Let's have a look at you!' Taking her by the arm he pulled her out of bed and to her feet, where she blinked, rubbed her eyes sleepily and stretched. 'What do you reckon?' he asked proudly.'

I looked her up and down – she was lovely.

'Go on, try her out while I'm having a shower. I won't look.'

'Some other time maybe. Go and have a shower.'

He laughed again – he certainly seemed happy – and left the room, adding that he liked my haircut.

At that hour the only customers in the Pudding Shop were local traders and other chancers sitting around drinking tea or coffee, waiting for the daily influx of green Western student hitchhikers to start.

Sat outside in the warm early-morning sunshine we watched the traffic slowly build up as the city shifted up through the gears – an hour later and the streets would be a deafening bumper-to-bumper snarl of hooting cars, lorries, taxis, buses and coaches, men and donkeys, water-sellers, beggars, waiters, itinerant street vendors, bazaar touts, money-changers, shoppers, and a million other comers and goers all getting on with their lives in their own crazy way. By comparison, London streets were a haven of tranquillity, civilised and restrained, the height of northern cool.

'Tea or coffee?' Frankie brought me back from the Old Kent Road.

'Er, coffee. And two fried eggs and tomatoes with bread.'

He shouted the order to the waiter who was sitting talking just inside. 'So what brought you back here? I thought you'd gone for good.'

'I don't know. Living alone on a deserted beach is all right for a week or two but you begin to miss other people. Robinson Crusoe's not my style – not without a Girl Friday, anyway. And I need to make some cash.'

Frankie narrowed his eyes and looked down his thin curved nose. 'Oh, I see. It's money you're after is it, Spitz?'

'All I need is enough to get me to Germany and feed me until I get a job.'

'You? Job?' He looked amazed.

'I told you. I've packed in all this other stuff. I'm getting myself together and going out east.'

'Out east? What do you mean?' He looked and sounded sceptical, but then Frankie always did look and sound sceptical if not downright sarcastic about things he hadn't thought of first.

'East. You know, opposite to west.'

'What for?'

'Looking for wisdom. Wise men come from the east, and all that.'

'Staying on that beach all by yourself hasn't done you a lot of good. You should take it easy, know what I mean?'

Two girls with massive rucksacks staggered from the street onto the little terrace and dumped the bags two tables away. Frankie caught me eyeing them.

'You missed out on a lovely pair of Aussie sorts – I shagged the pair of them; first one at a time on the sly, then when they found out, the pair of them together. But I think they were lesbians. Well, put it this way: I don't think they were too fussed the way they were carrying on in bed. You should have seen them.'

'You're winding me up.'

'Straight. I had to scare them off in the end because they were wearing me out and Mustafa was getting the hump.'

'Why, you giving him one as well?' I joked.

But it didn't go down too well. Frankie eyed me for a long second before replying, which meant I'd either hit a nerve or he was brinking angry at the insult. 'As I say, you've been on your own too long, that's your trouble. Do a lot of wanking, did you?'

The waiter arrived. 'Two kahve, and egg and tomato with bread two time.' He placed the food on the table. We ate silently for a while.

'As it happens, me and Mustafa have been doing very nicely.' He forked a piece of bread dripping with yolk into his mouth.

'Doing what?'

'There's this Irish cat who buys local produce – as much as we can supply. He shifts it in London and Dublin. I'm the language link. Every deal I arrange over the blower I get a nice cut.'

'What sort of produce?'

He looked around, as if to make sure no one was listening, but that was Frankie. 'Carpets, silver, copperware, that sort of stuff.'

'You just make all the arrangements.'

'Yeh.'

'Paperwork?'

'I act as the Irish geezer's agent – it's easier that way.'

'So when they find half-hundredweight of powder wrapped up in a carpet it's all down to you. Sounds as if your mate Mustafa's got it sussed.'

He laughed uneasily. 'What's the matter with you, Tommy? You're definitely losing it, you know that?'

'Just thinking about you, old son. Have you ever seen any of the goods that go out? Course not. How's the money paid?'

'What do you mean?'

'I mean when Paddy pays up, how does he pay?'

'I don't know. Into a bank account I suppose.'

'And Mustafa pays you.'

'Yeh.'

'I didn't realise you were such a prick. What happened to the girl-napping idea?'

'The what?'

'Mustafa wanted you to collect girls for him.'

He laughed. 'We had a bit of a problem. That Jenny turned up again giving it all the big traveller number, so I thought, right you flash cow, you can be number one, but her bloke turned up just as we spiked her and we had to do a runner before she fell over.

He called the gendarmes, Mustafa got captured and I took off for a few days. But Mustafa was sound – he blagged his way out and put the frighteners up the pair of them and they cleared off. I expect she's back in Surbiton by now. Anyway, we had to drop the idea after that because Plod was getting excited.'

'What happened to Mary?'

'Went with her, I suppose.'

'Shame. I could have done with some more of her right now.'

'I told you, you should have borrowed Nilüfer.' He looked suddenly thoughtful. 'Anyway, what do you mean, I'm a prick?'

'You've been set up. You'd be better off carrying the stuff back yourself – at least you'd get all the cash. The way it is they make the money and you take the risk.'

Frankie paused. 'Between you and me, I'm off in a couple of weeks anyway, but if you see Mustafa don't say anything.'

'I'm not going to be saying anything to Mustafa now, am I? Where are you going?'

'Morocco probably. There's a lot of people getting there. Place called Marrakesh. Why don't you come?'

'No. East is the only way to go. But as I say, first I need enough cash to get me to Germany.'

'What is it with you and Germany? Stay here and do the money-changing again. You're halfway there, why go back?'

'I hear what you're saying, but I just want to see a bit more of Europe before going, and there's something about Germany. I can work there until Christmas, go home for a week or so, then split off again.' The only reason I wanted to go home was to show off my tan, believe it or not, and make everyone sick with envy.

'I tell you, Morocco's better. There's a scene down there. Some cat told me a few people are getting there now – you can live off nothing.' I noticed Frankie was getting into his 'cats'. I'd have to start picking up the vocabulary as well.

'You can live *here* for next to nothing, but you've already turned it into a place you've got to get out of . . .'

'Give us a break, will you?'

'All right, enough said. How much money can you lend us?'

Frankie opened his mouth wide in disbelief – we play-acted

most of the time. 'Oh, I see . . . the dodgy money's all right to borrow then.'

''Course it is. It'll save you blowing it on Dildo or whatever her name is.'

'Nilüfer. I'm thinking about taking her back with me when I go. She'd earn a fortune up the West End.'

'I thought you said you were going to Morocco. Is she really on the game?'

'Just started. She's the little sister of someone who owes Mustafa money. Nearly a virgin.'

'Nearly.'

'Yeh. Mustafa broke her in as part payment.'

'Charming. She must have had a sore ring for a week.'

He shrugged. 'You think you're joking. No, it's all about family honour. The geezer should have paid his debts.'

'Well, I don't know about that – seems a bit rough on the girl, seeing as it weren't her debt.'

'Goods and chattels mate. Daughters rate lower than the family dog over here. They just use them for labouring or whoring depending on whether they're lookers or not. Even if they get them married off they have to pay for the privilege, so most families tend to avoid that sort of thing by keeping them locked up. Then the old man and the brothers knock them off instead.'

'Which explains all the weirdos you see about. I saw some geezer in Antalya the dead spit of Humpty Dumpty – with one big eye the size of a chicken's egg in the middle of his forehead. Scared the life out of me.'

'You wait until you go to India. I've heard the place is full of them.'

One of the two girls looked across. 'Hi!' she said, all teeth. 'Do I detect an English accent?'

Frankie wasn't going to answer, so I did. He's a bit offhand with confident women, preferring the more vulnerable ones. 'I suppose you could call it that. Where are you from, America?'

'United States of,' answered the other one. 'California.'

Silly me. You don't call it America. It's The States. In London we call dodgy-looking women 'states'. But these two were far from dodgy.

'I'm Barbara, this is Diane,' said the first one, a dark-haired athlete with beige shorts and serious boots. Diane was a blonde cheerleader type with freckles. A couple of good, clean, wholesome college girls.

'Nice. I'm Tommy, this is . . .'

'Bernie,' answered Frankie. 'You just arrived?'

'Yeh,' they chimed.

'We just got in from Bari, southern Italy,' explained Diane. 'Took the boat. It's a pretty good trip if you don't mind the company. Are you from London?'

'No, the Isle of Thanet,' said Frankie, 'It's an offshore island famous for its legendary one-eyed python.'

'Wow!' gasped Barbara looking astonished, 'is that near the Hebrides and the Isle of Man and all those?'

'Spot on. In fact, on a clear day you can see the Hebrides from the bog if you leave the door open.'

'And the snake? Does this have its roots in the slaying of the dragon; St George and St Patrick?'

Ignoring her, Frankie changed the subject: 'Have you changed any money yet?'

'We changed some in Italy, but we're going to need some more, that's for sure,' answered Diane. 'Where's the best place?'

Then they all started talking rates of exchange and I got bored as Frankie fired himself up to make a few bucks. Taking the key to his appartment I got up to go. 'Don't forget what I said about Nilüfer,' said Frankie. 'Have one on the house.' Then he added, 'Oh, d'you want that dosh now?' and handed me $100 and some Turkish lira. 'We'll sort it out later.'

When I got in, Nilüfer was sitting by the window smoking, staring at the crowds strolling around Sultanahmet Square. She was wearing Levis and a T-shirt and could easily have passed as a London girl, although her pale skin, raven hair and bright blue eyes might have given away her foreign roots.

I said hello but she didn't look round, just carried on staring through the window at the free world outside.

'You speak Ingiliz?' I tried.

Without looking she said, 'Little,' and drew on her cigarette.

'How little? Do you understand what I'm saying now?'

'Of course.'

'Amazing. Where did you learn?' I asked, moving alongside her. Thoughts of sex were the farthest thing from my mind as I stood looking at her, despite her profession. She was extraordinarily good looking, but maybe a bit on the skinny side for Turkish men who tended to treat fat women with more respect, as they did fat men.

'Books and radio. And now Frankie.'

'I'll teach you if you want.' Blind leading the blind here, I thought.

She showed the first sign of interest. 'Please. I like learn quick.'

'I like *to* learn quick. I want *to* speak English. I like *to* eat fish. I want *to* drink tea.'

'I want to drink tea.' She smiled at last.

'Okay. We'll go to drink tea. Now.'

'And Frankie? Is good?'

'Frankie is my friend. No problem.'

Suddenly at ease, knowing that business wasn't on my mind, she leapt from the chair with a childlike expression of joy on her lovely face. 'Okay. Now we go drink tea. Now we go *to* drink tea.'

'Good. And we'll buy a dictionary.'

'I have.' She skipped across to the side of the bed and retrieved a small book from the floor. 'Here. Türk–Ingiliz dictionary.'

'Bring it with you. We might need it.'

'From now on you speak only English, okay? Pretend you're American.' Seeing the lack of understanding in Nilüfer's eyes, I tried again. We were sitting outside a little tea-house in a far corner of the Grand Bazaar, well away from unwanted observers. 'You now American. Pretend American.'

'Pretend?'

I opened the dictionary. 'Pretend – Yalandan yapmak. Gibi yapmak. Iddiada bulunmak.'

She giggled aloud and took the dictionary to read what I was trying to say. Her face lit up. 'Amerikan oyniyalim. Okay. I understand. Why?'

I had an idea running around my head, but until I knew her feelings about it I'd have to keep it to myself. 'Because you understand Turkish. When I'm bargaining with the dealers they're always talking together and it would help if you tell me what they are saying. Also it's the quickest way for you to learn English, okay?'

'Okay.'

'Right.' I took a sip of sweet tea from the glass. 'Are you happy?' Something about the girl brought the knight in shining armour out in me. I held nothing against Frankie for what he was doing, but the thought of her being friendless was disturbing. Anyway, I was beginning to fancy her myself.

'Happy?' She laughed cynically. 'Now, yes. Yesterday no, tomorrow no. Is not possible, happiness like this, how do you say, selling sex.'

'You want to finish selling sex?'

She laughed again. 'Of course. But not possible. I go, I dead.'

'If I go I will be killed,' I corrected.

'Yes. If I go I will be killed.'

'Say it like an American girl.'

'Okay,' she said, elongating the vowels, 'If I go I will be killed.'

'Great!' She was a natural. I held her hand across the little table, and could feel the old familiar madness welling up inside me. 'Listen. If I can get you out of Turkey, would you like that?'

Her jaw dropped as she realised what I was saying. 'Where? It is not possible. I have no passport. No money. And my man – he me kill.'

'He will kill me. Your pimp will kill you.'

'Pimp?'

'Your man. Mustafa. A man who sells a girl's body is called a pimp.'

'My pimp will kill me,' she drawled aloud as an American couple dripping with camera equipment hove into earshot. The woman gave me a mean look and they moved on.

'Nobody need know. You go,' I waved my hand dismissively, 'never come back.'

'Where I go?'

'Where will I go? To Germany. With me.'

She gasped. 'Germany! I have friend in Germany, in München. Please. You take me to Germany, I love you.'

That evening I found Frankie sitting with Mustafa outside the Pudding Shop. I'd arranged to meet Nilüfer the next afternoon at the same tea-shop in the bazaar, but hadn't expected her to be the subject of conversation that evening. I'd told her to carry on as usual to avoid any problems, although the thought of Frankie being with her again made my stomach turn over.

'Tommy! You like coffee?' asked Mustafa with an olive oil smile.

'Cheers, Mustafa.' I dragged up a chair. All around us in the soft evening darkness sat a mixture of young travellers and Turks. Three tables away sat Barbara and Diane, surrounded by a little mob of polished and over-coiffured local boys who stared hard at me when the girls waved.

Mustafa clicked his fingers at a waiter and pointed almost indiscernibly to the empty space on the table before me. The waiter disappeared inside the restaurant and reappeared almost instantly carrying a coffee probably meant for someone else. On this patch, Mustafa came first.

Frankie spoke with a grin that wasn't quite true. I knew him well enough to be able to tell when something was on his mind. 'Did you get your leg over?' he asked.

I sipped the coffee before answering. 'What are you talking about?'

'The bird. Nilüfer. Have you seen her?'

'Yeh. Of course I've seen her. But in answer to your question, no. Not after you and him have been there.' I laughed trying to sound matey. 'No, we went for a walk along the seafront then she split, saying she had to see someone. Why?'

'Because my little girl is gone,' said Mustafa deep in thought, playing jacks with a solitary sugar cube, tossing it in the air and catching it on the back of his hand. He looked across the table at me as if he had a dog turd stuck under his nose. 'What she say to you?'

'Not a lot. She just showed me some of the sights.'

'Sights?'

'Things tourists look at – you know, mosques, the zoo . . .'

'You go in the zoo?'

Mustafa's attitude was getting to me. 'As it happens, I popped in to see if they had a spare cage for you.'

Frankie nearly spilt his coffee. 'Cut it out for fuck's sake. The geezer's only asking for a bit of help.'

'No we didn't go in the zoo. We walked past Gulhane Park then down towards the Bosphorus and along the seafront, okay? What is this anyway, some sort of interrogation?' I overdid the anger because I disliked Mustafa and would have liked the chance to slap him.

But Frankie intervened, 'No, no, she's gone missing and Mustafa's wondering if she's gone back home or been kidnapped or something. Nothing personal.'

'Better not be, otherwise I'll have to give him a spank.' I kept to London-speak to prevent Mustafa understanding what I was saying.

'Leave it out – the man's only worried about his investment.'

Mustafa smiled at the word. 'Investment, sure, I worry. This girl, she no good. But no problem. I make her – how you say? – see a light.' Then he leaned back in his chair as if he'd solved a problem, but the chair gave with the pressure and shattered his composure as he overreacted to its unexpected backward movement. To reassert his authority he bellowed for more coffee. A donkey brayed somewhere in the distance.

'Not for me, Mustafa,' I said standing up. 'I've got to say hello to someone.' I'd noticed the two American girls about to leave, trying to evade the young Turks who were all over them. And I needed their assistance.

'See you later,' said Frankie without looking up.

Weaving through the tables I caught up with the girls who were now shaking hands grimly with each of the boys. 'Jesus,' gasped Barbara, 'how the hell do you get these monkeys off your back? What's a girl have to do to find relaxation around here? It's either the goddam traffic or these jerks.'

'Come with me. With a bloke around they'll soon clear off.' Forcing myself between them, I shoved the two girls out onto the street and led them away down the hill towards Sirkeçi and the Galata Bridge.

'Phew!' hissed Diane, 'I thought Italy was bad. These guys beat them hands down. We'd better check nothing's missing. Barbara, check your purse.'

They looked through their shoulder bags, but everything seemed intact.

'Hang on!' whispered Barbara stopping in her tracks with a bemused look on her face, 'I think my virginity is missing.' She wiggled her arse as if checking. 'No. It's still there.' Then the pair of them shrieked with laughter and walked on.

Acting for all the world as if I knew the place, I led them into a tiny restaurant, actually a floating boat moored to the piles of the bridge, and forked out a couple of dollars for fish kebabs and cold beer all round. The setting for romance couldn't have been better. Not love and sex romance, if you get my drift, but foreigners-in-a-strange-land-with-the-moon-and-stars-twinkling-in-the-water kind of romance, where friendships are forged and memories born, as they say. The only snag to all this romantic stuff was that I had other things on my mind at the time and had a problem coming across as totally sincere, but not knowing me from Adam I assumed they couldn't tell if I was being sincere or not.

Diane shoved her blonde hair back over her head. She liked herself a lot. 'Your friend Bernie said that you lived on an island. That must be really beautiful. I have family that live on Cape Cod and the closeness of the sea makes a hell of a difference to their outlook on life – they're far more relaxed, more spiritual in their approach to life.' As Diane went on, Barbara pointedly concentrated on her fish to let me know she'd heard it all before. As I guessed, there was a tiny rift between them – traveller's rift.

'Bernie was taking the piss.' I replied.

'Taking the piss?'

'Yeh, I come from London.'

'What do you mean "taking the piss"?' asked Barbara.

'Joking. He was joking.'

'Strange thing to joke about. Does he come from London too?'

'Sure. He lives opposite the Tower of London.'

'Oh, wow,' they both chimed with admiring glances, not thinking for a moment that I too might be joking. There was no point in explaining that Frankie came from Cable Street, a rough part of London just a block away from the Tower. But it was obvious that their sincerity was skin-deep and designed to encourage further revelation, so I gave them a brief outline of my own home, based on childhood memories of Charlton House and grounds. When Diane asked what I'd 'majored' in I ground to a halt. I was slowly learning that these people spoke a different language. They explained that 'majoring' was your main subject at university, so I bluffed and countered that London kids studied within the City and Guilds System of Advanced Education and that I had gained the equivalent of a degree in Colloquial English and Modernism, but it didn't work and my rating with them took a hard knock. Efficiently adjusting their line of approach, they recategorised me as being of a different social type. Now filed as Non-Uni in their minds, I realised that despite a contempt for education and the system, I had quite a hang-up about my lack of it, and that sooner or later I'd have to do something about it – not my lack of education you understand, but my hang-up.

But of most concern to me right then was whether they'd be up to another meeting tomorrow, because that's when I planned to steal Barbara's passport. With a haircut, a rucksack and a pair of shorts, Nilüfer could pass for her, and as long as she kept smiling and drawling unintelligible American-sounding words, I was sure we could get past the guards on both the Turkish and Bulgarian border. The Greek border would be far too risky.

About nine o'clock Barbara and Diane decided it was time to get back to the Youth Hostel, so I brought up the subject of the next day. 'You mentioned islands earlier – do you fancy taking a trip to the Marmara Islands tomorrow? I hear they're beautiful and traffic-free. Ideal for relaxation.'

Then fate took a hand. Diane spoke first. 'I have to go pick up some traveller's cheques and make a few phone-calls so count me out. Maybe some other time.'

But Barbara was game, she wanted to go and said, 'Sure, I'd love to go.'

We arranged to meet next morning to catch an early boat.

Büyükada, or big island, was a little way off the mainland and special in that it had no cars to disturb the peace. The only public transport was horse and trap, and for a dollar our driver took us to the far side of the island dropped us as close as he could get to the water's edge, fifty feet down at the foot of an eroded headland.

Slipping and sliding down clutching fresh bread and bottles of Coke, we clambered through a barrier of rock pools until we eventually found a beach of dry, yellow mud where we both stripped and put on swimming gear. Barbara – or Babs, as she now wished to be known – had no objection to showing her body but stopped short of nude bathing in case any locals were about.

'You can never tell with these people. They could end up stoning me to death,' she shouted as she ran and dived into the deep blue sea. But it wasn't the Turks she had to worry about. Like an Olympic champion, she swam swiftly out into the depths of the Sea of Marmara, then turned and waved for me to join her.

Knocking the cap from one of the bottles of Coke, I gulped some down then took Frankie's little bottle of knock-out drops and poured in enough to do the trick – he'd said a couple of drops would do, but I counted in half a dozen just to make sure, screwed the top back on and shoved it back into my jeans pocket.

'Hey, Tommy, come on in!' she shouted again, her voice sounding strangely detached across the water, 'It's beautiful – so invigorating.'

Taking hold of the doctored Coke with my thumb over the open neck, I stood up and charged into the water like any young bloke looking for a bit of fun. A minute later we were bobbing about together like kids, splashing and giggling, and I passed her the Coke. 'Hey, what a gentleman,' she spluttered, her eyelashes all sparkling with seawater, and took a long pull from the bottle. I watched her Adam's apple bouncing up and down and prayed I hadn't overdone the dose because she was a sweet girl and didn't deserve any harm coming to her.

Within seconds she'd passed out. Grabbing her under the arms, I began the short haul back to the beach where I dragged her into the shade of a large boulder beneath the cliff. Inside her bag I found her passport and student ID card and a ball-point pen, then took a blank sheet from an address book and wrote: 'Babs. If you recover before I get back, this note is to say that I've gone to get help. You passed out on me in the water. Lucky to get you back to dry land. Instead of walking back the long way, I'm going to try to swim across the bay – it'll be quicker. I hope I can make it. I've left all our stuff here, obviously, but I hope nobody comes along and steals anything while I'm gone. I didn't know what else to do. See you soon. Love Tommy.' I folded the note carefully and stuffed it under the edge of her bikini top.

By running and walking intermittently I made the quay minutes before the ferry set out for the mainland. By my reckoning I'd arrive at the tea-house in the Grand Bazaar, after picking up my rucksack at the flat, with barely time to spare before Nilüfer showed. It had to be that way: public appearances had to be kept to a minimum.

For two Western backpackers, one bogus, the least dangerous exit from the country had to be quietly by train to Edirne, then by road, hitch-hiking across the border into Bulgaria. Having come in by that route with Mary I'd noticed that the guards seemed far too preoccupied with motor traffic and smugglers to bother much with young foreign hikers.

Back at the flat I took Frankie's rucksack and sleeping bag, a sweater and a couple of T-shirts, and four pairs of socks for Nilüfer to carry. I considered leaving a note with some sort of explanation but it would only have compromised him with Mustafa – I mean, what could I say? The less he knew the better. On the way to the bazaar I bought a small but very noticeable flag of the USA to stick on her rucksack, and a plastic pakamac in case it rained. Boots and shorts would have to wait until she was with me to try them on for size.

By the time we met, over two hours had passed since I'd spiked Barbara and we had no time to spare – I had to assume that she had already contacted or would be close to contacting the police and that every minute counted. I felt certain we'd make it, but plenty of stamina was going to be needed and I could see that Nilüfer was already feeling the strain having stayed up all night, hiding at a friend's house. She'd cut her hair shorter but had smothered her face with make-up thinking that looking like Joan Crawford might help, so I had to make her wash it off before we could leave. Grabbing some old American army boots, thick woollen socks and khaki shorts from a surplus store we dashed off to Sirkeçi Station and jumped on the 1412 to Edirne just as it was departing. Then she fell fast asleep with her head on my shoulder and remained out cold until we pulled into Edirne later that afternoon. I woke her by whispering 'Beautiful Barbara' softly in her ear, but instead of a friendly exchange or a 'Thank you, I love you Tommy' when she opened her dazzling blue eyes, her pale face was a picture of terror. Still half asleep she searched my face until something registered. 'Sorry . . .' she said finally in a soft Texan drawl, 'I much sleep . . . where we are?'

'Edirne. We have to move fast now. This is the dodgy bit.'

'Dodgibit?'

'Dikkat.' I used the Turkish word for 'caution' you see on traffic signs. She grabbed her rucksack.

'Okay, let's go.' Out of the station we went, past two armed police who gave no indication of being on the lookout for anyone, and set off down the road. The thought then hit me that Barbara might still be lying on the beach at Büyükada, dead. And suddenly I felt sick. What's the point in saving one and killing another? Why hadn't I just nicked her passport and gone back to make sure she was all right after giving it to Nilüfer? – I could still have blamed the theft on the locals and walked away with a clear conscience, but it was far too late to go back now.

Minutes later we stopped the first vehicle that came along, a Turkish-owned VW Camper tantalisingly on its way to Germany. But to risk going through customs with its two male occupants and suspect baggage would have been stupid. Nilüfer kept her mouth shut and acted the shy girl for an hour until we reached the border, when the camper was directed into a fenced compound for inspection. Now came the hard bit. We thanked them for the lift and marched purposefully towards Passport Control.

Grabbing Nilüfer's hand I looked into her eyes and said, 'Okay, Miss Barbara Nicholson, of Boston, Massachusetts, United States of America, you are going with me, your English boyfriend, to England. Okay? Don't look frightened. Be happy. Tired maybe. But not frightened. Okay?' Seeing the guard eyeing us through the window I laughed confidently and pointed like a good tourist to the hills in the distance.

'My name is Barbara Nicholson, of Boston . . .'

'Keep smiling.'

She smiled. '. . . of Boston, Massachusetts, United States of America. I am going with you, my boyfriend, to England.'

The border guard scowled at our passports, glanced briefly at both of us, then gave us an exit stamp. Bold as brass I said 'Teşekkür ederim'.

He half-smiled, 'Bir şey değil.'

'Allahaısmarladık!' said Nilüfer cheerily, sending my heart into overdrive. The silly girl had forgotten her role! I couldn't believe it.

He stared hard at Nilüfer.

'I practise my Turkish. Thank you very much, officer. Bye,' she drawled, and grabbed me by the hand. 'Okay, Tommy, we go now.'

'Güle güle,' he murmured behind us.

And away we marched. We'd done it.

The Bulgarian guard was more interested in a transit visa costing $5 if we stayed less than 24 hours in the country, but I explained we'd be lucky to get through in that time, and away we marched again, two silly foreign hitchhikers with nothing better to do.

At each border we received exactly the same treatment as anyone else, offhand but friendly, and as Turkey became more distant with each border passed – Yugoslavia, Italy, Austria and, finally, Germany – Nilüfer relaxed further into the cool beauty she probably was before Mustafa appeared on the scene. But far from our relationship blossoming into something more, if anything it became like the memory of Turkey – more distant. And now that she was free she had to me become unapproachable; any move had to come from her. Having played the white knight, I'd painted myself into a corner and knew that I'd seriously let the side down if I tried it on. She just didn't need it if her faith in life was to be restored. At every cheap hotel and hostel we stopped, we slept apart, and not once did I try to force the issue. All the while in my mind a tiny flame of hope flickered which said, 'Don't worry, play your cards right, old son, and she's yours.'

Whichever way I looked at it, this was the first time I'd had to treat a girl as a friend and not an aid to ejaculation. Come to think of it, I didn't know any male who beneath all the crap and clever words wasn't driven by lust when dealing with women. But given the ingredients of our relationship the outlook seemed pretty barren. After her experiences with men, and overjoyed simply to be free, Nilüfer wasn't about to throw herself at anyone, and we carried on as friends, the issue of any sexual contact between us dying slowly through lack of nourishment. Even worse, deep inside, way beyond all the excuses and reasoning, I knew she didn't fancy me, and that was a blow to my idea of fair play, after all, she owed me – I'd rescued her from hell, hadn't I?

But wasn't I acting for the purest of reasons, to help a maiden in distress?

If so, why did I leave the real Barbara out cold minus her ID on a remote beach in a foreign land? Why hadn't I just enrolled her aid, and told her about Nilüfer's plight? We could have got her into the American Embassy and asked for help. But would it have worked? They may have thrown her out as a waste of time. Had I done the right thing . . . ?

Or was there some other motive? Would I have risked so much if she hadn't been so beautiful? And what is beauty in a woman, but the promise of better sex? If I'm really honest, I wouldn't have bothered if she'd been sub-standard in the looks department.

We reached the German border at Salzburg and presented ourselves and our passports for inspection. This being the last obstacle before Nilüfer's long-dreamed-of reunion with her friends in Munich, she was nervous.

'Then forget about your friends,' I said, 'and come with me to England.'

But she wouldn't. These friends, whoever they were, meant a lot to her.

The guard stared at us for a long time, and even cocked his head to one side at Nilüfer as if he knew her from somewhere, but in the end he let us through because he fancied her too. Then a car stopped and took us to Munich and my chances with Nilüfer were over.

It took an hour to find her friend's address, a flat in a miserable concrete block, and when the door opened I was taken aback to see a handsome young man standing there, about the same age as me. Nilüfer rushed at him and they kissed and hugged, then he stood back to look at me in that expressionless, Asian way. They spoke in Turkish, she pleadingly, he looking increasingly awkward, then finally she turned to me and said, 'Mehmet, my boyfriend, he want to say thank you very much. Would you like come in for some tea? Sorry, like *to* come in . . .'

FIVE

Hot, cloudless German day on the main road leading north. There's no sea for hundreds of miles in any direction and the pressure's beginning to get to my brain. I don't particularly want to live by the sea but it's nice to know the water's not far away. You feel you could go mad here in central Europe, surrounded by land and people and heat, but maybe it's all in the head. Everything seems to be in the head lately. Turks. Money. Deception. But maybe I deserve it because I crapped on the American bird.

I'm wavering each day between what I was, what I think I'm becoming, what I'm actually becoming, and what I want to be, and every one of me catches me out.

Like when I'm sitting in the shade of a large old oak tree by the side of the road just enjoying the peace, listening to the buzz of insects and the birdsong and the hollow tonking of cowbells between traffic, and smelling the sun-baked cowshit beyond the hedge and wondering about life and feeling the freedom and soaking up the keen beauty of the mountains. Then a car stops with a beautiful woman in it – they're all beautiful these days – and I'm back on the same old track wondering if she's up for it, trying to get a glimpse of her tits as she stretches over to the glove compartment when I think she's not watching. It's like there's a demon in my head, an evil spirit that occupies me, controlling my brain when I'm not vigilant. Look, look, look, a nipple showing through the material of her summer dress.

The thing is, part of me thinks it's pathetic and small-minded, that part of me that wants to be cool and unfussed, man, but until it actually happens and the lust thing stops, I suppose I'll just have to pretend to be cool.

Then a car stops, a weird-shaped Renault which doesn't exist in England, driven by a blonde woman. Next to her is an older man who looks like a tired old film star. 'Wo gehen sie?' she asks, leaning across him towards me, showing cleavage.

'Comment?' I reply.

'Ach so. Vous êtes Français?'

'Non. Je suis Anglais.'

'Ach so. You are English. Where are you going?'

I tell her I'm basically going anywhere, but towards Stuttgart will do and she says they are going to Karlsruhe which is beyond Stuttgart, so jump in. I'm half glad of the lift and half irritated because I was enjoying sitting by the road and I don't feel much like struggling with communication problems but she looks a bit cheeky and who knows . . . ?

'Why are you in Germany?' she asks efficiently as we accelerate away.

'I'm looking for work.'

'Ach so.' She translates to her bloke who is much older than her. 'Er sucht Arbeit.'

Then they gabble away for a minute or two before she comes back to me. 'What do you do?' she asks shamelessly. Germans don't beat about the bush.

'I'm an engineer,' I lie.

'Engineer! But that is impossible. You are too young.'

'Not in England.'

'You have been to university?'

Here we go again. Better pretend. 'Yes, I went to City of London University and majored in telecommunications. I was a child prodigy.'

'Ach so. Telecommunications,' she translates this to her bloke and they gabble on again.

We're zooming quietly through beautiful wooded countryside at great speed and I'm impressed by the car which is like some futuristic space-capsule. Another eager-looking hitchhiker is stationed by the roadside with his thumb stuck out but they ignore him and suddenly I feel special.

She glances at me. 'His name is Ernst, and my name is Frieda.'

'Pleased to meet you.'

Silence.

'And your name?'

Should I tell them the truth? Maybe I'll nick something from them later on. But no, I've changed all that now, it's all behind me. Where *does* this stuff keep coming from? 'Tommy,' I answer.

'Ach so. Thomas. Hello, Thomas.'

'No. Tommy. Or Tom. Not Thomas.'

The Germans have a little joke about this. And it's easy to understand exactly what they're saying by where they stick the variations of my name into the sentences. Ernst ends the short, humourous exchange by looking into the distance with watery eyes and saying, 'He is young.' And she agrees. Then they have another more serious conversation followed by a short silence as Frieda prepares herself for a speech.

'Ernst ist mein Chef, my boss. I am his personal secretary. He has a Fabriken where is made Autoradio, you know . . .' detecting a lack of comprehension behind my look of interest she points to the car radio. 'He makes these. The best in the world.'

'He's got a car radio factory.'

'Factory. Yes. He has said to me that you can work there if you want, and you must learn to speak German. Do you want this?'

I've stumbled straight into a job – somebody up there likes me. 'Well, yes, I am wanting this very much,' I say.

Outside, the autobahn blurs by and I doze intermittently as we head north and west until suddenly we turn off into the countryside and pull up in a car park packed with limos outside a big hotel masquerading as a Swiss chalet. Inside I'm booked into a room, told to prepare for dinner and left alone for half an hour, I assume to give Ernst leisure time with Frieda, lucky bastard.

The receptionist is a beautiful, blonde-plaited, blue-eyed, very German female who can recognise a bum when she sees one, and when I arrive at the desk in but a change of T-shirt, smelling strongly of house shower-gel and lived-in boots and jeans, she sweeps me into the centre of the packed and unfriendly dining-room, deposits me at a table laid for three, and walks out again with her nose in the air as I'm about to ask for a beer.

Doing my best to look unperturbed, I relax awkwardly back into the chair and survey the scene around me. The dining-room is some sort of baronial hall, every wall bristling with swords, muskets, axes and other weaponry, interspersed with the heads of deer and wild boar, each of which seems to wear its own particular expression of surprise. As if that isn't enough I seem to be surrounded by their killers and young at feed – hefty carnivores in rich tweed, handsome Aryan liberals in expensive casual gear, politicians and businessmen in hunting green, and tanned blond super-kids who are staring suspiciously in my direction. One word out of place here and they'll be on me, tearing me apart, and already I can feel icy rivulets of nervous sweat trickling from my armpits, coursing a trail down my rib-cage. But suddenly I catch myself in one of the mirrors on the wall and realise I have nothing to fear, because as yet I haven't opened my mouth, and to a stranger I could just look like one of them.

So why does the fräulein on the desk hate me? Despite her arrogance she'd be the perfect partner for hitching. Put her in little leather shorts and make her up like Mae West and we'd stop everything on the road between Düsseldorf and Kandahar.

Kandahar, Afghanistan – I've made up my mind to go there in the new year, as soon as I've made enough money and got Christmas out of the way. Some far-out geezer I met on the road in Klagenfurt when I was with Nilüfer said Afghanistan was cool, so as I liked his style, I've decided to go there and pretend I discovered it first.

Ernst and Frieda turn up looking flushed. She keeps snapping at him, her boss, and he looks like a sad little boy.

'Vy do you not hef a trink?' she asks me, as if I am insulting their hospitality, but before I can answer she calls a waiter who ignores my existence.

'You like a whisky or brandy?' she asks, while Ernst discreetly requests something behind her back. Ah, I see now. Among other things he has a drink problem, so I ask for a beer, a large, cold beer. She orders chilled mineral water for herself and they at last sit down so that I can relax between them knowing they will protect me if the other diners turn nasty. Already I can see nostrils twitching. One hunter in particular is huge and keeps glancing hungrily in my direction, sniffing the air.

'So. Are you liking the idea of working with Autoradio Ernst?' asks Frieda.

Of course I am. It means I can save money to fuck off east after learning German. Five months will be ample time in this place. 'Is the factory far from here?' I ask sweetly.

'Oh, another hundred kilometres or so. On the edge of the Schwarzwald – the Black Forest. It is very beautiful there.'

The drinks are delivered, carefully to them, carelessly to me, and I think about the Second World War. But Ernst and Frieda aren't like the others here and as if she can read my mind she suddenly says, 'These people are not the same as all Germans. There is a division here in Germany between the Schwäbische people,' she looks about, 'and the rest of us.'

'You're not a swedebasher?'

'Schwäbische,' she corrects, 'hah nein, Ernst isn't either.'

He asks what we are talking about and she explains. As if to endorse things he looks about the room and laughs aloud. Frieda hisses at him. But if anything his outburst brings renewed respect from the other diners because they can see he is rich and doesn't give a damn what they think.

'They are a sort of, how you say, superior peasants,' she explains. 'You must learn to live with them, because where you will be staying they are the same.'

Later, after Ernst is helped to bed, I lose my mind on schnapps and ask Frieda if she will be nice and come to bed with me, but she laughs and says don't be a silly boy.

In my crisp Teutonic bed I sleep and dream of big wide streets and tall white buildings with German men in grey, and big white skies and restless red and black flags and tortured iron, clattering and screaming over old shiny cobblestones. Then I say 'goodbye' to the girl from the reception desk who is my wife in the dream and we cry and I am terrified by our separation and wake myself up as gunshots shatter the peace and bullets spin from Doric columns.

Outside the window a cricket whirrrrrs in the warm dark and suddenly I feel deliriously happy to be free of the dream, but devastated that I've left her behind.

For a while I drift in and out of the dream – in when I want to see more, out when I get scared – hoping that I can pick up again with my wife and maybe get to make love to her but when I reach the right street and the right house she's gone, everyone's gone.

And the cricket whirrrrrs on. And I feel horribly sorry for it, alone in a vast universe, crying out for company.

A hundred kilometres further on they install me in the Birkenhof Gästhaus on the edge of the Schwarzwald in a village full of suspicious locals. Here I am to live as an undesirable immigrant in a little village full of people dependent on the Ernst Radio factory. And as I am Ernst's blue-eyed boy, his Englander friend indeed, they have to remain polite at all costs – at which they're very good. In fact they're very much like the good old salt-of-the-earth English country folk I remember as a kid, kind to a fault when they have to be, but entirely untrustworthy and ready to grass you up as soon as look at you if it means a pat on the head from his lordship.

But I'm not alone. In the village lives another social outcast, Eva, a girl with pale features and jet black hair, a bit like Nilüfer, who likes to walk about in the middle of the night speaking to the moon and stars, singing and laughing. One day we meet and she gives me the come-on and says visit me after dark. She speaks English but according to the locals she is also insane.

The house in which she lives belongs to her parents who live elsewhere, and every night instead of having sex with me she goes on about infinity and the seven levels of consciousness. And about the necessity of eating vegetables as opposed to flesh. And astrology. And bringing the dead back to life. And reincarnation. And about all sorts of other weird stuff including a book called *The Kama Sutra*, which describes how you can reach enlightenment by worshipping each other's genitals – seems enlightenment is definitely a key word these days – and when I wonder to myself if she might be prepared to become more active in a physical sense she says she can read my mind and whispers she will come to me later on the astral plane, one of the seven levels of consciousness about which she has spoken.

When I see her the next day and ask why she didn't come to see me she says time has no meaning on the astral plane and that she could turn up unexpectedly at any time or any place, adding that in reality there are no boundaries.'

Now I don't mind all this spiritual stuff, especially if it's going to get her into bed with me, but if the truth be known some of it gives me the willies, the heebie-jeebies, you know what I mean? And I feel that my privacy as a human being is in danger of being jeopardised. And this infinity thing, well, what can I say? It scares me shitless.

'Look,' I explain, 'I've managed to live my life so far without knowing about all this stuff, and had a pretty good time to boot, but I think you're wasting your time, *liebling*, because I just wanted to be friends . . .'

'I know, I know,' she says, putting her hand reassuringly on mine, 'but our meeting was meant to be.'

'Oh, Eva, just to bed please with me come, if only to practise the things in that book you have me shown.' I'm also learning to speak German, and doing pretty well because, according to her, I'm reincarnated from a German family, jawohl.

She looks into my eyes. 'Let me see your hands.'

'What for?'

'I want to read them. Show me.'

So I hold them out.

For some minutes she studies the lines closely, making little marks with a biro and squeezing them in different places. Eventually she speaks, but when she looks up into my eyes, all the fun seems to have gone from her face. She is in her element. 'Okay. You say you are 21, right? Okay. There are many things here and I will not waste your time saying things you know already, but I can tell you that you will travel . . .'

'I'm already travelling.'

'. . . and that the travel will make you have many changes.'

'Like travel broadening the mind.'

'Yes. But maybe more than you expect.'

'But that's what I want. I feel I've been wasting my time for years. I need to get away from my past and . . .'

'Discover yourself. Okay. But that applies to most of us.' She squeezes my thumbs gently. 'There is a, what is the word, *possibility*, no . . . there is a *tendency* towards violent behaviour in you which has caused others pain in the past . . .'

'I used to box a bit.'

'Not just boxing, you are aggressive, perhaps when in the wrong company, and have hurt people in the past.'

'You said you didn't want to waste our time talking about my past.'

'But there is a link here with the past and future, also a friend – see this little line here coming from your life line – this shows the influence of a friend in the future, perhaps to do with the death of somebody you know. It is difficult. But my intuition says you have unfinished business, but for you it will be resolved in the best way.'

Frankie's the only one who comes to mind, and I'm worried about his dealings with Mustafa. 'Is it the death of a friend?'

She looks again. 'Maybe. Maybe not. That depends on you. But definitely a friend is involved, perhaps two, and between the three of you there is a death. Maybe I should do the cards.'

Do I believe this rubbish or not? I pull my hands away with a cheesy grin.

'No, that'll do. Any good news, or is it all doom and gloom?'

'Hah, doom and gloom, I like that. No, it is not all doom and gloom. Otherwise your hands are very good. They say also that you will have a very important meeting soon, next year, with God and he will change your life.'

I laugh aloud. 'With God! Is that all? No one higher up the ladder, you know, with a bit more sway, like the Queen, or Prince Charles? I hear he's getting into all this stuff as well.'

'Who knows?' she snaps, 'All I'm trying to say is that these little upward lines on your life, head, and fate lines indicate a meeting of spiritual significance. You must not laugh at this.'

After that night I didn't see her again; she went off to visit her grandparents in Berlin – at least that's what the neighbours said. But things weren't the same after those meetings because she'd infected my simple life with an infinite variety of complications. Now there had to be a question and an answer to everything – and reasons. There was a need to be *aware*. Relaxation would be impossible until I knew the answer to everything or at least until I believed I knew, or pretended I knew. Not even sleep would be simple because now I had the astral world, and zombies, and levels of consciousness and death to think about.

So I got into learning to speak German and drinking beer, gallons of it, week in week out until the time came to catch a train back to England.

SIX

Nothing much has changed. Still cold and damp. And dark.

Thankfully I get fucked by a couple of old girlfriends who appreciate my fading tan and find me amusing now that I've something exotic to talk about, but there's a problem when they find out about each other and I'm accused of two-timing. Two-timing, I ask you. These girls are still passing notes at primary school. It's free love now, love and peace, man.

And the blokes are still bragging about fighting and fucking. Even worse is the current pub fashion for sleazeball singers – Frank Sinatra, Matt Monro, Tony Bennett, Dean Martin and Sammy Davis Jnr are their heroes now and children's hour gangsterism is their style. Seduced by their own sad fantasies of stardom and the mafia, nothing presents a more unnerving sight than these phoney mobsters big-timing it in cheap-skate boozers. But what else have they got to live for? Any mention of anywhere else in the world apart from their own tiny patch just produces blank looks and questions about foreign women and whether they 'do the trick' or not. So having got the Christmas bit over I find a job stacking biscuits during the day and enrol to study sociology and philosophy at night because I'm now a cool geezer and all this other stuff is below me. I move back in with Mother and Father to avoid having to fork out on rent, cooking, laundry and other bills, and for a week all goes well, but when I begin playing Ravi Shankar and Himalayan temple music the strain begins. Om mane padme hum.

'Why don't you go and find yourself a decent job?' is the familiar hint of a problem to come from my mother; soon to be followed by well-meaning advice, yet again, on getting my hair cut, because by now it is almost on my shoulders and 'only mental cases wear hair that long'. As the days pass she expands on this: it makes me look like a 'silly boy' or a 'girl', or someone who's 'not all there' but I refuse to take the bait because my new angle is strictly tolerance and understanding and failing to be either is uncool.

Frankie hasn't been seen or heard of by anybody, and I feel that he's shown more of the true traveller spirit than me by disappearing altogether, and when I secretly seek out Beryl, my mature ex-lover, to find out what's going on it turns out that she's done a runner from Ray, her old man, and has gone to live in Italy. She wasn't pregnant after all. And when I run into him soon after, he's bordering on friendly and obviously unaware of what's been going on – he even calls me 'son' when he asks what I've been up to and says that it's nice to see a youngster doing something with his life for a change. Well, well, well, all my fears of persecution, torture and death were groundless.

And as for Michael Mouse – I saw Waller and he says nought's come of it, so my conscience is clear . . . No, I don't mean that . . . What I'm trying to say is that my immediate personal risk cupboard is nicely short on skeletons. I can walk the streets safely. I mean, if Michael Mouse shows up with a little team and they give me a retaliatory kicking, so be it, but as for sleeping nights, well, ask me how I really feel about it and I have to admit I wish I'd stayed in that night – I badly hurt and demoralised the guy, wrecked his dignity, and I'm sorry.

Evening classes. Sociology and social idealism, liberty, justice and equality. Social rules. Mores – did you know you look at your watch when you're waiting on the street corner for someone just to let strangers know you're not a weirdo? Social responsibility. Human action and free will. Free will and responsibility?

And philosophy.

People get paid to spread this crap. So I ask for my money back and they tell me to fuck off. When I say I need the money for my ailing grandmother they say tough shit, don't fuck with the Sociology and Philosophy Department. But the girl in accounts comes out for a drink and gives me a blow job. While we're at it in her father's car, I check my watch as a couple stroll by so they don't think I'm a weirdo. They think I'm timing her.

Finally, I manage to get enough bread together to leave, and after a stand-up argument with Mother and a frosty handshake with Father I walk out of the house with an ex-army kit bag over my shoulder containing a couple of pairs of underpants, socks, T-shirts, a jumper, another pair of Levi needlecords, washing and shaving kit, a map of Europe and Asia, my old feather sleeping bag, and three books: *The Shape of Things to Come* by H.G. Wells, *Fathers and Sons* by Ivan S. Turgenev and *The Bhagavadgita*, a sort of summary of Hinduism in easy-to-read form for beginners.

I also carry a large page-a-day diary in which to write important things and attempt to express myself.

If I'd known the way things would go I'd have left everything behind but the change of clothes.

* * *

Cold, dark rain at Dover. Out on the empty iron, wood and polished-brass ferryboat heading for Ostend. Rough sea makes the few passengers friendly with each other but I remain aloof, concentrating on Bazarov's philosophy as outlined in *Fathers and Sons*, which seems a good one to bone up on should I meet any intelligent people I feel the need to impress. 'Have you read *Fathers and Sons* by Turgenev? (pronounced Toorgayniev) – do you prefer Bazarov or Arkady? Oh, yeh, nihilism, man, too much.'

And the *Bhagavadgita*. Ooh la la. I have to read it over and over again to get the meaning; at least, I think I get the meaning. And my fellow passengers must be impressed at my detached attitude by now.

> I told thee purest Lord, there are two ways shown to this
> world;
> Two schools of wisdom.
> First the Sankhya's, which saves in way of works
> prescribed by reason;
> Next the way of the Yogi, which bids attainment by
> meditation, spiritually.
> Yet these are one.
> No man shall escape from act by shunning action;
> And no man shall come by mere renunciation unto
> perfection.

So up yours, Bazarov. Or up yours, *Bhagavadgita*, dependent on which viewpoint you happen to be into at the time. With a bit of concentration and dedication, not to say meditation, I should soon be able to get across a fair imitation of a cool freak. The danger is if I should happen across someone who knows what he or she's talking about, someone who starts hitting me with facts and smart arguments. I suppose I'll just have to put on that bored, couldn't care less, superior attitude, and pretend I'm above it all.

And H.G. Wells. Mmm. From what I've read so far, it seems like the bloke couldn't make up his mind whether to be serious or not. Sure, he's putting himself out on a limb trying to predict the future, but the Second World War being started by a Polish salesman getting an orange pip stuck under his dental plate didn't come true – or the great fever which followed in 1955 and wiped out half the world's population.

Might have to abandon that one or use it as toilet paper.

Read the next paragraph over and over again as I'm now trying to catch the eye of a nice little sweetie who keeps glancing in my direction, but she's with some old people who are embarrassing her by being there and I'm glad I've left all mine behind. They keep trying to buy her drinks and cakes and all she wants is freedom. But yes, she's spotted me so I give her a superior little smile touched with humility which always gets 'em and she responds by staring back. Then the old people drag her away somewhere – but she glances back again before disappearing forever.

Pitch, lurch, crash and boomph, with an occasional shattered drinking glass for a few hours, then the waves suddenly flatten out and instead of sea mist there's foreign-looking houses outside and we're gliding sedately into Ostend harbour as if the crossing never happened.

At last: foreign ground beneath my feet again; what a relief. As much as I'm getting to like some of the changes taking place back home – the Beatles getting all groovy instead of being a pop group and Flower Power festivals at Woburn Abbey among other places, there's still that horrible feeling that someone's going to pounce on you when you're least expecting it and lock you up for something you know nothing about. I know there's a big movement going on and that everyone is apparently getting emancipated and liberated but it scares me because I don't trust the people who are broadcasting the good news. According to them it's Swinging London and a Whole New Scene, you know what I mean – we've never had it so good and it's getting better – but the only pictures are of Lord or Lady this or that or the Earl of something else poncing about in Mayfair clubs with one or two working-class Uncle Toms thrown in to keep the peasants happy.

Back on earth, Jacko's still resorting to burglary to pay his rent, and Jimmy Mac's still battling with our own kind of people at the dole office for a handout of his own money despite the brain damage they're trying to accuse him of inflicting upon himself for being a passenger in someone else's car when it hit a lamp post. And Dinger's still 'accidentally' dead after being murdered. And I got beaten up in Paddington Green nick for laughing at an officer of the law, so I'm glad to get out, glad to be a foreigner again. As long as you don't step over any of the sacred boundaries out here they leave you alone, because foreigners like me mean endless paperwork followed by demotion and ridicule unless they get it exactly right and prove that all the effort involving everybody up to the head of state was really worth it.

Through Passport Control and Customs without the slightest problem and minutes later I'm striding the freezing Ostend streets looking for the youth hostel. Damp ice underfoot soon seeps through the leather soles of my mosquito boots and frozen breath collects on the bumfluff around my mouth making me feel like an explorer. But the cold is *cold.* For some silly reason I thought it was going to get warmer the moment I crossed the Channel.

The hostel's warm. Apart from one solitary Dutch girl who refuses to talk, I am alone in a cream and green gloss world of creaking and straining hot water pipes and clanging bedsprings. I wish the girl would creep into my dormitory in the middle of the night and ask me to cuddle her but she doesn't, and I feel too cool to wank now, especially after reading the *Bhagavadgita* for supper. Maybe I'll do this next bit when I get out East, practise a bit of meditation.

> In isolation he should sit steadfastly meditating, solitary,
> His thoughts reined, his passions hid away, without belongings.
> In a fair, still place, having his seat neither too high,
> Nor too low, let him be,
> His sole possessions a cloth, the skin of a deer, and the Kusa grass.
> There, concentrating his mind upon The One,
> Controlling self, silent and at peace, may he find Yôga,
> And gain clarity of vision . . .

I get a bit concerned with the way they have to use capitals for 'The One'. It puts me off reading it. Blind reverence was never really my number, although I was quite reverent about Maureen Hall, at one time until she went out with another kid with more spots than me. But that was a sort of first-year-at-school infatuation which coincided with one of my earlier experiences of enlightenment where I'd been advised by a friend to try rubbing my dick up and down the next time I took a bath. Astounded in fact. But getting back to the capitals, it seems a bit small-minded to highlight your religious beliefs with grammatical statements.

Funny what you think about lying in a strange bed.

And then suddenly it's morning and snowing, and you get ready, wrap up as best you can, put on an extra pair of socks and march out into the blinding-white day with your kitbag over your shoulder and hope someone gives you a lift before you freeze to death.

These continentals know their winter-driving, though. Chains and studs and powerful snow-clearing monsters – while back in England we're sliding all over the place, freezing our pensioners to death and blaming everyone else.

A nice woman stops and gives me a lift for a few miles, then a bloke in a van, and I think I'm not doing too bad despite the weather, but by nightfall I'm still only in Brussels and have to crash in the youth hostel then get a bus the next day to Aachen, where I soon get onto the snow-clear autobahn fit and ready for those fast German super-people who can whisk me back down to Austria. The next night I stay at Nürnberg youth hostel and practise German on a noisy crowd of 15-year-old boys by ordering them to be quiet – and the most amazing thing happens, they immediately fall silent. No chance of that in England.

And the next day a fat man in a big Mercedes buys me lunch in a motorway restaurant – jägerschnitzel and chips – and I sit there eye-flirting with a beautiful blond businesswoman at the next table who winks goodbye when she finally leaves with a man who has arrived with a large spanner to throw into my fantasy. The plan was to abandon the fat man and stand hitching at the exit until she came along to take me off to a Black Forest motel, but it didn't happen so I reconsider the *Bhagavadgita* while having some gâteau and cream and another beer, which the fat man insists on.

> There are three gateways to hell through which men
>   pass to ruin –
> That of Lust, that of Anger, and that of Greed.
> Let the true man shun them.

81

Capitals again. I'm not sure about this *Bhagavadgita*. I'm searching for some sort of special enlightenment tailored just for me which no one else has tried, but this stuff sounds just like the Bible. I need a sudden and vast input of mind-blowing energy which'll turn me into a living god; something so powerful I'll be able to change the world to suit me, whether anyone else likes it or not. But maybe that's not allowed. In which case just what is enlightenment? Jesus could walk on water, why can't I? I'm a son of God as well, you know, despite my faults.

Faults. I thought I'd come to terms with that on the beach – it's everyone else's fault. Parents, teachers, school bullies, employers and other thugs, and life in general, are all to blame. For example, this fat geezer's turning me into a glutton and the businesswoman turned me into a slut, so how do I achieve enlightenment with all these other diversions around to corrupt me?

And didn't Krishna say, 'No man shall escape from act by shunning action, and no man shall come by mere renunciation unto perfection'?

'Do you think man can achieve spiritual perfection living in the modern world?' I ask the fat man.

He eyes me warily, mumbles something about the time getting on then disappears into the men's lavatory. When he comes out again he goes to the phone booth, has a long conversation with the machine then comes back and takes me to Innsbruck. All the way we barely exchange a dozen words and I'm beginning to think that maybe he's some sort of weirdo or that I've somehow said the wrong thing by mentioning spiritual perfection, as he could be Satan on one of his business trips to earth disguised as a fat bloke.

'What did you say your line of business was?' I ask.

'I didn't,' he says. 'But as you ask,' he adds, 'I'm in meat.'

'Ah. What exactly?'

'Wurst.'

And then he drops me off in the slush of some town centre square and drives away watching me in his rear view mirror. Definitely a pervert. I reassure myself by deciding that he probably eats too much meat and is either reincarnated from a pig or is heading in that direction. Could it be that in me he saw that blinding purity of spirit which casts demons from mens' souls and freaks out the impure? Too right. But I'd better go easy on the spiritual stuff because Granger told me that one of his aunts had turned very strange after trying to get in touch with her dead husband. The doctor said she needed help and had her locked away for safekeeping. Apparently, he said, this happens a lot to people who try to contact the dead or speak with God, so I imagine that as God is all-powerful, he must have decided that it was time for these people to be locked up. And going on from there, if God is all-powerful does sin exist? When our religious education teacher said God was all-powerful and I'd muttered 'silly whore', she wasn't amused at my reasoning that it was God, not me speaking, and smacked my head. A beating from the head of department followed, despite my protests that their sweeping statements about God seemed to be a bit one-sided, favouring them. He pointed out that what I was experiencing was a fine example of God 'working in a mysterious way', a statement my grandmother always used to explain everything that hurt.

Well, the wonder of it all is that now I'm standing in Innsbruck, still no nearer to divine wisdom than the day I was born. I mean, I don't even know what wisdom is, let alone divinity – all of it seems like some pointless mental exercise invented by lunatics. I'm quite happy as I am, thank you very much. Only the ignorant crave enlightenment. Mmn. Only the ignorant crave enlightenment. Yeh, I like that one. Time to use all these books for bog-paper. Ha. Where's my lift? It's snowing again. Carry on trudging through the deepening snow.

Having just decided that if the worse comes to the worst I'll walk back into town and kip in the station, a Mercedes sports car with chains and a playboy driver stops and takes me madly on into Italy, grinding and gushing through snowdrifts and on into a white dreamland called Cortina. This delightful town comes complete with sweet woodsmoke, horses and sleighs with bells, coloured lights hanging from iced fir trees, a fountain in the town square frozen solid, and hundreds of beautiful people the like of which I never knew existed on this planet. But I know my limitations on this one – sixty quid to see me through to India – and get to the bus station as quickly as possible for a brandy and an espresso coffee before I blow it all on another fantasy.

The café is warm and cosy and wood panelled with glittering coffee machines like old American cars and I have to wait until ten past midnight, which I don't mind, for the bus to Venice to arrive. I figure a few lira spent on a ticket will be cheaper in the long run and warmer than hanging about or trying to hitch through the night.

So far, the only thing I'm missing is other travellers, who seem thin on the ground in January, but I'm bound to come across some between here and Istanbul. Beyond there, who knows?

* * *

By the time the bus got out of the mountains and onto the coastal plain the snow had disappeared and an anaemic yellow sun was pushing its way up through the Venetian fog. I thought I'd get to grips with the day by dropping in and reviving a few memories of the last visit when I was with Nilüfer and we'd sat and ate the cheapest spaghetti on the menu by the side of the canal and watched the kids diving into the water to cool off. Now the place was grey and cold, besieged by floodwater, and as dull and quiet as the day after Christmas. Gone were the colourful crowds, the packed tour boats and alleyways, the singing gondoliers and beautiful women; now there were just Venetians in raincoats, and you could have lost every single one of them in Soho. Even the tiny bar where I sat over an empty espresso cup for an hour could have been lifted straight out of Wardour Street.

Nilüfer. What a mess. You risk life and limb for a complete stranger because some screwed-up corner of your brain is screaming 'Do it! Do it! You might get your leg over!' And at the end of it all she's even unsure about inviting you in for a cup of tea – a cup of fucking tea – because suddenly she's got someone else to think about. It could almost be funny.

Now I'm in some sort of wintry limbo, a frozen wasteland between West and East, forcing a passage between the past and the future.

As it is outside so it is in – I mean, look at the landscape now, snow-swept sepia, huddled bundles of rags they call people.

Zagreb, Belgrade, Sofia, all frozen, in slow motion, people wary, too cold to relax, too cold to struggle. The only vibrancy is mine and I'm marching on through, a ruddy-faced apparition with nothing but direction and a sense of humour, because soon I'll be there, in Istanbul, by the fire. And out of it.

* * *

When the train finally steamed into Istanbul Sirkeçi I left the West and the past behind in second class and slipped out up the hill towards the Gulhane Hotel. I wasn't going to look for Frankie as I couldn't be sure about anything – especially if Mustafa had found out it was me who'd liberated Nilüfer – and I didn't want to be side-tracked into any of his little schemes either. But I guessed sooner or later that curiosity would get the better of me.

The Gulhane was now the haunt of the year-round traveller, who tended to be more road-worn and less scrubbed than the summer version, and I was secretly gratified to get a friendly greeting from Salim the proprietor and his boy who recognised me the moment I walked through the door. There were at least half a dozen interesting-looking people sitting about who'd observed this familiarity and I could see they were impressed. With apologies and an explanation that business had unfortunately never been better, I was taken upstairs and shown into an occupied room with a spare bed.

The other bed, a double, I soon discovered was being used by a secretive Italian couple who whispered together in a mixture of Italian, French, German and English, the idea being, I suppose, that it would fool everyone, but the actuality was that everybody was able to understand everything they said all the time; if they'd stuck to street Italian they'd have fooled us all. But I guessed the idea was his because girls just don't play silly games like that. She was tasty in a sort of boyish way and, I suspected, friendly, given the chance, but he was jealous and suspicious and made a big point of letting me see the gun he carried – an ancient revolver that would probably have exploded as soon as the trigger was pulled. Embarrassed at this silly display, his girlfriend met my eyes for the first time without supervision as he spun the chamber to check it was fully loaded, and instantly we became friends. I'd picked up a battered paperback from the table in the common room with the title *Dead Fingers Talk*, so laying back on the bed with my boots on I made a big point of being far more interested in the book than his gun.

Mustafa was in the Pudding Shop as usual when I finally plucked up the nerve and dropped in for egg and chips, but instead of his usual flash offhand self, he was friendly in the extreme, 'Tommy, how are you?' he gushed, and I knew he was up to something. 'Where have you been? How is London? You make plenty money?' But there was no mention of Frankie. So I didn't ask.

After, I strolled across the square to our old apartment, but Frankie wasn't there either. As usual, Ali was asleep under the stairs. 'Hey, Ali, good to see you again. Where's Frankie?' I asked, slapping him on the back.

Ali looked furtive, bothered by my presence as if he felt someone might be listening. 'He go. Big problem with girl.'

'Which girl?' I hoped it wasn't Nilüfer.

'American. She say you take passport. Police come, take Frankie. Mustafa pay. Frankie go.'

'Where?'

Ali shrugged. 'Maybe London.'

Istanbul in winter was cold and damp, threatening snow, and smoky. Wood stoves had been moved into the colder hotel rooms, and these became the focal points around which the evening smoking sessions took place. One night a couple of days later I found out for the first time what it was like to get stoned – sure, I'd mucked around with tiny bits of brown stuff in silver foil back in London, but I'd never noticed any effect. My room-mates, Rico and Gina, Redman the draft dodger, American King John, Indian Amin and two French girls, Corinne and Francine, had gathered round the stove to try out Redman's dope which he claimed to have bought from the best source in town. It wasn't long before you could see it taking effect. Rico was getting loud and cocky in between periods of paranoia – 'You have to be careful of the pigs around here'; Gina was giggling quietly to herself; King John was staring into space with his mouth wide open; Amin was rigid on his back on the floor, staring at the ceiling; Corinne kept asking Francine if she was all right; and Redman was telling tales so vividly outrageous that I started laughing and couldn't stop.

PART II

ONE

Cockroaches and red-gloss walls through tears of laughter. Stinking bog, no chain, no paper but only urinating anyway. Good old Gulhane Hotel. Rico passed this way and threw up his guts after showing off and smoking too much, trying to force the girls to smoke more than they wanted. Everyone's crashed out now except me because I'm too stoned to lay down. I tried earlier but had to get up again and now I badly need to eat to settle my stomach which is like an echoing cave sending out nervous tremors and little waves of fear which trigger my brain into overactivity and self-concern. Tried reading *Dead Fingers Talk* again but like the *Bhagavadgita* most of it is beyond me, but for different reasons, having been written by a middle-aged American junkie using in-jokes and obscure words which mean nothing. Can't see the point. Climb on seat to pull cistern lever to flush away chocolate pudding, tomato skins and oil, and my bright orange piss, and it works first time, kerlonk . . . whoosh . . . Get down, switch off light and ricochet off the walls to bedroom.

Gina's in my bed and Rico's sprawled out and unconscious in theirs so I squeeze in next to her and pass out almost immediately, but with a powerful awareness of the female next to me who, in her night-time wanderings and the need to keep warm, is getting about as close as she can get. Images of a rusty revolver and a passionate Italian male keep flooding in. So, after the passing of immeasurable time and slow emergence from stonedness with an urgent erection, I very quietly roll out of bed, take a cover and go to sleep on the settee in the common room.

Later, as dawn lightens the dark corners, I catch a blurred glimpse of Rico leaving, with his suede and tassels and high boots for all the world like a backwoodsman. He is off on a train to meet his hashish contact somewhere between here and Ankara

91

and expects to be back before midnight. I know all this because I overheard him yesterday, filling in Gina with the details before warning her to be faithful. So I fall fast asleep again only to be awakened up by an evil-looking Mustafa shaking my shoulder.

'Tommy! Tommy! Here.' He presses a small piece of paper into my hand. With a nasty smile he adds, 'You come. If not come . . .' Then he runs a finger round his throat.

So I look at him stupidly and groan, 'If I don't come you are going to cut your throat. You ought to be in Charlie Chaplin films, you know that?'

The smile evaporates from his face. 'Not me die – you. You finish.'

'When you want me to come? Where? You're a pest, d'you know that?'

'Today.' He looks insistent.

'Yeh, yeh, what time?'

'You come three o'clock, okay?'

I'm getting irritated by his pushy manner. 'Three o'clock's no good. I have to read my *Bhagavadgita* at three o'clock every day because I'm majoring in enlightenment.' I know he's too proud to ask me what I mean, but despite the little joke I still want to know what the fuss is about.

'You know why,' he spits. 'Your friend Frankie no good.'

'What Frankie gets up to is his problem. It's got nothing to do with me.' I'm waking up properly now.

'No, no, also your problem. Where girl?'

Oops. 'What girl? What are you talking about, Mustafa?'

'Turkish girl. You take.'

'I don't know what you're talking about, now go away and leave me alone before I have to head butt you.' I throw the scrap of paper back at him just as Redman walks into the room, good old Burl Ives Redman.

'Hey, what's going on?' He looks at me, surprised and concerned. 'This motherfucker hassling you, man?'

'I wish you wouldn't use that word,' I groan.

'What?'

'Motherfucker.'

His eyes light up. 'Hey, does it kinda turn you on, man?' He turns on Mustafa. 'How about you? Does the idea of screwing your mother turn you on? Hey, I bet it does.'

Mustafa glares at me. 'I see you later.'

'No, Mustafa. I've got nothing to say. Maybe some other time.' He leaves.

Redman looks suddenly serious, but then he tends to, it's all part of his facial pantomime. 'You don't want to wind these Turkish guys up, man. They're vicious bastards.'

'Yeh, I've heard it all before. My grandfather was at Gallipoli.'

'Oh, yeh, your lot really fucked up there. The only way anyone ever beat the Turks was by annihilating the motherfuckers. So what's it all about?'

'Last year I smuggled one of his girls out of Turkey.'

'One of his girls?'

'Yeh, she was on the game, given to him in part payment for her father's debts.'

'What, you got her out for him?'

'No, he didn't know anything about it. He didn't at the time anyway.'

Redman's jaw dropped. 'Jesus. If I were you, I'd leave. Like now.'

'No, bollocks . . . I wasn't in the wrong.'

'No, not in your eyes, man. These fuckers are still in the sixteenth century. If you don't get outta here now, someone's gonna find you with your throat cut and your severed dick stuffed up your ass. It's their idea of fun.'

I have to laugh. Redman's bearded face has that slightly mongoloid, quizzical look about it which makes everything he says seem funny.

'I've had a bad night, man,' I moan. 'I'm going back to bed.' I'm quite pleased with the way I drop 'man' in without it sounding too contrived, because so far I've been feeling a bit uncomfortable using the new lingo, but you get more respect if you do. Maybe I'm mixing with the wrong people.

'How come?'

'Gina was in my bed last night, so I had to sleep down here.'

'Hey, man, she's got the hots for you . . .'

'Leave it out, Redman.' But it's a tantalising thought. I could do with an ego boost right now. Come to that, my ego always needs boosting. 'What makes you say that?' I ask.

'Oh, I can tell – the way she was looking at you last night when Rico was too busy mouthing-off to realise what was going on – the erect nipples, the damp patch on the carpet when she got up . . .'

'Fuck off . . .' Giggling again, I drag myself back to the bedroom where I find both beds empty, which is disappointing because I'm intrigued about Gina now. Then I notice her clothes hanging over the end of the bed, so she has to be around somewhere.

I drop a couple of logs onto the glowing embers in the stove, undress, get into bed, and read *Fathers and Sons*, which is easier than *Dead Fingers* or the *Bhagavadgita*, while in the background the muezzin wails and the catching wood spits and puffs against the sooty glass panels of the stove door.

Five minutes later Gina enters the room wrapped in a towel, her hair wet, fresh from the shower. 'Hello,' she says cheekily, now that Rico's miles away, 'why did you go?'

'Why did I go where?'

'Last night. From this bed.'

'Because of Rico's gun.'

She laughs and looks suddenly like Mia Farrow with tits. She also has that strange dark yellow, burnished-gold hair colour that some Mediterranean females have. 'Oh, he would never use it. He is a showman, you know.'

'A jealous showman.'

'All Italian males are jealous.' She rummages around in her rucksack. 'Shall I roll a joint?'

I hate tobacco in the morning, but say 'Yeh, sure', to avoid sounding like I care about something. I'm laid back, you see.

So she gets a tin out and skilfully makes a three-paper joint as if she's been doing it all her life while I pretend to read.

'What are you reading?'

'*Fathers and Sons*.'

'Who is the writer?'

'Toorgayniev.'

'I don't know it. Is he Russian? Must be I suppose with a name

94

like that.' She lights the joint without ceremony and sits on her bed.

'Yeh, but he went to live in France later, and died there.' This I found out from the write-up inside the cover.

'Read me some,' she says dreamily, casting the towel aside, and comes across to join me in bed. 'Here.' She passes the joint.

'Thanks,' I say, trying not to sound anything. Her getting into bed with me has seriously disturbed my inner cool. But she's done it so naturally I wonder if it's the way she normally carries on – if it's the way all these people carry on. Just because she's got into bed with me doesn't necessarily mean that I have any right to expect sex, so I'll play it cool, and test the water by looking into her eyes at exactly the right moment, if I can find it. If a kiss follows naturally, well, the rest should be right behind. It's just that all this bed and bedroom sharing and walking around half naked has temporarily *blown my mind* – is that the right way to put it? Maybe a bit strong for what I mean exactly. It's *fazed me* – that's the one. *This cool chick who's got the hots for me has fazed me by getting into the sack starkers, man.* 'Mmn, where'd you get this?' I ask, as if the knowledge would make any difference.

She turns on her elbow to face me – my chance to eyeball her. 'Rico got it from somewhere, I don't know, but it's quite good.' She takes the joint gently from my mouth and says, 'you want a blow back?'

What's she talking about? 'Sure,' I say, 'go ahead.'

'Open your mouth.' She puts the lighted end of the joint into her mouth, and blows a jet of smoke into mine. It's nice. A bit cooler. Then I do the same for her. Then she lays back dreamily and says, 'I want to fuck,' in a lovely Italian way.

Outside, the sky has turned a dirty yellow, a keen wind has got up, and flurries of snow are dancing at the window. So we do.

Later I'm in Jener's café with Gina – avoiding Mustafa in the Pudding Shop – when he walks in with two mates. Seeing me he makes a beeline for our table and sits down without invitation. 'Hello, Tommy. Good you come.' He looks at Gina. 'You introduce me to your charming friend?'

'Mustafa – Marilyn; Marilyn – Mustafa.' Acknowledging my stare, Gina goes along with my little deception – I just don't want her caught up with him if I can help it – and offers her hand.

He gets down to business. 'Your friend Frankie also owe me money. But because of you.'

'I don't understand.'

'The girl – Nilüfer, she use passport of American girl. American girl she tell police. Police come and take Frankie. I pay for Frankie out. So, two thousand dollars for Frankie, and three thousand dollars for girl. You owe me.' He grinned.

I sit back and stare at him, doing my best to look as if I'm in control, but actually I'm still stoned. And five thousand dollars – the guy's a maniac. 'I don't know what you're talking about and anyway where am I going to get that sort of money?'

Mustafa looks smug. 'You not have?'

''Course I not have, you wazzock. Anyway, as I say, I don't owe you anything. The girl went of her own accord; I didn't force her.'

Mustafa doesn't understand.

'I not make girl go. She go to see boyfriend. She owes me money for passport. She not pay. So, she owes you money. Five thousand dollars. Okay?'

'No, Tommy. She owe you. You owe me.'

'No, Mustafa. She owe me, Frankie owe you.'

'But Frankie is in Morocco.'

'Then that's your problem, Mustafa. Go to Morocco. See how you get on there.'

Mustafa stands up, unconsciously pulling out the creases on the arms of his brown man-made fibre suit jacket. 'No, Tommy. You owe me. You pay in one week.' Then he puts on a tough guy face, looks Gina up and down like a piece of meat, and walks out followed by his buddies.

Some days the city is bitter cold and dark, others, the cloud blows away and a sharp Asian blue sky backdrops the fabulous skyline of domes and minarets. From both the Eastern and Western land masses freezing winds from the interior whip through the streets, but the worst howls down from Russia, across the Black Sea, whining its own bone-chilling dampness into the Gulhane Hotel through the old warped windows and doorways, gusting down the stovepipes and filling the rooms with smoke.

Rico's back, so Gina and me have been back on stranger terms for the best part of a week. I've a day left, 24 hours, to find five thousand dollars or discover what Mustafa means to do about it. In normal circumstances I'd have worked out some sort of plan, either flight or confrontation of some sort, but to be honest, I don't much care, as an odd apathy seems to have descended upon me. Just thinking about the problem – if that's what it is – is too much to contend with, it's not important, and anyway, I know something will turn up. I think this lethargy has something to do with the hashish I'm smoking, but as it's not unpleasant in itself, I carry on smoking and behaving in an uncharacteristic manner: indifference is the new one, a new style, a display of detachment for the benefit of the rest of the screwed-up universe. I like it. This is hip, pretty baby.

Indian Amin rushes into reception where we are all sitting in a smoky circle and says, 'Does anyone want to go to Teheran?'

I knew something would turn up. Of course I do. And Redman after a moment of deliberation decides he's up for it too.

'Some Iranian guys need company for the journey,' he explains, 'and they'll pay us for going.'

An hour later we dump our bags into the boots of three Mercedes cars parked outside a hotel a stone's throw from the Pudding Shop and Mustafa and his gang. A light snowfall fails to make much impression here in town, melting as it lands and damping the sidewalks but little do any of us realise the weather that lies ahead. Everything packed, the Iranians happy that all is in place, we double up, each trilby-hatted Iranian driver with a hairy freak, and roll away watched by Gina and King John who have come to see us off.

Down to the Galata Bridge, across to Taksim then follow the curve of the hill round to the ferry. All the time my driver is cracking and eating pistachios and pecan nuts as if to distract himself from the business of driving. Grunting something, he gesticulates that I should help myself. The pistachios are good, a bit bacony in flavour, but the others, the fake walnuts, make me want to puke. Then he offers a cigarette and demonstrates the limit of his English language – 'zigarette goot' – so I try German and discover he can speak a fair bit of that. Explaining that the cars have been bought in Munich for resale in Iran, where they need to be imported on someone else's passport, he adds that they do the trip at least six times a year without any problems.

Disembarking from the pitching ferry a little while later in Üsküdar, I feel a vague sense of relief that Europe and Mustafa are now on the far side of the Bosphorus. Getting back's going to be the only problem. Behind us the other two Mercs look menacingly robust as we plough through the slush pits in the road leading east towards Ankara, and Sami, my driver, points out proudly that they are the only cars capable of handling the journey in winter.

After a long day of freezing mud and battles with lorries and other road users, we're installed in a soulless concrete block hotel in Beypazari with Turks, Iranians, Syrians and naked light-bulbs in every room.

Redman's already unhappy, having been terrified every inch of the way by the bad driving of his partner, 'You should see him, man – he's like a fucking three-year-old with a toy. All he does is blindly follow on, whether it's safe or not, with a big grin on his stupid face, playing with the heating and the radio and the gear column and the steering wheel; eating, drinking and smoking, giving no thought to anyone or anything else on the fucking road. I'm gonna die before Teheran – I can feel it, man – killed by some motherfucker with a brain the size of a peanut. This is not good.'

According to Amin his driver is almost as bad, and won't talk or share a thing. By contrast, Sami seems pretty good. The other two then try to pull a fast one by suggesting we take turns with the drivers, and to shut them up I agree to discuss it with Sami the very next day, but I've already made up my mind that I'm not moving anywhere because the further east we go, the worse the driving conditions seem to get, and if anything I'm looking for ways to increase not decrease my chances of survival. Besides, by asking me to share the risk they're also asking me to increase my share of the risk and illustrating quite clearly that they don't care too much about me – anyway, I don't want to insult the gods by attempting to determine the course of fate, so looking after number one it is, then.

After a bad night of scrabbling cockroaches, snoring men with strong feet and armpits, automatic farts and persistent coughing, we climb back in our cars and head on out towards Ankara. 'Don't forget to talk to your driver,' Redman reminds me.

But Sami won't have any of it, especially when I let him know it isn't my idea and that I'm more than happy to continue map reading in the lead vehicle with him. Anyway, he prefers the Englishman, so the next time we stop I say I'm really sorry folks but as hard as I tried he still won't let us change vehicles – it's something to do with me speaking German.

It seems that with each mile that passes something happens to remind me that Europe is over and long gone: a dead dog here, its guts trampled into the muddy tarmac by passing lorries; a dead horse there by the side of the road; another pile-up; odd-looking locals staring hungrily at us as we pass; and police and army armed to the teeth looking dangerously in control. Each mile brings with it a drop in temperature until we reach Ankara, a grey and meaningless place, where it begins to snow in earnest, and by Yozgat, 120 miles further east we're floundering in a white-out and left with no choice but to stop until the blizzard blows over. Sami takes this chance to get chains on, and when we can see again the traction's good enough to enable us to get up speed despite the thick snow. In places the snow is so deep that only a foot or so of the roadside telephone poles remains visible, and in another, where the narrow ice-covered road runs alongside a deep ravine, we have to inch past a waiting bull-nosed tipper truck with such care that the slightest error of judgment would send us straight to our deaths hundreds of feet below. Thinking it might be safer to take a chance on foot, and ignoring Sami's advice to stay put, I try to get out but find there just isn't enough ground left on which to place a foot. Carefully closing the door I contemplate leaping over Sami and out his side, but the truck is too close and I realise I'm trapped. All it needs now is a tiny landslip, a crumbling of whatever makes up the edge of the road surface and we're done for.

But we make it, inch by inch: Sami a picture of concentration, his mind focused on the potential value of the Mercedes. Once past we have to stop and get out to guide the other two, and the second driver, alone and abandoned by Redman who is following on foot until the danger has passed, has to keep reversing to realign the car after continually screwing up the angle of approach. Suddenly I understand the danger of being in the lead vehicle and make pains to point this out to Redman once he's gingerly negotiated the truck himself. 'Fuck, man,' he says, 'I don't know how you made it – your tyres were right on the edge of the fucking road.'

And the weather isn't improving. At Sivas, where we stop for the night in another concrete block caravanserai there's a howling snowstorm that lasts all night, and in the morning, far from being deterred by the deep virgin snow Sami insists that things can only get better. So we plough off into the blinding whiteness each of us wondering just how far we can get.

Once back on the main road the going improves, yet despite this our target of Erzurum is becoming increasingly unlikely as constant snowfall continues to force Sami to keep the speed down. In wild and remote countryside somewhere outside Erzincan we are followed by a pack of wolves who keep racing ahead to stop at the roadside to peer through the windows at us as we pass, checking, to make sure there's something edible inside. At this point Sami pulls a large automatic pistol from beneath his seat and points it playfully in their direction. 'Wolf nix gut,' he says, 'Sie wollen uns essen.'

Now it's dark and we're still a long way from Erzurum, but Sami's keen on proving that he's invincible, that he's the man for sticking to schedule, so we're going to charge blindly on into the few yards of blurred whiteness that lie ahead within the range of our snowed-up headlights. Wallowing and churning in and out of snowpits, up inclines into blackness, around bends skirting empty voids, the strain is beginning to tell and Sami's tiring fast. I talk endlessly just to keep his brain from wandering prematurely back to his wife and a warm bed in Tabriz, but I'm beginning to hallucinate with the constant strain of staring ahead. Even keeping the eyes open has become a struggle. Twice Redman's driver has missed the road altogether and ploughed into snowdrifts, but now at last the terrain seems to be flattening out as we approach Erzurum.

For some time we've been following a strange red light some distance off to the left which appears to be running almost parallel with us. At first I thought it was a reflection on the window, and then when I couldn't find what was causing it, some sort of low-flying aircraft, but by the time I realise that the mystery object is in fact a light on the front of a train and shout to Sami that our paths are converging, his brain seems to have stopped. Then the road bends sharply to the left and up a short incline to the ungated level crossing I've been expecting and Sami, instead of braking, just carries on. But the wheels spin on the slight uphill incline and we slither and grind to an involuntary halt a couple of feet from the track just as the 1,000-ton, mile-long bacon-slicer roars by. Asleep with his eyes open, Sami is still staring blankly ahead with his foot on the accelerator as the back wheels spin in the snow, chains biting slowly into the packed ice, seeking something to grip. Lunging across I shove his foot from the pedal, and the car stalls, saving the car and both our lives. Emerging from his reverie, Sami stares at me as if to say 'Who the fuck are you?' then remembers and curses the train for getting in the way and slowing us down.

By the time we reach Erzurum, both Redman and Amin look to be in a state of shock. The temperature's even lower now and the region gives out a strong vibration of malicious and unpredictable danger. 'Kurds,' says Sami. Stopping to refuel just outside town, the three of us had grabbed the chance to get a coffee in a nearby tea-house but had been confronted inside by a wild-looking drunk waving a revolver. The café owner had thrown him out, but the damage had been done and now I'm listening to Amin and Redman going on and on about it like a pair of old women.

I roll a joint in the bedroom which we have to ourselves for the first time, but they don't want to know, so I lay in bed reading and smoking, listening to the silence broken only by the occasional roaring of the wood stove and Amin's nocturnal whimperings. And I fancy I hear gunshots in the distance, but who can tell?

The grapevine says that Iran and Afghanistan are wilder still than Eastern Turkey – although according to Sami, Iran is heaven on earth – but I'm at a loss to see how much wilder a place can get in terms of sheer menace. The whole area feels harsh and hostile: the country itself, the weather, the wildlife, the people; and the underlying but very real vibe of imminent danger creeps right into your gut to instil a sense of unease that few Europeans get the chance to experience. But I'm not afraid. Excited maybe, but not afraid. And I wonder how anyone can choose to travel in fear.

Finishing *Fathers and Sons*, I feel momentarily desolate as the full weight of the book hits me after weeks of apparent meaninglessness. I declare the book a masterpiece and leave it behind for someone else to discover. *The Shape of Things to Come*, and *Dead Fingers Talk* are still in Istanbul where I left them to go their own way but the *Bhagavadgita* I shall save to see if it works any better in it's homeland. I like the idea it's trying to get across, but feel in my stoned wisdom that you can't beat a path to the truth. *Fathers and Sons* drops you right in it without warning, leaves you wallowing not knowing whether to laugh or cry – and I have a feeling deep inside that truth has the tendency to sneak up on you rather than to sit coyly at the end of a gated track waiting to be visited by the chosen few.

Even the dogs don't bark tonight.

Somewhere between Agri and the Iran border, in sight of Mount Ararat, a lonely snow-covered cone, we're flagged down and forced to stop at a road accident where its victim, an old man with a badly smashed face, is standing quietly waiting, hand clamped to face, for help. Someone else asks if we can drive him back into Agri for treatment, and while Sami argues the toss, exclaiming angrily that he has his precious schedule to meet, the old man looks on through his sticky fingers. Slowly Sami comes to his senses and realises that his thin reputation as a human being is looking more doubtful with every excuse and finally he gives in. With ill humour he bundles the victim into the Mercedes after first spreading out an old blanket to protect the seat from bloodstains and speeds off back towards Agri.

The cold is almost solid – breathing is a dangerous pastime and hurts the lungs. A brilliant blue sky overhead and the dazzling white snow which spreads away as far as the stinging eye can see in all directions leaves us awestruck. And the strange silence.

Feeling the raw power of the frozen land we wait for Sami's return and share a joint together, trying to defuse the moment with a measure of lightheartedness, but Amin and Redman seem to be slipping into some sort of forlorn state, as if they've given up on life and its surprises and are meekly waiting for the end.

'Jesus, man, these people are like fucking animals,' whispers Redman. 'They have no compassion or feeling. That guy's injuries were enough to kill any normal person.'

'In my country people die on the streets all day long.'

'Yeh, but you're a fucking Indian . . .' growls Redman, irritated at Amin's pointless observation, '. . . dying's a trade out there.'

The severe cold makes thinking an effort.

Pause to puff.

'Are you taking any of this stuff through into Iran?' Amin asks.

Seeing my hesitation, Redman chips in that I'd have to be crazy to think about it. 'Turkey – 30 years; Iran – death. All for an attempt on Nirvana.' He makes it sound like a crack at Everest.

'Nobody's going to worry about a tiny bit of hash. You're talking junk for the death penalty anyway. Heroin.'

'Well, fuck you. Just keep well away from me, okay?' Redman's paranoia leaps out unexpectedly. Amin keeps his mouth shut, not knowing who to side with now that he's seen Redman lose his cool.

Sami returns and we get under way for the last leg before the Turkish border, into a massing bank of slate-grey snow clouds and the oncoming night.

The border point is a nightmare of wire fences, locked gates, floodlights and bored soldiers armed with machine-guns. To one side three large wooden huts stand in a sea of freezing mud in which sit a dozen or more trucks awaiting clearance. Beyond this a pound packed with forlorn-looking, confiscated vehicles, half-hidden beneath a layer of snow and ice, sends out a clear message to anyone thinking of breaking the rules.

Parking opposite the largest of the huts Sami tells us to stay put until called for, so I get out to stretch my legs and roll another joint.

'You're fucking crazy, man!' Redman hisses, edging away. 'These motherfuckers'll shoot you if they see what you're doing.'

I laugh at his serious face. Amin laughs nervously and looks around at the guards who are watching us. I'm going to have to get shot of them because their fear's beginning to take the sparkle out of everything, polluting the newness of each day. I walk about in full view of everyone, smoking the joint until it's done then grind the roach into the mud.

Sami comes out looking under pressure. 'You,' he says to me, 'come and speak to the officer.' Pulling the collar of my jacket up against the cold I follow him across the slushy courtyard towards the main wooden hut – even if they search me and find the hash I know I'll be able to talk my way out of it. Behind us stand Redman and Amin, babes in the wood, frozen together by cold and apprehension. Sami glances sternly at me and tells me to look serious.

Inside is a long wooden room with muddy wooden floorboards, a few seats and tables, and at one end a large desk with a fat, uniformed officer sitting behind it. Sami directs me towards him.

Still standing, I try to look friendly as he studies me until suddenly he speaks, 'The Mercedes car outside – it is yours?'

Glancing at Sami I confirm this. Technically the car was mine.

'Okay. Please let me see your registration papers.'

I glance at Sami again, and he tilts his head almost indiscernibly upwards and closes his eyes in a slow blink, a gesture for me to say what I like and not to worry about it. 'I don't understand,' I say.

'Your International Carnet?' continues the customs officer.

'Beg your pardon?'

'Insurance. You have insurance?'

'Er, no.'

'Driving licence?' he asks, his voice becoming flatter and dropping in volume.

Smiling inanely, I mumble, 'I left that at home.'

He laughs incredulously and suddenly I realise the potential depth of the sea of shit I'm paddling about in. I hope Sami knows what he's doing – just my luck now to get shipped back to Istanbul, or worse get put in Sagmalçilar nick where Mustafa's mates can carve me up at leisure. 'So you come all the way from Munich with Mercedes car, through Austria, Yugoslavia, Bulgaria and Turkey without papers. Ha ha ha ha. You very clever boy, how you do this?' Then twisting his little black moustache he beams and sits back to wait for my explanation.

A long couple of seconds tick by on the wall clock, but fortunately Sami steps in and takes over, and I'm told to wait outside again while the officer interviews Amin and Redman in turn.

When Amin comes out, he's white, shocked to the marrow. I could hear the Turkish officer banging on the desk, shouting at him like he was some sort of low criminal, but this wasn't entirely unexpected, as everywhere we go Amin gets picked on by the Turks, who seem to regard him as something from the wrong end of the social scale. 'We've had it, man,' he whines, 'fucking bastards. I knew we shouldn't have got involved in all this.'

'It was you that got us involved, what are you talking about?'

'Roll a joint. If I'm going to go down, I might as well go with a smile on my bloody face.' Amin has rebelled, and nothing is going to 'jolly well' stop him.

So we smoke another joint until Redman reappears looking dumbfounded. 'Nothing anybody says in there makes any sense whatsoever. We are blatantly in breach of all the rules, yet all of them are arguing the toss about it. Give us a toke on that.' He fills his lungs. 'I think we'll know in the next few minutes which way all this is going, because I've said I want my passport back or I'm making an official complaint. They can argue with good old Uncle Sam.'

Just as he finishes talking, the three Iranians file out of the customs shed looking pleased with themselves and head straight over to us brandishing our passports. 'We go,' says Sami handing me mine.

'How did you manage to . . .'

He raises his hand like a prophet. 'Baksheesh. Always baksheesh.'

The gates are unlocked and pulled back allowing us to pass on through into the no-man's land between the two countries, and a short while later we come to the Iranian border. This time Sami's smiling because he's on home ground. Again we have to wait while Sami does the business with our passports, only this time he emerges without them. 'Okay. We go,' he says.

'Passports, Sami?'

'They are keeping them to process. We pick them up again in Tabriz. Nix problem.'

TWO

On that last stretch to Tabriz, I thought we'd landed on another planet. From horizon to horizon stretched a barren sea of ancient rock – red, brown, mauve, grey and yellow, brutalised into morbid hills and lifeless valleys by a powerful force which still maintained an invisible but tangible presence, manifesting itself every few miles in the shape of some wrecked vehicle or other. On one long bend around the curve of a bare, purple mountain no less than 17 broken trucks littered the valley bed below, each one of them the victim of a road which continually twisted the senses with drama. The scale alone of the landscape was enough to disorientate anyone, but combined with the freak discolouration, the bizarre and unexpected contrasts of dark and light, and the corrugated surface of the track which effectively screened out every glimmer of reason in the struggling brain, it was a wonder that anyone ever made it to Tabriz.

When we finally rolled into town mid-morning of the next day all of us were tired beyond words. Sami fixed us up in a hotel across the road from the bazaar, and laid money on me to buy food. He added casually that the passports might take a few days to come, but in the event it took nearly two weeks – two weeks with Redman and Amin who had by then, with the shock of being separated from their passports, withdrawn almost entirely into their individual shells.

Driven finally by some inner desperation, Redman at one point took the chance of exposing his whereabouts as a draft-dodger by looking up the diplomatic residents of the town, such was his need to talk once again with his own kind, but he soon came back when it became clear that his company wasn't required. Amin on the other hand just ate and slept, stricken down with apathy brought on by anxiety, and I remembered the jungle rats that I'd read about who chose to lay down and die when confronted with a hopeless situation.

To avoid getting into pointless arguments with them about who was to blame and whether we should report the whole thing to our respective consuls I took to wandering about the town and making friends, spending hours in the bazaar drinking tea and fumbling around languages, but it was a weird all-male world darkened by hints of lawlessness, homosexuality and rebellion. Many of the men carried daggers and most of them seemed ready to use them, but the overriding vibration among men both young and old was of discontent rather than mischief, a discontent with the way in which the nation's wealth was being shared out. Justice, they said, was non-existent, corruption a way of life and torture and murder commonplace. Nobody trusted anyone. Everywhere, people were struggling just to exist, and resentment and hate was being drummed up by their religious brothers who had other plans for the redistribution of power when the great revolution came. If the terms 'cut-throat' and 'cloak and dagger' had any geographic origin, it had to be here in the bazaars of Tabriz.

'Jesus, man, I've never heard of any passport control taking this long. I think it's about time we started calling the shots. You should get along to the British Embassy and tell them that these motherfuckers are holding our passports. It's illegal, man.'

'You go along to your fucking embassy and tell them.'

'I'm a draft-dodger, man. They'd probably turn me over to the Iranian authorities as an undesirable alien.' Even on the verge of tears Redman looked hilarious.

Amin continued to sleep as I giggled hash smoke.

'Anyway,' I said, 'the embassy is in Teheran and I'm not moving from here until I've got my passport back.' At least Sami was dropping in to see us every day, and he'd promised to pay me fifty dollars – unlike Redman and Amin whose lack of faith alone constituted in his mind a valid reason not to pay them. So I wasn't about to start rocking the boat.

In fact I felt quite happy with life as it was going. February in exotic Tabriz, bitter cold but all bills paid, and an excellent chance to see local life in the raw – after all, Sami was known and respected locally, and providing I didn't do anything daft it was a real chance for me to put a finger on the Middle-Eastern pulse. And beneath it all, this wild little town was actually quite benign.

Then one day Sami turned up in a hurry and rushed us round to the Offices of Customs and Excise where we were each interviewed by a suave and well-educated officer of the Shah. He too was astonished that we'd brought the cars this far without documents, but was prepared to do us all a favour and clear the whole thing up by permitting the sale of our vehicles for a nominal fee to Sami. An hour later and fifty dollars richer I was bargaining in the bazaar for a warm goatskin overcoat and thick socks in readiness for the next stretch of the journey which everyone said was out of the question, the only road being snowbound and therefore impassable for the foreseeable future.

After getting the coat for ten dollars instead of fifty dollars I grabbed my things and set out for the bus station to see if anyone was going to attempt the 250-mile stretch of road south-east through the mountains of Sharqi and Zanjan to Teheran, but as everyone had said, nobody was going anywhere because the road was blocked. About to give up and walk back to the hotel, I was almost run down by an old blue coach which unexpectedly materialised in a cloud of black smoke. As it chugged to a halt, the co-driver jumped out waving a bundle of tickets and began yelling, 'Teheran! Teheran!'

Nobody moved except me, and when I went ahead and bought a ticket, I could see many a knowing grin among those battered Arab faces which spelt out 'foreign lunatic'. But within half an hour Redman and Amin had joined a growing contingency of lunatics, and by early afternoon we were away.

Until the sun went down somewhere over Syria, the three of us sat silent as the immensity of Iran revealed itself, and dwarfed the lives of the people who scratched about on its temporarily frozen surface. During the summer months the very same land would be scorching hot, seared and dessicated by the burning sun. At each village or settlement, old men, children and goats stood watching as we passed, expressionless and silent until the driver blasted them with his klaxon. Then they'd all wave. Sometimes exuberant kids and dogs chased us, spurred on by the rare glimpse of foreigners staring back at them through the windows. But hanging over everything was still the heavy air of oppression – both by man and by nature itself.

In one village I smoked a joint by the side of the road and watched a dog and bitch knotted together after mating, trying to escape a ragged band of stone-throwing kids. I yelled at them to stop and they stared at me like I was something from outer space, debating in their minds whether to stone me or not. These kids with their nightmare inbred faces stared like *I* was weird – and according to local opinion they were right.

Deep in the hills that night the snow began falling heavily and the two drivers had no choice but to get out and strap on wheel chains. Inside, the other passengers, aware of the danger ahead began praying aloud in unison while Redman and Amin reacted by wrapping bath-towels around their heads to keep warm. They had in adversity finally united as a couple, believing I'm sure that there was safety in numbers. When the bus started away again into a wild, raging blizzard, the prayers continued in earnest, rising in pitch and volume with each new hazard. Amin and Redman got their heads down in an attempt to obliterate fear with sleep.

Later we were attacked by bandits. After hours of slewing through snowdrifts, battling up and down soft white inclines and negotiating hairpin bends, a wild-looking man suddenly appeared in the headlights waving a sword. Another appeared and wrenched open the side door to climb in, but the co-driver, a large man obviously hired for this sort of work, leapt on him and a struggle began. Despite the efforts of the first bandit to wave down the bus, we were still spluttering and growling along at five miles an hour. Far from being forced to stop, the driver was now trying to run the man down, while inside, silhouetted against the headlit snow, the struggle went on like a magic lantern show until the villain was finally ejected. Half a dozen others had arrived, and were running alongside the bus waving daggers and cudgels, but gradually we made headway and left them behind shouting and gesticulating in the snow. Redman and Amin slept through it all.

An hour later, at the height of the storm, when vision ahead was almost impossible, the bus slewed to a halt and everyone filed out into the freezing darkness. I sat there for a while feeling the chill seeping in, but getting nothing but moans from Redman and Amin when I tried to wake them, got up and followed the rest of the passengers. Outside, the snow was thigh-deep and the blizzard vicious, but by groping through the dark I found that we were parked alongside what seemed to be a large heap of snow with a wooden door. Unable to find a handle, I hammered until someone opened it from the inside and dragged me in.

Inside was a single large room lit by a paraffin lamp, and in the middle, surrounded by all the other travellers staring blankly in my direction, stood a roaring cast-iron stove with a kettle on top. As it came to the boil, its lid chattering in time with my teeth, a silent group decision seemed to be arrived at and I was shoved gently towards the stove to warm up. Someone then passed me a glass of tea.

Then the questions started, the words and gesticulations, the attempts at mime. They hadn't heard of the Beatles or Bobby Charlton or Elvis Presley, and how you mimed your reasons for being there was beyond me, not least of all because they had little idea of distance or geography. So we made up things and made each other laugh with the faces we pulled and the sounds we made until we gave up trying to be serious and began believing what we wanted. The co-driver then pushed his way through the crowd to act as translator.

'What is your name? Ah, Tommy.'
'Are you married?'
'What is your religion?'

Usually I said 'none' or 'atheist' but remembering where I was I explained carefully that I believed in one God, one God for all men. This information was translated back to a hushed crowd and suddenly, as if a bomb had been defused, I had a roomful of friends around me. Someone muttered a prayer, and smiles began lighting up the room. More tea was poured, more questions asked, and even the women relaxed their face scarves so that I could see a bit of them.

Then without warning the door burst open with a crash and there stood Redman, panting heavily with his back to the door, ready for a fight. 'Hey, man,' he growled, 'keep away from them, they're dangerous!'

I couldn't believe my eyes and ears. 'Have you lost your mind? Either come in, drink tea and be friendly, or fuck off back to the coach where none of us have to look at your face.'

He looked shocked by my response. 'I've come out looking for you because we were worried about you.'

'Well, there you go – I'm all right. D'you want tea or are you going back to the coach?'

He took the tea, but in bad spirit, and stood with his back to the door silently watching everyone in case they should suddenly turn violent.

The further east we went, the more peculiar, the more withdrawn Redman became, as if the geographical vibrations were affecting his stability in some way. Back in Istanbul he'd been the life and soul of the party, but out here his humour was failing. 'This country is seriously fucking weird, man,' was one of his repeated observations, but instead of enjoying it, trying to get his head around the weirdness, he saw it all as a plot to destabilise his rock-steady perception of the order of things. His world was crumbling all about him. Amin meanwhile carried with him an air of resigned desperation and did his best to avoid upsetting anyone, but by the time we reached Teheran even he was tiring of Redman's constant lamentation, and the three of us had taken to sitting apart on the bus. Only occasionally would we talk across the other passengers. Redman's hip humour had deserted him and his straightness was showing like an old petticoat.

111

He was going to join the Peace Corps somewhere in the north of Afghanistan, he said, but Amin simply pointed out that everyone knew that the Peace Corps was a cover operation for the CIA. I asked Redman if this was true, hoping to find out what the CIA was without showing my ignorance.

'No, man, of course it's not. What we're hearing here is good old Indian paranoia.' 'Indian paranoia?' Amin chuckled. 'If there's one nation with a shortage of that western sickness it's India. We might get a bit restless sometimes, but paranoia? No way, man. In fact I'd go as far as to say it's an American sickness.'

'Maybe,' Redman conceded, turning to me, 'but you Europeans are infected too, you know. You haven't got off scot-free. It's what we call media-induced paranoia. It's a way of life. Paranoia sells, man. Half the fucking planet's paranoid: paranoid about commie bastards, fascist bastards, bastards in general, washing machines, instant coffee, the strength of the dollar, racial integration.' He paused. 'The frequency and duration of the female orgasm. Cars, colours, fat, tobacco, penis size, crime figures, Vietnam, JFK, Johnson, the CIA, the Threat of Red China, the Threat of Cuba, the Threat of The Rest of the World, drugs, unemployment, parental abuse, homosexuality, and just about every other motherfucking thing you can think of.'

'What do you mean by "media"?' I asked. Sometimes I got left behind in these discussions because the words were new to me.

But Redman thought I was being specific. It hadn't occurred to him that I didn't know what the word meant. 'The whole fucking thing – television, newspapers, radio, billboards. Whichever way the assholes feel they need to get their goddamned message across to the people. Like fear. Stick by us and you'll be all right. That sort of thing.'

'Right.' I liked being included in all this intellectual stuff, it made me feel sort of special – a hangover from early schooldays when I'd felt honoured to be spoken to by a teacher as a human being. The only problem was that I'd be so overcome that I'd instantly lose my mind and blow it by saying something like 'thank you, sir' in response to a chummy observation of the weather conditions. The sixth form was even worse. It seemed that I was incapable of understanding what anyone was talking about, whatever the subject – as if they were speaking in a foreign language. By the time I'd worked it out and come up with something to say they'd moved on to something else. Being able to talk to someone like Redman, a graduate, was quite a thing for me because as I say, it made me feel important. And I was picking up a lot of good stuff for the future.

'So why does the CIA bother you?' I asked Amin.

'They murder people and destabilise the world, that's why.'

Redman thought about it. 'You may be right. Or maybe not. We'll never know.' He looked at me. 'Our Central Intelligence Agency is exactly like your MI5. Whatever he says, man, we need 'em.'

'And where the natural trends don't fit in with their plans, they remove the trendsetters,' added Amin. 'The so-called Peace Corps in northern Afghanistan and Pakistan is the CIA. They're trying to destabilise the area and get the Russians blamed for it. Everybody knows that.'

I didn't. And to tell you the truth I didn't care – I was bored already. Being English, I'd been weaned on intrigue and gossip, and the last thing I needed was further education in it. I rubbed the condensation from the window – outside were more houses than I'd seen for days.

Teheran, one of the crossroads of the Middle East as they say, was grotesque, an unpleasant mixture of the old and still-being-built new. Beautiful New Teheranians in silk suits and mini skirts played their money games surrounded on all sides by mad priests, dire poverty, and sinister armed police.

The fortunates hung out on a tree-lined grand central avenue which housed all the banks and luxurious hotels, just a street away from the filth everyone else had to put up with. So at one end of an alley you might find a blind beggar with a weeping skin disease, whereas at the other you could brush shoulders with a beautiful, milk-skinned girl straight from the pages of a fashion magazine (being a Westerner it was all right to do this).

The hotel we found, close to the main station, was a warren of brown and cream gloss-painted corridors, swarming with bearded men in long robes, dangerous-looking women, and wailing children. At every corner you were assailed either by boys demanding baksheesh, women demanding right of way or religious freaks threatening the wrath of God, reminding me of a visit I once made to a mental hospital where a friend was being treated. Oddly in the middle of this bedlam I felt at peace with the world. No one was going to get me here because this was hell on earth – this was way beyond anything I'd ever known, light years beyond the treacherous sanity of my own culture. Here in Teheran was rebellion and revolution in the making, and as long as you kept a low profile I couldn't think of a better place to hide.

Redman, however, thought differently, believing – justifiably I suppose – that we were sitting on a powder keg, while Amin stayed resigned, although more calmly now, to his impending martyrdom at the hands of the 'muslim devils'.

'. . . although this is not unlike the chaos of India, so I suppose I have to admit that there must be some feeling of familiarity which helps me relax,' he muttered thoughtfully, pulling deeply on a joint. My Turkish hash was almost finished.

'Jesus, man, how can you even think about relaxing in this fucking place? This is probably the most dangerous situation I've ever been in in my whole life including being held hostage by Creoles down by the Tombigbee River. And those motherfuckers know how to scare a man.' Redman was off on one of his fables. 'I tell you, I can smell danger, and this place stinks like the asshole of the Great Whore of Babylon.' He was lying stretched out staring at the ceiling through a layer of smoke.

A tap at the door stopped me having another fit of the giggles.

'Fuck off!' bellowed Redman.

The door opened and in came the cringing shape of a man in his forties or fifties with a large curved nose, a small black skull-cap, grey flannel trousers and sandals, a collarless white shirt frayed at the edges, and a sleeveless knitted Fair Isle jumper, similarly frayed.

'Excuse me,' he said in heavily accented English, 'but I heard there were some foreigners staying here so I thought I'd come along and offer my good wishes.'

'For what?' growled Redman.

I offered the man the joint, and he readily accepted it. 'Thank you,' he said, ignoring Redman. 'Are you staying long? No, of course not. Just long enough to get your Afghan visa. Who'd want to stay here?' He chuckled. 'The funny thing is I was supposed to be passing through – just like you – but got caught up in it all. There's a reasonable living to be made, you know, although I must say things are looking a little unstable at present.' He half-sat very carefully on the edge of my bed, acknowledging it as my space but pushing his luck.

Amin asked the man where he came from. If you'd have asked me I'd have guessed Brick Lane – he was the spit of old Fagin who used to fence our stolen gear.

'I come from Armenia. A beautiful country, but the communists are destroying it slowly.'

'Where's that?' I asked.

Redman butted in – he loved showing his knowledge. 'You remember that road accident just before the border? Mount Ararat over to the left? It's behind that.'

Amin asked why he thought Teheran was unstable. We knew – or at least had heard things, like the Shah was unpopular – but he was stoned and talking for the sake of it.

'Because the mullahs want to take power from the Shah.'

'You mean the inequality between the few rich and the millions of poor is finally coming to a head,' added Redman.

'That is your . . . western . . . view, my friend. It is ironically exactly the same view as that of the perpetrators of the communist tragedy in Russia. In fact most people live quite happily in how might I put it . . . unequal circumstances. For thousands of years people have been content. Providing they can feed and clothe the family,' – he pointedly eyed the joint – 'smoke a little tobacco now and again and remain unmolested there is no problem. No. The problem now is this incredible change in mentality. "Why can't I be rich too?" they ask themselves. So instead of mass contentment, we now have mass discontentment. And the explosion will be fuelled by the mullahs who are similarly discontent, but for different reasons. They are not just after an improvement in living standards, but after the throne itself. After all, how can God take second place?'

I asked what he thought had caused the sudden change in

mentality; if it had been some sort of mass enlightenment. Had they all got up one morning as a nation and shouted, 'We are no longer content – in fact we are discontent and demand a sudden change for the better'?

'Not quite, my friend. Modern technology: the ship, the plane, the car, the bus, the telephone, the radio – and now the television have all contributed. News travels faster and breeds discontent.' He paused. 'Which is why I am here. No doubt you are discontented with the official rates of exchange in the banks. Well, I can give you double what they can offer . . .'

That evening I left Redman and Amin to themselves and went out to post a letter home and take a wander around town to see what went on at night, but after posting the letter I became caught up in a running battle between students and police. As a small gesture of defiance to the traditionalists, these students wore a western-style uniform of white shirt and dark trousers, which provided an easy target for the police. Bullets began flying, a police car was overturned and set alight, and for a while it looked as if the revolution itself had started. Gangs of hysterical males waving clubs and knives then began roaming the streets screaming in defiance against the Shah and looking for someone to pick on, so I thought it best to keep out of the way. Using the moment as an excuse, I slipped into a busy, neon-lit restaurant where I sat down and scoffed a shocking-pink, rose-scented pudding sprinkled with desiccated coconut, followed quickly by a white one, vanilla I think, sprinkled with hundreds and thousands, to satisfy my dope-fuelled craving for something sweet. As I finished, a knot of students pushed their way in supporting a fellow friend who was bleeding heavily from a stomach wound. Seeing me sitting there they hesitated, and one of them muttered something under his breath to the café owner, but he shrugged and told them to go through into the back of the building. Outside, the crowd was getting louder and crazier, and it looked as if I might have a problem getting away, but seeing my hesitation the owner grabbed my arm and led me through into the back of the building where I followed a trail of blood along a corridor and out into a dark but quiet backstreet.

'You must be fucking crazy, going out in this, man.' Redman

had adopted a mother hen attitude, and was chiding me for getting back late to the hotel. After I'd left the restaurant I'd wandered down Pahlavi Avenue to see what the rich dudes were up to during the civil unrest (not a sign of them), but he thought this was irresponsible and uncool. 'Sometimes I wonder where your fucking head's at. Those motherfuckers are killers – I've told you before.' He paced about, anxiously glancing towards the window every time he heard a gunshot or an explosion. 'How do you know you weren't followed back? For all we know they could be forming a lynch mob right now.'

Amin was laying on his bed facing the wall. Outside in the corridor one man was screaming at another. Then a woman started. And a child. From below came the crashing of glass. I rolled another joint, lit it, and laid back on the bed, blissfully happy.

* * *

I'm on a bus to Meshed, second only to Mecca as a place of pilgrimage for all good Muslims and I'm sitting with this colourful band of pilgrims rather than Redman and Amin, because suddenly I prefer their company. I too am a pilgrim. Despite the lack of a common language we are communicating, and again the veils of the females are slowly relaxing as they realise I'm all right. They seem to decide when it's time to unveil, not the men – in fact they seem to have a lot more say in things than I at first thought.

A kid of about 17 with long eyelashes has taken a liking to my hair and keeps touching it, offering me his prayer beads to finger. This amuses the older men, but I know he wants more because he keeps rubbing his dick absentmindedly as he stares into my eyes searching for a sign.

'Hey, he wants to fuck you, man!' Redman's voice crackles over the atmosphere. I tell him to fuck off, but say 'goodbye' to the pilgrims anyway, as the kid's persistence is beginning to get on my nerves, and rejoin my two fellow travellers.

'Looks like you've got it made there,' says Amin with a cheeky grin.'

'Yeh, bollocks,' says I. But I have to admit that any flattery is better than none at all, and girls have been thin on the ground since Istanbul.

'Listen, man, you'd fuck anything after a few weeks without women,' growls Redman.

'You might.' I say.

'I'm just saying that the sexual drive of the average male will overcome all obstacles under all circumstances.'

I had to think about it. 'So you would then – that's an admission if you're an average male and there's nothing . . . out of the ordinary . . . about you.' I mean to say *abnormal* but can't immediately think of the word, and Redman obviously doesn't like it, being obliquely referred to as 'ordinary', because he sticks out his jaw and looks offended. He likes to admit to being one of the people, to being ordinary, but hates being called it.

'Well, hey, fuck you, man,' he says, 'the trouble with you little Englishmen is that you walk around with your heads stuffed up each other's asses. Being sexually inclined in any direction whatsoever is no big deal. And for your information, I am not homosexual.' He looks away, out of the window, and out of my life. But all I want to do is laugh – even now his face looks funnier than ever. And I thought he was objecting to my suggestion that he was nothing out of the ordinary – but it was a homosexual thing.

Amin glances at me and grimaces, then looks back out of the window. 'We've just passed the grave of Omar Khayyam,' he mumbles, absent-mindedly.

Meshed is a holy city, a place of pilgrimage and the streets are running alive with prophets. Jesus was here, is here somewhere, I'm sure.

The West petered out way back and we're in a different universe now, with a rarefied Islamic atmosphere, and are being treated as undesirable aliens. This isn't our manor. We're trespassing. Keep out. It's skull and crossbones danger stuff.

Redman and Amin have moved camp and buddied-up with a couple of straight American archaeologists who are physically into digging people's graves while I have found more far-out camaraderie with a bunch of freaks from other parts of Europe who are also heading east. We've holed up together in a concrete-block hotel built in a sea of mud which is the bus depot and there is a strange atmosphere caused by this mix of nationalities and individual temperament. First we have the Iranians who run the place and whose friends keep coming in on the offchance that a western slag, male or female, might want to fuck them or throw money in their direction. Then we have Prince Stanislavski, a Swiss guy with two devotees, who sweeps around in a maroon velvet cape and jackboots like one of the three musketeers. Then we have King John – who's turned up again after taking a train most of the way from Istanbul – revelling in pain from stomach cramps because 'hey, man, I haven't eaten in over two days'. Fasting is a sign of the spiritually strong, apparently. Why, I don't know, but some travellers love to boast about how little they've eaten. Then there's Dutch Paul, a tall guy from Amsterdam with a secret stash of dope, two very straight Swedish blokes going to India in a London taxi and, finally, a morose French girl on her way back to Europe who refuses to speak.

For those going east into Afghanistan there is a two-day wait until a bus is ready to take us the last part of the journey through a no-man's land policed, so the story goes, by murderers and bandits, so other than sitting about waiting all day there's little to do but explore the town which, given that this is a place of religious fervour, is a dangerous pastime. The general feeling is that we should all keep our heads down in the common room of the hotel until the bus is due – but to me living under siege in such a seedy hole is demoralising.

The beds, however, are fairly clean, and after a fruitless attempt to gain the confidence of the morose French girl who just sits staring at the bare table top before her, I go off to sleep and dream unexpectedly about Michael Mouse who is dying with a punctured lung after the punishment he received. Shocked, I wake myself up and struggle to adjust again to my surroundings, believing at first that I was in an old girlfriend's bed-sit in Hackney.

Whether we deserved to be attacked the next day and chased through the streets of Meshed by a screaming mob of religious nuts is arguable. At least, it is if you're like Redman and his

119

archaeologists, who've elevated themselves above the level of our low 'hippy' existence as one of them calls it, a term they've discovered in a newspaper.

'Right on,' says Dutch Paul, 'ze term is "hippy" now for zose that choose to reject zat part of society, zat machine which they sink attempts to control zem. Ze machine has invented a word to capture ze spirit. Now ze spirit will be slaughtered systematically by zat killer of free expression called 'fashion'. But what the machine can't understand is zat ze spirit is beyond all understanding. You can't bottle love, man.'

Mmn. What's he on about?

'But where did your love get you when you tried to get inside the holy mosque?' asks Redman with a smart look on his face. 'Strikes me you need a bit of practice.'

'You can't practise love – it pours from ze heart, from ze centre of your being,' continues Dutch Paul in his excellent English.

I try to work out where the centre of my being is and consider quoting something from the *Bhagavadgita* – which would probably fit in quite nicely at this point and single me out as a turned-on geezer – but I can't remember any of it.

'Intangible crap,' says an archaeologist from behind his *Herald Tribune*.

'No. Ze only crap is in your brain, man, zis brain of yours that needs to dig up ze past to see into ze future. You people are the ghouls of ze spirit.' Paul's trying hard now, glaring through his shattered glasses, a result of our stoning at the mosque, but I keep my mouth shut because I don't really understand what anyone's talking about. Love was always a mystery to me. So is the word 'intangible', come to that.

'There you go again – more crap.' Redman's grinning.

'Don't rise to the bait, man,' says King John to Paul, 'it's tainted with profanity.'

'Oh, he is not ze fisherman, I sink, just a little boat wiz a big hole in ze bottom in an ocean of scepticism.'

This is all getting a bit too much for me, and the best I can do is sit there trying to look smart or bored, so I wander off to try talking again to the morose French girl who is sitting alone fiddling with her hands.

'Hello. I'm Tommy,' I begin. She glances up. She's about 20, pretty and well-formed beneath a camouflage of old jumpers, smelly jeans and grubbiness. 'We tried getting into the mosque today,' I say cheerfully, 'but they threw stones and chased us away. Smashed Paul's glasses.' I wait a few seconds for a response. With a scrub and a change of clothes she'd come up quite nice. 'Where are you heading?' I ask.

'Home,' she whispers.

'Where's that?'

'France. Paris.' She still doesn't look up.

'You coming from India?'

'Oui.'

'Alone?'

'Yes.'

'When did you leave France?'

'Last year. Maybe nine months ago.'

'Alone?'

'No. With a friend. But she is gone back home.'

'You've had enough?'

'What?'

'Now you go home because your holiday is finished?'

'No. Because I have many problems.' She looks up and begins to communicate. 'At first it was fine, then I begin having trouble with men. After my friend leave – she had problems at home and had to go back, but I wanted to stay on – my money was stolen by an Indian man. I went to the French Embassy to ask for help, but they said they do not help overlanders who get in trouble. It is my problem.'

'So you're trying to make your way back.'

'Yes, but it is difficult alone. The only money I have is what people give me. And everywhere I go I have trouble with men. In India I was raped by two men who give me a lift. And in Pakistan the same thing also. Afghanistan was not so bad, but still I have some problems. If you are a western woman alone they fuck you if you like it or not. Now I just want to go home to my parents.'

I can't give her any money – I haven't got that much myself – and say so, but she accepts that. The fighting spirit is almost dead.

'It is okay. I will get home, I think.' She tries to smile but can't hold it. The poor girl is desperate and still has 4,000 miles to go; 4,000 miles of men who, where sex is concerned, will overcome all obstacles under all circumstances.

Unable to say much to reassure her, I wish her well and leave. The least I should do if I had any sense of moral obligation would be to abandon my personal number and escort her back home, but instead, I'm going to drive out any feelings of what a stout character might do and concentrate on myself, show a strong single-mindedness, a strength of purpose that will see me safely past these distractions. That's the best way of putting it, anyway.

Gandhi said something about depriving people of the right to suffer – I read that in a book on India I picked up in the library – like suffering was an honour. But the thing is, I can't work out the logic of it unless you believe in reincarnation; after all, what's the point in suffering if death's absolute? You might just as well kill anyone that gets in your way and live like a king while you can, like our leaders. And my religious education teacher, the one who smacked my head, said that belief in reincarnation was sinful. So none of it makes sense. What I do know is that when my grandmother died, her body looked much the same – it just wasn't living, that's all. It didn't speak or breathe, but just laid there in the coffin. Still. Like an empty building.

'You think too much, man.' King John's voice shatters my thoughts, brings me back to the strange hovel in which I'm staying. 'Too much thinkin's a bummer.'

We used to call queers bummers. And our sort of people are 'freaks' or 'heads', not hippies as the papers are saying. One misplaced word, one indication that you don't understand the way to use the current language and you've blown it, what a joke. Who cares anyway?

I do.

I try to be relaxed and not let this silly protocol affect me but I can't; I need to impress like anyone else, because not impressing means no credibility which equals no chicks. To pull women, you have to impress by conforming to their requirements – or blow their minds, which is actually better because they respect you for it. But apart from the French girl there are none about to practise on, and she's definitely out of the question, to me at least. As with

Nilüfer, I can't make a move on her without seeing myself as an unprincipled lecher. So we're back to being cool . . . man.

And the presence of western people is slightly disturbing. This need to form into groups is the result of fear of being in a foreign land – but I'm relieved to be in a foreign land, so my relationship with everyone here is slightly unreal, as if I'm looking in from the outside. I need to find people I'm happy to be with, people who are happy to be with me, not those who create, consciously or unconsciously, a divide.

'I'm telling you, you think too much, man.' It's King John, jumping into my pool again. 'There's a bus leaving in an hour.'

'An hour? I thought they wouldn't cross the border at night.'

'They said we should make it before nightfall. Depends how we get on with the Irani border guards.'

'So how wide's this bit of no-man's land?'

'About twenty-five miles according to our archaeologist friends. Twenty-five miles of bandit territory. It's the same on the other side, going out into Pakistan, like the whole country's controlled by wildmen. They decide if you go in. They decide if you go out. Nobody's ever managed to tame them, man.'

And here we are, using Afghanistan as the main through route to India. Unlike others who were taking the route south into Pakistan, avoiding Afghanistan altogether. But then you miss the drugs. Rumour has it that Afghan hashish is the best in the world and I can't wait to try the stuff, but King John's a bit nervy.

'They don't fuck about, man. These guys graduate in killing at the age of three. And the women are worse.'

We set out just after midday in an old green bus; half a dozen weird-looking Westerners among a crush of weird-looking Easterners, but by the time the hilly landscape has changed into a flat wilderness of freezing rock and mud, most of the locals have got off the bus and disappeared into nowhere.

The border point is a brick shed by a wire-mesh gate in a wire-mesh fence that stretches as far north and south as the eye can see. To one side of the brick shed is a cage and a kennel containing an addicted drug-sniffer Alsatian on a bad come-down, and to the other an emptiness leading into thickening dusk over no-man's land and Afghanistan.

And we wait.

Nearly an hour passes before the guards choose to swagger out of their hut to take a look down their noses at us. Another hour later and they're still arguing with the driver that it's too late to cross. While we wait, Redman points out again that in Iran the penalty for possession of heroin is death. Possession of hashish . . . well . . . it depends on their mood at the time of capture. It could be the amount of baksheesh you pay, or whether you've got a nice face or not and whose dick you suck with it. If there are any political problems between Iran and your own country forget it. Twenty years wouldn't be unusual. Twenty years in a hole that would make Brixton nick look like the Promised Land.

'It's legal in Afghanistan,' says Dutch Paul, trying to boost spirits.

But in the end, with the arrival of nightfall, they drag open the gates and let us through, into the darkness.

THREE

Twenty-five miles of bumpy, unmetalled darkness and constant loud prayers to Allah by our remaining Muslim friends on board sees us safely past the bandits and into the Afghan customs compound where a little building with golden lamplight streaming through its windows gives the impression of an English country cottage, and I'm the first to jump up from my seat, keen as I am to get inside.

'I'd stay put if I were you,' advises one of the archaeologists imperiously, 'it's always best to let the Afghans make the first move.' He looks meaningfully at his fellow archaeologist and Redman and adds, 'Their social codes to date have proved singularly unreliable,' as if this were a gem not worth sharing beyond their own inner circle.

'Yeh, well, maybe you're right,' I say, 'but my grandma would have said that this was a case of Mohammed going to the mountain, so I'll see you bunch of fairies later.' And off I go. I'm proud of that one and feel warm and smug as I cross the courtyard towards Rose Cottage.

After knocking on the door I wait a few seconds and a voice inside says something non-aggressive so I go in.

'Hello, I've come to see if you'll check my passport and stamp it for me please,' I say. Before me, seated on a fabulous carpet, are two smiling, grey-bearded guys dressed in white robes and turbans smoking a large water-pipe. One of them gestures to me to join them.

Pulling off my boots and standing them up to one side I make up the triangle and take the pipe that is offered. 'Hashish?' I ask.

Both laugh. And one of them with a milky eye, the one who seems to be in charge, puts his wrists together. So Dutch Paul got it wrong. I laugh quickly to show I was joking and take a long pull of the cooled tobacco smoke . . . wow . . . good flavour. It even makes my head spin, like when I took my first draw on a cigarette in the cemetery behind Greenwich church – the same cemetery where I squeezed June Butterworth's tits and drank a bottle of brown ale. It was the only place to go if you wanted any privacy.

The Afghan with the milky eye asks a question and gestures to something outside, so I look stupid to let him know I don't understand. He waves my passport benignly at me and in the general direction of the coach and I take it that he's wondering where all the other passengers are, so I shrug and glance to the heavens, indicating that the others are nothing to do with me. I make a move to get up anyway, to go call them in, but he waves me down and nods at the pipe and for half an hour we smoke and gesticulate about Inghilistan and Afghanistan both being excellent places.

There's a soft tapping on the door. Gently it opens and in comes a fearful coach driver clutching a handful of passports belonging to the other passengers. 'Please, please, effendi,' he whines, 'can you clear these passports and stamp them so that my most esteemed charges may get on their way?' Or something like that. But Milky Eye and his mate are having none of it and tell him to leave the passports on the side and get out. 'Oh, and by the way, tell the others we want to see them all, not just you, you cretin.' Or something like that.

The coach driver backs out like a dog expecting to be beaten. And we carry on smoking.

A few minutes later, everyone else files sheepishly in and stands staring in disbelief at the scene before them of King Tommy at the Afghan Court. For me it is a moment of great satisfaction, a moment of 'I got it right', and the two Afghans begin to giggle in a strangely childlike way at the group standing awkwardly before them. 'Come sit down with us' they wave, and seeing this the Europeans and King John and Amin kick off their boots and do as they are told, but the archaeologists and Redman stay put like martyrs making a last stand before the heathen.

Ignoring them, we pass the pipe of peace around for another five minutes until finally Milky Eye gets up, lays out the open passports in a line and stamps them all one after the other with a brilliant *rat-tat-tat* action which brings the house down. Even the Americans are impressed.

Around midnight we unload into a Herat hotel, an inn without beds, and for a couple of pence I'm given a rolled-up carpet and a small cell with a tiny window high up in the wall. The carpet is my bed. My kitbag is the pillow. And I crash, as they say . . . man . . . into a deep, deep, Bhagavadgita dream hole brought on by reading it before bedtime.

After a weird bit where I'm using an elephant as a water pipe, I sense that God is about to reveal himself to me:

> Take a gander at me
> Whose powers are many and varied.
> I am the kingdom, the power and the glory in every
>   creature;
> Out of me they come; by me they live, and at my word
>   they go.
> Fucking hell . . .

'Wake up you lazy bastard!'
I know that voice.

'Is that you, Elephant God?'

Then I recognise the chuckle, that silly little girly chuckle.

But hell, am I dreaming or is this real? Best open my eyes and cast off this elephant. This is a shame, because the dope inside the elephant is monstrous: the first draw through the twin barrels of its trunk has scrambled my brain.

'I guessed it was you as soon as Daoud said an ugly Englishman was staying here.' Frankie was standing over me holding a candle and looking down with a big grin on his face.

'Daoud?'

'The geezer that runs this place.'

'I thought you were in Morocco.'

'I said that to throw Mustafa off the trail.'

'So did I. What are you up to out here?' I prop myself up against the wall.

He sits on the floor next to me and begins rolling a joint using a pliant and dark lump of hash half the size of my fist. 'Mazari. From a bloke called Aziz Ullah in Kandahar. One of the best,' he explains, seeing me staring at it. 'I'm knocking out dope to the overlanders – the ones who haven't got the time to suss out the scene theirselves. It's so cheap they don't believe it even after I've put on my bit. A key for twenty pounds. I've just done two keys for an Aussie couple driving into Iran; sealed inside peach tins.'

'The dogs won't suss it?'

'No – it's been tried and tested. The stuff's sealed inside cellophane bags and then the tin's filled up with sugar water so it sounds pukka if they shake it. Even the labels have been printed in English, saying "Made in Australia". Loads of 'em do it; it pays for the trip.' He passes the joint.

'Mmn. Nice one. Fffft . . . fft . . . ffffft. Nnnnnnnh . . . aaaaaaaaah.'

'That's why I'm here in Herat. There's two German geezers I'm working with who go up to Mazar-i-Sharif and buy the stuff. They bring it back and I do the selling.' He takes back the joint I'm holding out to him.

The dope's strong. I lay down again from the propped-up position. Frankie lays next to me and we stare at the flickering ceiling.

'So what are you into then?' he asks.

127

'Spiritual evolution.'

'Spirit what?'

'Spiritual evolution. The growth of the soul.'

'The growth of the fucking soul?' What are you on about? You don't believe in all that do you?'

'I don't know.'

'How can you believe in something like that? You of all people Thomas. You'll be going to church next.'

'Not quite.' It's hard to explain what I mean. And I'm getting increasingly stoned and can't get my words together. 'It's not a matter of believing,' I say, 'it's like, a sort of natural thing, a change, like something that happens and you can't do much about it.' Pause. 'So how did you get here? By bus?'

'Something that happens and you can't do much about it? Fuck off. You're cracking up.' He's leaning on his elbow now, staring at me. 'I took the train out of Istanbul, then train and bussed it all the way except for a lift with some Paki geezer to Teheran. Did you get to see Mustafa again? Oh, yeh, you said you did – what did he have to say?'

'About what?' I don't know how much Frankie knows about me and Nilüfer.

'Anything. He reckons I ripped him off with that Turkish bird.'

'What do you mean, "ripped him off"?'

'She did a runner and he reckoned I'd helped her.'

He doesn't know. But Mustafa did, because his contacts in Germany must have told him that I'd helped her get out of Turkey. So Frankie split before Mustafa had found out it was me, but I've no real reason to hold back from telling him apart from the fact that it had probably been the cause of his fall out with Mustafa. This could upset him. 'Is that why you and him fell out?' I ask.

'What, Nilüfer? No. She was just one of the things we fell out over. You remember them American birds? One of 'em had her passport nicked and the Old Bill gave me a pull, so Mustafa paid to get me out. But I didn't pay him back because a) it was fuck all to do with me and b) he'd burned me on a skag deal. Then he tried to set me up with the pigs to get his own back by arranging a dodgy pick-up and I had to get out quick. But not before I had him over for the gear.' He laughs. 'As it happens, it was you the Old Bill were looking for. They reckoned you'd had the passport away, but I told 'em I hadn't seen you.'

Which was why they'd arrested him. They knew I was involved because the American girl would have told them about us on the beach. Unless they thought maybe I'd drowned after I'd left the note saying I'd gone to get help. Whatever. It's all over now, and I've no intention of going back to Istanbul. I'd have to be crazy. Crazy.

And I can't see the point of telling Frankie, except that I'm beginning to feel talkative now that the first wave of stonedness has passed, so I change the subject. 'Who are these two German geezers then.'

'Fritz and Heinz I call 'em – a couple of prats. No, they're all right, they're just German, that's all, but they keep having the Afghanis over, you know what I mean? Doing deals on credit and not going back. Every time I see 'em they're boasting how they've burned someone else – they think it's funny, but sooner or later they'll pay; it's the way these fucking tribesmen carry on. They like it if you rip 'em off because it gives 'em an excuse for a bit of revenge. And they do like a bit of revenge.' He laughs again. 'You know, if you shag one of their women, they'll kill her – and you. In fact if you manage to get a look at one they'll probably kill you.'

'Which is why they're all so fucking menacing, I suppose, because they're mad with frustration.'

'I wouldn't say that. They're into boys.'

'Fuck off . . .'

'Straight. It's part of their culture. I mean, not all of them, but a fair few. Some of the boys are prettier than the girls.'

I want to ask if he's tried it, but I'm afraid to in case he says he has – I wouldn't put anything past Frankie. Okay, I've got a bit of a moral problem here: half of my brain's trying to imagine what the attraction could be, while the other half's trying to shut the process of imagination down on the grounds that it's something I've been taught to see as wrong. But the dope's confusing me and I'm beginning to think that maybe I'm just a bit too precious about the whole body thing.

'Everyone to their own thing,' I finally say.

'Fucking right. But you wait until one of these kids starts making eyes at you – you'll know what I'm talking about then.'

'It happened on the bus. There was some young geezer there kept showing out, just like a bird.'

'There you go then, you know what I'm talking about.'

'Yeh, well. I fucked him off, anyway. You're not telling me you'd get into it?'

'Fuck off. What do you think I am?'

Relief. I laugh as I gain the advantage. 'Come on, own up – you've been shagging boys; I knew there was something funny about you . . .'

'Give us a kiss,' he says leaning over, pulling a grotesque face. So I pull a face back and we both collapse with the giggles.

Frankie sits up. 'I gotta go. I've left a woman in bed. She's probably wondering what's happened to me.'

'What sort?'

'Some Dutch girl I met this afternoon.'

Lucky bastard. In the candlelight he looks like an emaciated Christopher Lee with long hair, and I wonder again how he manages to keep pulling the women. I'm a lot prettier, but maybe too nice – they seem to go for danger more than looks. 'Look,' I say, 'I'm leaving early tomorrow for Kabul. I don't know what your plans are, but if I don't see you, take care.'

'You know me, old son. See you about.' Then he stands up with a strange look in his eyes as he realises that I'm still bent on going my own way. 'Keep up with the soul searching; you never know, you might discover yourself one day.' And he walks out, closing the door softly behind him, leaving me in a strangely hollow space where I toss and turn all night, flitting in and out of an endless stream of imagined situations. Frankie always does that, leaves you feeling like you've let him down somehow, or failed to complete something, but I'm also partially relieved because this is my trip and I'm going to work it out. It's strange how he walks in and out of my life – it's like only yesterday that I last saw him. No big hellos, no big goodbyes – it's like we know better than to worry about silly things like time and space, as if our relationship was formed in an altogether bigger place.

Still stoned. And the early morning Kandahar bus adds yet another angle to the Afghan mentality – how could such a violent race of people produce a work of art like this that wouldn't look out of place in Swinging London or Haight Ashbury? (Redman's told me all about Haight Ashbury). This must be the original Magical Mystery Tour bus, a confusion of primary colours and symbolism that clashes absolutely with everything around. Surely the buses here should be camouflaged and bullet-proof?

Inside, the dashboard's completely hidden beneath the driver's personal collection of trinkets and charms, bits of jewellery, wood and plastic religious objects and precious photographs of his family. You might even expect de luxe buttoned plush seats to round off the general feeling of excess that the decoration suggests, but no, for the 400 or so miles we have to travel to reach Kandahar, we have nothing but hard, slatted wooden seats on which to sit and freezing lino-covered floorboards on which to place our feet. Passengers are clearly an afterthought, an inconvenient burden, inconsiderate and small-minded enough to need to travel at all. The rich and powerful, they say, the most respected of the tribe, should, except in times of war, have no need to move anywhere.

Travellers are sad bastards therefore.

But the idea of someone travelling for the fun of it is a new one to them and until they learn otherwise they regard us young Westerners as an unknown quantity, to be observed and treated with respect. Knowing this, I blag the best seat up front near the warm engine, and settle in for a long day.

I've only the *Bhagavadgita* left to read now, but it takes a bit of studying – I think I can see what it's getting at, but at the end of the day it's nothing but words. Like the Bible. I want instant enlightenment, not something you have to do nine to five all your life, like a long boring job with a pension at the end. And I can't start worshipping, or being devoted, because I don't believe in anything other than me.

I thought I'd cracked it back on the beach in Turkey, but as time goes by you start becoming the old you again, obsessed by sex and fear.

And I realised last night that fear had crept back into my life when I thought about returning to Istanbul. And the boy thing. That made me uncomfortable for a while – and what's being uncomfortable, other than being afraid?

So I lay there and thought and thought and thought. Where does it all keep coming from? You sweep the house out and before you know where you are, it's dirty again – it struck me that whatever happened on that beach has to be done every day.

The thing is, I can't work out exactly what did happen on the beach. I know what the result was, that I felt free and invincible by understanding myself for the first time – at least I thought I did – but I've moved on again in my head and need to understand more about the way I tick now.

Could this then be an endless search? With a constantly changing outlook, nirvana seems just as far away as it ever did; reaching it is like trying to find the horizon or the end of a rainbow. Detachment's one way, they say. Or rather, non-attachment, because if you think you're detached you're really attached – attached to being detached. Or something like that.

Maybe King John was right: I do think too much, a strange thing because thinking was never my strong point, why should I start now?

I think the smoking's got something to do with it.

I think. Here I go again.

But no, seriously, before I smoked hashish I didn't think too much, just roamed around like some sort of violent beast, not necessarily violent as in fighting, but violent as in going for it like there's no tomorrow: violent in eating, violent in sex, violent in communication of every kind – you know, talking without thinking, predatory. When I ate I wolfed it down and wondered how much more there was for me; when I had sex it was all about me, not about she; when I conversed with anyone it was all about what I was saying and nothing to do with listening. Everything was me, or is that what being young's all about?

Far in the distance, according to the map I borrowed from one of Redman's archaeologist mates without his knowledge, I can see the south-western fingers of the Hindu Kush, a secret place of steep green fertile valleys lived in by ancestors of Alexander the Great, Genghis Khan and Tamerlane. Must be some crazy people. We did Alexander the Great at school and I wished I'd paid more attention, but at the time Christine Smith's tits seemed more important.

Despite what I said about King John and his belly-aching I haven't eaten now for over 24 hours and I'm feeling pleased with myself too. Eating's one of those things frowned upon by top freaks, so you have to creep off and do it in secret. But not eating makes you kind of light-headed until you get used to it, then your stomach shrinks along with your cheeks and arse – although in my case, having done a couple of years boxing training and having run hundreds of miles building up stamina, there isn't much to come off in those areas anyway. But being skinny's definitely where it's at, because it means you don't care, that you're not self-indulgent and weak; and the last thing chicks are looking for is a self-indulgent fat bloke, unless he's rich.

Around midday we stop at a roadside eating house, and seeing as I'm the only Westerner on the bus and unlikely to be discovered eating, I slide off and grab a plate of goat and rice and a glass of tea for about two pence and indulge myself, quietly at peace with the world. Nobody bothers me or even looks in my direction with any sort of abnormal interest. Nobody stares and pesters or looks menacing or lecherous, or hateful because I'm an infidel, and for a moment I stumble on that happiness again, alone in a desolate wilderness, inhabited by murderers and cut-throats. The problem here is that I can still feel the effect of the dope I smoked with Frankie, which means that my perception of the world probably isn't altogether realistic. And the mountains look little more than a short walk away, an hour or so by foot, but according to the map they're 100 miles distant, 100 miles of extraordinarily clear air.

Last night I realised I was no longer certain of anything, and my stomach turned over. The statement I saw scratched on the hotel lavatory wall this morning that 'everything's an illusion anyway' has done nothing to help. I have no doubt that this is an easy view to cope with either completely stoned or completely straight, but right now I'm in that halfway house between the two, and I find the idea destabilising and scary.

Because of this, my body has discovered an automatic defence mechanism against these disturbing thoughts: it makes me need to shit. This occupies the brain until either I manage to go or the pangs subside. Three times before lunch stomach cramps have prevented me from thinking too deeply, and forced me instead to concentrate on the scenery or the people around. I've been offered oranges and dates, grubby dried apricots, sticky raisins and various mysterious and very gooey sweets, all of which I've accepted on the grounds that I'm not going to get paranoid about my state of health. Sooner or later on this kind of journey you have to give up worrying about getting sick because most of your mental energy's occupied full-time trying to cope with the constant assault on your senses.

As soon as we get to Kandahar I'm going to go out and buy some hash, score some dope I mean, so that I can free myself from my head and get on with the important things in life like music, laughter and women.

The bus roars into action, a strangely loud but disembodied horn blasts through the icy air, and everyone clambers back in. But here there are no rules and someone's nicked my place.

The only free seat is next to a lone, sweet-smelling female covered from head to toe in a bright green burkha. Looking apologetically around to make sure I'm treading on nobody's nuptial toes, I sit down gingerly beside her and immediately feel her warmth. Remembering Frankie's words about Afghan women I then stare everywhere but in her direction until I can feel the mood inside the bus slowly relax.

After a little while it becomes apparent that there's a child hidden somewhere within the burkha, and as I listen to the thing feeding happily on those forbidden breasts I become aware that she's watching me. After several stops and still an hour or so from Kandahar a strange thing happens: by now everyone has left the bus except for the two of us and the driver, so out of politeness I move to another seat nearby to allow her more room. Suddenly uninhibited, she lifts the burkha over her head to reveal the most beautiful female face. She must be 18 or 19. Her long hair is jet black, her skin ivory, and her eyes an astonishing bright green. I am stunned. Staring me straight in the eye she lifts her shirt to reveal a perfect breast and fixes the baby onto it and I smile like an idiot. And she smiles back.

'Hello,' I stammer.

She makes the slightest of head movements in acknowledgement, then lowers her eyes shyly before looking up again to stare at me. I'm irretrievably hooked – I could live forever with this person, in a hovel in Kandahar, or take her back to London and show her off. But I've probably already overstepped the mark by setting eyes on her, by ogling her breast; somewhere there has to be a husband, a dark-eyed maniac with a very sharp knife, waiting.

Heedless I move across to sit in the seat in front and turn to face her. At least it'll give her the opportunity to react negatively and put me in my place, but if she doesn't it could mean that I'm in with a chance. All she needs do is pull the burkha down and I'll know the score. Also, by not sitting next to her, I'll not compromise her in any way, because I've noticed the driver glancing back from time to time, and who knows, he could be the brother-in-law.

Smiling pleasantly I introduce myself, telling her my name, where I'm from and going to, and go on to praise her incredible looks and her bonny baby, even going so far as to dare to stroke it gently on the cheek with the knuckle of my middle finger. Her breast is two inches away and she smiles again. Madness is in me, and I want to lean forward and kiss her beautiful mouth and for a moment the tension is almost irresistible, but alarm bells sound in my head and I draw back.

What am I doing? What the *fuck* am I doing? This is Afghanistan. The men here are killers. She has a baby.

I think I know what has happened – something has seriously affected my sense of right and wrong, that instinct that stops you from doing dangerous things. This – on top of being fazed by her beauty – has caused me to lose my head. The thing is, I'm wavering, between 'so what?' and 'how can I get away with this?' and don't care too much about repercussions. The main thing is, I want her.

The issue is solved by the bus grinding to a halt at the roadside to allow a small group of Afghans aboard and I have little choice but to turn away and face the front. She pulls the burkha gracefully over her head and resumes anonymity for the rest of the journey.

As the bus pulls into the square at Kandahar I get up without looking back, make way to the front and jump out. Fifty yards away the old city walls tower over little crowds of itinerants and tradesmen, so I melt into the background and head for a small triangle of shadow cast between the wall and a turret by the lowering sun in the clear blue winter sky. Here on the edge of the southern desert, or the Dasht-e-Margow, as the map calls it, sounds have a disconnected and remote ring to them; nothing reverberates. But even the drop of a pebble can be heard clearly at some distance. Combined with the almost absurd clarity of vision which makes the judging of distance difficult, everything has an entirely unreal but very direct feel to it. The old city wall for example, about 50 feet away, feels as if it is but an inch from my nose. I seem to have lost a dimension.

Leaning my kitbag against the wall I turn to sit down and face the bus to see if anyone, an armed warlord perhaps, or an insanely jealous father, has come to meet her, but she's already here, standing silently in front of me holding a bundle in one arm and the baby in the other. I look quickly about, but no one's taking any notice of my major drama so I look back at her behind the veil.

'Okay,' I say, picking up my bag, 'come with me.' Am I insane? No, I'll take her to the nearest hotel, install her and the baby in a room, and find a translator. At least this way I'll find out where she's coming from: whether she's alone, on the game, just being friendly, or some sort of head-case. Anyway, now that she's back under that emerald green sheet the attraction I felt for her is diminishing as the image of her face becomes a memory. At the same time I desperately want to see her face again but fear I'll fall apart if I do. Why don't I just go while I can? I think of Nilüfer.

But this one's doing the chasing, wanting to make contact, whereas Nilüfer didn't want to know.

I wonder what her name is.

Halfway across the square I turn, poke my chest with my thumb, and say, 'Tommy', and smile.

A small voice comes through the facial lace, 'Masumah.'
'Masumah,' I say, and do a tiny bow, which seems in order.
'Tommy,' she says.

The owner of the Khyber Hotel looks suspiciously at Masumah but takes my money for a double room before getting a boy to guide us to the second floor past a chaotic first floor which seems to be occupied by young Europeans on their way to India. You can tell the novices because they're bright-eyed, talk too much, and crave experience. Oh, and they're dressed all wrong. My sudden appearance among them with an Afghan female in tow sends me straight to the top of the credibility charts, alongside the intravenous drug users and those eccentrics that have lost their minds somewhere en route. Knowing that these two are the only groups to occupy this exalted position, and knowing also that I am not an intravenous drug user – although, no doubt I will be if the chance arises – it seems to me that I must in that case belong to the eccentric or lost-mind group, and at last I feel that I've made it.

The room is small and basic with two single beds and a stove which the boy immediately lights causing woodsmoke to puff from every little crack in the ironwork until at last the thing begins to roar and crack and radiate heat. Masumah says something sharply to him and he nods obediently and hurries out. Quickly he returns, with a screen of all things, which he erects around the chair and table in one corner of the room. Again she snaps at him and off he trots, this time to return in a few minutes with a teapot and two glasses on a tray. With a flourish he places the teapot on the stove, and already I can see great advantages in having a wife here who speaks the language. Maybe I'll just rest awhile and enjoy the luxury before I start delving into her background.

After yet more orders the boy bows out leaving us alone together with my beating heart. Laying the sleeping child down gently on one of the beds, she removes the burkha, and again I can see her incredible face. She smiles. Beneath the robe she's wearing white cotton trousers and an embroidered white cotton top with a knitted light-brown woollen cardigan edged with a pattern of blue flowers. On her feet over a pair of woollen socks she's wearing red embroidered leather slip-on shoes with slightly turned-up pointed toes. She's almost as tall as me.

'Chai?' she says, then giggles, adding, 'Tommy . . . Tommy . . .' and turns to the stove and the steaming teapot. Taking two glasses she pours out the tea and offers one to me.

'Thank you.' I take one with a lump of sugar and sip.

Sitting on the edge of the two beds we face each other wondering what to say next, but there is a soft tap at the door and she gets up and moves quickly behind the screen. Again the boy enters, this time carrying a tray loaded with food which, at my suggestion, he places on the bed. Then he leaves and Masumah emerges from behind the screen to share out the flat bread, meat and rice. With the arrival of food the baby begins to whimper, so she attaches it to a breast and we eat together.

'Yum, yum,' I say, smacking my lips.

'Mmmn,' she responds. I look up and suddenly we meet, without the barrier of language, and I want to throw myself at her. But we eat some more, and from time to time I say things like, 'You're gorgeous,' or 'You've got the most beautiful face I've ever seen,' or 'What am I going to do about you?' or 'Will you sleep with me tonight?' And in return she says things I don't understand, and makes almost indiscernible but what I interpret as flirtatious little movements with her mouth and eyes, lowering her eyelashes and running her tongue along her lips. Changing the baby from one breast to the other she again makes no attempt to cover up, but I don't know the social score here in Afghanistan when it comes to tits – is it a come on, or just a mother feeding a baby?

Thoughts of getting some of the local hashish still pass through my mind spurred on by erotic memories of screwing with Gina while stoned, so after I finish the food, while Masumah is concentrating on cleaning the baby, I grab my coat and tell her as best I can that I'm going out for an hour. Frankie's friend, Aziz Ullah, shouldn't be too hard to find.

She looks intently at me. 'Dollar,' she says, holding out her hand. Then she points to the baby's red arse. I've got about $15 left, about five of them in Afghanis, and curse myself for not borrowing more from Frankie while I had the chance. I give her a wad of Afghanis, take a $5 bill from inside my passport for the purchase of dope and chance a kiss on her mouth, but she deflects at the last instant and takes it on the cheek.

Aziz Ullah's pad is only a few narrow alleys and streets away from the Khyber Hotel but it takes nearly an hour to find after getting poor directions from the hotel owner, and I'm almost on the point of giving up when a small boy accosts me saying 'Smoke, mister?' Running in front he leads the way through an alley just wide enough to take a donkey, then into a dark doorway to one side. Wary of attack I follow him further. In the light of the matches that he is striking for my benefit we go up a stone stairway and along a short corridor until we come to a heavy iron door before which he hesitates, listening. Satisfied at whatever it is he can or cannot hear he knocks and pushes it open.

Inside, the scene is breathtaking. There before me sitting on the floor behind a low wooden table is an Afghan male dressed in white robes, sporting a white turban. His skin is olive and his long wispy beard jet black; a beard to die for. The room, apart from the little table, is furnished solely with carpets – on the floor, the walls, and even the ceiling, carpets so richly coloured they trigger a rush of joy, a sensation of great warmth and happiness at being there. The only source of light, suspended by a long chain from the ceiling, is a brass oil-lamp which flickers subtly as I walk in, just enough to make the walls dance and everything appear entirely unreal.

'Please come in,' says the apparition as the small boy departs closing the door gently behind him. 'Welcome to the house of Aziz Ullah. Please sit down if you wish.'

I thank him for his hospitality and sit on a layer of carpets that feels about six inches thick. And the colours – deep reds, violet and midnight blue, gold and russet, deep orange-yellow, touches of vivid pink. One carpet, with a complex and intricate pattern, reveals a tree with birds and butterflies before a domed building, a mosque maybe.

Words are a waste of energy, but I feel that I have to say something. 'Wow,' I groan, 'these carpets are too much.'

He smiles indulgently, obviously used to this sort of mindless western observation. 'Many things in Afghanistan are "too much". We are a people who love beauty.'

A couple of minutes of silence pass as I take it in. The vaulted carpet warehouses of Tabriz, mind-blowing relics of the past, have been distilled here into the spirit of a dope-dealer's mind.

'You have come for hashish?' he asks softly.

'Yes.'

'Then you have come to the right man. I supply and deliver all over the world, to Europe, America, Australia. I was in Amsterdam and Copenhagen. I send it in musical instruments, in shipments of skins, dried fruit, wood carvings and pottery. Even in shoes.' He waits for my approval.

'Amazing.' This is my first real one-to-one with an Afghan of his stature and I'm a bit overawed. I expected some dodgy geezer with a scarred face and a hook nose, but this one's suave and almost saintly, with the gentlest of mannerisms. His hands move slowly and expressively and all the time he is looking deep inside my head with those dark, dark eyes.

'You would like to try hashish?'

'Er, yeh – thanks very much.'

'I have different qualities, different types from different regions. You like something gentle, or a little stronger, maybe?'

'The best you have?'

He laughs patiently. '"Best" depends on taste, does it not? But usually your people mean strongest when they ask for the best.'

'Okay, the best for when you go with a girl.'

'Girl?'

'Lady. Female.'

'For love-making.' He laughs again and opens a drawer in the table. 'There is no such thing without the flame of desire, but if the flame is there . . .'

Now he's getting poetic. I love these people. They seem to have retained something we lost when . . . when . . . When what? That's the question. But I haven't got time to think about it because he's passing me a piece of light-brown hash about the size of the top of my thumb.

'Please. Try this. It is from the hills of Kunduz.'

I skin up a small joint, light it and offer it to him more out of politeness, but he declines by slightly raising the fingers of his right hand, and closing his eyes for about a second. Makes a nice change from explanations and excuses.

So I smoke it all to myself. The flavour is tangy, herbal, and almost foxy with a very slight, burnt edge, and I begin to feel a creeping relaxation of the body and a sense of ease and peacefulness. I think of Masumah, and my willy twitches. Not that I need dope to feel horny about her. And the room has also taken on an intensity and depth that causes another shift in my perception. The space between the walls – the room – has become filled with a labyrinth of colour, and my body seems to have become entwined with it.

My voice says, 'That's good,' and I laugh distantly. Aziz Ullah's beaming at me, his face radiating light from the lamp.

'You would like to try another?' he asks.

'Sure.'

Dipping his hand into the drawer again he pulls out a darker piece, about the same size as the first and places it on the corner of the table nearest me. 'This is from Mazar-i-Sharif, in the north of Afghanistan. Some people say it is "the best" as you put it.'

'Mazari . . . my friend Frankie gave me some that he brought from you.'

He looks more pointedly at me. Do I detect a slight frown? 'Frankie? English Frankie is a friend of yours?'

Whoops. 'I met him in Herat. When I say a friend I mean like anyone who comes from the same country as yourself who you meet on the road, not friend as such but someone you meet. Thanks.' I take the piece of Mazari dope and begin rolling another joint. 'You know him then?'

'Do you know his two German friends?' he asks, ignoring my superfluous question.

'He mentioned them – they're in business or something together. But I haven't met them. I was only in Herat for about six hours. That was where I met Frankie, in the hotel.'

Fuck this. Just fuck all this. Here I go again, getting defensive because of Frankie. Sure he's got his uses – like when I need money or information on some dodgy scheme, and we have a friendship of sorts derived mainly from background and shared experience, but that's as far as it goes. And this astute Afghan must realise that a one-off six-hour meeting in a hotel isn't going to produce the sort of information I've just revealed unless I already knew the bloke.

I offer Aziz Ullah the joint but he refuses again.

'I don't know whether your paths will cross again, but if you do, tell your friend that his German associates are in a very precarious position – they are, how do you say . . .' he chuckles, 'skating on thin ice?'

The new hashish is oilier and heavier, stickier and less easy to crumble than the last. Again I finish the joint alone but I feel no awkwardness about this because the man I'm with expects nothing of me except that I enjoy his hospitality.

'Why are they skating on thin ice?' my mouth asks from a great distance. I'm getting stoned.

'They insult Afghan hospitality. So far, allowance has been made because they do not understand our ways, but their error has been pointed out to them and still they continue taking advantage of our trust and refusing to honour debts. It is little concern of mine as I do not trade on credit with strangers, but they are dealing with men who will not hesitate to balance the books in one way or another.'

'They've ripped someone off?'

He looks at me, a little mystified by the phrase I learned from King John.

'Cheated somebody. Not paid up.'

'Rip . . . how do you say it?' He's a keen learner.

'To rip someone off. To be ripped off. Or you can say, for example, if something is far too expensive – it's a rip-off.'

'I like that. So yes, they've ripped off somebody – who is very likely to rip off their ears.' He began giggling. But there was a sinister undercurrent in the humour. If the devil lives anywhere on Earth it has to be here in Afghanistan. 'But my hashish is not a rip-off. I will sell you "the best" at the best price.'

The Mazari is strong. I recall others coming into the room at some stage and voices and carpets, and then the crisp night air and alleyways and a vast open square and stars above, billions of stars above creating silver and black shadows below, and silence interrupted only by boots crunching on frozen mud. And the barking of distant dogs. Could this be the loneliest place on

Earth? The feeling of being stuck by the soles of my feet to a huge ball spinning in space is overpowering.

Dark room. Strike a light. Light a candle.

But something's wrong, the room's empty. Oh, no. Not even a sign that another world existed here just a short while ago. My kitbag is still in the same place, but the screen is gone and the stove is almost dead. Checking the kitbag I find my passport, but the $5 bill is gone, as is a pair of boxer shorts and a T-shirt.

Masumah has ripped me off. But I can't believe it.

Spinning round I see something on a pillow of one of the beds. A rose. A red paper rose. But I'm too stoned to do much about it. What can I do anyway?

I can ask the hotel boy, asleep downstairs, if he's seen her.

'Hey, boy! Where's woman?'

Sleepy face, hair sticking up all over the place, but no fear. I read amused insolence in those young eyes and silent words that say 'Sucker. Don't mess with Afghanistan.' 'Woman. She go,' he says.

'Where?'

He shrugs.

'Okay. Police. She take money.' Is this unchivalrous of me? I wouldn't really call them, but where's my love now, eh? This female who stole my heart has also stolen my money, and I'm indignant, a small-minded tosser who is rattled at being taken for a sucker. Worse. Being taken for a sucker by a beautiful girl. Major blow to the ego here.

'Okay, you fetch. I sleeping.' Then the little turd walks away. He's probably in on this with her. They've probably been ripping off half the overlanders between them. I wish I'd never mentioned 'rip off' to Aziz Ullah – I feel like I've put the mockers on everything now.

How can such a promising start end up like this?

'Oy! Boy! Woman. She go alone?'

The boy's mystified by 'alone'.

I try again. 'Woman go with . . .'

'Gwth?'

'With. She go with . . .'

'Hweeth?'

'No no. She go *with* someone? With man? With other woman? Oh, fuck off.'

Back in bed I dream Masumah is here all the time, hiding behind the screen which is in another part of the room, and I am about to do it with her doggy fashion when the ever-vigilant dream-spoiling part of me says 'you're only dreaming'. So I lay and think all night about her and Aziz Ullah and Frankie and her again, and think maybe my self-esteem's at a bit of a low ebb.

And should I warn Frankie about the German blokes? If I spend money bussing back to Herat he might not be there anyway. Then I would've wasted valuable cash. I've got five dollars and some Afghanis left, enough to last a couple of weeks if I'm careful.

Then what? Who knows? Who cares? Something'll turn up.

FOUR

Current state of head: a bit odd. I can't put my finger on it, it's too confusing, I mean my head's not confused but the world is . . .

Listen to this: I'm in Kabul now, in the Bamiyan Hotel just round the corner from the Khyber Restaurant. Not the Khyber Hotel which is in Kandahar which I did a runner from early this morning (If they can't tell me where the Afghan chick is, I'm not going to pay, you know what I mean) but the Khyber Restaurant, a modern cafeteria, just like you find in London that sells chips – and apple pie and fried eggs and baked beans. And curried goat.

In the Bamiyan Hotel, which is above a tea-house that plays loud Eastern music, are twenty or so Europeans, all about my age, either coming from or going to India. Everyone of them looks or is mad, except for the four who are women.

These four females have a room to themselves and are called Elizabeth, Marie, Penny, and some fraülein whose name I forget, maybe Gerlinde. Actually, Marie isn't a European at all, but a New Zealand Maori and is one of the sweetest girls I've ever met. Elizabeth is Swedish and blonde, and sweet as well. Beautiful actually – well, stunning; Penny is Dutch I think, looks like Rita Tushingham and is also sweet. And Gerlinde is blonde and sweet. There is another girl with a mass of frizzy dark hair who might be sweet but she's with a bloke and both of them are German and unapproachably cool. No one can get near them without freezing solid. Actually, I think I could get near her if he wasn't there, but he always is, guarding.

In my room are four other blokes: Dirk, a tall, thin, crazy German; Hulm, an emaciated German junkie and Patrick and Christian from Paris, also junkies. Christian has long, very blond hair, Patrick long brown. Together they're returning from India, while Hulm and Dirk, who are not together, are going. Well, Dirk isn't too sure what he's doing, but right now, sitting opposite me on his bed, he says he is *going* to India.

Adding to the strong feeling of community that exists here is the requirement that we stay in the hotel whether we like it or not. None of us can go out, now that it's dark, because there's a curfew on, and tanks and other armoured vehicles are on the streets shooting anyone they come across. Christian, who seems pretty clued up about everything, says there has been, or was almost, a coup, and that the army's feeling pretty mean. While a curfew from dusk to dawn is inconvenient if you fancy going out for a kebab or to pay a social call to the Noor Hotel where I'm told there's another group of Europeans, the outbreak of cholera which has also just occurred in the city is one of those things that you can't be sure how to handle. Staying in won't necessarily save you, nor will going out necessarily mean that your chances of living are going to decrease, but knowledge of its presence adds a touch of uncertainty to the already highly unusual situation.

But I'm jumping the gun. When I arrived earlier, everyone was out. I was shown to my bed next to the window on the first floor overlooking the street by the hotel boy, and crashed-out with exhaustion, only to dream about Michael Mouse again. He was about to introduce me to his girlfriend, a sexy bird with sexy lips that I already had designs on, when the music started.

BOM BOM BOM BOM BOM . . .
You're probably wondering why I'm here
And so am I, and so am I . . .

What the fuck is this? Where am I? What's going on? What is this weird music?

I sit up and Kabul Afghanistan 1968 begins.

Facing me is a tall skeleton of a male sitting on his bed, holding a strange pipe a foot long which is belching smoke. He offers it to me. His wrist bangles jingle and jangle. He wears an apple green velvet suit over a floral blouse. His hair, dark blond, has been cut just above the shoulders by a drunk with a pair of blunt scissors. His head is massive and upon his broad nose rests a pair of wire-framed glasses with very thick lenses.

He laughs aloud, infectiously, at me. 'Hello,' he says in a thick German accent, 'Welcome. My name is . . .' He looks slowly around at the other four males in the room before gazing motionless into the distance as if overcome with pride by what he's about to say. Then suddenly puffing out his chest, he spreads his arms wide, and booms, 'Dirk!'

Full of smoke from the chillum, I stare wide-eyed at him as he stares wide-eyed back like a grinning simpleton.

'Pleased to meet you,' I hiss, expelling smoke, 'My name is Tommy.'

Everyone nods and smiles as I suck again on the bottom end of the pipe which has a damp cloth around it for filtering and cooling purposes.

'No, no, man, here . . .' The guy on the next bed, long dark wavy hair, moustache and little beard on the end of his chin, gets up and crosses the yard or so of faded lino to my bed. 'My name is Hulm, this is Patrick, this is Christian – oh, and Guy, but he doesn't live in this bedroom. He is how you say? Visiting. Here . . .' Then he shows me how to hold the pipe, which is called a chillum. The rag also has a name: the safi.

And I try again. Much cooler this time than sucking straight through the bottom. Then I pass it to him. 'What's the music?' I groan after expelling the smoke.

'Dunno, man.' He asks Patrick.

'The Mothers of Invention. Freak out.'

Weird shit. Never heard anything like this before. I like it. A bit different to The Temptations. I'm prone again, staring at the ceiling, aware that the chillum is heading back towards Dirk. He taps and scrapes it out, dumping the ash into the top of the woodstove which stands in the centre of the room, then refills it, using one of a dozen large lumps of hashish on a tray on the floor. He dampens the safi from a jug of water, wraps it around the pipe, and passes it to me to light. 'You want to fire this one up?'

'Sure.' I sit up. They're either checking me out or giving me a hero's welcome; in which case it has to be a check out, so I take a few long tokes while Dirk holds a lighted taper over the pipe. Shit. I'm swallowing vast amounts of very potent smoke – the first pipe alone has destroyed my brain. Enveloped in a cloud, the glow from the pipe is hot enough to smelt iron, and I pass it on again.

For a period after the chillum is finished, everyone is silent. Then Hulm sits up and says that he's hungry, and does anyone else want anything? Dirk is lying rigidly staring at the ceiling, his arms by his side, his feet neatly together, but at the mention of food he sits bolt upright like Frankenstein and booms 'Chappattis and jam. With tea. I-must-have-tea. I-MUST-HAVE-TEA!' Then lies back down again.

Deciding on flatbread, jam and tea all round, Hulm bangs on the floor and bellows out for Sardar, the boy. Within seconds he is there at the door humbly taking the order, and I lay back and think I could get used to this way of life, being waited-on for a pittance.

Soon the food arives on a tray followed by another tray of teas in glasses. Hulm erupts at Sardar, 'Where's my milky tea, you fucking Afghan kunt?' he screams. 'I told you I wanted western tea, western tea, you fucking kunt. Go and get it now!' He throws himself back on the bed, fuming, staring at the ceiling while everyone else looks away in amusement. They're obviously used to these outbursts. Sardar creeps out of the room and closes the door quietly behind him.

Unable to hold myself together any longer, I burst into laughter and break the silence. Dirk sits bolt upright again, beaming, looking at me in mock adoration, gasping with delight that I'm giggling – but it's the dope of course.

Hulm explains his outburst in heavily accented English, 'Fucking stupid kunt! Always he forgets I don't like Afghan fucking tea!' Then he too starts laughing and the room relaxes.

'You know, you must really stop screaming at the Afghans, Hulm. Sometimes you go too far with them. Maybe you get your throat cut next time.' Christian gives a warning in good humour.

'Ach no, it is all they understand. You have to talk to them like this otherwise they have no respect for you,' explains Hulm.

Dirk begins chanting 'Fucking Afghan kunt' in a deep voice, waving his gigantic bony hands like a temple dancer and staring pointedly at the far corner of the ceiling as if he can see something astonishing there. The guy's flipped somewhere along the line, but whether it's the dope or my desperate need for humour after the destabilising events of the last twenty-four hours I find him contagiously funny. Slowly his head swivels until he is staring at me. He pulls grotesque faces ranging from extreme surprise through anger to longing to fright and finally outrage – in which mode he freezes as if the wind has changed. This expression he directs at Hulm who says, 'You're fucking crazy, man,' as he gets another chillum together. I go and put 'Careful with that Axe Eugene' on and get stuck into the bread and jam.

Patrick has a beautiful sitar inlaid with ivory which he plays softly along to the music. The chillum goes round again and Guy picks up some tablas and begins to accompany Patrick. Then the door opens and a beautiful girl with long white-blonde hair enters followed by a darker girl with brown hair. They all greet each other and the two come over to me and introduce themselves as Elizabeth and Maria, then Elizabeth sits on the bed next to me while Maria goes and gets some bread and jam. Sardar eventually returns with Hulm's milky tea, which he accepts with better grace after asking why it took so long, and the drumming and sitar begin to build up in volume as the chillum is filled yet again. By this time I'm in another world, thinking that maybe I'm in heaven – after all, it's all just an illusion – and Christian takes up another set of drums to accompany them. More people come in, notably two more females, Penny and Gerlinde, with more drums. The air in the room becomes thick with hashish smoke. Dirk looms around as the unofficial passer of the chillum, dancing as he goes. Elizabeth is lying next to me, jutting her tits into the air, telling me softly about India and other bits of her life she thinks I need to know. She met Maria, a trained nurse, in Madras, and they're travelling back together – at least, she's travelling back whereas Maria's on her way for the first time to Europe. On the way east she met and fell in love with an Afghan guy and lived with him for a while but it didn't work out because their cultures where too far apart, whatever that means – probably something to do with toilet paper – but you could tell she was besotted; it was just a shame she wasn't besotted with me.

Then she sits with Dirk for a while before moving on to Hulm, Christian and Patrick.

Marie is kind hearted, with no side to her and says she wants to see the world before going back to nursing, that maybe she'll find a job in London and suggests we all meet up there some time in the future. Dutch Penny's training to be a journalist, and like Maria, refuses to smoke the dope. Gerlinde, from Hamburg, speaks very little English so we talk in German. Hulm overhears and is impressed, 'It is good that an Englishman bothers to learn to speak German,' he says, and we become friends.

Out of all the girls, Gerlinde shows the most promise because she has a way of looking into you that makes you feel good. Marie, no way, too puritan. Penny's deep and unfathomable. Elizabeth? Well. The most agreeable but not showing out to anybody. She's just Swedish-cool, that's all.

Pipe dreams. Back in London: a girl who was going out with Jacko, one of my mates, always gave the impression that she wasn't interested – she hardly looked at me, especially when they were together, and I must have known her for a couple of years. It was an on-off relationship, sort of on one week and off the next, but she really put it over that there was no one else in her life other than Jacko. Then one night I met her at a party when Jacko wasn't around and she came on really strong and we ended up shagging like crazy in the garden trying to make up for lost time. After that she was just her same old cold self again when he was about and I did my best to avoid her, feeling a bit guilty about things, but from then on whenever the chance presented itself, on she came again, like I was *her* bit on the side. In the end she gave Jacko the elbow because he was an unreliable piss-head, and married some other geezer, and to be sure it broke him up, but she was a nice shag . . .

Memories, vivid ones at that. I feel I can conjure up any scene I want, and go walkabout in some sort of dream world . . .

And that amazing pull I had one night when I went out with Vince, the older brother of one of my friends. He had a Jag. Everyone else was either staying in or out already and we were at a loose end so Vince said 'fancy coming out?' and off we went. I was only nineteen, and felt very smooth sitting next to him in his motor. I think he was showing off a bit, too, letting me know what it was like to be cool. Older cool. Anyway, it was a nice summer evening and we drove out of town to a little pub called the Tiger's Head on Chislehurst Common, and straightaway he starts chatting up these two birds, one of whom is very tasty indeed, a tiny bit like Marilyn Monroe, and he's making a play for her. To cut a long story short, she pulls me – not him, which does my head in (and his) because he's a really smart geezer, much more so in a sort of grown-up way than me – and takes me off in her car and shags me in the back of it. And she tells me she's engaged and wants a fling before she gets married. Anyway it was some fling because it lasted for a month leading up to the weekend of her wedding, meeting whenever and wherever we could, even one lunchtime on the roof of St Paul's. Then one day she said it was all over and that was that, I never saw her again.

When I come to in the morning, Gerlinde's in bed with me, but when I look around the room has changed shape, seems somehow smaller, and Hulm and Dirk are missing, so are Christian and Patrick. This is confusing. And I'm naked, as is Gerlinde, who is snoring softly. Where are my jeans? Ah. They're on the floor. I must be in someone else's bed. Gerlinde turns, opens her eyes and says 'Oh,' as if surprised, 'Good morning.' Then snuggles up. Outside the window, snow is falling heavily. The night before slowly comes back: the stoned shagging oblivious to the comings and goings of others – could this be what they call free love?

We'd gone to another room to escape the crowd which had gathered in ours, but the German freak couple had come in from somewhere else, switched on the light and said 'Entschuldigen Sie' and switched it off again but not after farting around for ages looking for a book. And all the while Gerlinde was going like the clappers on top of me and moaning and I wanted to laugh but didn't want to risk interrupting her in case she switched off. Then the German couple went to bed and started, then Marie came in, switched the light on, quickly turned it off again and left. And we all laughed and carried on, and I was so stoned in the darkness I thought I was with a Chinese girl in a room inside a pagoda. Even Gerlinde's words sounded Chinese and I was lost for hours until gunshots outside brought me back to Kabul and a pack of wild dogs or wolves baying, chasing something through the streets, tearing it to pieces. The roaring and screaming badly unnerved Gerlinde – I think the victim was another dog – and we lay cuddling, joined at the crutch, Gerlinde hanging on and wincing at every awful noise until it went horribly silent. 'Aber, mein gott,' she whispered, 'dass ist schrecklich!' Then she started moving her little bum again.

Quietly I slide out of bed as the winter sun slides between the snow clouds and creeps through the window. Dressing silently I go back to my room where Hulm is aleady fire-lighting while the other three stir in their beds. 'You want we go and get some breakfast?' he says in German, briskly loading the stove with dry wood.

'Ja, doch.' If I'd been back in England it would have been 'where've you been? Have you been shaggin that German sort? Come on – we know what you've been up to – did she do the trick all right?' or something like that. Here, nobody gives a toss, the cool is genuine and uncontrived. But then, most of these people have other things on their minds. Like morphine.

I take another look at Hulm and see that he is being over-attentive with everything he is doing, meticulously speedy, intensive to the point of being obsessed about every tiny detail: a piece of charcoal that drops on the lino he quickly picks up to put back in the stove then makes a meal of cleaning away every last tiny trace of soot from the floor.

Christian is now sitting on the edge of his bed, but beyond a perfunctory greeting he has other things on his mind: a burning candle, a sooty spoon, white powder, cotton-wool, water – I'm fascinated – and a silver and glass syringe. As the powder and water become a colourless liquid in the heating spoon, he drops a small ball of cotton wool into the mixture to act as a filter and sucks the liquid up into the syringe. Laying this carefully down he then wraps an old necktie around his thin left arm just under the armpit, pulls it tight with his teeth, and begins tapping the flesh around the inside of his elbow until a vein stands proud. Very carefully, after pointing the syringe upwards and shooting out any air, he eases the needle into the vein, allowing a curl of blood to seep back into the reservoir, then injects. Then he removes the needle carefully, placing a wad of linen over the tiny puncture, folds his arm, releases the tourniquet, and sinks back onto the bed with a sigh. Patrick's doing the same thing with his own treasured set of equipment, his works, and similarly collapses back onto the bed as the first rush of morphine hits him.

Hulm has already been through this stage and is expending his secondary rush on building the fire. When Christian and Patrick sit up a little while later they begin a crazy animated talk together, faster than anything I've ever seen with speed, and I have to laugh, but they're oblivious. Dirk seems to have gone back to sleep after making all the noises of getting up, so Hulm and I go out alone to eat.

Outside, the sun is shining on a sea of snow, slush and mud, but the raised wooden sidewalks keep you out of the mud. There are rails to tie horses and donkeys to, but instead of cowboys the place is swarming with Afghans on business, many of them armed to the teeth. As different as we might look, few take any notice as we stroll along the wooden boards peering into the open-fronted shops which sell everything from morphine to alarm clocks and lemons and tangerines to second-hand '50s American baseball jackets. One is selling live sparrows and starlings from cages so I buy two and release them to fly away over the rooftops, much to the astonishment of the seller and onlookers.

Weaving our way onwards through the beggars and street

vendors and ghostly women, we come to a long glass-fronted modern café, the Khyber Restaurant. Here, in contrast to everywhere else, are young people – students dressed as in Teheran in the western-style uniform of white shirts and black trousers. The girls too are similarly dressed but with daring dark skirts above the knee. 'Students from Kabul University,' explains Hulm, 'trying to climb their way out of the fifteenth century. It's very difficult for them. The girls get spat on, and some are killed – both boys and girls – because they offend Allah. But nowhere in the Koran does it say such things.' He laughs cynically. 'They make me sick, man, these religious madmen.' He spits in the road.

Just across the boulevard is a wide expanse of mud dotted with little heaps, tiny pyramids of shit, among which dogs scavenge and people wander or squat. A covered woman is among them. It is the public lavatory. 'You must be careful of these places in the dark,' he says. 'A few days before you came, when the curfew wasn't in place, Dirk fell over here and came back covered in scheisse. My God, did he stink!'

Inside the restaurant we order fried eggs and chips, but when it comes to paying Hulm can only just find enough to cover his share of the bill, so I ask him how he's going to survive, especially as he's on his way out rather than back.

'You don't need money,' he explains. 'Once you get into Pakistan and India the people just want to feed you all the time. They love us, man.'

'And the junk?'

'Not expensive. Everyone shares it anyway. But I have a friend who is living in Lahore – she will give me money until I get some sent over from Germany. My friends send me money, and I will pay them back. But in India it is possible to make money if you really want.'

But I can't imagine it, seeing the poverty that exists.

'It is true. With our links to Europe it is easy to become an agent for export, or to earn commission by attracting buyers to shops. But fuck, why am I talking like this? I don't know what I am going to do. Die probably. They keep telling me I'm going to die.'

'Who's they?'

'Christian and Patrick. They are going home for a cure. They say I should too, but who cares? Next time I will be reincarnated as a mosquito.'

Two tables away a pretty Afghan student girl is looking at us, but Hulm warns me off and I think of Redman. 'They kill you for looking at them here.'

I still smile but she looks away.

And despite everything, the western-style lavatories installed here in the restaurant, the first I've seen since Ankara, are still used like holes in the ground because the arse cannot be dirtied on a seat used by others. These students, these young modernists, climb onto and crouch over the bowl with their filthy boots on the seats rather than sit on them. Some have even crapped on the floor rather than risk using this devilish modern contraption. And I see the logic.

Outside the restaurant we almost fall over a man minus a body from the waist down balancing on a wooden board with roller-skate wheels on each corner. How he shits I don't know. With huge arms he propels himself about among the crowds at knee height, every so often tugging at someone's pantaloons to beg for alms.

A dying dog lies in the gutter wheezing its last as kids throw stones at it while amused adults look on and suddenly I begin to pick up on the feel of the place. This is the opposite to everything I know and understand and my values now count for nought – I mean, most children are cruel, but to see them encouraged in their cruelty by adults is new to me.

These people tolerate us, look at us with a cold eye, knowing that anytime they wish they can do anything they want. They can rob us, hurt us, kill us – and nobody would do a thing about it because law here is almost non-existent. Okay, there is a law, but the people only tolerate the law while it suits them. The army's loose on the streets now because some tribal lord has decided to show off, and rumours of a coup or attempted assassination are doing the rounds, but what worries me are the soldiers – toes poking through their boots and comical to look at, they are brutal in the extreme.

154

One of them has just battered a man to death in front of us, while people stand watching. He was clubbed to death because he was begging in a teashop and the owner complained. Thwack, thwack, thwack, thwack, thwack . . . while he was unconscious, dead, on the floor. Until his skull caved in.

I can't believe it. My system is numb.

Hulm is in a rage and begins screaming at the soldier but I have to drag him away because he's sure to get the same treatment if he persists. 'You fucking kunt!' he screams – Hulm loves this English term – 'You have killed him, you fucking bastard! Look! You fucking animal, no, you are worse than a fucking animal!' This is a big insult to an Afghan and I hope no one can translate, but the soldier just stands there looking stupid, bemused by this long-haired screaming foreigner.

When we get back to the Bamiyan Hotel, Marie adds fuel to the fire by telling us about the massacre of the British Army in 1842. The entire army was besieged in Kabul, demoralised, spooked, and finally allowed to retreat back towards India through the Kabul Gorge only to be ambushed and slaughtered to a man. Well, almost – they let one live to tell the tale.

Just before the siege they'd butchered a couple of the British envoys who'd tried to do a deal, and hung their quartered bodies in a butcher shop in the bazaar for everyone to see, alongside the carcasses of goats and sheep.

'Even now,' she says, 'no one'll use the gorge at night because of the ghosts.'

That's another thing – the feeling of death. The country's full of it. When I came through Ghazni I had the worse feeling I've ever had in my life, like a feeling of foreboding and darkness. In fact it had started just after I left Herat, but with sunshine and scenery the feeling had worn off. And then Masumah had turned up and I'd forgotten all about it, but when I passed through Ghazni the next day it all came flooding back . . .

Christian thinks it's something to do with past lives, and the thought gives me mixed feelings, like, if I really was here it gives me the willies, but I'm relieved it's all over. But is it? Just how far does this illusion thing go? The next thing I get is a strong urge to get out of the country before it's too late again.

Patrick says you can screw yourself up thinking about reincarnation and past lives, and I believe him: he met a guy in Benares, another French guy, who recognised the Burning Ghats from a previous existence and destabilised back into the past. Now he's living on the Ghats covered in ashes like one of the local madmen unable to get back into the present.

This is very unsettling. This is the first time I've come across this weird shit and I find it a bit disturbing, like it bends your mind. But it also seems to be the thing that everyone's into so I'd better learn more about it.

The chillum begins its rounds and another day and night of stonedness begins with people coming and going. Around nine in the evening we all choose to go out, despite the curfew, to a tea-house Guy knows which serves hashish in waterpipes to Westerners. To fortify ourselves for the journey we each swallow a handful of amphetamine pills, wait for the buzz to start then leave in pairs. I go with Elizabeth.

Outside in the freezing darkness we listen for the sound of army patrol vehicles, and hearing none, dash across the street into the shadows and head down towards the Kabul bridge which we have to cross. The other thing to watch out for is dogs, because according to Guy they attack if they suspect you're unarmed.

Surprisingly at the bridge there's no guard, but as we run across we suddenly hear the roar of a diesel engine and the rumble and squeal of tracks and have to dart into a stinking alleyway full of shit. The lavatories on the upper floors of the houses here empty out through the walls, onto the street, and you have to be careful where you walk.

Hugging closely together, I become very conscious of Elizabeth pressing against me, and her grip is encouraging, but the speed has already taken effect and I'm out of action for the night. An armoured car passes and I can just about make out someone in the turret but it is gone almost immediately and we dash out again. This happens twice more before we reach the tea-house, and a few streets away we hear a burst of automatic gunfire.

Inside the tea-house it is packed. Dozens of armed tribesmen sit about on raised carpeted platforms, and to one side leaning up against a roof support is a stack of rifles placed as umbrellas might be back in England. We spot Guy and Patrick already drinking tea in an alcove to one side, so nodding to the crowd who seem a friendly enough bunch we take off our boots and join them. Guy explains that the alcoves are generally used for hashish smoking while the main area is used for tea drinking, tobacco smoking, and gossip.

Guy orders. He has a smattering of Pashto.

Soon, a crafty-looking serving boy comes to fill a fresh pipe and I notice that everyone is watching. Guy lights it and takes a deep draught but explodes into a coughing fit and is unable to continue. Suggesting that someone else has a go because perhaps he's been smoking a bit too much lately, he passes on the pipe and each of us tries in turn, but with similar results. The feeling is unanimous – the dope's no good. But before we can shout for better hashish, a nearby tribesman jumps to his feet, strides across and kicks over the pipe. A rumble goes through the room and for a bad moment we look at each other and wonder if we've done something terribly wrong, but the proprietor scurries over cringing like a dog and changes the pipe, putting new hashish in the bowl. Towering over him our guardian then watches as we savour the cool smoke, the sweet hashish which should have been served at the outset to us as honoured guests of the Afghan people. To one side the proprietor wrings his hands, hoping desperately that we are satisfied, while outside in the dark night, a tank groans and clanks its way past.

When we get back, two German guys have arrived in a VW caravanette, on their way to Herat from Mazar-i-Sharif. It's a small world – they are going to meet Frankie.

The taller of the two is wary when I introduce myself – I suppose I'm a bit out of it and too druggy for anyone half as straight as he is – but eventually he relaxes and after midnight tea and pancakes they agree to give me a lift back to Herat in the morning.

Almost out of money, I feel the only choice I've got other than the Hulm route of trusting in providence, is to get a sub from Frankie. I get around this in my mind by telling myself that he owes me more than enough from way back – he still owes me a hundred quid for the Mini he wrote off – anyway, what are friend for, if you can't tap them now and again?

I'm not letting myself down am I? Especially after slagging him so much, like, yeh, he's a waste of time but his money's okay. I don't think so. If the truth be known we use each other to suit our own ends.

But there *is* a nagging doubt, and it goes back to begging money and favours from parents: It's About Time I Learned To Look After Myself, and all that. I'm reliant upon others. Inadequate. A ponce. And a hypocritical one.

I do this to myself sometimes, not deliberately, but as a sort of undesirable extra-curricular activity to my normally cheerful existence. Thoughts pop up like weeds, hang around for a bit, then wither and die when I spray them with humour, when I laugh at the things I call myself in these grey moments.

It's snowing again outside. Big flakes are falling vertically through the light from the windows and packs of dogs are baying again just a few streets away. I hope they don't come too close and rip something to bits because the screams of a dying dog are unbearable. I saw a bug Labrador run down, squashed by a lorry in Camberley, and the screams were terrifying. Someone threw up. Father said he'd seen men like it in Normandy, but I don't want to think about that right now.

Why am I being plagued with bad thoughts? They don't go well with a lot of dope smoking, and I can feel fear creeping back into my gut like a black snake. Maybe it's the speed come-down, but I thought I had that yesterday. Or was it? Hang on, I'm losing track of the days here. A tremor passes through me and I start to get flashes of doubt about going back to Herat.

It's the journey back to Herat that's unsettling me – I think. And Ghazni. Thoughts of Ghazni seriously give me the horrors.

But in the morning, after I awake in a panic because the sun's streaming through the windows with a ten o'clock smile on its face, the decision's been made for me because they're gone. They've left already, the bastards – I knew they weren't to be trusted. And Aziz Ullah said so too. They could have at least come and given me a call – I'd only have been two minutes getting ready.

Despite the relief that they've gone without me, I'm pissed off that they obviously don't think I'm worth worrying about. A clear case of lack of respect. Here I go again, putting myself down. Is this yet another painful stage of self-discovery, doubt and self-dislike? No, of course not . . . I'm much better than I used to be on that front . . . When I was 13, I thought I was an insect, the creature from the Black Lagoon, because I was adolescent and pubescent and confused, and ridiculed and despised by every adult I met – so things have improved. But self-esteem takes a backward step when I'm on a low. When I'm on a high I can take anything, but when I'm down all it needs is for some passing female to look at me in the wrong way, or worse still not at all, or for someone to try to short-change or deceive or mislead me, or even for me to *imagine* that something like this is going on, and darkness descends. So I try to remain on a high, and drugs seem to be a pretty good way of doing it. The only thing about this is that certain hashish makes me question everything, forces my brain to churn over and over about little things, so I have to make sure I smoke nothing but the best, which tends to wipe out negative thoughts, leaving you empty but content and looking at the world from a different angle.

After a chillum livener, I go with Dirk and Patrick to the Kabul Ministry of Health for a cholera jab which is now compulsory if we want to leave the country. Similar in style to the hotel across the road from Teheran Station the building is running alive with children and adults in all states of health and mentality. Being what we are we soon attract the attention of nurses and doctors and are each given injection in the arm plus and a booklet containing details of the shot and a very impressive magenta stamp.

Leaving Patrick and Dirk in the bazaar buying secondhand clothes I wander off into the backstreets, then across town and out up towards the heights to the north to take a closer look at the ruins of the Bala Hissar fortifications, which run along the top.

I'm fine until suddenly the realisation dawns on me that I've been wandering for about an hour along the ridge without taking very much notice of anything, as if I were walking a route I'd walked before, almost taking it for granted, and in that moment I'm suddenly overwhelmed at how much everything's changed. I see myself with sandy hair and a drooping moustache, and a bright red tunic and I can smell and taste blood and there's a woman crying and a strong smell of burning, like fireworks, and suddenly I've got the shits real bad and I'm running back down the hill gasping for breath, shocked.

This feeling passes almost as suddenly as it came, like gates have opened and closed, and the terror passes to leave just a touch of intrigue concerning the woman in the vision: I can't put a precise image to her face, but I sense a huge sadness there and have to stop thinking about it because it brings me down badly.

Back in town I'm dodging through yet another side-street dotted with heaps of human shit when a stampede of long-horned steers forces me to turn and run, almost into the arms of a man striding fearlessly on towards them. He is over six feet tall, with long golden hair, fair skin and blue eyes. He wears a turban and the usual Afghan garments, beaneath crossed bandoliers of bullets and a rifle, but on his back he is carrying a dead wolf. He stares hard at me, trying to work out what I am, then continues on towards the herd who have now shuddered to a halt at the sight of him and are panicking, trying to get away backwards down the street. When they finally charge off down another sidestreet I notice that the Afghans chasing them are also extremely wary of this strange fair man, and back away deferentially, avoiding his eye as they go.

A hundred yards further on, after he has disappeared from sight, I'm baited by a band of kids who keep running up and pulling my hair and throwing pebbles, but as I near a little fruit-stall, the vendor sees the problem I'm having and steps out to slap the leader full in the face, knocking him to the ground. Without a murmur the boy jumps up and the little gang wanders off to find another victim and I remember the time in southern Turkey when a similar thing happened, but that seems like another life too.

'There's a girl from Pays-Bas here who knows about these things. You should talk with her. Maybe if you want she can hypnotise you to see.'

'Penny?' I've told Christian about my experience on the ridge. Dirk and Patrick are still out.

He laughs. 'Yes. Penny. But take care, I'm not sure if she's crazy. She says lots of things that don't make sense, and I think that *hypnotisme* is sometimes a bit crazy too. Just use your sense.'

It's an idea though. I know what I felt up there. If she's talking bollocks I'll soon be able to tell. But I must confess that the thought of the geezer in Benares is a bit worrying, losing his mind in the past as he did. The thing is, I'm not really sure whether I believe in all this reincarnation stuff anyway, but I suppose if I'm going to make a good hippy, I mean freak, I'll have to give it a go, man.

Like most of the Dutch people I've met, Penny speaks amazing English – better than me in fact – and is keen to talk, but she says we have to be alone and undisturbed, which I have to agree is a very good idea because if nothing else we might hit it off in other ways. She looks a bit weird with her diamond-tipped, turned-up little nose, but I tell myself that being in no position to bargain, most weird-looking chicks do the business. And with her hair up and glasses on she looks a bit like my old English teacher, Miss Turley. Dim lights and a strong chillum could make an old dream come true.

We get to borrow the empty room that Elizabeth and Marie have grabbed for themselves now that its earlier occupants have moved on, and sit down on a bed cross-legged, facing each other.

'Okay,' she says softly, 'start by telling me everything that happened.'

So I tell her and she listens, and I can just make out the two-tiered nipples of her sharp little breasts beneath her embroidered Afghan top and she says 'Okay, what I would like to do is take you back through the recent period prior to this life. Do you feel it would make you any happier if you understood more about yourself?'

A chance to show off bigtime. 'Sure. It's one of the main things in my life, self-discovery. The *Bhagavadgita* says . . .'

'The *Bhagavadgita* is a beautiful book. But if you wish to look into your past it will be easier if you try to forget the intellect for now.'

Showing-off time quickly over I ask her to explain the difference between the brain, the intellect, the mind, the spirit, and the soul, because I don't have a clue.

'Questions, questions,' she says. 'The mind invents questions and worries itself looking for an answer. When it arranges an answer acceptable to itself it files this away as knowledge for future use. This we call intellect, the relationship between the mind and the brain. Take away the mind and brain and you are left with your soul. And the source of life within that soul, the spirit, is common to us all.'

'So what is the brain?'

'A calculating machine with a large memory. On its own it is useless.'

So there you go, ask a silly question. It's all words to me. My intellect obviously needs sharpening. 'So where does all this memory of past life come into it? Surely that dies with the brain.'

'Every one of your memories is filed into the records of spirit, along with those of everyone else's. When your soul finds another body to inhabit, for whatever reason, it takes past memories along within the spirit. And it is possible to look through those files.'

'What if I get stuck in the past, and can't get back?'

She laughs. 'Most people are stuck in the past, if only they knew it. But no, if that happens, then that is your karma.'

She sounds authoritative, as if she knows what she's talking about, so I ask for her version of karma.

'It's what you deserve in life, okay? Now do you want to get to the bottom of this experience you had or not?'

'I'm not so sure.' And I'm not.

'There are two ways: I can take you back, or I can go back with your help. The first way, usually the best way, is when you go back and tell me. The second way is when I go back and tell you.'

'The second one appeals to me. Don't get me wrong, I'm not scared, it's just that I'm not sure whether I believe in all this stuff and I might not take it seriously enough.' And I'm still worried about the Benares geezer syndrome.

'Okay,' she says finally, 'but we have to work together. We hold each other's hands with our eyes shut. I guide you and we take it from there.'

And so we start. Holding hands, sitting cross-legged on the bed, eyes shut, and I'm thinking she fancies me – she must, holding my hands like this.

'Okay. Concentrate on the colour red of the . . . tunic you call it . . . that's all. Just fix your mind on that colour.'

So I see the colour just as if I'm staring close up at the tunic, and the smells and sounds begin to flood back in and I can feel her beginning to quiver and shake until she's almost bouncing on the bed and she squeals, 'Go back further!' and I wonder how to do this but then I imagine an army of horsemen and I'm one of them and she starts trembling again until she says, 'Come back closer to now' and I see the red again. Then white, and black and red, and I get a shiver up my back . . .

And when finally she whispers 'Okay, you are back in the Bamiyan Hotel. Kabul. It is the year 1968' I feel surprised and exhilarated, so much so that nothing feels real any more.

And what's happened to the time? Daylight has gone and we're sitting in the near dark.

'So what did you discover?' I ask, wondering at the same time whether she does shag or not. It's beginning to look like she doesn't. With me anyway. And I thought I was on to a good thing.

Lighting a candle and some joss sticks, she explains: 'Last life you were German; in the Gestapo after a spell as a soldier. You died in Eastern France as the result of a single bullet wound to the chest and drowned in your own blood.' She sees the look of surprise on my face. 'But you were not a bad man, okay? Before that you were an officer in the British army in India – also dying of a bullet wound to the chest, here in Kabul. The means of death sometimes repeat themselves. Just before that, during the same life, you made a mistake, an error of judgment, in a town south of here, and men died because of your mistake but you made it back to your wife in the garrison where you went today. Before that you were a small farmer in America; then some sort of mercenary in southern Europe, France I think; and before that a horse soldier with the armies of Timur. There were other impressions but the ones I have told you were the strongest.

Much of your life has been involved in violence against others and the time has come to change.'

'What, this life, you mean?'

'No. Your lives before. This is a chance to change your ways. You have no choice anyway. You've suffered very badly and paid for the things already done, so this time you start with a clean slate. Well, cleanish.'

That's what she thinks. I've already started out on the wrong foot and probably put myself back a life by carrying on the way I did before I left England. Anyway, I'm not sure whether I believe her – she could easily have invented all this on the sparse information she has about me. But I didn't tell her about the dream I had in Germany.

She gets up to leave, but turns and says, 'And incidentally, I don't fuck with just anybody like most people these days. That is a silly waste of energy.'

Before I can protest she's gone. And I never see her again.

'Wow, man, too fucking much!' Hulm's really going for it.

I'm telling my room-mates about the experience with Dutch Penny. Most of it, anyway.

'She cannot know such things,' growls Dirk, 'it is impossible . . .'

Patrick sits up. 'No, man, I tell you, it is possible. There are men in India who can tell you these things. You pay them a rupee and they tell you the secrets of life.'

Dirk gasps and mouths 'A rupee!' as if overcome, then gets carried away with the word itself and begins repeating it aloud in different tones and facial expressions backed up by sweeping gestures of the hand until Hulm tells him to shut up.

'I think maybe she is telling the truth,' Hulm adds.

'I think it's not wise to believe everything you hear,' remarks Christian through a cloud of smoke. 'But what do you think, Tommy? Do you think you were here before? And with Timur. Wow.'

I've already decided not to tell them about my last life as a Gestapo officer. 'I don't know. Maybe there's something in it. It was pretty weird up there today.'

'But maybe you just picked up on the vibes around the place. Afghanistan is a strange and very powerful place.'

And suddenly I'm thinking 'far out'. Here I am with a bunch of blokes I really respect talking about stuff that's turned-on. And then I think, but am I a fraud? I bet they're not thinking about being turned-on – because they *are* turned-on.

I feel honoured to be here with them, part of this amazing eastern trip, to be accepted as one of them, but somehow, yes somehow, I have to burn away this part of me which keeps dragging me to one side and saying, 'Look at what you're up to now.' It's like I haven't got a mind or a character of my own. All the time I'm wondering how I'm shaping up and appearing in the eyes of other people.

So feeling that some sort of commitment is needed, if only for my own benefit, I ask Christian to jack me up, but he tells me not to be so daft. 'Patrick and I are going back to Paris for a cure. It's crazy for anyone to start this.'

Hulm says it's okay but he wishes he hadn't started, and Dirk just shrugs because he only does it from time to time, he says.

'After three years of "time to time" you have a habit, man,' snaps Hulm. 'Think about it. I used to do it from "time to time" but the gaps just get smaller until that's it. You think you're in control but you're not. And when I try to stop, bam! It's no good. Now I am going to India to die.'

That night we have a party for Guy's birthday. Orchestrated by the girls, we spend the day decorating the room with coloured paper and cloth and dozens of candles. Dozens of incense sticks burn, their smoke scenting the air with Sandalwood, Mysore Nights and Bengal Rose. On a table to one side is a heap of hand-pressed dope surrounded by smaller piles of opium balls and speed and barbiturate pills. All around the room giant joints have been wedged into cracks like unlit torches, and in the centre, but not too close to the stove, stands a small table borrowed from another room laden with cakes and sweets from the restaurant downstairs. A pile of long-playing records is stacked alongside the portable player and Elizabeth is sorting the albums into their correct covers. Already we are passing a chillum around, and I join her after piling our stock of firewood neatly against one wall.

'Looks like it's going to be a good night,' I say for want of something else to say. I fancy her so much now that I find it difficult to think straight when I'm talking to her.

'I think so.' She seems to be thinking about something.

'How long are you planning on staying here?'

'Tonight?'

'No, before you leave for Kandahar.'

'We may not go that way. If the weather is good we may go through Bamiyan and Dowlat. The road is not so good but it is more interesting.'

'Be careful of bandits.'

'Oh, I have nothing they want.' She looks magnificent just then.

'So when are you leaving?'

'I don't know. One day. Two days. A week. Who knows? Why? I don't think you care when I go.'

Her change to the personal note suddenly changes everything. 'Of course I care. I'd come with you if you wanted.'

She laughs. 'Don't be silly. You are going to India, not coming back. Besides, I have Marie with me.'

'I'm not particularly going anywhere. I'm a free agent. Maybe I'll go to India, maybe I'll go to Pakistan, maybe I'll go north to the Chinese border by yak. I don't know.' I'm desperately trying to come across as laid-back here, and it seems to be working.

'That's a good trip. I would like to do that also. They say the air is so clear you can lose your mind at first – you know, it is difficult to know distances with your eyes.'

'You lose your sense of distance. Yeh. I've experienced that.'

'Yes. But also the pure air has an effect on the brain.'

She is having an effect on my brain. I want the conversation to get personal again. 'Why did you think I didn't care when you were going?'

'You are always so . . . careless . . . that I think you don't like me.' She shrugs.

The room is packed. Cream, Hendrix, Captain Beefheart, Pink Floyd, Velvet Undergound and The Mothers – 'Fresh Cream',

'Disraeli Gears', 'Safe As Milk', 'Piper At The Gates Of Dawn', 'White Light/White Heat', 'Are You Experienced', 'Axis: Bold As Love' and 'Freak Out'. The music combined with unlimited strong drugs, eased us all a big step closer to eternal bliss. Dirk is dancing slowly around the stove, waving his bony arms about again, oblivious to everything. The Chief of Police with an armed guard waiting outside the door is eating cake and being nice to the girls – he's been invited by Guy to drop in, which has blown our minds and we've had to hide all the dope – while Sardar is constantly running in and out with trays of tea, dodging between the from the tea-shop below who come in from time to time just to stare.

Through the smoke I fancy that Elizabeth has been trying to catch my eye all evening and I'm beginning to wish I hadn't done speed again. In fact I've done both speed and bombers as well as the dope and I'm laughing too much at the sounds and choking on the smoke, but somehow managing not to fall into unconsciousness.

After a while, his social call over, the Chief of Police leaves and we are able to relax into a state of loud ecstasy. Elizabeth looks across the room at me and pointedly at the door, then gets up slowly and eases her way out of the room, so I follow. But the amphetamine defuses any lust I might have had, and we sit on the bed alone together in her room talking about nothing, with her dropping wasted hints about being on the pill, and free love being a way of life in Sweden until she gets bored and I get disgusted with myself for not being able to tell her why I'm holding back. Why I couldn't have said 'Sorry, but my penis won't stand up because I'm speeding' I don't know. But there it is, and I have to continue this charade of being too cool to want to fuck. So she says let's go back to the party and that's the end of it.

When we get back there's a problem with Dirk – he's overdosed on everything and appears to be on the brink of death in Christian's bed, groaning and convulsing in tremors and pulling grotesque faces as he shits himself. With the music turned down – not off, just down – the rest of us try to continue the party while Marie applies her nursing techniques in an effort to save Dirk's life. She's talking to him constantly – 'don't worry, don't worry I'm here to look after you' – and mopping his pale forehead with a wet towel, in between getting angry with the rest of us for being so useless. Beyond trying to put on a sympathetic front, none of us really cares that much because after all, this is Dirk and this is his style.

Hulm is also unconscious, and slowly, the room empties until just Dirk and Marie, Hulm, Christian and myself are left.

The music stops. Just one candle burns. And I feel that I could give it another try with Elizabeth. Softly I creep from the room, along the corridor, and tap gently on the door. Eastern pop music drifts up from the restaurant, and the dogs are hunting in the streets again. Marie's not there because she's with Dirk so I gently ease open the door and slide in. But inside, Elizabeth has a visitor. I recognise the long, dark wavy hair – Patrick is screwing her. Slowly I ease myself out again and stagger back to bed out of my mind with grief and confusion. I mean, how could she? I thought . . .

All night, Marie tends Dirk, and by daybreak he is sipping tea. She's changed his clothes and stripped the bed, washed him down and dressed him again in clean clothes, but something has snapped in his mind. Now he just sits and stares ahead with a blank look on his face, as if all joy has gone.

Hulm is throwing up green and yellow slime into a chipped, cream enamel bowl he keeps under the bed and Christian, brewing his morphine, says again, 'You're going to die, man, if you don't stop. You should see a doctor or something.'

Patrick is back and sleeping soundly and I feel madly jealous, which is strange for me. Why am I affected in this way? Maybe the excessive dope, or the opium, or the other stuff, or the combination of them all – I tried Morphine in pill form last night too. Or maybe it's Afghanistan and its strange vibes, or my past lives, or maybe I'm just feeling a bit low.

Then who should turn up but Redman. Fucking Redman.

In a way I'm pleased to see him but he jolts me back to the past with his Montana drawl. 'D'you hear about those German guys?' he asks us all, taking a seat on the edge of Patrick's bed.

'What German guys?'

'Two German guys have been murdered just outside Herat.'

'What! Who by? What happened?' My stomach's churning.

'Two German guys in a VW caravanette. Had their fuckin' heads cut off and stuck neatly on their chests facing the traffic alongside the road as a warning to everyone.'

And here we all are, trapped in Kabul, the Kabul Pass blocked with snow.

Redman didn't hang around long, just long enough to infect us with paranoia which seems in turn to have infected the Afghans with a sneering disrespect. In the bazaar their hostility has become open, as it has in the Khyber Restaurant where they're now refusing to serve Hulm, Dirk, and Austrian Freddy, an arrogant son of a bitch who looks like Hitler's grandson, right down to the jackboots he wears. And the proprietor of the Bamiyan Hotel is making demands daily for his now long overdue rent and refreshments bills to be paid. And Hulm, visibly wilting with each passing day, finally loses it very badly with Sardar who instead of running away turns on him and threatens to kill not only him but the rest of us as well.

Twenty-four hours later Hulm goes down with acute diarrhoea, followed by each of us in turn until we are bedridden, or trying to make it to the one lavatory on the landing, outside which there is a permanent queue of the groaning sick. There's another queue outside the shower cubicle which is being used for both cleaning up and as another lavatory.

Inside the lavatory, the pan and floor are covered with multi-coloured shit and vomit, as is the door, because whichever way you face, it spurts out the other end, and the stench of bad eggs which fills the whole of the building would be unbearable except that none of us has the strength or will to do anything about it. For three days we suffer this, and suspicions of having been poisoned by Sardar diminish when we learn that he too is a victim. Marie thinks we have cholera and says that we'll be all right providing we drink plenty of water, but for a while it looks bad.

Then one by one we slowly begin to recover, and the sun comes out again with the overpowering reek of disinfectant which has been sprinkled along the corridors.

Strength almost back to normal, I drift round to Poste Restante and find a letter waiting for me from Mother. Inside, neatly folded like a personal message is £20! She's worrying about me and says I should be thinking about coming back home. But sorry, wrong direction. Twenty-four hours ago I was praying for home, but now, well, I feel good again. Even better with the twenty quid. And I've still got $5 and 110 afghanis to go. And almost a kilo of hand-pressed hash.

The thing is, since poring over the map I've had a real strong urge to go to southern Pakistan, Karachi to be precise, where word has it that you can take a boat round to Chittagong on the other side of India for next to nothing. From there I could go into Burma and Thailand and make tracks across to Australia, where I could work for a bit. Or I could head back into India from the opposite direction, find a guru to enlighten me then spend the rest of my days wandering as a holy man and living on hand-outs. One thing's for sure, I need to get out of here, or at least away from big gangs of hippies, because sooner or later they attract trouble. The thing to do is arrive, move in on the chicks and move out again before the locals get their teeth into you.

But as I say, you've got to look the business to attract the females, so you can't go around looking like a straight tourist to keep the locals happy if you're on the pull.

And here Tommy has a cunning plan: as soon as I hit Karachi, I'm going to sell everything I've got and buy Pakistani clothes, then sit in my hotel room or mud hut and get stoned silly and wander about in the tropical sunshine. This way I'll get my tan back to full strength and with the aid of the hashish try to burn up that last little bit of my head that's clinging to the past, the bit that hides away for days then jumps out on me when I least expect it, saying things like, 'You look pretty cool' or 'Everyone's watching you' or asking dumb questions like, 'How do these people see me?' or 'Am I saying or doing the right thing?' or 'Do people like me?' and if they don't, 'Why Not?'

You see, I have to be sure of myself, confident in what I am, but the trouble is, I still don't know what I am – I'm not a doctor or a scientist or a musician or a painter or a dentist or a shoemaker or a dustman or a train-driver or a carpenter or an electrician or a blacksmith or anything recognisable. I mean, if I'd been trained as something at least I'd have a head start and be able to give it up – as it stands I can't even drop out like everyone else because I was never in . . .

Shit. I've just walked past a bloke with half his face missing, a gaping hole where his nose and mouth ought to be.

What was I saying? Yeh, I can't drop out because I was never in . . .

But of course! The answer's staring at me. I could weave all sorts of bollocks into the fabric of my make-up by reinforcing just that – the fact that I've never been tainted by being stuffed overlong into one of society's rancid pigeonholes. Too right! I am one of the undefiled.

This revelation has made my day, my year, my life. Now I know where I'm coming from. At long last! To celebrate, I buy a small plate of chickpeas and onions from the guy on the bridge and stand watching the women and urchins picking through the mud below.

Hulm is waiting for me at the Bamiyan. He beams. 'What's happened to you, man? You look blissed out.'

'I am. I belong to nobody. My life is my own and I'm free.'

'Someone sent you some money.'

Hulm is just about hanging onto it. He's wearing a plain white, collarless, cotton shirt, tight black jeans about six inches too short in the leg with a busted zip fly held together with a safety pin, blue and white woollen football socks and a beaten-up old pair of black leather Oxford shoes without laces.

'Can I come with you, man?' he whispers.

I'm just about ready to leave Kabul. There's a bus at ten going to Jalalabad, and from there you take another one through the Khyber Pass into Pakistan. But I hadn't planned on going with anybody.

'Where?' I'm stalling, looking for a way out. Hulm, I like a lot, but getting through Pathan country where it's not unusual for buses to be ambushed and robbed at gunpoint and then the Afghan and Pakistan border points with him in tow might not be as simple as I'd like. He's a penniless junkie out of his head, who's not going to be able to answer any questions or fill in any forms, and he'd be sure to argue with any bandits we might come across, but he's so desperately ethereal, and I love him for it.

'To Pakistan.'

'Have you got a bus ticket? Only it's leaving in an hour.'

'Marie's gone to get me one. She's a beautiful lady. If I wasn't . . . if I was a different person . . . maybe she would make a good wife.' He chuckles softly to himself.

Dear Marie. I'm going to miss her most I think. Elizabeth too, but she shagged Patrick. Gerlinde's already gone – just like Penny, my past-life lady. I wonder where she is? Probably on the back of a yak or telling fortunes in Samarkand.

'Yeh, well, as long as she's back by half past nine, that's cool.'

'Dirk wants to come too.'

I laugh. 'Yeh, I know. If you can get him out of bed, good luck.' Then I walk away to settle up with the hotel keeper. I can't see how Dirk's going to get it together to go anywhere: he's still sitting in bed staring at the wall, doing everything he has to do, like go to the bog, in slow motion, like he doesn't trust the floor beneath his feet or the hand at the end of his arm. He'll probably spend the rest of his days here in Kabul. As soon as the money runs out they'll kick him out of the hotel and he'll have to go begging on the streets, picking through the river sludge in slow motion. Hulm's borrowed money from Christian to get to Lahore where he says he knows someone, someone who'll look after him, but I've got a horrible feeling he's not going to make it much further than that. He's too ill. His vomiting every morning is getting worse, and most of the day he's in pain unless he's just jacked up. But as I say, he's a cracker – unless you're Sardar. Sardar just gloats over Hulm's sickness, giving him the evil eye every time he sees him, wishing him into an early grave, and I'm still not 100 per cent certain he's not poisoning him.

The bus leaves more or less on time, after blowing its horn for five minutes to attract the last few stragglers, and off we go. Hulm's already fidgeting, making sure he's not forgotten his morphine or his works, as if he would, and settling himself in so that he can jack up en-route without being seen. His syringe is full, ready for a quick fix when the time comes and he looks pleased with himself when at last he is absolutely sure that nothing's been forgotten.

Until I saw him panic a couple of days ago when his works and junk were accidentally locked inside someone else's room I hadn't realised how much the stuff meant to him – I thought mainlining meant you didn't give a toss about life, that it was the ultimate gesture of defiance to all the creeps that run the world. Well, maybe that's true, but show me a smart-talking, cool, seen-it-all-before junkie, man, and I'll show you a screaming wreck inside a few hours. First he tried to break down the door, but didn't have the strength. Then he paced up and down screaming abuse first at the door and the absent keyholders who'd been thoughtless enough to go out. Within minutes a crowd of grinning spectators brought up from the street by Sardar were standing watching him in his agony as he tried to control his panic. Grinding his teeth and ageing visually by the second, he snatched Austrian Freddy's alpine walking stick to help him march the length of the corridor and back again, up and down, up and down, like an automaton out of control, banging the stick hard on the floorboards with every step until someone at last arrived with a key. By now in the grip of uncontrollable terror, he snatched the key, but in his desperation couldn't locate the keyhole. Finally, if only to bring Sardar's fun to an end, I pinned Hulm against the wall while Freddy unlocked the door to let him in.

A few miles out of Kabul we begin the switchback through the Kabul Gorge, a roadway without safety barriers hacked out of perpendicular rock, and I look down into the deep crack in the earth where the British army and its followers, forty thousand men women and children, were wiped out by tribesmen using sniping and hit-and-run tactics. I can see their descendants sitting among the rocks now, watching our bus labour its way up and down through the pass. The worst bit is when you get a glimpse of the road far ahead on what appears to be an inaccessible part of the gorge and you think surely we can't be going up there. But yes, we are, and the diarrhoea demon announces its return with sobering pangs deep inside the gut and I've no choice but to hang on and grip the edge of the seat tightly. The giddy location of our struggling bus becomes meaningless in the shadow of this unexpected setback and when you feel the hot liquid churning inside your colon you know you are but a cough, sneeze or sudden jolt from disaster.

But as I've already discovered, it discourages negative thought, and by the time the ache has passed we're through the worst of it and on our way down – down towards warmth, sunshine and a Jalalabad spring. From the slush, ice and snow of upland Kabul, we're entering another world of fruit trees, green grass and promise.

Hulm's jacked up again and is back in his morphine-sulphate world, so there's no point in talking to him until the first rush has worn off. I, on the other hand, have been eating Mazari since leaving Kabul and by the time we hit Jalalabad both of us stagger from the bus, mouths agape and staring in astonishment at the incredible change of scene. Lorries, buses, donkeys and camels, horses and beaten-up old cars, and thousands of turbanned men and covered women are all trying to get somewhere at the same time. Like us, many are looking for somewhere to eat, but movement in any direction is hampered by someone else already being there. Allowing me to take the lead, Hulm follows meekly along as I wander, increasingly stoned as the Mazari takes a grip, from one restaurant to another, from café to tea-house, examining the diners and what they're eating – but most of the food looks the same, sort of brown and white.

Finding one with less surly clientele we take seats at a table and are soon served with curry and rice. Hulm toys with his in between mumbling on about something, 'You know, man . . . in Lahore . . . crazy skag deal . . . Copenhagen . . . she blew it, man . . .,' but knowing we've a bus to catch I finish his food for him. As we are about to leave, a Pathan with mascara and black teeth leaps in from the street, screams something unpleasant, spits in my face, and tries to stab me in the neck with a curved dagger. Another local jumps to shove him away, but instead of giving up, the man attacks again, this time trying to stab Hulm who's standing there oblivious to what's going on around him, discussing a bum skag deal with his shoes. Again the attacker is fended off and eventually restrained, and when I ask why they say it's because he thought we were CIA agents. Far out, like I mean, do we really look like CIA agents?

By the time our bus reaches the border I'm wondering whether carrying a kilo of hashish in my bag is such a good idea after all.

Because of armed and paranoid madmen, the border guards are on alert and keen to prove just how ruthless and efficient they can be. As we're queueing for clearance out, I somehow stray too close to a laden orange tree and a guard cocks and aims his gun at my heart. Hulm by now is coming out of his stupour and mumbles that a guard is pointing a gun at me and that maybe I'd better put my hands in the air and give myself up. Smiling pleasantly I move slowly away from the tree just as Hulm notices the oranges, 'Hey, man, look at these!' he gasps. But the guard's already there, poking him in the belly with the gun barrel. 'Ach du scheisse! Was machen sie? Don't touch me, you fucking kunt . . .'

The official in the office has an ant on his face which disappears up one nostril and emerges from the other a few seconds later. He stamps our passports with a suspicious glare then waves us away. Goodbye Afghanistan, I love you.

On the Pakistan side we have to parade before a slick officer behind a desk who politely asks Hulm to complete a two-page form. Being an Englishman and a member of the Commonwealth I don't have to do this, so instead I fill in Hulm's for him as he is clearly incapable and swaying from side to side with a silly downcast smile on his face. He seems to be destabilising rapidly, now that the junk's almost gone. Putting him down as having two hundred pounds sterling, I add that he receives regular payments of similar amounts from his parents who are the Baron and Baroness of Pforzheim.

'But why can he not complete the form himself?' asks the officer.

'It's the coach trip. It makes him sick. And his English isn't too good.'

'What's he saying, man?' asks Hulm as if it's the most boring thing in the world. He speaks English well but refuses to listen when it suits him.

Outside, the guards are on the roof of the bus, checking the baggage for illegal goods. Seeing me watching them the officer asks if I am carrying any drugs.

I laugh lightheartedly and say that anyone would have to be crazy to think about bringing anything through this border control, and he seems pleased with this, taking it as an observation of his own efficiency. On the roof of the bus the guards are checking every container except my beaten-up old kitbag. If only they were to glance inside . . . but khaki kitbags are invisible to border guards.

'And why are you coming to Pakistan?' asks the officer.

'I've heard a lot about your country and the people,' I lie.

'I suppose you are passing through on your way to India,' he sighs.

'No, not at all – I'm going down to Karachi.'

This bit of news cheers him up, and he gives me a welcoming smile and goes on to describe how hospitable his people are. He wishes me all the best, and says if ever I have any problems I can always refer people to him, Captain Hussein at Torkham Khyber.

Back on the bus I remind Hulm to check out Lahore Poste Restante for me in case Frankie or someone else has sent a letter and ask him to forward anything to Karachi. The advantage – or not – of having sudden changes of plan is that no one knows where you're going to be, but how else can it be if I've cut loose? I don't want people to know where I am, do I? Okay, Hulm knows, but I know that he'll say nothing, because he has far more important things on his mind. I also know he'll keep his word, because despite being a junkie, he's reliable.

Muttering that I have nothing to worry about he then jacks up the last of the junk and retreats back inside himself until Peshawar where we part company. Unpleasant and difficult, I feel that I'm losing a real friend. Awkwardly we shake hands and I give him a few rupees and he wanders away. Looking back suddenly he waves, then disappears out of my life.

FIVE

Euphoric in a warm and beautiful country I sit on the tarmac platform and smoke a strong joint while watching sparrows peck around the track. Take away these men in turbans and skull-caps and baggy clothes and it could be any rural English train station when I was a kid, right down to the carved wooden frieze around the station roof. Even the spring sunshine, heavenly after the deathly cold of Afghanistan, has the feel of a warm English summer and my mind drifts back to posters of Sunny Worthing and Bournemouth, the Isle of Wight and Glorious Eastbourne. Warm creosote-scented wood and the smell of dry grass add to the illusion and only the arrival of the train prevents me becoming lost in the moment. Slowly it rolls in, a great matt black steaming monster with a red star on the front, the carriages behind covered with dark people in light cotton. Momentarily phased by this intrusion, I grab a red-turbanned porter with a big white moustache and ask him to find me a space, and incredibly he unlocks an empty compartment and lets me in.

Inside are four rows of wooden benches along the length of the carriage, two down the outside and two in the middle back to back, with luggage racks above all of them. At one end is a lavatory – a cubicle with a water tap and a hole in the floor through which you can see the track. Meanwhile my man is standing outside stopping anyone else from getting in, holding firm against a crush of passengers with parcels and babies, shoving and pushing, trying to squeeze past; but he is resolute.

Throwing my bag up into a rack I arrange myself comfortably along one bench which I can also use later as a bed. On the side of the carriage away from the platform is a sliding door which, once the train is under way, I'll open to watch the unfolding panorama of Pakistan's sub-tropical beauty. Or something like that. But right now I'll relax and roll another joint. Shit, this is the business. You feel you can really level out here, sit back and enjoy the order, the easy-going but organised feel of the place, the legacy of the British.

Weird. The ticket office looked as if it had been built by the same people that built Cranbrook Station and the cross-Channel ferry, all wood and brass and green and white paint and signs saying Women Only or Private or First Class. As a white man I'm still treated with unreasonable respect, like they've not learned that the world's changed since they were handed their national freedom. It seems they've been indoctrinated, brainwashed by the marauders who came here and nicked everything. And I was one of them according to Dutch Penny. Now I've returned to what was once India, the same place I was in, like 120 years ago. And I have to say it is very familiar in an inexplicable way, perhaps because it's like England when I was a kid except for the brown faces, palm trees and turbans. A lot of the buildings wouldn't look out of place in London either, and a drain cover I saw had Birmingham England stamped on it.

Now the train's moving and Peshawar's behind me, so I can pull back the sliding door and let the warm air and sunshine flood in. The green fields look like paddy fields and behind them are the tallest palm trees I've ever seen, great long stalks with a feather puff on top. What a life, sitting here in the late afternoon sun watching women in brightly coloured saris bent double, working in the fields.

The trip south takes 36 hours, passing Rawalpindi, about 100 miles away, Lahore, Multan, Bahawalpur, and Hyderabad before terminating at Karachi on the Arabian Sea. I've figured I can either go on to Chittagong by boat or just hang about for a bit and see what comes up, maybe take a nice little break before carrying on finding myself. Or find myself first, then take a break.

I wonder where I'm at now, finding myself-wise? I mean, I wonder just how turned on or not, just how aware or unaware I am right now? Maybe I'm getting very close to Buddhahood and don't know it; maybe the lotus is about to unfurl and reveal the miriad radiant facets of its mystical splendour . . .

Then the train slides quietly to a stop and a million people crowd into my head. We've already come to another station and all the world is getting on. I scream 'Fuck off, this is *my* carriage' and try to shove them out again, but within seconds I'm crammed between a mad mullah who looks like Charlie Chaplin's fat arch enemy with the dark eyes, and someone else who looks like the Artful Dodger carrying a pudding basin in a cloth. Opposite is an exotic female wrapped in bright red cloth so that just her eyes show, but I'm afraid to look because she is with a murderer, a man with a gigantic turban and a rifle who keeps glaring at me with a mixture of hate and fear. Baluchi I think. Someone told me they were worse than the Afghans when it came to carnage. The carriage is now packed so tight that no one can move without everyone else joining in, but a small gap left in front of me so that they can all take a peek at whitey and be entertained for a few miles. This makes life difficult for me because my eyes keep meeting Mrs Baluchi who stares at me at an angle so that Mister Baluchi doesn't know.

Then the mullah tries to strike up conversation – I think he's asking if I'll get up in the luggage rack with him – and Artful comes to the rescue by speaking in English.

'What is your name?' he asks suddenly in that weird frog-mouthed way that these people do. I tell him.

'Where are you from?'

I tell him.

'My cousin is in London. His name is Imrat Yamin. Do you know him.'

'Yes. He's a wanker.'

'I beg your pardon?' Then he unwraps the pudding basin and reveals something inside which looks like brawn which he says I must eat with him otherwise it is not polite, so he spoons some onto a piece of flatbread and gives it to me. Watched by everyone I eat the stuff as he eats his, and when we finish he says that I must give him a gift in return as it is the custom in his country, especially as he is a Shunter Grade Three, so I offer him a cigarette which he accepts, but only as a token of what he apparently should be given – money or an article of jewellery such as a watch or ring. So I tell him to fuck off which he comprehends, by the look on my face, and he goes on to tell me that I am not a good person and that it is customary to give gifts. Then the mullah starts touching my leg and making eyes – and do I detect just a touch of a smile from Mrs Baluchi as she watches me getting angry? Her scarf slips away a little and I can see her pretty face but her bloke is eyeing me again, just waiting for the chance to shoot me in the forehead.

The train's banging along now, at last really under way, and soon my position as star turn evaporates as everyone gets into doing their own thing, like eating or making their way to the lavatory or feeding kids. Mrs Baluchi has a new baby which she is breast-feeding, but Mr Baluchi doesn't seem to mind this in front of an infidel. It's the eye contact he doesn't like. I can stare lovingly at the baby while trying to sneak a glimpse of nipple as she changes over and he doesn't mind one bit, but just a hint of eye contact and he's on the alert, bristling, his three-foot handlebar moustache twitching, black eyes narrowed to pinpoints of hatred. To pass time I try to work out how Mrs Baluchi and me could have a secret liaison in the lavatory. Maybe at a stop when he is outside on the platform buying food from any one of the hundreds of vendors that besiege the train – or I could bribe Artful to get him removed from the train altogether then claim her as mine. We could settle in the desert, in a tent under the stars, and make endless love . . .

After dark I climb into the luggage rack above to get my head down, and being exhausted, I'm soon sound asleep.

Some hours later I'm awoken by the train's lack of movement and discover that we have stopped at a station somewhere. Cups of tea are being passed into the carriage, and seeing me lift my head Artful passes one up. It's good stuff, sweet and milky, the first tea with milk I've had since England – condensed milk maybe, but still milk. Now I understand why Hulm was so keen on it with Sardar. Jumping down onto the shoulders of the people below I buy more through the window and shout out to a cake-seller who rushes over and sells me half a dozen for less than a halfpenny – this way I'm able to share them among my neighbours and regain a bit of credibility as a human being after being so unpleasant in the first place. The train starts again, but everyone reassures me that the cups won't go astray because the teaboy's mate will be at the next stop to collect them.

People get off, others get on. I climb back to reclaim the rack and fall asleep: a strange sleep of stopping and starting and coming and going and long periods of darkness and short periods of bright light from station lamps only to wake up around dawn with Artful's feet in my face. He's at the opposite end of the rack, snoring. Down below, Mr and Mrs Baluchi are still there packed in among the rest, but she has relaxed and uncovered her head, no doubt with Mr Baluchi's consent, and everybody seems happy.

The mullah's gone, and his place has been taken by two thinner men.

Not long after sun-up the carriage is beginning to overheat with the change in latitude, so I climb down and open the sliding door to sit with my legs dangling from the train. Here the scenery's flat and green and we're following the course of a big brown river, with wallowing black buffalo and small brown boys and more women in red, and yellow, and pink, and green, and every other bright colour you can think of, and I'm feeling really good to be somewhere that I've only seen before in picture books. Red and yellow and pink and green, da ditty da ditty da da da. Artful comes to join me and says that he's getting off at Multan and that I'd be welcome to come and see his family, but whatever I decide, it's important, he adds, that I give him my address in England so that he can write me a letter. Using paper and pen borrowed from a travelling salesman who looks like a tiny brown version of David Niven, I give him Frankie's last address in Soho, where his old girlfriend Norma lives – which should give her something to talk about for a while if she's still alive.

Who knows? She could be brown bread, the way she was carrying on. It seems like a million years since all that London stuff: the grey skies, amphetamines, pubs and wet pavements. And Beryl doing a runner with a Yank . . .

I wonder if anyone back there's thinking about *me* now?

Meanwhile, David Niven has squeezed in next to me and started the same old conversation rigmarole – 'Hello, where are you from? what is your name?' etcetera. So I ignore him and Artful tells him to fuck off in Urdu, because I am *his* Westerner – borrowing pen and paper doesn't give the newcomer any rights over me. Then Artful demands a gift for being my protector and I tell him that the only gift he'll get from me will be a poke in the eye, but he doesn't understand so I ignore him as well. In the space of less than 24 hours my tolerance is waning because they're on at you all the time, and while at first I thought it was because they were a bit over zealous with their welcome, the constant pestering's becoming a strain. I mean, how can I begin to find myself if everyone else is begging for attention?

'Excuse me, I have brother in England . . .'

FUCK OFF!

Diddly Da Diddly Da Diddly Da Diddly Da Da Duckety Duckety Duckety Da Diggety Da Diggety Da Diggety Diggety Diggety Da Oh, I do like to be beside the seaside Oh, I do like to be beside the sea . . . Da Diddledy Da Diddledy Da Da Da . . .

Got the tune stuck in my head now . . .

'Excuse me, sir . . .'

'WHAT?'

'What is your name? Where are you from?'

In the end you have to ignore 'em, completely ignore them until they go away. But you can't relax for a second because if you do someone's straight in there with more of the same: 'What is your name?', 'Where are you from?'

It's not so much that, but generally speaking they don't even know what they're saying, they've just learnt it parrot-fashion like I learnt how to say parley-voo when I was eight, and if you answer they just grin and ask you again, intrigued and amused by the gibberish you're uttering.

Artful eventually gets off and I'm alone again for a few seconds – but David Niven takes it upon himself to look over me, and his breath stinks, so I have to push him away and threaten him while the others gaze on mindlessly. These people appear to be unaware of themselves as living beings, their brains operating at minimum tick-over, the body at base level. If you shout and wave your arms they shrink back but carry on staring, waiting to see what you do next.

And so it goes on. Throughout the day and night. And everything would have been more or less fine except that my stomach problems have returned. And trying to squirt through the hole in the floor of a rocking train then trying to wash your arse with water from the tap without getting soaked would be difficult enough without being stoned. But I've been eating dope again in an attempt to isolate myself from this thing called reality. Or at least from the people around me who are slowly blowing my mind – not just with their odd attitude towards me, but with, well, everything. Among themselves they seem fairly normal, although their facial expressions are something else, but as soon as the attention's turned on me they assume that vacant stare, like they switch-off because the image they're receiving is too much to cope with.

Next morning, again sitting with my legs hanging out of the sliding door, I'm watching more kids playing in a river when a man who boarded at the last stop gets up from his seat to tell me to move away from the open door. Thinking he's trying to exert authority for the hell of it or nick my place I tell him to fuck off, and carry on enjoying the scenery and the cool breeze. The weird thing is he just shrugs and goes back to his seat. Maybe I'm overdoing the aggression, I tell myself, and make a small gesture of compliance by sitting cross-legged in the half-lotus position. Seconds later the train roars into a station with a high platform, level with the carriage floor. Jumping up in surprise I turn and thank the man profusely, but what astonishes me is that having warned me of the danger he was then quite prepared to sit back and watch my legs get mangled, like, don't say I didn't warn you – may God have mercy upon your soul.

This is all a bit of a shock because I've been raised to believe that life has been designed to look after my best interests – now I have to get used to the idea that I must take responsibility for myself. And far from making me feel good, this dramatic realisation makes me feel very small in a very big and dangerous place.

Outside Karachi Station, a man in baggy, blue cotton clothes approaches and says, 'Hey, Johnny, you wanna smoke?' So I say okay and follow him into the back streets. Nazir's about 40, with dark, pock-marked skin and a curved nose and thinning swept-back hair and he's going to be my personal guide for the rest of my stay.

A few streets away he invites me to sit on a kerbside charpoy, a sort of communal wooden bedstead for layabouts. He removes a brick from the adjacent wall and pulls out a small chillum and a lump of dope. Sitting next to me, he breaks a piece into the pipe then carefully places on top a coil of hemp string before shouting something to a boy across the street. Disappearing inside a house the boy reappears minutes later with a small jug of water with which to wet the safi. Striking a match, Nazir then passes the chillum to me to light and watches with approval as I demonstrate the skills picked up in Kabul. 'Atcha,' he says. Nice one.

Now I've got a new word to use. 'Atcha'. I can use that with 'Salaam Aleikum' and 'Aleikum Salaam' which I hear people say to each other as a greeting. That way I'll become really far out and cool. And when I get some Pakistani clothes to wear I'll be the business. All I'll need to do then is blow my mind so that I'm a bit weird and I'll be able to pull all the hippy chicks between here and, well, anywhere you like. This dope's good. Makes a nice change from Afghani which is cut with a bit too much opium for my liking.

I take a piece of Afghani from my bag and show it to Nazir. He sniffs it and asks where it's from. I tell him.

'No good,' he says, 'Afghanistan hashish no good. Make crazy.' He stirs his temple with his finger then points to a zombie trudging along the road, mouth wide open, staring into space. 'He smoke too much. Afghani hashish same.'

'Me like crazy.'

'You like crazy, you get crazy.' Then he starts laughing, but with a straight face.

Soon another man joins us, a fatter one who looks like an Italian barber, and he refills the chillum. I notice that he too is interested in my smoking. I suppose it's a bit like watching a Pakistani drink ten Light and Bitters in the Brown Bear in Deptford High Street. So for their benefit I give it a couple of really good tokes and hold the smoke in, swirling it around the bottom of my lungs until I'm ready to burst. Then I coolly exhale without a sign of discomfort or urgency and carry on as if nothing's happened.

The Barber hails a thin old man wearing a turban and nothing else but a cloth over his nuts, and metal bangles on his wrists and ankles, and asks him to show us his wares. Pieman, pieman, what have you got there? I'm feeling hungry as it happens, not having eaten since around midnight when I had a curry on the platform of Khanpur Station. Or was it Sukkur? Anyway, the old guy gently places his basket at my feet and flicks open the top for me to choose a cake. But as I lean forward to look in he blows on a fat pipe and up pops a large snake, a large glistening gunmetal cobra with hood and flicking tongue, which sways there watching me with one beady eye and him with the other. This goes on until we get bored and he stops playing and the snake collapses back into the basket. Giving him a rupee for the performance, Nazir says it's too much and replaces it with an anna from my handful of change. Rupees? Annas? Pice? Suddenly I realise I gave Hulm annas instead of rupees when we parted, barely enough to buy him a meal.

Both Nazir and the Barber agree that the Dilkusha or Heavenly Garden would be the ideal hotel for me, but having passed on the information neither appears to feel like moving so I wish them all the best and stagger off with my kitbag over my shoulder, through the passing throng to search for it. The passing throng. What is all this bollocks? Throng. What sort of language is that? The thing is, I've started writing again because it adds an arty dimension to my otherwise meaningless existence, and now, when I get stoned I get word fixations. Throng. Writing also tends to give you a bit of space: when I wrote a few notes on the train for want of something better to do the crowd went silent and watched in amazement. So I'm continuously trying to compose sentences that might appeal to my English teacher, Miss Turley, and come up with lines like, 'A sea of multi-coloured turbans bobbed before me as I attempted to negotiate the intricacies of Karachi's renowned spice market. Wafts of cinnamon, clove and nutmeg assaulted my nostrils as I twisted and turned through a labyrinth of shady alleyways before once again emerging into the sun-drenched splendour of Hafizullah Square . . .'

A few streets on I ask a sugarcane seller for the Dilkusha Hotel, but he stares at me as if I'm mad. Instead I ask one of his customers, who's wearing a western white shirt and grey worsted trousers, reasoning that if he dresses like that he's bound to speak English, but he stares at me too after taking a couple of steps backward. Then a third man joins them and they all start arguing loudly until a fourth, attracted by the noise, comes up and says, 'Excuse me sir, what is your name?'

Oh, no, not again. 'Tommy Spitz.'

'Tommy Spitz. Where are you from?'

'London.'

'What is your name?'

'Look, you prick, I'm looking for the HOTEL DILKUSHA.' Then, exasperated, I wag my head and say 'Hotel Dilkusha' again, but with a Pakistani accent, and suddenly they all understand what I'm talking about. It's the accent you see, not the language. So it would seem I even have to sound like them! Heavens above.

Incredibly, the Dilkusha is just around the corner – the distance from you to your goal generally being proportional to the weight of your luggage – and on the way, escorted by a small army of well-wishers, I buy an engraved brass waterpipe to aid my spiritual journey.

So far, so good. If there's anywhere in the world I can blow my mind it has to be here in Karachi, because it's weird and miles from anywhere. All you can do from here is go into the desert or the sea. And there are no overlanders, hippies, or tourists who might distract me or bring me back to my own head, so I can just get on with getting stoned and losing my mind.

'You have room for me?' I ask with a Pakistani accent. I must try not to think in this accent because I might become confused or schizophrenic, like Blokk, the kid at school who came from South Africa, nicknamed the 'white wog' because he sounded black. Don't want to end up being called something silly like that instead of Satguru or Enlightened One.

The hotel-keeper shows me through a door into a courtyard open to the sky with rooms all around on two levels, the upper level being skirted by a communal landing which looks down on the courtyard. My room on the upper level is equipped with a single bed, a small table, and a chair. Nothing else. An unglazed window, about two feet square, looks out over a small sloping roof of red clay tiles to the rooftops and skyline of the old quarter.

Here I have a white-painted cell ideal for my purpose, and at only a dollar per week, I've got enough cash here for about two years' worth. Food I can beg, like all true disciples.

'I thank you very much. Salaam Aleikum.'

'Aleikum Salaam.' And off he goes.

Then a boy appears, or rather a young man, in baggy whites and an embroidered white skullcap, and asks me if I want anything to eat or drink, so I order a jug of water and tea with sweet pancakes which he brings back in minutes. Closing the door, I fill the pipe with water, heat and crumble a large lump of dope into the bowl, and smoke it between sips of tea until there's nothing left but ash. Hulm says you can jack up the ash if there's opium in it, but as I'm not into that I mix it with the tea and drink it. Ugh. Won't do that again. But it seems to work because suddenly the room's changing shape. Or maybe it's the waterpipe that's done it, who knows, but for sure I'm wedged up against this wall and can't move. Good job I'm on the bed.

Through the window the blue sky becomes more and more intense until a star appears, first one then billions until the night sky is alight and I'm aware of the landscape of the room in blue shadow. Through the window float the distant sounds of people and bells and carhorns, and a sweet-voiced girl singing of unrequited love, betrayal and death, accompanied by penny whistle and orchestra. Over the rooftops a man with a beautiful voice is calling, beckoning the faithful, through a loudspeaker, so I move and shock myself back into my body.

Outside is a warm night full of warm people. Plunging in I drift back towards the railway station where I recall seeing food being cooked in open-fronted restaurants but lose my bearings and find instead food being cooked on the pavement over roaring petrol stoves by wiry little men on their haunches, so I squat with them and eat curry and rice and chapatis with right hand. But oh dear, through the mists I feel the shits coming on again, real urgent this time, so watched by a thousand eyes I rush into an alleyway and unload, wiping my arse with my left hand which I then wipe on the wall. This happens once more before I make it back to the Dilkusha.

Running up to the washrooms on the roof, I strip off and shower, then scrub my jeans which are splattered down the legs with yellow crap. While I'm standing there naked beneath a single light bulb, I hear, 'Excuse me, sir' and turn to see two young men watching me, students by the look of it, in tell-tale white shirts and dark grey trousers.

'Yes?' I snap.

'Good evening, sir, where are you from?'

'England.'

'Why are you coming over here, raping our women and stealing our wealth?'

'What?' Maybe I'm not hearing right. And there's no need to put on an accent with this guy because he speaks reasonable English. His mate appears to understand too – wagging his head in agreement but ready to run should I turn nasty.

'You come over here to exploit us and rape our women,' says the talking one.

'No I fucking don't.'

'Oh, yes, you do, you and your damn capitalist brothers.'

'I haven't got any brothers.'

'A figure of speech . . . your fellow capitalists. You come over here . . .'

'Hold on, hold on. I'm not a capitalist, I'm poor.'

'Well, that's it then, you come over here to exploit our generosity and rape our women.'

'I'm not raping any women.'

'It is the way of your people. Always you come and . . .'

'Why don't you fuck off . . .'

His jaw drops open. 'No. You jolly well fuck off.'

I can't help myself, I have to laugh at the way he says it, wagging his head – and then I can't stop. Then he starts. Then his mate. And we scream with laughter together.

When we finally stop, he says 'Welcome to Pakistan' and the pair of them walk off satisfied.

At daybreak I shout for tea, load another pipe, and set aside the things I'm not going to sell. I've made up my mind to be ruthless and get rid of everything: the sleeping bag which I haven't used for months, the embroidered goatskin coat which is worse than useless in this heat because it stinks and has lice, the suede jacket, the Levi cords, a jumper, an old polo shirt, a wristwatch I won't wear (because it's uncool to wear a watch, I mean, you've got to be insane to walk around with a machine for telling the time strapped to your body), and with difficulty, my old faithful suede mosquito boots. All I'll have left is washing and shaving gear and the clothes in which I stand which I'll sell as soon as I'm wearing the new stuff. I prefer to do it this way rather than break into my stash of money because doing that's a bit unsettling – what if I buy a load of new gear and can't sell the old?

Apart from the clothes, I want a kilo of Paki hash to tide me over because it doesn't feel right smoking Afghani hashish in Pakistan.

The wonderful tea's arrived and Shaukat – the 'boy' – is pleased to see me, a good start to the day. I ask him where to sell my things, excluding the watch, because I know he'll be on me if he knows I've got an English watch to sell.

'In market. Many places buy.' He waggles his head.

'How much?'

'Good price. Maybe ten, twenty rupees.'

Just a couple of dollars – but it's no good thinking this way. A couple of dollars is two weeks' rent or a month's food – back in England that would be a good price for some old clothes.

And twenty rupees I finally make on the deal, but the kitbag has to be thrown in as well to clinch it. Now I have the clothes I stand in, thirty pounds sterling, and about forty rupees.

A few crowded streets away – streets full of the same inquisitive onlookers all chiming 'What is your name?' and 'Where are you from?' – I find a tailor, a machinist of cotton clothes. Existing in tandem next door is a drapers where, followed by about twenty-five onlookers who are roughly ejected by the owner, I choose a bright orange cotton for the proposed shirt and white for the pants. Clutching a sample of each I return to the tailor and allow him to measure me, pointing out how long I would like the pants to be and the length of the side slits of the shirt. At twenty rupees the lot I feel I've been ripped off, but there you go, and accept on the understanding it is finished and ready to wear by the following morning.

That done, I wander off to find Nazir, who usually hangs out by the station or on the chillum charpoy. I've got to get some Paki dope, like as soon as possible, because I'm sure the Afghan stuff's not good for this climate – I mean, it's good, but it sort of puts you in an Afghan headspace when you want to be in a Pakistani headspace if you get my drift. It's speedy by comparison to the stuff I smoked on the charpoy – at least it is once you've got over being slaughtered, whereas I want something that's going to make me melt into the place, help me become invisible in an orange shirt.

Nazir's on the charpoy talking to Fred Astaire. The weird thing about Karachi, or maybe the whole of Asia, is the way men fall into facial types. It's not so much that – we all seem to fall into facial types – but one of these types is what I call the Film Star, where they resemble someone famous, but not quite. I mean, being brown makes a difference for a start, but they're also different in other ways, like they might be very short or cross-eyed, or insane, or crippled and begging in the gutter, but they still have the look . . .

I've noticed that George Formbys, Errol Flynns and Cary Grants are quite common.

'Nazir! My friend. How are you?'

'Atcha. Thank you, thank you. Please meet friend, Hossein.'

I shake hands.

'My friend Hossein want learn English. Write English. You write letter for him.'

'No problem.'

'He stay at Dilkusha – he speak after.' Then he says something to Hossein, like, it's okay, Johnny will see you later, and dismisses him.

I tell Nazir I want to sell the watch or swap it for a kilo of dope, whichever's the best deal. This may be a silly move, but I'll be happy with the kilo, and believe it or not I trust Nazir and hope that he makes something for himself out of it. He asks to see the watch.

'Mmn. This good. No problem. You come.'

He stops a scooter rickshaw and we jump in and hurtle off to what seems to be the other side of town. We trundle along a wide, cobbled highway which could easily be the street by the Spread Eagle pub where my paternal grandfather sometimes drank when he wasn't sitting in the back room by the fire smoking his pipe. Or it could almost be by the Elephant and Castle pub on Woolwich Market Square where my maternal grandfather drank when he wasn't drinking somewhere else. A little further on there's a massive brick wall around an industrial depot which could easily be the one around the coal yard on the lower road to Greenwich, and thinking about it, my maternal grandfather may have had sea-faring links with this very same port. For some reason it makes me feel good yet oddly disembodied, like I'm seeing it through his eyes.

'Okay, Johnny, you wait.'

I'm wrenched back to reality. We've pulled up on another long stretch of wide cobbled road next to Karachi Docks. You can see for hundreds of yards in both directions. Nazir clambers out with my watch, and strolls off down a side street. On his instructions I sit and wait. And wait. Twenty minutes or more. At least I think it could be around twenty minutes or more, but I seem to be losing track of time lately. Then half an hour. And the rickshaw driver keeps talking in Urdu and smoking and looking back and talking more and saying Inglistan and Great Britain but I haven't got a clue what he's talking about because I'm dreaming up ways of finding and murdering Nazir: it's obvious now that I've been a very silly boy – I mean, why was I so stupid? I should know by now that you can't trust foreigners.

Then Nazir comes back with a flat brown paper-wrapped parcel about a foot long and six inches wide and an inch thick which he plonks in my lap as he gives the order to drive away. Ripping open the end I take a long sniff of the black stuff. Yeh, right on, man, I knew I could trust him. You can see it in his eyes – he's an honest guy.

Back at the Dilkusha I unwrap the parcel carefully. Inside are two half-inch thick slabs of soft, dark-brown hashish, each stamped in gold with a slogan in Urdu, probably 'By Appointment to Her Majesty the Queen'.

Twisting off a piece the size of my thumbnail, I load the pipe and light it, drawing the smoke into my lungs as far as I can. Then I wait. Expelling the sweet smoke I shout down for tea. Outside the temperature is in the 80s, although it's not yet April, and mosquitoes are beginning to put themselves about: upstairs on the roof there are mosquito larvae coming through the water taps from every one of the water tanks, but as far as I know there's no malaria risk here. Who cares anyway?

Just as I'm getting to the end of the pipe there's a gentle knocking on the door and Shaukat enters with the tea, looking slightly troubled.

'There is woman to see you, sahib.'

Sahib! I've been called sahib! But I don't know whether I like it or not, now that it's happened. I thought I was getting accepted into the gang.

'My name's Tommy, call me Tommy. Or Johnny. My friend Nazir calls me Johnny, not sahib, Shaukat.' But he fails to understand, or decides to ignore me.

Then what he's said hits home – woman! Woman?

'I send her up?'

'What she want? Where she from? European?'

'No. From Pakistan. She thinks you holy man.' He touches his hair and points to mine. 'Some people think that this is holy man.'

I see. Golden locks means holy man. 'Okay. Send her up.'

He goes, and shortly after there's another very faint tap at the door. I shout out, 'Come in', and a woman shuffles through, pushing a small boy before her. She is about thirty, swathed in an old faded green sari and the little boy is about five or six. She seems in awe, and the boy's eyes are wide with terror at the sight of me.

'Hello, is there something I can do to help you?' I ask softly in my best holy man voice, but as soon as I speak she casts down her eyes and shoves the boy towards me. Bending down she lifts his grubby gown and reveals on his right leg an open sore just below the knee. Taking the jug of water, I pour a little over the wound and use the safi cloth to pat it dry, but I have to admit I'm a bit overcome by it all. If only I had some Dettol. The sore looks pretty ordinary to me, but then I don't know, and I'm not even switched-on enough to give him some sort of blessing or whatever it is that holy men do. All I'm doing – yet again – is thinking about me, yes me, and it makes me feel depressed because I'm a small-minded prick. But the woman seems grateful enough, and smiles beautifully before whisking the boy out and closing the door quietly behind her. I could also have given her some money. Or if that was over the top I could have offered to come to her house and treat the boy daily with some sort of antiseptic from the chemist.

But all I did was sit there overcome by the thought of being regarded as a holy man.

And I need all the money I've got to see me through, don't I? I can't go around dishing out cash to everyone – I'd end up like them.

Fill up the pipe again, that's the answer. Pheeoow . . . if I can manage it. That last one's just caught up with me. Better lay down now.

But just as I do there is another tap and Fred Astaire comes in, all buddy-like.

'Hello, Johnny,' he says, auditioning for a film. I expect him to break into a dance routine.

'Hi, Fred, where's Ginger?'

'Please, you write letter for me?'

'Sure.' Groan. Why I can't just say fuck-off-and-leave-me-alone-can't-you-see-I'm-stoned, I don't know.

He taps across towards me clutching his top hat and walking stick which turns out to be a bag full of papers and a pencil. 'Please, I am receiving this letter. I want to write. But you are better,' he beams. 'You read please first.'

So I sit up and read the letter which is not only handwritten, but worded in a formal business style making it hard to understand. Furthermore my brain is trying to shut down for the day, and my heart isn't in it. In fact, I'm beginning to loathe it's bearer. 'Honourable Sir,' it begins, and continues, 'With humble ref. to your esteemed order of the 25th inst. this is to respectfully inform your kind self that the aforementioned order will not in fact be available for despatch prior to the date as offered due to acts of God beyond our humble control. We are however, able to despatch same on the aforementioned date as hitherto agreed. Kindly inform us of your esteemed wishes in this matter in order that we may expedite same as a matter of urgency.'

'I think they're saying they can't send your goods any quicker because God's put his oar in somewhere, but they're feeling urgent about it, like they're probably stalling for time, you know what I mean. But I may be wrong.'

'I beg your pardon?'

'God's blown it for you, man.'

'What?'

'D'you understand the letter?'

'Yes.'

'So what's the problem?'

'Can you write back to say that I accept but less ten percent for the delay?'

'But there isn't a delay. They just can't get the stuff to you any quicker than agreed.'

'But I still want reduction.'

This is all getting too much for me. I never wanted this guy in here anyway. Here I am trying to get to the core of my being and be at one with my true self and instead I'm discussing Fred Astaire's attempts to manoeuvre a reduction in the cost of washers, steam hose couplings for the use of. 'Look,' I say, 'can you please go away? I'm feeling a bit under the weather.' And I have to say it all with a Pakistani accent.

He looks at me malignantly, and says, 'The trouble with you Westerners is you smoke too much hashish. I will write letter myself.' Then he stands up and leaves, glancing back as he goes through the door. 'Be careful,' he says, 'police here very bad.' And injects a touch of paranoia into things.

Just what I need right now, a touch of fear. But apart from the initial jolt to the gut when my brain suggests that there might be an underlying threat in this last piece of free advice, the fear doesn't come, and I settle back and close my eyes for a bit of pipe-dreaming, a wander into the unknown, or rather the forgotten, and find myself back in London's West End, cutting through Walker's Court into Berwick Street.

The odd thing is, the crowds of passersby are taking no notice of me – whereas if I was dreaming they'd be part of my imagination, under my control, and reacting to my presence as I'd expect. But this time I'm invisible. I can even get into the Raymond Revue Bar and past reception without anyone challenging me, then up and along the carpeted corridor – all reds and blues again, a bit like Aziz Ullah's pad but with chrome and coloured neon lighting – until I reach the auditorium. Drifting past the seated punters up to the little stage, I check out a redhead peeling off a sequinned bodice who is totally unaware of my presence before moving on backstage with the rest of the girls. Suddenly there's a tapping – tap, tap, tap – where's it coming from? Things become hazy and I'm drifting somewhere else, losing the picture, damn. Tap, tap, tap.

I'm in a room about ten feet by ten, walls painted white. Before me is a door, a red door. Tap, tap, tap. I sit bolt upright, a wave of confusion spreading through my brain.

The Dilkusha. Karachi. I'm in Pakistan for fuck's sake. Almost lost it there.

'Yes?' I snap.

Shaukat comes in again. 'There is girl. She want to see you.'

'Someone else wants to see holy man?'

'No. She prostitute. Over.' He points across to the opposite landing.

'Is she nice?'

'Very beautiful indeed. She say you go or she come. Special price.'

Shaukat's acting the pimp here. If I'm going to be seeing any girls it's going to be on my terms. 'Okay, Shaukat, thanks for the information.'

'You go?'

'I don't know. Maybe.'

'I tell her you come.'

'You tell her nothing. You hear me? Nothing. Maybe I see her, maybe I not see her.' Wandering about inside the Raymond Revue Bar has caused a reaction in my pants, and Shaukat glances down. 'Okay, Shaukat? You go now. No – on the other hand bring some tea.'

He smiles craftily and backs off.

A Pakistani whore eh? Probably the same as whores anywhere else, but I must say, some of the women I've seen here are stunning.

I wait for Shaukat to bring the tea. In the meantime I reload the pipe and slump back against the wall to consider whether I can afford to spend a couple of rupees for a few hours insight into the Karachi version of the Kama Sutra. Glug, glug, glug, glglglglug . . .

There's another tap at the door.

'Yes, yes! Alright bring it in!' But who should come in but a raven-haired apparition in a bright red sari. She is gracefully carrying two cups of tea on a tray.

Then she says something in Urdu, the only word I understand being 'chai'.

'Thanks, put them on the table.' She looks pretty good under the sari too, because as she leans forward I can see a shapely light-brown waist and breasts gift-wrapped in red silk.

'Take a seat,' I say, indicating to the chair.

Sitting slowly down she stares at me with dark eyes – she's about 18 or 19 with an extra ten years' worth of make-up on her face; but Shaukat's right, she's beautiful. I discreetly look her up and down as she looks away and wonder if she's, well, disease free. According to my old sociology lecturer, johnnies aren't in great demand over here. Funny how these useless bits of information come back.

Then she says something else in Urdu with the word 'rupees' thrown in a few times, so I shrug to say I don't understand and she comes to sit next to me on the bed and begins counting on my fingers. I think we finally agree on twenty rupees for something, although I'm still struggling with the idea of paying for sex, but the deciding factor is the irresistible scent of roses, her perfect full lips and dazzling teeth, her radiant golden, coffee-brown skin. How can I resist?

Now the *Bhagavadgita* floods back into my mind, the bit about greed, anger and lust, but I sling it out, preferring to risk hell rather than miss a chance like this.

Taking her arm I try gently pulling her towards me, but she resists and stands up, making little circular movements in the air with her hand and tilting her head to one side which I take to mean she's going to come back later. Then she leaves.

I'm inflamed, she'd better hurry up. She can't leave me now. I'm going to have to chase after her and offer more money, maybe another ten rupees for a steamy no-holds barred afternoon session . . .

And then there's another tap on the door: please, please, let it be her again.

But instead a white bloke comes in, a fucking white bloke! Just what is going on here? The dope's getting me confused. Or is it me getting the dope confused? I stare at him, astonished, wishing he'd go away.

'Doctor Livingstone I presume . . .' he says with a pronounced south London accent, 'someone told me there was an English geezer staying 'ere, so I thought I'd come and find you.' Then he sits down on the end of the bed without so much as a by your leave and stares smugly at me, and if there's two things I can't stand it's being taken for granted, and smugness. 'So what brings you here?' he asks, with a cocky grin on his face. He's as straight as they come – but obviously not that straight otherwise he wouldn't be in Karachi, unless he's out here working or something. Or spying for the CIA. His light-brown hair is neatly cut, and he's dressed straight, a bit dated, in beige sta-prest slacks and a Fred Perry-type shirt. He must be about the same age as me.

'I could ask you the same.' I say, building another pipe, and watch his eyes bulge out of their sockets, his composure disintegrate, as he realises what I'm doing. Yep, he's straight all right, and now he thinks I'm a drug addict.

'Well,' he says, eyeing the pipe like it's an unexploded bomb, 'I jacked my job in – I was working in the print in Fleet Street – and thought I'd travel around Europe a bit, you know what I mean, but I was in Italy and I met this Paki bloke who was coming here so I just got a lift with him. And here I am.' He looks pleased with himself but a bit surprised, like he's just woken up to his whereabouts. 'How about you?'

Shit. I don't feel like explaining myself to anyone. 'D'you want some of this?' I offer the pipe but he declines.

'What is it, opium or something?'

'Hashish.' Gurgle gurgle gurgle.

'No, fuck that. They taught me at school to leave that stuff alone.' He laughs at his joke. 'So how come you're here then?' he asks again.

'I'm on my way to India.'

'How you getting from here to India? You're a bit off track ain't you?'

197

I decide to lie to him, 'I'm taking a boat to Burma, then coming back into India through Calcutta.' I don't want anyone knowing my plans, least of all some person who's here by accident. And Karachi seems to be getting a bit busy for my liking: first invalids, then Fred Astaire, then whores, now some London prick who wants to know my life story. And if he won't smoke my pipe he can walk. 'Look, I don't mean to be rude,' I say, 'but I'm not 8,000 miles from Fleet Street because I particularly want to be reminded of it, you know what I mean?'

He seems a bit stunned by this revelation. 'Er, no, sorry. I was just . . . I thought you might have been interested. That's what travelling's all about ain't it, sharing experiences?'

'It might be to you, but before you start sharing you should ask yourself if that's what the other person wants. In my case it's not, so if you don't mind I'd rather be left alone right now.' My whore might be on her way back, and his presence could well screw up the whole thing. He might get off with her and I'd have to kill him. Anyway, if I was back in London he'd be the last sort of character I'd want to know . . .

He stands up reluctantly, unable to believe his ears. 'Okay, I understand you want to be left alone, Greta Garbo,' he says with a slight smirk – if he's not careful I might just have to revert to old ways and give him a kicking – 'but can I ask your advice?'

'On what?'

'What's the best way to get back to Europe?'

Cunt. What a complete tosser. 'Have you got any money?'

'About twenty quid,' he laughs, looking embarrassed at himself.

Unless someone holds his hand I can't see for the life of me how he can get back. Afghanistan, Baluchistan or even India would be out of the question for someone of his calibre and mentality.

'You'll have to go to Afghanistan or Baluchistan. Or go on to India where you'll find a larger community of Brits to help you. Why don't you go to the British Embassy here in Karachi?'

'It was them that told me about you.'

Later, when he's gone, I try to assess this piece of information but I'm too stoned to make very much of it despite the intriguing question it provokes: how do they know I'm here? Is it through information from the frontier – Captain Hussein – or a local informant? This makes up my mind for me: I have to move on. Give it two or three days and I'll split off to Korangi Creek a bit further up the coast, get my head back into the Bhagavadgita and burst my way out of sanity. Sanity. The guy who's just left is what they call sane and doesn't have a clue about anything. He's having to ask around to find out. Like er, excuse me, could you help me out of this nightmare of ignorance that I somehow find myself in? I'm only any good at pouring ink into a machine that prints bollocks and suddenly I'm in this place called Kar . . . what's it called . . . Karachi? But I'm sane. Oh, yes. And I can prove it – you ask my doctor.

Om. Om. Om. Om mane padme hum. Om mane padme hum. Om mane padme hum. Fifteen steps to the ground floor, the red sari woman failed to show so I jerked off instead. Just had to. The expectation, imagination and dope overpowered me until I almost went looking for her but bottled out, so now I'm out on the wander thinking that maybe I could liven up the evening by checking out Karachi nights.

This dope seems to get stronger the more you smoke.

Out into the night. Faces, faces, all staring, camels with bells, open-front lamplit shops, stalls, shiny cobblestones polished by countless feet, dark-eyed women and crafty men, turbans and skull-caps and the din of thousands of voices and wailing gramophones – you are my heart's desire how could you leave me for another I cut my heart out and offer it to you sweet sugar my body and soul are yours why do you desert me for the dawn? Hey, Johnny, this way Johnny, that way Johnny, fuck off, you buy, you give, what is your name? where do you come from? what is your name? what is your name? what is your name? Through the dark warmth of a thousand spicy alleyways, in and out, close to pock-marked brown faces and rancid breath and incense, out into another square . . .

And my mind goes blank.

The state of being I've been searching for has happened. I know I exist, I know I'm here, wherever here is, but I have no explanation for anything. No name. No address. I do not know who I am or where I come from. I am disembodied but trapped inside a body and need to escape from it. Or do I? Isn't this a big step? Is it not death? Where am I?

The brain attempts to fire up, trying desperately to lay everything out in clear fashion to understand what is happening . . . but is unable to operate. The body is still functioning as it should, the legs are working, arms swinging slightly, eyes looking about, breath coming evenly. I stop to touch fruit on a stall and understand the texture but the name of the fruit won't come, despite its familiarity.

I can feel the brain getting worried now, trying to send out fear signals. But as long as I continue to stand apart from it and don't get caught up in its cogs and wheels I'll be all right, because this form of consciousness is exhilarating – exhilarating way beyond the threatening fear.

And instead of pestering me now, these crowds draw back when I look at them. Ha! The power! The power! Do they see me as a madman now? What's happened to change their opinion, their judgement? Five minutes ago they were all over me. Now, yes, they draw back, almost in awe it seems.

I command them away and they disperse, leaving me alone to wander from stall to stall, alley to alley, street to street.

I recognise this street now as the very one that leads down to Woolwich Ferry, Hare Street I believe, because across on the other side is the dark brown grocery shop with wooden floorboards where I used to go on Saturdays with my mother and watch a man with a white hat and apron slice rashers of bacon from a hock. Sacks of sugar and beans with brass scoops stood around on the floor, but I can't see them just now. And yes, up ahead I can make out the dark-brown drapers, smelling of cotton linen, where a woman puts money in a brass canister and it whizzes across the ceiling on wires to a secret office where they collect it and send back a receipt. All so comforting. But it's blurred, the image indistinct.

Now we get to the greengrocers: cabbage and greens, the earthy smell of King Edward potatoes, and a big brass scoop to weigh them. But instead there are unidentifiable fruits and vegetables, sweet incense and odd dark-brown men with funny little hats and turbans. Something is wrong. A bolt of fear rips through my gut like electricity and I take off back up the hill towards Powis Street – I can make it along towards Market Square and catch a number 75 bus to Charlton where I live, that'll sort it out. The fear grips as I tear along through the strange-looking crowds until suddenly the brain kicks in again, firing on all cylinders.

It's okay, it's okay. I'm in Karachi, Pakistan, I know now. Feel a bit sick. What happened? Like I lost my mind for a bit there, like after that dream about the Raymond Revue bar, but longer, just what I've been looking for but scarier than I expected it to be – I thought losing my mind would have been something cool, but shit, man, it's heavy duty.

At least I know now that when the brain's not in control, life goes on. In fact those few minutes were far out until I started thinking again. It's when the brain thinks it's in control and discovers it isn't that the problems start. All the time it had me placed in Woolwich it was happy, but when the pieces didn't fit, when it couldn't force the pieces to fit, when it saw the turbans and brown faces and smelt the incense and stuff, it freaked.

It's what I guessed all along: the brain doesn't give a toss about the truth as long as it's comfortable in whatever belief it happens to be going along with at the time.

And now that I'm back to Earth, I'm being pestered again: excuse me, what is your name? where are you from? blah blah blah. FUCK OFF!

The best thing I can do now is find my way back to the Dilkusha.

The orange shirt and white trousers look the business. As soon as I get out in them I notice that I'm not being pestered so much by crowds of inquisitive persons keen to practice their English. A pair of flip-flops takes the place of the old-faithful boots, and a dashing white embroidered skullcap completes the illusion or whatever it is I'm trying to achieve. Nothing seems certain since the little run-in with the brain yesterday, and activity in that region now seems to fluctuate between the mundane and the crazy, the down to earth and the unearthly, as if it's trying to restore order in a shattered mental environment. I feel that somehow I've broken through the shell of my identity, for what that identity was worth, so that I no longer have strong views about anything. But the experience has left me feeling a bit weak, a bit depleted.

To make up for this I buy a thick silver dancing anklet with bells so that I jingle my way about. A few cheap bangles on each wrist and I've got to be the farrest-out geezer between here and Mile End Road, probably beyond as well. All I need now is to get the clothes a bit more lived-in looking, and . . . hang on, this is all about spiritual growth and attaining the Godhead, not whether I look the part or not – what am I doing?

I'll have to find Nazir because he said something about a holy man being around somewhere. Perhaps he'll take me along to see him, or at least give me his address – although somehow it doesn't seem right for a holy man to have an address – but if not he should at least be able to help me find him so that I can learn about the truth of things and more easily settle into a new identity.

The Dilkusha again. Another waterpipe, and I still have 99.9 per cent of the stuff left, which gives me an idea: after seeing the guru, I'll take a walk to Karachi Docks and hitch a ride with the first passing ship back to Europe. There I can sell the hash at vast profit and fly back to Bombay or Katmandu . . .

There's another tap at the door, tap tap tap. Who is it this time?

'Come in.'

The door opens and there stands my sari girl but in rich blue silk with a printed silver edging. And she smells of Chanel No 5 instead of roses – she obviously means business.

'Come in, come in. Here, sit on the bed, you look far out, d'you know that?'

Not understanding, she smiles and floats in looking at my new get up, then does a little laugh in Urdu before sitting down next to me. Does she like my new gear or is she taking the piss? Pulling the scarf from her head, she says something about rupees again, and runs her hand lightly up the inside of my leg as if examining the cotton material of my new strides. This is it, the moment I've been waiting for. Taking her hand away she stands up and slips off the sari. Underneath she's wearing a long-sleeved blue silk top and long blue pants, both of which she slips off to reveal surprisingly Western-looking underwear: I half expected her to be wearing some sort of loincloth or nappy, but she could have bought these in an Oxford Street store.

Expressionless, she removes first the bra then the knickers and stands displaying the goods, waiting for approval. I've never seen purple nipples before, or a shaved crutch come to that, and the look of surprise on my face must come across as a thumbs-up because she smiles and sits down close to me. I'm not too sure how to go about things either, being in a delicate mental state and unused to eastern girls, so I offer her the pipe and to my surprise she takes it, drawing deep and holding in the smoke. Then she leans forward and starts to touch my face softly with the tip of her tongue, first at the sides, then around the neck and ears, blowing little puffs of smoke into my hair, but when I try to kiss her gorgeous lips she turns her mouth away and twists her body to pull me on top. In the same movement she undoes the drawstring which holds up my new cotton pants and pushes them down a few inches. Within seconds I'm inside her and out of control, coming before I want to, completely overwhelmed by her sexuality and, oh no, my weakened guts give up on me and simultaneously explode over my pants. Quickly I slide to the floor where I kneel and try to extricate myself from them without causing any further mess, but things aren't made any easier by her standing up with a look of disgust on her pretty face and demanding rupees, fucking rupees. Carefully I feel under the mattress where I've stashed the money, and hand her twenty, making a mental note to change the hiding place as soon as she's gone, because she could well be in league with Shaukat, waiting to rip me off. Dressing quickly while I'm hopping about on one leg, she leaves without looking back, and I wonder momentarily what sort of impression I've made. Was I the first Westerner she's met? Whatever, it hasn't done my self-confidence much good. Finally I get the pants off without dripping too much yellow crap over the floor, but the absurdity of it all gives me the giggles as I suddenly feel very stoned again. Cleaning up on a dry patch of the pants, I roll them into a ball before grabbing the money and hiding the dope outside the window on the rooftop. Now I climb into my old jeans, grab the bundle and make a dash for the roof to wash up.

'The holy man lives on Keamari Beach. There is small red temple there. He is inside. But you must take gift – fruit or flowers.'

I'm sitting on the charpoy talking to Nazir, back in the orange and white after spending half a day washing and drying the pants and shirt – some had got onto the shirt too, but it didn't show so much being of roughly the same hue. I was a bit concerned to see blood in the shit, but I've passed it off in my mind as being the real thing – at least I'll be able to say I had real stomach problems and not just the usual diarrhoea that everyone seems to feel the need to boast about. I suppose I should see a doctor, but to tell you the truth, I can't be bothered, everything's too much – I don't know whether it's the heat or the dope or a combination of the two, but whatever it is I feel my energy is being drained away to nothing. On the way here I dropped into the Post Office to see if any mail had arrived, but after an hour and a half of begging and threatening they told me Poste Restante was closed. Leaving in a state of exhausted rage, I lost control when the first person I met outside – the dead spit of Clark Gable but for a wart on the end of his nose – came up and asked, 'What is your name?' quickly followed by, 'Where are you from?' Even worse was that he walked away without waiting for an answer. Mad, I ran after him, grabbed his shoulder and screamed, 'Oy! My name's Tommy, d'you hear me? And I come from England!' But nothing seemed to register with him or the crowd that instantly formed and they all just stood staring until I gave up and marched away.

Then a bearded giant of a man walked up alongside me and said, 'You mustn't get so annoyed with these people, you know, they are only trying to be friendly.'

Relieved to find someone who could speak English I explained that the Post Office clerks had been giving me a bad time.

'Oh, they did indeed, eh? Well, you come with me and I'll jolly well sort them out.'

Saying that, he grabbed my hand and marched me back into the Post Office where he demanded to see the Postmaster. I don't know who my good friend was, but everyone jumped when he spoke, and within minutes I was presented with a letter by a fawning clerk.

Nazir says the man was a mullah – he recognises his description. But I still haven't worked out the contents of the letter, which is bothering me. It's from a girl called Anna. Her short note says: 'Dear Tommy, Hulm asked me to send you this which he picked up from Poste Restante Lahore. He is not well and says he is dying. Om Shanti.' And with it is a letter from Frankie postmarked Delhi, which says:

> Tommy, I finally saw the light when my business partners lost their heads, ha ha. You were right, I should have cooled it, but there you go. Then I looked for you but you were gone, and I don't know whether I'm talking to myself or not, because there's no way of knowing if this'll reach you. But anyway, I've seen the light, everything's divine, you were right and he is mine. Jai sat chit ananda.
> Love and Peace,
> Frankie.

Fuck. Frankie's finally flipped. Of all the people. And what's he doing in Delhi? And the foreign language bit? 'Nazir, what does this mean?' I ask, showing him the letter.

He scrutinises the wording. 'Jai sat chi ananda . . . this Hindi, not Urdu, but is praise to the holy one. You say this to guru.'

So that's it. Frankie's found a guru. I don't believe this, the bastard's beaten me to it. I know what'll happen now: he'll come back full of himself and try to convert me to what I've been telling him for months. I'd better get to see this local holy man as soon as possible – at least I'll be able to say I've found one too. For all he knows I could well have been with my guru long before him. I mean, it stands to reason, because I left Afghanistan first. Therefore I found my guru first. 'Where did you say this local holy man was, Nazir?' I ask again, taking another long pull on the chillum.

'Holy man on beach.'

'What, sunbathing?'

'No. In temple. There is red temple on beach.'

'Which beach?'

'You not listening. Keamari Beach. But holy man not like visitors. And not to forget gift.'

'Not like visitors?'

'No.'

'No?'

'He want be alone. He very dangerous. Make crazy.'

'What, he makes people crazy?'

'Yes.'

I take a rickshaw to Keamari Beach, argue with the driver for five minutes about the cost of the two mile ride, pay him a third of what he originally demanded, which he gloats over, then head towards the sound of the breaking waves. I've been dropped off on the land side of a long line of dunes through which leads a sandy track. Apart from a rusty barbed-wire fence half sunk in the golden sand and a lop-sided corrugated iron hut there's no other sign of a building. The best thing to do is get on the beach and look back landward along the shore.

The day's beautifully hot and a cool breeze off the Arabian Sea is flapping my pants and shirt, so looking about to make sure no one's around I strip off, run into the warm waves and plunge in, tasting the salt . . . ahh . . . bliss . . . blue sea through diamond eyelashes, swim out, way out of my depth, exhilaration, then remember sharks and swim quickly back. Stumbling through the surf I notice to the left in among the dunes what looks like a steeple, a stubby red steeple, or at least the triangular red top of a building. But first I have to do a little sunbathing to dry off. Laying my body carefully down upon the sand, arms and legs stretched out, I close my eyes and feel the sun soaking into my face and body, the glorious hot light filtering through the blood of my eyelids.

But suddenly the light and heat fades from the cloudless sky. I look up and see a circle of brown faces looking down in amazement. I sit up. Around me, standing in a circle are a dozen inquisitive males, just staring, blocking out the sun.

'Yes?' I ask, looking at each in turn.

One wags his head and says, 'What is your name? Where are you from?'

But the mullah has told me how to handle this one, 'Salaam Aleikum,' I say.

'Aleikum Salaam!' they chant together, their faces beaming. Now they understand: I am human.

Getting up I quickly dress and push my way through the circle, heading off in the direction of the red pyramid, which seems to deter them from following me. Hearing one or two shouts I glance back and see they are calling me away, but if nothing else, walking in this direction has got them off of my back, so I continue.

Stuck in the middle of the dunes, the Red Temple, a red stone building maybe forty feet square with a pyramid-shaped roof, looks more like a mausoleum built to house the bodies of some long-forgotten dynasty. Cautiously I approach the entrance knowing there could be anything inside, stray dogs or cats, scorpions, cobras, who knows? Maybe even a madman.

I take a single wary step inside and wait for my eyes to adjust to the gloom, there being no windows, but I'm pretty sure I can make out someone sitting or crouching in the far corner. Also, there is an intermittent hissing sound, like someone breathing deeply.

Gradually I'm able to make out the figure of a naked man sitting cross-legged. His white hair is shorn almost to the skull, and his brown body doesn't carry an ounce of fat. I'd give him sixty years or more.

The atmosphere is very heavy, eerie, and I'm tempted to leave, but as I'm standing there something moves in the right-hand corner and I see what looks like a trickle of water or oil running towards me. But it is a large snake. A cobra.

The creature stops in front of me, rises to chest height and stares up into my eyes, its tongue flicking in and out picking up scents as I wonder what to do, whether to back off slowly, keep dead still while staring mesmerically into its eyes, sway from side to side chanting 'Om', grab it by the throat and wrestle it to the ground, or make an undignified dash back out onto the beach.

Before I can decide, a voice comes from within the temple and the snake draws in its hood and withdraws back into the shadows.

'What do you want?' the voice asks sharply.

'Can I come in?'

'I said, "what do you want?"'

'Someone said you are a holy man. I want to ask questions about, well, spiritual things.' I remembered then that I hadn't brought a gift.

'You haven't brought a gift. It is customary and respectful to give holy man gift.'

And Shunters Grade Three. 'I'm sorry. I was so keen to get here that I forgot.'

'So keen, eh? Is that why you were making a fool of yourself lying on the beach, because you were keen? No matter. Come in and sit down.'

I am still trying to get a better view of this person, but for some irritating reason I can't focus on his face.

'No! Don't sit there. There is scorpion. You will make him angry. Over there.' He directs me into a corner where there is a large smooth stone on which to sit. I look for the scorpion, and see something move into a crack at the base of the wall. 'Good. Sit down. What can I tell sahib . . . the secret of life, perhaps? The truth about everything? Or maybe I should just give him a brief outline of the future, an inkling of things to come?'

Do I detect a note of sarcasm in his voice? His command of the English language is refreshing, but I don't know quite where to begin. 'Do you live here all the time?' I ask, more as a way of starting up some sort of conversation.

He laughs aloud. 'Live? Time? All? You Westerners don't have a clue, do you.'

'Just making conversation.' My turn to get pissed off.

'Please sir, don't come here making conversation. It would be better if you shut up or go away.'

Somehow I have to get this guy on my wavelength, otherwise I can see him telling me to fuck off. 'The snake is your guardian?' I ask politely.

'Snake? What snake?'

'The cobra that barred the way before you called it off.'

'There is no snake. You conjured him up.'

'There's a snake in the corner of the room.' I can still see a coiled heap in the shadows.

'If you wish.'

'It's not what I wish – in fact I wish he wasn't there.'

'But your fear and belief insist he stays. You are in darkness, sahib, if I may be permitted to say so.'

'Prove he's not there then.'

'Very well. But can you possibly be quiet for a few seconds?'

'Sure.'

'Good.'

I sit waiting for a few seconds, then a few minutes, wondering what he's up to. Then the time seems to stretch into what must be a good hour until I finally get bored and speak. 'Look, I don't want to interrupt your meditation or whatever it is you're doing, but . . .' And then I realise that the room is much lighter than it had been, and that the coiled snake is in fact nothing more than a pile of rocks. I look about. The holy man seems to be shining, radiant, like a medieval picture of a saint or the baby Jesus.

'Ah, at last. You people are such hard work. Now you see. No snake.'

I laugh in disbelief. True, the sun has shifted so that it reflects more into the temple, but it's not just sunshine illuminating the room. And the snake is definitely a pile of rocks. I know I've experienced all sorts of weird shit while stoned, and delusion is now run of the mill stuff for me, but how does that explain the snake when it reared up before my very eyes? But I decide not to mention it again because Gandhi here seems to think it was an illusion, a silly western idea.

'Gandhi was not Maharishi.'

'Maharishi?' I ask. Is he reading my mind?

'Great Sage. I am Great Sage. And also a mere nothing. Gandhi was crafty politician. But necessary politician to free Great Britain from the burden of India, to allow Great Britain to go into decline. It is karmic law. Every dog has its day. Great . . . ha, ha . . . Great Britain is now Small Britain. Which is good for your country. It shows maturity and growth. At last. Like an egotistical child, it has grown up. Now it is your turn.'

What *is* this guy going on about?

'What I am saying is that sooner or later everyone has to face up to the truth. Not in some silly imagined way where he or she goes off in search of some guru or other to satisfy the needs of the ego, but where one comes face to face with oneself. And that can be most exciting.'

'In what way?'

'Not Dan-Dare-Superman-Roy-of-the-Rovers-exciting; but mixing-acid-with-alkali-applying-heat-to-dynamite exciting. Which is why I say "sooner or later". Facing the truth can only happen when the time is right, otherwise you might disintegrate with the shock. And more often than not you cannot force the issue. I say "more often than not" because sometimes it is one's path to seek and find the truth, to force the issue, but now it is fashion and many people waste time seeking truth. They would be better off washing dishes. As Jesus said in his heyday, it is like casting pearls before swine.'

'What do you mean disintegrate? I mean, why should the truth or self-awareness cause disintegration?'

He sighs. 'This truth is not an intellectual thing. It cannot be told. One can talk in parables, but it is poor medium.' He grabs a handful of dust from the floor and holds it out. 'This is handful of dust, is it not? But if you care to magnify this dust a billion times, – and my hand with it – you will find a universe, no, an infinite number of universes within universes with immeasurable space. You see, our scientists, being what they are, have not yet discovered that atoms too have an infinite structure of even smaller atoms and so on. It is too much for their minds to grasp. So you might ask why doesn't the dust fall through the fabric of my hand? It is because the *idea* of the hand and the dust exists. The *idea* is what makes so-called reality. And truth is being aware that the idea can be changed.' He holds up his hand and releases a sparrow which flutters about then escapes through the door. 'But to come to this great and wonderful understanding you have to abandon all preconceptions, and this is particularly difficult for you Westerners who are imprisoned by what you call sanity.'

I gasp. Surely it has to be hypnotism? Did I just see a bird fly from his hand?

His vague face seems to be staring intently at me. 'As I said, casting pearls before swine. Now you are thinking I hypnotised you.'

This is all good stuff. But I still don't quite see what he's getting at. I mean, I know that a wall's a wall, and if I try walking through it I'll end up with a flat nose. And who's idea is it that a hand's a hand, or dust, dust? Or a bird?

'Relax and cast belief aside. Cut loose from your moorings. Enjoy yourself. Have some fun. That way it may be less painful when you finally lose your mind.'

Lose my mind? Somehow the way he says it is a bit scary.

'Don't be afraid. Everyone loses their mind sooner or later. You came here looking for a way to blow your own mind, as you youngsters put it these days, and you have found it. Your dreams and desires have shaped your future whether you like it or not. Now begins the roller-coaster of the reformation of your being. As is the dust, so are we.'

Outside, the Sun has shifted further, leaving him in deep shadow once again.

'Can I ask your name?' I wait for an answer. And wait.

Something has happened to my sense of time and suddenly I'm not sure just how long I've been sitting here. He seems to have stopped communicating now, and anyway, suddenly I feel that I've heard enough for one day. A nice strong pipe will just about round off an amazing day. Standing up slowly I do a little bow with my hands together and back out of the temple into the sunlight.

On the other side of the dunes is a shack selling fish in curry batter and suddenly I realise I'm hungry. The man looks at me carefully, picks a large piece from the smoking iron pan and says, 'Enjoy yourself. Have some fun.'

'What?' I ask. 'What did you say?'

But he doesn't speak a word of English. I must have misheard him.

I wander, fishy-fingered, through the strange roads, through the rows of '30s houses of suburban Karachi, a world apart from the shacks and mud brick hovels of the old town which I prefer. This subtropical Welwyn Garden City is subtly disturbing;

211

instead of soft green lawns are baked brown lawns; in place of delicate roses are hard, vicious roses; and in place of privet and bay or gentle forsythia and hydrangea are harsh and prickly shrubs and bushes inhabited by nasty-looking spiders with thick webs. I've been here before in childhood nightmares of loneliness, where nobody knew me and love didn't exist.

Moving quickly on and back into the old town and real life, I bump into Nazir who drags me away to another quarter where, he says, I must meet some important friends who wish to see me. A few streets on he drags me into the backroom of a general store where he tells me to wait. On the walls are pictures of eastern holy men with halos and some very elaborate decorated writings which probably say something incredibly profound or explain the meaning of life, but there you go. I've just had it first hand.

Soon he comes back with a couple of old men dressed in white who seem very interested in me. One is carrying a huge chillum, the largest I've ever seen, about eighteen inches long with a top diameter of about three inches, while the other has a box which he opens to reveal a lump of hashish the size of my fist.

'You want smoke?' asks Nazir.

Five minutes later we're all sitting outside on a charpoy puffing away on the huge chillum and, according to Nazir, they're astonished at my capacity.

I hadn't realised it, but by the time the chillum is dead a small crowd has gathered and is watching with fascination, but something even more interesting has caught my eye – directly overhead in the sky is a circular rainbow.

Jumping up and pointing I shout, 'Look! Look, a circular rainbow! A rain circle!' and the crowd is very amused. Soon an even larger crowd gathers to watch as I dance about exclaiming that I've never before seen such a thing and the old guys in white are laughing and clapping. Of course nobody can understand what I'm saying but they can all see what I'm staring at.

Or can they? It occurs to me that I might be imagining things, and when I look up again, well, it's gone. Glancing back at Nazir I ask him to confirm that what I saw was real, but all he does is laugh. So I laugh and everyone laughs all the more and they fill the chillum again.

Back at the Dilkusha, sari girl is no more. Shaukat says she has moved on which is a shame because I feel I could do with her company right now – after apologising for my lack of manners previously of course. But instead I read the *Bhagavadgita*. And discover something called *Pralyas*, or periodic occasions when the universe is dissolved.

And it describes evil people as those who don't see that there *is* order to the world, people who believe that it 'has no law nor order nor a lord', people who believe that 'the world has not arisen through cause following on cause, in perfect purposing.'

Those who don't accept a Theory of Evolution are earmarked for hell apparently. This is freaky stuff.

So we evolve through millions of heart-breaking years, from amoeba to air traffic controllers and have to find enlightenment before the universe is arbitrarily dissolved and we have to start again. You could be on the brink, about to become the new saviour, when you suddenly cease to exist because The Highest One wants to go home for tea.

God's too much if I have to believe all this. I mean, what sort of vicious bastard would terrify his offspring with threats like that? Like, do as you're told or I'm going to vaporise you periodically – in fact, I will anyway, whether you like it or not.

Compared to all this stuff, Gandhi back at the beach really has got something going for him. I must get back tomorrow and learn more, especially about this universe within universe stuff, and the space–time thing. According to what he was saying, me sitting here on this bed in a hotel in Karachi loading up another pipe with top-grade hash is only an *idea* in some other mind inside which lives my awareness, like early man in a cave of thought.

And those stars outside could well be the inside structure of someone else's hash-pipe.

'It puts things into perspective, does it not?' asks Gandhi the next day. 'Makes those things which seem important suddenly very insignificant. The way of the master is to transcend this worldly illusion and rise to heaven.'

'Easier said than done.'

'For those that are not masters.'

'So how do I get to be a master?'

'You wait in the queue until it is your turn.'

'And what about pralyas, the end of the world? What if I almost get there and I'm suddenly sent back to "Go"?'

He laughs aloud. 'You have been reading too much. Forget your pralyas. Understanding that would be like trying to explain the effect of an atomic bomb to a microbe, if you get my meaning.'

'But I need to understand what life is about.'

'You cannot. There is nothing to understand. The human brain invents reasons and explanations for everything, but it is all nonsense. If you wish to be able to see more you must master the brain, get it under control and use it when *you* need it – not be ruled by it. All I hear from you is impotent chatter, childish demands to know more. "I need to understand, I need to understand, I need to understand." What you are actually saying is that you are frightened, that you are in pain without an explanation for everything. Lack of knowledge frightens you. Your unruly little brain must have an explanation, otherwise it will sulk and make you feel depressed and miserable.'

'So what should I do?' I ask. There's no doubt about it, the man is making sense – at last someone agrees with what I'd thought all along, that all the clever bastards at school had it wrong.

'Do you not learn? Yesterday I said, "Relax and cast aside belief. Cut loose from your moorings. Enjoy yourself. Have some fun. That way it may be less painful when you finally lose your mind."'

'But I still think about things.'

'Think about the material world only. The biggest fools are philosophers: they are trying to start a fire with a bucket of water. Use your brain to work out the train timetable or how long to boil an egg, but please don't waste your time philosophising on what might be.'

'So how do I control the brain?'

'It is helpful to know first what life is like without the brain. Would you like to experience that?'

I'm about to say 'yes' when a warning bell rings and my stomach turns over.

'I would expect hesitation,' he says sharply. 'Your brain would of course object to the suggestion.'

'How would you . . . I . . . do it?'

'Any way you like. You could continue drugging yourself to insensibility – but you tend not to remember things that way. You could ask a butcher to cut it out, but the shock would probably kill you. You could recall your very early childhood, moments after you were born when you looked at things around you, undisturbed by the movement of the brain . . .'

I say that I can't remember that far back.

'Of course, your brain makes sure you cannot remember a time without it, tyrant that it is. You could meditate, practice a method of mind-control for the next god knows how many years. Or you could allow me to show you.'

His face is still vague within the shadows of the temple's interior.

'How will you show me?'

'By helping you to die.'

'By helping me to die?'

'I will hold your hand through death and bring you back. While dead you will understand how it is to exist without a brain.'

'But what if I really do die? What if you don't bring me back?'

He laughs again. 'Don't worry. Your time isn't up yet, but you will wish it was when you see.'

I laugh nervously, not knowing whether to be reassured or disconcerted. 'How can you tell my time isn't up?'

'Just by looking at you. Are you ready for this, or are you going to sit there all day thinking about it with that silly brain of yours?'

For some insane reason I agree to give it a go. 'Okay. Where do we start?'

'First you take a drop, just a drop of this water. Keep it by your side, you may need a drop more.' He produces a gourd and tosses it to me.

'What is it?'

'Holy water.'

The water is cool and sweet. I place the gourd at my side.

'Now close your eyes.'

Eyes shut tight I sit and wait.

Blackness.

Swirls of red and blue, little flashes of white break through. Then, I feel something messing with my brain, like an electric shadow passing over it but when I try to open my eyes, I can't. Nor can I move or speak.

A wave of panic sweeps through me, but I sense a friendly smile and the warmth of reassurance from a friendly source I take to be Gandhi. 'My name is not Gandhi,' comes through clearly, but not in words, 'it is Brama.'

'Okay, Brama, I'm paralysed and scared. Now what?'

'Now there will be a clash of vibrations as your non-physical state passes from the physical. As they vibrate at a different rate it is inevitable that there will be disturbance as they separate. Beyond that there will be a no-man's land to pass through, you call it "hell", a barrier designed to discourage comers and goers in the physical world. Don't be afraid as we pass through. I am with you all the time.

The vibration begins, becomes like an earthquake, then settles into an agonising drawn out rattle until suddenly I feel that I'm floating through a warm blackness. Then there's a very real sense of danger all around as I begin to notice living or at least moving shapes approaching. As they come closer, I see faces, some grotesque, some acceptable, some beautiful, but all emanating menace. Some of them I recognise – I see the two German boys who were topped in Afghanistan, but Brama tells me to ignore them. And a stunning girl, very much like my sari girl, gets close enough to touch me – her eyes are beautiful beyond words and I want to stay with her but again Brama pulls me away, saying she too is illusion. My own illusion. 'Don't get caught up with it. Remember this the next time you pass through.'

And suddenly we are through and into a world of light, pure warm light and joy. Now I see Brama quite clearly for the first time: he is indescribably beautiful. 'Look,' he says, and as I adjust I see green and trees and warm grassy meadows with running streams and beautiful familiar people sitting about in the grass, and distant music and birdsong and the fragrance of a million flowers, and I feel big, big love, and know that I am back home where I should be. But then Brama is there again, in front of me, staring intently into my eyes. 'We must go back.'

'But I want to stay. I belong here.'

'Not right now you don't.'

'But this is home. I recognise it. And those people – they are my family. I want to stay.'

'Recognise this state. The no brain. Now we go back.'

Before I can object, I realise with a jolt that I'm sitting on the cool dusty floor of the temple. And I'm stunned, unbearably miserable. 'Why couldn't I have stayed?' I eventually gasp.

'Because you must be here. You will return in good time.'

'But what's the point in all this here if there's that there?'

'Regeneration and movement. Growth and Love. All you need is love, ha, ha. I tell you, go out and enjoy yourself. Don't get caught up with the brain. Use it only to run your body and add up two and two. Be firm with it. Order it to look after your body. Then you will find freedom. Just remember those woods and fields and streams, and the music if you can. Meditate on them whenever your brain becomes too unruly, for it surely will.'

'You think so?' I look for the water but it has gone.

'I don't think so, I know so. You have interesting times ahead. I will pose you a riddle.' He produces the gourd again from the shadows and tips the contents on the floor. Using his index finger he draws a line across the puddle. 'Water equals pounds, shillings and pence. You must cross it first, then give it to your enemy. In so doing you may find the key to a longer life.'

Now he's beginning to sound like a gypsy fortune teller. 'I saw family and friends back there, and people I know but haven't met here yet. And how come my family are there and here at the same time?'

'I told you – this is an illusion, a place to come and train, a place to develop yourself as an idea, to recharge and grow.'

'Are there any rules?'

'Only the brain needs rules.'

'But if my brain says, "Don't put your hand in the fire because you will get burnt", surely that's a valid rule.'

'As valid as you want to make it. It's a good job Jesus didn't listen to his brain when he went walking on the water. Fire! Pah! Look at me.'

Smoke begins to bellow from beneath him. Suddenly flames envelope his scrawny form and I see his skin beginning to blister and char. The heat is almost overpowering and I have to move back, but as suddenly as they appeared, the flames die away to nothing, and he sits there intact and smiling. 'Like the Phoenix from the ashes!'

Far from feeling enlightened by all this stuff I wander back into town feeling oddly jaded, like I've had my life ripped away. Life seems pointless now, second class, like a B movie before the main film. And if I'm honest about it, the heat and the bustle and craziness and dope are beginning to get to me again. Having seen some sort of vision of paradise, Karachi seems a long way off. In fact I can't think of anywhere on earth that might fit the bill and I'm momentarily at a loss as to what to do next, feeling disinclined to get involved any more.

In the Dilkusha, a welcome refuge from everything around me, I load another pipe and sit back to think over the day.

Gandhi, or Brama, said that the things he showed me would change my life forever and that the best was yet to come; that I would lose my mind and rediscover it as I grow from one being into another. He said that I was never to worry about my sanity as 'one man's sanity is another man's living death', and that I was to meditate on paradise if ever I felt I needed strength. The Yoga of Madness he called it.

But now I've found it, I'm not so sure I want it. Already I can feel the jaws of uncertainty gnawing away at the foundations of my life, at everything I believe in, and I feel lost, adrift in a sea that washes up against the shores of that other dark place through which he led me. It's not easy to forget. But I know the place is me. And it's real. As real as anything in this great illusion, this conundrum of minds, this melting pot of ideas and false beliefs, but I wish I didn't know it because now I realise that my only hope was in ignorance. Now that I've been told the score I can't plead it any more, I really am accountable for myself.

There are times when you realise you can never go back, ever again, and this is the biggest so far, like I know hell is for real and waiting. Listen, man, I saw those faces – they're real all right. Yeh, okay, an illusion, but still real enough. I mean, if this life's an illusion, that one's real enough for me.

Thinking about it's making me real scared. I feel I've been defiled, somehow ruined by the insight. I call Shaukat – anything normal will help, and Shaukat's always reassuring in a nice, 'Yes Sahib' kind of way. But someone else comes and my paranoia turns into the desperate need to shit, so I rush past the new boy up the tiled stairs to the roof where I squirt more yellow and red liquid into a stinking hole. Why I have to go upstairs to shit downwards I don't know. What a waste of energy. Mosquitos are landing on my thighs, and probably my white arse too, as my stomach tightens itself into spasmodic knots, but I'm afraid to swat them in case it gives me bad karma and increases my chances of going to hell. One is so fat on my blood it can barely fly away and almost falls into the mire but I manage to scoop it away and out of danger – surely that'll count in my favour?

After washing, using the watercan method, I trip back downstairs to my room and collapse damp onto the bed. I really do need to get my act together, get out of Karachi and back to some sort of normality where I can appreciate everything that's been going on, maybe get back into women or take up night school again, or get a real job, something worthwhile, settle down and have kids. Fuck all this spiritual stuff.

But the moment I close my eyes to go to sleep I'm flying, first over rooftops, then into that weird place with the faces, but I wrench myself away and sit up in bed awake, soaked with sweat. The *Bhagavadgita* is too unnerving to read now, so I do another pipe and settle back down for the night, toying with the idea of destroying the book. First thing I'll go and see Gandhi – sorry, Brama – and get him to straighten me out. I'll explain that I was only being frivolous in my quest and ask to be returned immediately to a state of ignorance. Then I'll go and find a boat sailing back to Europe: cross the water, as the man said. The rest of it, the bit about giving it to my enemies for a longer life, I'll forget, because I don't understand what he meant.

Exhausted after no sleep, I make my way at first light back out to Keamari Beach and the Red Temple, but when I get there something isn't right. For a start there's old rusty barbed wire all around the building, and the sand has blown up much higher than it was before. Perhaps there's been a storm overnight? But the barbed wire . . .

I climb through between the strands and approach the door.

'Brama, Brama, are you there?' Peering into the gloom I can see nothing, so this time, armed with matches, I strike one and hold it out to light the far corners of the temple's interior, but there's nothing. Inside is a small sea of wind-blown sand and human turds of varying age and decomposition.

Head spinning I step back out into the morning sunshine. There must be another temple – there has to be. Perhaps there are two guarding this particular stretch of the beach.

Nearby two of the local males are standing gawping at me like I'm a lunatic.

'Hey, you know another temple here?'

'Hello, what is your name?' The speaker's face is incredibly ridiculous but I don't feel like laughing because I'm sure he's from hell.

'No, no, temple like this?' I shout. 'Other temple?'

'Where are you from?'

Ignoring them, I rush first in an easterly direction for about half a mile, then back again and head west for another half mile or so, but there is no other temple.

Oddly enough, after the shock and then the disbelief, a warm rush of relief hits me as I realise it could all be little other than a nightmare. Somehow I've lost track of time and dreamed it all, and I'm off the hook.

Heading straight for the port, I wander past the gate guards with a cheery 'Salaam Aleikum' and begin searching the quaysides for a ship going to Europe, asking from one mooring to the next if they need a hand.

By midday, and strengthened by a breakfast of bacon, eggs and sliced bread from a British boat on its way to Hong Kong, I find a Greek registered ship, the *Saint George*, bound for Greece via the Cape of Good Hope. 'Yes,' the Chief Steward says, 'we want mess boy. We pay too. So you go Piraeus and you have money, good money, plenty money. But you be quick, okay? We go today.'

So this must be the pounds, shillings and pence part of Brama's conundrum – crossing the water and getting paid for it. Not quite so mystical as I expected.

I pay and thank the owner of the Dilkusha, but can't find Nazir anywhere, so I have to go without saying goodbye. And despite my strange relationship with Karachi, I feel sad and uneasy as the *Saint George* steams off into the Arabian Sea, because as much as I kid myself otherwise, I know, yes I know, that everything I experienced was just as valid as the deck I'm standing on now. Everything that little dream man said and did has taken root deep inside. He was there. He was there, believe me. And the snake. And the little bird. It really happened.

SIX

The voyage across the water began with chicken and chips and beer and cigarettes served by the chief steward in the crew's canteen. No one else was about, occupied elsewhere as they were with the rigmarole of leaving port, and after months of goat and rice the western food was incredible, the cold beer out of this world.

Standing at the ship's rail later, watching Pakistan disappear into the heat haze radiating from the lowlands of Sind, all the earlier misgivings evaporated and suddenly I felt extraordinarily content despite my mental and physical health. Before me stretched two and a half months of dishwashing, messroom scrubbing, corridor mopping, and cleaning officers' cabins, and I felt sure that by the time we reached Europe I'd be fit again. Being shacked up in my own cabin – the old sick bay – inside an iron castle surrounded by a very large moat, I even felt safe enough to getting into Brama's meditation between shifts.

* * *

Now I'm not so sure. It's next morning and I've met the captain, who I've nicknamed Napoleon, and he says my hair has to come off. Nobody said anything about this when they took me on and I'm unhappy about it because it's halfway down my back now, well almost, and cutting it is going to be painful. I mean, why is there always someone who needs to inflict himself on you? It could be that he finds something uncomfortable about long hair on another male? Maybe there's a sexual thing going on here, or a threat to his position as the main man, like 'I've got longer hair than you' type of thing.

Ten minutes later there's Mister First Engineerios, a big bloke with arms like my thighs, together with Mister Bosun who looks like Captain Hook, escorting me to a solitary wooden chair stuck in the centre of the deck, while all around sit the rest of the crew, waiting to be entertained.

Napoleon struts forward with a smirk on his face. 'Meester Tommy, klopsy klopsy.' he says, using two fingers as scissors to make the point, and I learn my first Greek word, klops. First Engineerios guides me to the chair with strong hands, Hook wields the real scissors, and within minutes I'm shorn, so I take a bow and the crew cheers and claps me for being a sport. One up to me. I don't care anyway, now that it's done, but as Napoleon examines me with a look that says 'I may be short but I'm in charge' I just know that before the voyage is over I'll get a glimpse of the real him.

Then the work begins.

Fetch breakfasts from galley and serve in mess to captain and six other officers: coffee, ham, eggs, bread rolls, butter, honey and jam, fruit, more coffee. These Greek men like their food and obviously miss their mums, you can see it.

Afternoons I have to make the coffee as well, each one individually in a little brass pot over the gas. That's fun. And the Chief Engineer, a tall gaunt man like Laurence Harvey with piles, is very particular. So is the Radio Officer, a Bob Dylan fake, and the Chief Petty Officer (James Stewart minus a brain) who likes one third of a level teaspoon of sugar in his. After Karachi, everyone I look at seems to resemble someone else.

When they finish stuffing themselves and wander off, I clear the wreckage, wash and polish the table, sweep and mop the floor, wash up the dishes and cutlery, take plates back to the galley, snivel around the cook who must be fêted for perks, joke around with Alecco the galley boy, swab corridors around the officer's quarters and make the individual bunks in the cabins. All the while there's the steady dombity domb dombity domb dombity domb of the engine way below which is beginning to drive me nuts after sounding briefly reassuring at the outset. One of the disadvantages of being quartered amidships is the noise from the engine room, which I can hear while I'm deep in sleep. The upside is that there's less sea swell and no squabbling to put up with from neighbours. Back aft in the crew's quarters all you can hear is the driveshaft whining below and unknown things bashing against the iron hull outside as the ship cuts its way south through the Arabian Sea.

The crew seem all right. There's Hook, Alecco, Moussaka Joe the cook, two grumpy old men who don't appear to do anything, dodgy Tharnassus, Eric the Austrian, Hassan the Egyptian, and a couple of greater or lesser engineers and stokers.

Eric the Austrian has taken it upon himself to be my guardian as he seems to think that we two are the sole representatives of civilisation on the boat. 'The Greeks are okay,' he says, 'but don't turn your back on them. Any trouble, you watch out. Don't trust the little cabin boy Tharnassus – he's mischief. Alecco's okay. And the big first engineer, the one who cut your hair, he's okay too. And Hassan. But the rest? Well, they're Greek. This boat is a very old Norwegian boat, an icebreaker and very strong, but these Greek shipowners buy old boats, take big insurance, and wait for them to sink, so be careful.'

'Oh, yeh, like I can be careful. What can I do?'

'Just stay by me. I look after you if there is problem. I have a gun and an axe in my cabin.'

Some blokes are too honourable for their own good. Eric's on the run, or at least he has debts back in Austria caused by a dodgy wife and a hotel business that went down the pan, so he's working on boats to save the cash to pay his creditors.

Black Hassan is strong and cheerful. The two boys, Tharnassus and Alecco, keep one or two of the officers company when they're off duty, and Hook wanders the decks in his spare time with a .22 rifle looking for birds or sharks to shoot. I hate him for it. The other day he shot two doves which had landed on the radio aerial for a breather and I called him a wanker, which he didn't like one bit. And when he's not working, the cook hides himself on one of the starboard gangways and smokes reefers to calm his temper. So far I've smoked no dope because I need my wits about me, and slowly I seem to be coming out of a fog.

Meanwhile, the Captain struts about with his chest puffed out on the bridge. I know because I've just had to take coffee to him, on a silver tray, all the way from the galley which is two decks down and halfway along the ship. 'This coffee is cold,' he says, pulling an irritated, spoilt-kid face. It's a long way I say. 'You come quicker next time,' he snaps back, then turns away like I'm dismissed, the pig. 'No,' I say, 'you bring it yourself next time.' And he says he is the Captain and what he says goes and if I'm not careful I might just end up swimming back to Europe. And suddenly it dawns on me that no one knows I'm on the boat, and that to get rid of me would be very easy indeed.

From that point on I imagine animosity from everyone, as if the Captain has told them I'm dead meat. So each night I wedge a chair under the handle of my cabin to prevent anyone from sneaking in and cutting my throat.

And every day it gets worse: this coffee's too sweet, this one's too strong, or not strong enough, or too cool, or not sweet enough, and all the officers want them before everyone else, just like kids. Three times in one evening the Chief Engineer sends his back, and the Radio Officer is screaming for more bread while the Captain shouts for water. Even Alecco is being non-communicative, and Eric the Austrian is keeping well out of the picture because it's clear that they are planning to kill me.

Yesterday I saw Moussaka Joe putting white powder into some of the dinners. And when he hands me the plates he is always very specific about who has which: 'This one for the Captain, this one for the Chief Engineer, this one for the Radio Officer,' and so on, despite them all appearing to be identical. So I swap them about to see what happens and all becomes clear – cook has been spiking his enemies with laxative powder and, judging by their recent behaviour towards me, I've been getting the blame. But now that I've changed the order of service, the focus of attention is taken away from me.

I'm learning that the Greek thought process is a complex thing, something my school teachers vainly tried impressing on me years ago: Moussaka Joe is punishing Napoleon and friends because of some dispute, probably pay. Napoleon and friends who have been suffering badly from the shits have got it into their heads that I am the cause of this, but now that they are feeling better and have noticed that the cook's friends have the shits instead, they seem to accept quite illogically that I am not at the root of it after all. In fact Napoleon asks me if I've swapped the plates about, but I say I can't remember, just to confuse matters further and to ensure that they keep an eye on cook.

But after a week of fun when I discover the true meaning of dashing officers, Moussaka Joe susses what's going on and corners me in the galley with a boning knife. 'You bastard!' he hisses. 'You change plates! You give Chief Engineer the plate of the Captain!' So I ask what difference it makes and he has to lie about making sure the Captain gets the best food. But he knows that I know, and the spiking comes to a stop and everyone's friendly again.

Many boring equatorial days go by until one morning the wind gets up and the sea gets bigger and bigger, until by midnight we are crashing our way through a hurricane. The Radio Officer who failed to pick up the warnings because he was asleep says the wind force is off the Beaufort scale and suddenly everyone is very frightened but also extremely friendly – being in the same boat. Eric says Napoleon is on the bridge bawling his eyes out, so I take up an unexpected coffee just to gloat. From the galley, along the deck and up two flights of iron stairs I take his coffee, hanging on every inch of the way, without spilling a drop, through a hurricane, to find him wailing at the sea ahead. 'This is no good,' he screams. 'Sea too big for little ship. No good. No good. We go down.'

'There there,' I say, 'have a nice cup of hot coffee. It'll warm the cockles of your 'eart.'

'Cockles?' he sobs, bracing himself against the chart table.

'An old London saying. Means it's just what you need.' I don't tell him I've nicked some of Moussaka Joe's laxative and dosed it with that just to keep him on his toes. At least it'll take his mind off the storm for a bit.

'Thank you,' he says gratefully, sipping at the poison. And beware of Englishmen bearing gifts thinks I – I'll teach you to cut my hair you strutting little pimp.

Later he has to be rescued covered in shit from his private lavatory where he's been thrown to the floor by the force of the storm. While this is happening I'm at the nodding donkey back end of the ship with Hook trying to cut free several drums of oil that have come loose and are threatening damage as the ship rolls around. It's not that I'm brave, but I'd rather do anything than sit with the rest of the crew who've gathered amidships to frighten themselves with talk of doom and disaster. At every lurch, thud or shake of the boat they glance at each other and stare horrified at the ceiling as if waiting for the sea to smash its way in. On the bridge, Eric is steering her alone now, nobody else being up to the job, while Napoleon continues to run knock-kneed and weeping between bog and bunk.

Dombity domb dombity domb dombity domb uphill, domb domb domb domb domb domb domb downhill. Dombity domb dombity domb dombity domb BANG! BANG! uphill, dombombombombombombom bangity BANG! downhill as the engines labour and explode under the strain. And all the while the screaming of wind and the crashing of seawater against the hull and superstructure and you would never believe waves could be so big. The *Saint George*, 120 yards long, is struggling through a mountain range of water. One moment you can't see anything but the night sky, tilted first this way, then the other; the next and there's nothing but massive walls of black water all around. Finally, overcome by the scale of it all and the tension among the crew, I go to my bunk.

Dear God, I know that I've doubted you in the past (well, I've never really doubted you) but if you can see your way to getting me out of this

226

*one, I'll spread the word wherever I go. I mean it. I'll never doubt you
again, dear Lord, please spare me from this. I thank you. Amen.*

I'd better include my fellow men in this otherwise he'll think
I'm being selfish and ignore my prayer. *'And my fellow men O
Lord. And anyone else on the sea who is suffering. Thank you. Amen.*

I'm even having to brace myself in the bunk now. The
engine's still exploding, and the structure's beginning to creak
and groan like it's breaking apart. Om mane padme hum. Om
mane padme hum . . . Meditate like Brama said – picture the
green fields and feel the bliss, the love, the overwhelming feeling
of belonging . . .

Silence.

Silence?

Sitting up I realise the engines are switched off. The ship is
rolling gently in a minor swell and I'm alive.

Outside it's light, and while I've been sleeping *à la* Redman
and Amin on the coach to Teheran, trying to miss the dangerous
bits, the crew's rigged up a crane to remove a piston from the
engine – a piston larger than me that somehow got bent in the
storm. First Engineerios is doing his greasy bit showing just how
strong he really is, while all around the boat, seals show off and
do acrobatics in the deep blue water.

Eight hours later and we're under way again, heading north
this time, back up towards the equator, dombity domb dombity
domb, but the mood has changed and everyone's very friendly
except Captain who's in disgrace and hiding.

Up the west coast of Africa, round past Morocco and back into
the Med, but Radio Man says we've new instructions: we have to
go to North Yugoslavia instead of Piraeus, which suits me fine as
it's much closer to home.

On arrival, Napoleon gets his own back and pays me in
Yugoslav dinar at bank exchange rate instead of the agreed
American dollars, which means that I lose about 75 per cent of
the value of my wages because I have to convert it into Italian lira
first as I leave the country before being able to convert it into
dollars in Italy. And then the thieving bastard deducts more
money for 'customs charges' incurred in Karachi. He says he had

to bribe the officer to let me through without papers – maybe he did, but I wish he wouldn't rub it in so much because I feel so happy about getting off the ship that I don't want him to spoil my day. But at least I've got the hashish hidden in the bottom of my little Pakistani shoulder bag.

All I need to do now is get it back home, or somewhere I can convert it without fuss into $1,000, then take off again, maybe for Mongolia because nobody's been there. It'll be a first, like, Mongolia wow! Cool, man, come and tell me all about it then shag me. The chicks love it if you've been somewhere outrageous. I'm looking forward to getting back on the road again and meeting up with a few women – the Afghan card alone should see me through until Mongolia. I think of Mary and Jenny in Trieste, and Nilüfer and the two American girls, Barbara and Diane. A year's gone by. What are they all doing now?

Of course! Why didn't I think of it before? Nilüfer must know someone in Munich who'll buy the dope. That'll save me risking British Customs at Dover. Once I'm out of the port here in Koper it'll be a doddle: 300 kilometres across the Austrian Alps, a day at the most, and I'll be on her doorstep. Let's just hope the boyfriend's not at home.

SEVEN

When you get off a boat after a long time at sea, it feels as if the earth's moving around beneath your feet. So while the Yugoslav customs man is laughing at me swaying about and waving me through without a check, I'm having my own little laugh knowing there's almost a kilo of top-grade hashish a yard from c the gold braid on his cuffs.

'Welcome to our country,' he says with a smile.

'Yeh, yeh, I know,' I say with a bigger smile, remembering the thugs in Belgrade who didn't seem to care whether they shagged Mary or me. And the dogs.

Out on the sunny deserted road again, quick spliff in mouth, relax into the vibes man. Would you believe it? Here I am back in Europe, dressed like a Pakistani with dancing bells around my ankles and bangles on my wrists, and feeling very happy indeed. Few can parallel my experiences. I am a far-out freak. From Munich I'll fly back to Karachi, or Bombay, or Katmandu, and do another dope deal. Outer Mongolia will have to wait.

First things first, get a lift. And by the sound of it a car is coming this way. Yep. Thumb out, look pleasant, car slows down . . . and cruises by as the driver stares hard at me in amazement. Then another drives past sticking his finger in the air and shouting abuse. And a couple of minutes later another.

Come on then, you Yugoslav bastards, stop the car and get out, let's see how tough you are.

But thinking about it, maybe I do look a bit odd.

Well, who cares? If need be I'll walk. I have all the time in the world. It's far more important to look the part, to be one of a select group of travellers who know no bounds, physically, mentally, or spiritually. Om mane padme hum.

By nightfall I've at least managed to get the few miles across the border into Italy and into the Youth Hostel at Trieste, where my arrival has created some interest as it is obvious that I have travelled far and wide. But I play it cool, and wander about looking blissed-out and enigmatic when people ask me questions like, 'Are you coming back from the East?'

Looking sort of distant, I open my mouth just slightly, dip my head a touch to the left, and say softly, 'You could say that', in the best far-out voice I can muster.

Soon I'm laying it on real thick with some big-titted Californian chick who's getting bored with her know-it-all boyfriend, and I'm just enjoying being a bastard because, would you believe it, *he's* actually telling *me* about the dangers and pitfalls of Asian travel despite never having been there. The way things are going I'll be with his girlfriend before the night's out while he's creeping about with a long face inflicting his wisdom on somebody else, and I just can't wait – in fact I'm getting a hard-on sitting here on the terrace talking to her, but it's easy enough to hide beneath these baggy cotton pants and long shirt.

'Oh, wow' is her catchphrase, but the boyfriend resents her sharing it with me. 'And you went through the Khyber Pass? *Oh, wow*. Were the natives okay? I mean were they friendly, or were they really like they say in books, you know, kinda mean?'

'He wouldn't be here now if they'd decided to get mean, would he?' interrupted the jerk. 'Those guys are past masters at murder and intrigue. Just look at the way they kicked British butt back in the 1800s. Not that kicking British butt has been confined to Afghanistan, ha, ha, ha.'

I've heard that before somewhere. 'You fancy giving it a go then?' I'd just love the chance to stamp in his mouth, but Big Tits gets there first.

'Have you finished the washing up yet?' she snaps at him.

With this he blows it by telling her to do the dishes herself and walks off, so I seize the moment and suggest we take a walk around the headland to see the fabulous castle which stands illuminated high above the rocky edge of the sea. '*Oh, wow*,' she says.

On a beach nearby we share a joint and she asks for my name and a brief history and tells me hers is Toni and that she comes from San Jose near San Francisco and then we fuck, first too quickly because I'm sex-crazed, then again a little bit later. I think some sand must have got in somewhere because she goes all gasping and squirmy on me for a bit before making it loudly. Then she wants to go swimming in the moonlight, while all I want to do is lie there and feel pleased with myself – hoping that Big Mouth heard her come – but I give in and splash about with her and we screw again, this time standing up in the water, which is a new one for me.

'D'you know,' she says, 'I wouldn't mind tagging along for a bit, if that's okay with you. Wayne's getting to be real tiresome. Oh, he's okay, but I think we've been together too long. It's enough to try anybody.'

But sadly she doesn't fit into my plans. I mean, any chick that ready to dump her man in the middle of nowhere has to be some sort of liability and, anyway, she's too Miss Wholesome-Brash-

California: all teeth and tits. She definitely doesn't fit the image of the kind of female I want as the other half of a freak double act – although I suppose with a few more drugs and a bit of deprivation she'd probably come up to scratch. But no, something a bit more exotic, with a touch of mystery, is what I'm looking for. Someone like Nilüfer or Masumah, the Afghan bird. I can see Nilüfer now, rid of her boyfriend, waiting for my return at the window of her Munich tenement – I come along, rescue her for the second time and she realises that I'm the one for her. Da da . . .

'That'd be really nice but I have to go to Germany on business. See some man about a deal. And I have to go alone.'

'We could go together and I could wait somewhere until you've done the business, whatever that might be,' she says, wiggling her butt with both legs around my hips.

I can feel my feet sinking slowly into the sand beneath our combined weight, so I have to stagger into a new position.

And she's prying already, hoping I'll tell her what I'm up to. 'It's not that easy. It could take a couple of days or a month. Depends.' Pause to think of a lie. 'The thing is, I'm dealing with political refugees and the underground, so anything could happen.'

'*Oh, wow*. Refugees. I'm majoring in politics and human rights – this would be just amazing stuff. I won't get in the way. And I have a really useful allowance which could help. I mean, we could take the train instead of hitching.'

Too much. I've never met an American girl like this before – they're usually really clever with their money – unlike English girls, who'll blow it all on a one night piss-up if the mood takes them. And at least it would mean unlimited sex until Munich, where I could lose her or fix her up with a nice Turk.

Hey, what's happening to me? I'm thinking evil – what's brought this on? It must be her boyfriend winding me up that's done it. 'Look. I'll tell you what I'll do. Which way are you and your boyfriend heading?'

'He's not my boyfriend. But as you ask, we were going to take in Venice, Florence, Rome and Naples, then cut across to Athens.'

'Okay. When you get to those places, check out the Poste

Restante when you arrive and when you leave. I'll mail you as soon as I'm free to move on, and we can meet up somewhere.' Then I stagger up the beach and finish her off before she can think of another way round it.

'You'll need to know my full name, won't you?' she asks as we lie there studying the stars.

Gorizia, Udine, Villach, Badgastein, Salzburg, Rosenheim, and Munich. A single day. Three hundred and fifty miles of beautiful mountainous countryside, a dozen lifts and no aggro.

Except for one or two Italian catcalls and strange hand gesticulations, the Pakistani clothes seem to be a novelty rather than a provocation now that I'm back to civilisation, and I'm pleased to note that other freaks I've met on the road treat me with considerable respect. I hope I appear to these strangers as Dirk and Hulm appeared to me when we first met – far out, weird and beautiful.

The old confidence is coming back. Here I am jingling through a German city street dressed like this and everyone's staring, wondering where I'm at, and I love it. At the end of the day, as they say, it's all about having no fear – yeh, here we go again, fear. It's no good wearing the best gear in the world if you're going to stand in the corner trembling, is it? On the other hand it's no good trying to be flash if you're strutting about in clothes that went out of fashion the day before yesterday – you'd only just get away with it in Okehampton or Hyderabad. If you want to be right up there you have to frighten people, make them respect you by wearing clothes that scream *Approach With Caution*.

Up ahead I see Nilüfer's dismal grey apartment block blotting out the blue sky, guarded by a small gang of urchins who have stopped kicking a tennis ball about to weigh me up as I approach. You can see their minds working overtime as they clock my gear, wondering whether to put me to the test, but Asia has taught me how to handle gangs of kids. Deadpan, and ignoring their presence, I stick a Rössli cigarette in my mouth and in passing startle them all by asking if they've got a light. Of course the biggest one has and I thank him with a little glance of respect and walk on while he keeps the rest of them under control.

Tap, tap, on Nilüfer's fading blue door. Is she still here? A year's gone by. Will her boyfriend be here? Friendly or aggressive? What if Mustafa's there? A quick getaway won't be so easy in flip-flops, neither will fighting come to that, and it looks as if someone's already had a go at the door because there are marks around the lock and indentations down the opening edge caused by a chisel or bar of some sort.

Then the door opens and Nilüfer's boyfriend is standing there eyeing me up and down with a 'fuck off' look on his face. He remembers me.

'If you're looking for Nilüfer she's not here,' he says in German.

'Is she coming back soon?'

'Work.'

I ask if I can come in to speak more privately.

'Sure,' he says, 'but not for long. Too many people around here talk too much, and you are a big problem.'

Ominous. Me a big problem? Once inside the scruffy little flat I'm led along a short corridor with doors either side to a room at the end which turns out to be the living room. The stink of long-term dirt, onions and cigarette smoke fills the air. At each end of the room the windows are covered with threadbare drapes woven with scenes of minarets and sheep, and in the soft multi-coloured gloom which filters through from the sunlit end I can make out a scruffy three-piece suite, a table covered with newspapers, dirty crockery and full ashtrays, a few hard chairs, and a large water pipe at which I pointedly glance with a knowing grin. 'You smoke hashish?' I ask, knowing there's no point in beating around the bush.

'Tobacco. No hashish.'

A baby starts crying in another room and he goes to sort it out. When he comes back he apologises, adding that it is his and Nilüfer's child. 'Salim. Nilüfer wanted to call him Tomi, after you,' he says.

I laugh to keep it light. 'I helped Nilüfer get out of Turkey. I hope everything is working out all right for you both. At least she has some work, you say.' I hope she's not been forced back onto the game, but it's not the sort of thing you can ask her man.

'She must do it. Mustafa Gölü is boss. You know him.'

Mustafa. The bastard's found her. Ah well, tough luck, I've done my bit. All I want to do is sell a kilo of dope. I keep my mouth shut and wait for a signal.

He continues, 'Gölü say you owe him money. And you shame her family.'

'What's he talking about? Nilüfer said she was in danger in Istanbul and wanted to escape to Germany, so I helped her because I thought it was political or religious persecution . . .' I can't really say she was Mustafa's whore either, without risking some sort of violent attack, because I don't know if she's told him. 'That's all. And how come I owe him money?'

'He say you steal money from him to buy passport for Nilüfer. Five thousand dollars. Now she has to work, to pay back.'

'And what about you? Why don't you tell him to fuck off? Who cares about $5,000 anyway? At least she's safe.' If you ask me the whole thing's his problem now anyway – he wanted his little girl back and he's fertilised her to prove it, knocked her up to place a claim on her.

He laughs unhappily. 'Turkish man like Mafia – worse. I say "fuck off" they kill me, my baby, Nilüfer's father or brother.' He shrugs. 'All the same to them.'

Oh, yeh, nice one. I have to be careful here in case I get dragged into some Turkish 'B' movie nightmare, where you end up dead and nobody knows or cares. In fact I could be very close to it now. Who knows what's going through this guy's ill-informed mind? For all I know he thinks I've been giving Nilüfer a severe seeing-to and has dreamt of disembowelling me for the last year.

And here I am trying to get into this new love and peace thing that's sweeping the planet. Even the Beatles have dropped out. I saw a picture of them in yesterday's Oggi with some Indian geezer – they all had beards, for fuck's sake. Everyone's at it, while I'm here in Germany wondering how to walk the next twenty-five steps and stay alive at the same time.

Then I make a big mistake. I should have risked the twenty-five steps and left, but I didn't. 'Look,' I say, 'don't misunderstand me, but I don't really know what you're on about. This Mustafa

Gooloo, I met him once in the Pudding Shop. I don't know the man. Nilüfer came here on a passport I borrowed from an American girl who then reported it stolen. That's all. I thought I was helping her. Where he comes into it I don't know.'

'So why you are here now?'

I try to look weary and hard done by. 'Because I don't know anyone in town and I want to sell some hashish.'

He looks long and hard at me. 'How much you got?'

'Just under a kilo.'

'You have?'

In for a penny . . . 'Sure, it's here in my bag.' And I get it out.

He sniffs it and twists a tiny piece from the used corner which he lights and sniffs again. 'Mmn. How much you want?'

'Thousand dollars.' This is cheap, but it has to be attractive for a quick sale. Going rate's about fifteen hundred. But looking at the two slabs now the price seems absurdly high.

'Okay. You wait. I take. Bring money if okay.'

'Oh, yeh? And then I don't see you again? You bring money, I give you hashish.'

'Not possible.' He shrugs his shoulders. 'I leave you with baby – why you not trust me?'

That sounds reasonable enough; he's hardly going to disappear and leave me with the baby. Anyway, I've got little choice. The strain of carrying a kilo of dope around under your arm begins to tell after a while, especially when the Polizei keep driving by and clocking you. 'Okay, you take, but be quick, I've got a plane to catch.' Before handing over the dope I tear off about half an ounce for the road, adding that he's got it cheap anyway.

Seizing the goods he leaves the room after telling me there is a bottle of warm milk in a pan on the stove should the baby wake up. 'One hour,' he says.

This has all the ingredients of a classic rip-off. How many times have I been told never to part with the goods until I've seen the money? I should have learnt by now.

Half an hour goes by, then an hour according to the gold plastic heart-shaped clock on the wall. Then I hear the door open and the sound of footsteps, female footsteps. They go into the bedroom and I hear gooing and gurgling and hungry whimpering, and suddenly Nilüfer bustles into the room carrying the baby.

'Nilüfer!' She looks even better, more mature with the larger breasts that come with having babies.

'Tommy!' she gasps. 'What are you doing here?'

'Me? I came to see you but your man said you were working.'

'Friday is early finish. He always forget.'

'He said you were working, to pay back money.'

'Sure I work – in factory. Half my money goes to Mustafa to stop him saying I am illegal immigrant.'

'But why didn't you just disappear? If what your boyfriend said is true about the Turkish mafia you must've known he'd find you if you stayed in one place.'

'It doesn't matter where you go if these men have their hooks in you. I know this now. But at least I don't have to sell my body.'

'No, just your soul.'

'You didn't say anything about Istanbul to Sukru?'

'Sukru?'

'My man – he doesn't know.'

'No, of course not.' So Mustafa's got her over a barrel then. I wish I'd never come back. But Jeez . . . she's so beautiful. Why did she have to have a boyfriend?

'So where's Sukru now?' she asks.

'Er, he's changing money for me.'

'Why you not do it yourself? There's no black market here.'

The door opens and Sukru walks back in looking very pleased with himself. He says something to Nilüfer and she leaves the room. 'Entschuldigung,' he says. 'Excuse me, but I have good message. Mustafa very happy man.'

'Mustafa? What's he got to do with it?'

'No, no, listen. I sell hashish to cousin of Mustafa. He make phone-call to Turkey. Mustafa very pleased you make business with him and say he can help you with import-export business. If you do this he will clear our debt and yours. And you have English friend also. He is with Mustafa.'

Frankie. With Mustafa? 'Did you get the money?' I ask.

'There is one ticket airplane to Istanbul. For tonight. You go.'

'No money?'

'Mustafa have. You go Istanbul. First you telephone, now. Then go.'

He gives me a piece of paper with a string of numbers on it.

'Okay. Nice work Sukru. Looked after number one all right then.'

'What?'

'Forget it. Where's the nearest telephone?'

'Down. Out on street.'

'Okay, see you later.' I leave the room and find Nilüfer waiting in the hallway. 'I'm going,' I say in English to exclude Sukru. 'If ever you change your mind about this creep, let me know.' I turn to Sukru. 'I need change for the telephone . . .'

'Hello, who is this?'

'Tommy in Germany.'

'Ah, my friend. Good to hear you again. You have some news?'

'Where's Frankie?'

'Here.'

'Let me talk to him.'

'Okay.'

'Tommy?'

'Frankie! What the fuck are you doing there?'

'I got sick in India and had the chance of a free lift back with some cat from Balham, so I took it.'

'And got pulled in Istanbul.'

'That's about it.' He starts talking Londonese. 'Keep an eye out old son. Best bet's to have it away like ASAP, these geezers ain't kosher. I'll look after number one, get my drift?'

'I've got to come back because he owes me money . . .'

Suddenly Mustafa's voice is back on the line. 'You listen to your friend, Tommy. You pick up ticket at Lufthansa desk then we meet you at airport. Don't forget. Frankie will be very unhappy if you not come.'

At Munich airport I check in, pick up the ticket as instructed, then change the flight for an earlier one, leaving with minutes to spare. The last thing I need is a bunch of heavies waiting for me. Why I don't forget it and meet up with Toni instead or carry on travelling the globe avoiding Istanbul I don't know. Frankie always looked after himself and wouldn't dream of helping me unless it suited him. Fair enough, I have to admit that he did tell me to steer clear, but I can't. Things probably aren't half as bad as they seem, and I'm sure we can bluff or negotiate a way out of it – if nothing else we can always resort to violence. Anyway, I want to see Frankie again.

A couple of hours later I'm in Istanbul and, as planned, being early there's no welcoming party so I jump in a taxi and ride into town.

Up the hill past Gulhane Park again, like old times, across the road and back up to the Gulhane Hotel where I could really put it about now if I wanted to, but I have to think about funds and take a space on the roof instead of a room because we might need every penny when it's time to leave. I'm down to about fifty dollars in mixed currency and it's just occurred to me that I've come through Turkish customs with a lump of dope in my pocket. What's happening to my head? A pull with that, small as it is, could mean eight years in hell. How could I not think of the risk?

The roof is packed. There must be thirty people or more up here, many of them camping beneath a large polythene sheet erected as an afterthought by the management. Others are camped elsewhere beneath their own little contraptions or in sleeping bags, but all I have is the blanket I stole from the youth hostel in Trieste which I now put down in a spare corner. For a pillow I can use my shoulder bag which'll make life difficult for anyone who gets ideas about thieving. Spartan stuff, but impressive to others, because out here your credibility is inversely proportional to the size of your bag. Rookies don't know this and tend to go for the big-is-beautiful approach, with multi-coloured rucksacks that tower over them like giant parasites fattening nicely on the away-from-home insecurity of the host.

A girl approaches. 'Hi,' she says. She's English, probably Home Counties by her accent.

'Alright?' I take her in. Short brown hair, average height, pleasant round face. And I can see she's a bit lonely and a bit out of her depth. Behind those eyes the message is 'I'm looking for a friend.' She's picked the wrong one here then.

'Where you from?' she asks.

'London.'

'Me too – which part?'

Wrong there then. 'Bermondsey. You?'

'Carshalton.'

'That's not London.'

'Well, Surrey. Same thing. Anyway, my name's Terry, what's yours? Where you going?'

'Hello Theresa, mine's Thomas but you can call me Tommy. Where am I going next? I'm not sure – maybe back East.'

As expected, her eyes light up. 'You've been there already? I suppose you must've done, dressed like that. What's it like?'

I ask you, what a question. 'Yeh, it's all right.'

The silly answer seems to satisfy her. 'How did you get there? D'you mind if I sit here?'

'Be my guest. I went from here to Teheran by car, and then by bus and train. Came back by boat from Karachi to Yugoslavia around the Cape of Good Hope, then hitched to Munich and flew from there to here. And here I am. D'you smoke?' I pull the lump of dope from my pocket.

'Yeh . . .' she says uncertainly, eyeing the brown lump, and I can tell she hasn't smoked hashish before, 'What's that, hashish?'

'Yeh.'

'I've never tried it before.'

I smile. 'A virgin.'

She laughs. 'Could say that.'

'How did you get here?'

'With my friend. She's the little blonde one over there with that big bloke.'

Sitting beneath the polythene shelter among a crowd of others is a tiny blonde girl entwined with a massive blonde Teuton. 'What, has she just met him?'

'Yes. Well, yesterday.'

'And you've been abandoned.'

'She'll get over it. She normally does in two or three days. I have to put up with it all the time.'

'Here.' I pass the joint.

She smokes some of it like a cigarette and passes it back, then we sit side by side and watch the few fluffy white clouds passing over the Bosphorus. Once again life's looking good: I have a new lady friend if I want, a few dollars, a good bit of summer left to play with, and a lump of dope. The only damper is this Mustafa and Frankie thing and I haven't a clue how to go about it. For a start I'm alone and on enemy territory. If I go to the British Consul Frankie'll probably just disappear and I'll follow him later after being told to get out and stop wasting staff time. People go missing here regularly and nobody does a thing about it, the attitude being that if you're silly enough to come to a place like Istanbul, it serves you right if it turns sour on you.

The only time they're interested is if you've got the right connections – if it's going to cause them problems later because they've done nothing about it.

I go over the thing again in my mind. As far as I can see, I can either do a deal of some sort, pay off the debt, find out where Frankie is and get him out, get Mustafa to change his mind somehow, or get rid of him. Now I've never murdered anyone before so the last option's unlikely unless it's accidental, and as Mustafa's demands are as yet unknown I can't do a thing until I've come face to face with him.

So as none of those solutions seems feasible I'm going to do a couple of tubes of amphetamines and anything else I can get my hands on the off-chance that maybe the chemical input will present a solution to all this by forcing me to think or act laterally. And besides, it might be the last chance I get.

'D'you fancy getting blasted?' I ask Terry.

She stares at me. The hash seems to be working. 'My mate's boyfriend's got some LSD,' she says with a surprised stoned-for-the-first-time look on her face.

'Far out.' I'm not going to admit that I've never taken LSD before. 'Does he want to sell some?'

'He doesn't sell it, he gives it away for spiritual reasons or something. He's got a little bottle full of it. He showed it to me – I thought it was water. You have to put it on a sugar cube.'

'Have you tried it?'

She nods over to her friend. 'Karen did but it terrified her for twenty-four hours, so I'm not too sure if I want to. Have you then?'

'In London, yeh,' I lie.

'Did you like it?'

'It was all right. Go and ask if we can have some. If not we'll score something else.'

She gets up and walks steadily towards Karen and her German, and I watch as she speaks to them. The German looks over, grins, and puts his hand up in greeting.

A few seconds later she returns and says the acid will arrive a little later, as someone is currently using it in a peace ritual.

At the chemist down by Sirkeçi Station, I buy a tube each of Ritalin and Romila. Terry takes three pills from each – despite my advice that you need to take at least half a tube to get anywhere – and swallows them with the help of a bottle of Coke. What the hell – I swallow the rest and chuck the containers into the gutter.

By now it's dark, and as we walk the crowded streets around the covered market I get the feeling that Mustafa's henchmen are watching from every doorway, from every dark alley and shadowy corner. By the time we get back onto the main street leading towards the Blue Mosque I'm beginning to get the first chemical rush and manage to convince myself that we really are being followed.

A few blocks on, and waves of paranoia are flooding through me and I'm walking faster and faster until Terry has to trot alongside to keep up. I feel perspiration trickling down my body beneath the sweaty and suddenly very lurid orange shirt and a tremor vibrates in my gut threatening to erupt into panic.

'Are you okay?' she asks, peering into my eyes and making me feel worse.

The panic's growing and I think it's probably as a result of swallowing the two tubes of pills: Ritalin were never a problem, but these Romila are a new one on me. What if they don't mix? Maybe the combined chemicals produce a mind-fuck. Maybe I'm going to die after a period of insanity, because I feel as if I'm beginning to lose my mind right now as it teeters on the edge of blackness. Hell is but a single tiny wrong thought away, and my breath is becoming shallower and faster.

'I don't know,' I gasp. 'I think this Turkish guy might have someone following me.' I have to keep my fear from her at all costs otherwise she'll think I'm a tosser and abandon me. I'm also just beginning to see a way through this unforeseen personal development – if I can get her to agree, we can check into another hotel for the night and see it out there. Just as long as she doesn't think I'm trying to get into her pants. I couldn't handle all that right now. 'Look,' I ask, 'are you into getting a hotel room with me?' I glance behind then up and down the street to see if anyone looks suspicious. On the other side of the road there's a young guy with a thin moustache trying to hide behind a newspaper.

'I wouldn't mind,' she says, 'I could really do with a bath or a shower and a clean bed for a change.'

'I'll get one with two beds, don't worry.'

'I'm not worrying. Where's the best place to get one?'

Taksim appeals to me, being on the far side of a stretch of water – albeit connected by a bridge – because this side is Mustafa country. 'Let's get over the Galata Bridge. I know a few hotels over there, nice ones with clean rooms and no cockroaches.'

I hail a taxi and in we jump, crammed together with another five people and their shopping, but it's hard going and inside a couple of minutes claustrophobia mounts and the old lady sitting opposite begins to take on the form of a black chicken in the gloom. Her eyes become shiny orange and red beads and her nose and mouth combine to form a beak. She is staring at me. The worse thing is that I'm aware of everything going on around me but can't exit from the fear state – the dam has cracked and burst and now I can't control the flood of terror as it washes through my mind, ridiculing and destroying reason with crazy images.

Terry keeps looking at me – I'm very aware of her too – but so far she's not changed into anything odd. I try to remain calm but waves of panic override the attempt until, eventually, to explain my distress, I'm forced to invent a stomach ache. This has the effect of bringing on a real cramp, so by the time we reach Taksim I also have the problem yet again of retaining the churning contents of my bowels.

Three hotels, one after the other, refuse us admittance, but the fourth, the Adana, says it has a double room with a bathroom and lavatory on the same landing. Teeth gritted I pay the man $5 and up we go – Terry to the bedroom, me to the hole in the ground.

The room is small with sickening gloss pink walls and a single window looking out over a busy backstreet full of night strollers. I think of my old London flat which looked out onto Brewer Street, but the recollection only causes more fear as the memory brings home exactly where I am. Inside the room are two single beds – which suits me as sex is the farthest thing from my mind. All I want right now is oblivion in the form of a dead sleep to get me through the dark hours.

'I'm going for a shower,' says Terry.

'Okay, you go ahead.' Maybe I'll have one after, but then she'll think the intention is sexual, and anyway, for some reason the idea of getting wet is frightening. The thought comes to me that I may have contracted rabies somewhere.

She's back ten minutes later in jeans and T-shirt, looking shiny and damp-haired, but I'm still being ravaged by paranoia. Outside, I'm sure I saw someone looking up at the window, so I wedge a chair under the door knob.

'Why are you doing that?' she asks, pulling off her jeans. She's wearing nothing underneath and feels it necessary to explain: 'There were no towels, so I had to use my clothes to dry on. Why have you wedged the chair up against the door?'

'It's okay, I don't mind. Take the lot off. These door locks never work. You have to watch out for thieves.'

'Oh. Are you going to shower?'

'I don't know. I don't know . . .' I decide to come clean about my condition – it's no use trying to pretend any more as I think I might be about to die. Every few minutes my mind's being flooded with inexplicable feelings of hopelessness, infinity and darkness. It's as if something dreadful has happened, like I've finally gone too far and lost the protection of the gods. Nothing will ever be the same again – something has snapped. The drugs were the last straw. I tell her about Mustafa and Frankie and the experiences in Karachi. 'I thought the boat trip had sorted my head out,' I explain, 'but it's all come back again. I don't feel good.'

Terry strips and gets into bed. 'Come in here,' she says softly, and how can I say no?

All night I'm cradled in her arms like a child in the dark, waiting for the fear to pass. I daren't close my eyes for any longer than a few seconds at a time in case the blackness swallows my mind, but Terry clings on with motherly tenderness until dawn breaks when I feel brave enough to risk sleep.

'I've got to go and sort out this business with Mustafa. I can either meet you back here or at the Gulhane.' After waking up sometime after midday I'm back on form but feeling strangely empty, not unpleasantly, but short on emotion. Twelve hours of paranoia and chemical fire in my veins interspersed with bouts of diarrhoea has weakened everything except the need to find Frankie as quickly as possible and resolve the problem. The snag is, I still don't have a plan.

'Shall I still get the LSD? We could take it tonight.'

And she's still right in there, despite my not coming across with the goods last night. I couldn't make it. Even the thought of sex had frightened me and I'd turned my back on her when her hands had started wandering. 'After last night? You must be joking. My nerves need a break.'

Suddenly, out of the blue, comes the voice of inspiration, 'Water . . . equals pounds, shillings and pence. You must cross it first then give it to your enemy. In so doing you may find the key to a longer life.'

Pounds, shillings and pence equals LSD. Terry said it looks like water. And I've already crossed it getting from Pakistan to here. Or did he mean back across the Galata Bridge?

Brama is talking to me. I have to get the water, the LSD, from Terry's friends, then I'll spike Mustafa when the time is right. But first I have to get a tiny bottle with a dropper from a chemist.

I hurry back to the Gulhane in search of the Teuton and discover both him and little Karen out of their heads and screwing beneath their zipped-together sleeping bags. Preoccupied, he doesn't think twice about handing me his bottle of acid. 'One, maybe two drops is all you need for a 12-hour trip, so take care,' he adds, absent-mindedly.

Sitting on the perimeter wall of the roof with them out of view behind me I transfer a good measure of the clear liquid into my own bottle, enough for maybe 20 or 30 trips. When I hand it back, the Teuton – still shagging Karen who seems to have passed out – just grunts and hides it away without checking the level. Now I have to find Mustafa, on neutral ground, and the most likely place is the Pudding Shop.

Terry says she wants to come with me after I give her a vague outline of what I'm planning to do, adding that she'll be a good independent witness if Mustafa tries anything. This may be so, but I don't bother to explain the way things work over here – that nobody'll give a shit about witnesses anyway and the chances are she'll get pulled in too because she's a pretty face. Every other night in the Gulhane the police come in and take someone pretty away, female or male, for questioning, so I've no illusions about fair play here.

When I see Mustafa in a bright blue man-made fibre suit sitting with a couple of others at a table at the far end of the café, I leave Terry waiting outside at a table and stroll in to confront him. 'Mustafa, long time no see. Have you got a minute? Talk private?'

He gets up and faces me. 'Good. You come. Okay, we talk. Where you want to go?' He says something to his mates who eye me sullenly, trying to work out whether the Pakistani clothes are some new western fashion that they'll have to try to keep pace with.

'Outside'll do.'

We walk together back past the counter and I guide him to the table where Terry sits digging into a chocolate pudding.

He eyes her up and down, and I can see his mind calculating how much he could make on her, one way or another. He looks back at me. 'You say private talk.'

'Yeh, private. Us three.'

'Okay.' He sits down. 'You want coffee? Tea? Gazus? Cola?'

'Coffee. Two coffees.'

He shouts the order to the waiter and we sit discussing the weather and the sights until the coffee arrives.

'You have my money?' he begins.

'You have my money and my friend?'

'Money, money,' he laughs. 'Of course your friend is very happy – he like Istanbul too much.'

We sit silently sipping at our coffee as a little gang of noisy student backpackers leaves.

'Listen Mustafa, this is the deal: you bring Frankie here for me to see first, then we have deal. No see Frankie, no business.'

'My friend, I make the business here. If you not trust the word of Mustafa then you lose. Not my problem. Already I have money back if I want. Police always like me if I give them drug dealer. Frankie drug dealer, you drug dealer, so you do as you wish – pay me or you and your friend go to prison. There not good. You choose.'

'I can't deal with you unless I see Frankie first, please yourself. Come on Terry.' I go to stand up.

'Wait, wait,' says Mustafa all smiles, 'if you want to see your friend, I show.'

'Here.'

'No. You come with me.'

'Then you capture me and you've got two for your police friends? No way. I must see him in a public place. Why not here now?'

It took him some time, about five seconds, to work out what 'capture' meant. 'Capture . . . good . . . if I bring him here now, how I not know you try to escape him?'

At least I now know that Frankie's being held somewhere not too far away. 'Look,' I say, 'can you think of a better idea?'

'Of course. Only way. Tonight you come to Alanya Café. You see friend.'

The Alanya Café was a drinking dive close to the Galata Bridge in the dodgiest quarter of the old town.

'How do I know he'll be there?'

'Trust me, trust me.'

'But I don't.'

'You have no choice. Now I go. You come tonight at nine.' He stands up and goes back inside. It's a quarter to five.

'Karen said she'd heard it was good if you use LSD in bed,' says Terry suddenly.

246

'Eh?' Here's me trying to work out how to solve this Frankie problem, and she's thinking about sex.

'Apparently . . .' she giggles, 'if the bloke puts it on his willy, it's supposed to be pretty amazing.'

'I tell you what, if I get Frankie out of there tonight, I'll let you put it on.'

From the outside, the Alanya Café is nothing more than a doorway in a dark narrow street, but inside, once past the bolted door and down a dozen steps, it opens out into a large bar packed with tables around which men sit smoking large water-pipes and drinking alcohol. As if expected, I'm shown to a table in an alcove on the far side of the room at which sit Mustafa and two other men. All smiles, you'd have thought they were welcoming a lost brother.

'Mister Tommy, you come, good. Very clever you come alone.'

I explain that Terry has to go and meet friends at the airport, friends of the British Consul. Maybe she will come later, I add.

The three Turks mutter together.

'I'm sorry but in here woman is "verboten",' says Mustafa.

'Well, never mind. She'll probably wait outside in a cab or something.' In fact she's waiting for my return back at the hotel we stayed in last night, but I need to make Mustafa feel uncertain, that I have back-up. 'Anyway, where's Frankie?' I ask.

'Ah, your friend. Let us have a drink.' He signals to a waiter who weaves his way through the tables disturbing the almost stationary tobacco smoke which hangs in the air and orders four beers with raki chasers. 'You like raki?' he asks.

'Sure. I drink very good raki in Greece.'

'Turkey raki good,' he smiles. 'Greece raki no good. You see. You try.'

Small glasses of raki are promptly delivered and we each down them in one as is the custom. Then a shirt-sleeved arm delivers a beer from behind and as I look up I come face to face with Frankie. He has that shifty look I recognise, the one he wears when he's in a tight corner.

'Beer for his lordship. I thought I told you to stay clear. What's the matter with you?'

Mustafa's all ears, but he can't understand.

I stand up and clasp his hand like an old friend. 'Good to see you, old son – spike 'em all with this extremely strong acid – how've you been keeping? Well, I hope.' And I press the little bottle into his palm.

'Yeh, cool.' He looks at Mustafa. 'My friend dogbreath here's being his usual old self, you know, friendly, helpful, good man, nice person to do business with.'

Mustafa nods and smiles benevolently.

'Anyway, I'd better get on. I'll see you later.' He walks away with the little bottle secreted in his hand.

Mustafa looks hard at me. 'You see, he work now, pay back, maybe finish in two three years, unless you bring girl or pay.'

'Before we start, where's the money for the stuff your mates nicked from me in Munich?'

He doesn't understand.

'Munich? One kilo? Where is it?'

'Hashish verboten.'

I swallow my beer. 'Alright – you owe me one kilo at Munich prices. Take that from Frankie's debt.

He leans forward over the table. 'One kilo only interest. You pay rest or big problem.'

I catch Frankie's eye and order another round of raki. Turning back to Mustafa I ask him to give me some idea how much he expects to be paid.

'That girl make a thousand dollars a week. Now she finish. Say she good for five years . . .'

'Hold on, hold on, that's . . . over a quarter of a million dollars reckoning it that way – there's no way I'm going to be able to pay that sort of money back, and you know it. What exactly do you want from us? I didn't steal her anyway – she escaped.'

Frankie arrives with four glasses of raki, placing one in front of each of us. Giving me a short deadpan stare which translates as 'job done' he walks back to the kitchen.

'Listen,' I say, 'we can make good business. I have plenty of money. We stay friends. Cheers.' And I hold out my glass to toast good relations and down it in one. Of course, they follow suit, and quickly I order a round of beer from another waiter to make sure Frankie's not the only one to have served us.

Twenty minutes to go. At about nine-thirty we'll see just how good this acid is, and I hope Frankie's got a good exit route because I can't see how we're going to get past the doorman – he must be over six feet tall and weigh a hundred kilos. Then I see Frankie pass him a bottle of beer.

Looking about, I make a quick mental note that some of the tables are older with turned wooden legs which usually pull off easily enough when needed. But I have to accept they won't be a match for guns if there are any about. Confusion and flight has to be the answer. Quickly and neatly. No bloodshed. Love and Peace, man. Ha, ha. Getting nervous now. Half the problem is that I've never taken acid, so I can't judge how it might affect someone else or how I can manipulate the effects to my advantage. Give me speed or cannabis and I'm your man, but I don't think I'd be spiking these nutcases with speed. And cannabis, well, the Turks know all about the stuff – they'd either realise they'd been spiked or not even notice the effect it was having on them.

'So, Mister Tommy, how you say we become friends? How you pay me?'

Having learnt that a bit of confusion and madness in the conversation can help destabilise someone on drugs, I say, 'I fuck your ring once or twice before Christmas in the snake-pit, and you get to kiss the donkey's foreskin,' very quickly with a cockney accent and a pleasant smile. This way he only gets to pick out some of the bits he understands. And if need be I can deny his interpretation and rephrase it differently with an exasperated look on my face.

Mustafa puts on a knowing smile – it wouldn't do for his mates to realise he hasn't a clue what I'm talking about – and says, 'Sure, we work it out okay.'

'And next time the crocodile whore fuck your sister's only brother, I say we must insert large snakes into Bobby Charlton's left nostril. A lot of money spiders. Beatles too.'

'Bobby Charlton good,' says Mustafa's nearest henchman.

'Beatles okay,' says his friend.

'You know in England, beetles are insects? Creepy crawly things that bite and sting and sometimes eat your heart out motherfucker says Redman my American friend.'

For a while we sit silently, listening to a recording of an ancient Turkish love song being sung by a male with an extremely deep voice. I think they've put the record player on one notch too slow, and everything in the bar seems to be slowing down.

Mustafa's sweating now. He's glancing nervously around the room, and his eyes are getting larger and larger. The guy next to him is also looking weird, but his eyes are getting smaller instead, and darker, more glittery like . . . I seem to have this beady chicken eye thing . . . strangely, his head of black hair has turned bright cobalt blue, or could it be reflected light from one of the coloured bulbs over by the bar?.

And Mustafa's head seems to be swelling under the strain, becoming purple. His hands are clawing like vulture's talons at the table edge as the magic water begins to take effect.

'Hey, Mustafa, look at those walls behind you, they're running with blood!'

He spins around horrified and stares at the walls.

I stand up and look more closely – they *are* running with blood. Fuck! Someone must be getting slaughtered upstairs. Maybe there's an abattoir above and they've just slaughtered a sheep, cut its throat, and the floor's leaking.

And behind me I hear a slow deep rumbling chuckle getting louder and louder – the doorman's finding something very amusing with one of the carpets on the floor. He seems to be following the pattern, giggling to himself like a young boy as he stares down, touching the curves delicately with the tip of his down-at-heel size 12 chaussures. Suddenly the third man at our table, a little guy with a shaven head, leaps up and rushes for the door but collides with the doorman who seizes him by the throat and begins strangling him. The guy next to Mustafa laughs aloud, but then can't stop and Mustafa is so phased by it all that his fingers bite deep into the table top causing the tips to burst under the pressure and spurt red onto the formica. Frankie comes back out with a big grin on his lizard face. He walks over to our table just as the room begins to pulsate slowly in time with the love song.

Something is very odd with him: his voice is out of sync, echoing and ringing in my ears. and the irises of his eyes have become luminous green.

250

'You're jealous, man – your eyes have gone bright green,' my mouth says of its own accord.

In front of the bar one of the waiters falls to his knees sobbing and wailing, and begins scrubbing the floor furiously with a towel until a hole appears.

'Where does that lead? Maybe we could get out there.'

Frankie looks hard at me. 'What's it like?'

'What's what like?'

'The acid. I had to put some in all the glasses in case Rigid Man there wanted to swap them about.'

Mustafa is rooted, immobile, to the spot, his mouth wide open in disbelief. Number two is still screaming with laughter. A roaring sound, the sound of low-flying jets, fills the air as the giant doorman lurches about the room clutching Mustafa's friend by the throat, eating his face like it was a cheeseburger with ketchup. A lip complete with moustache comes away and drops to the floor, but before anyone can put their foot on the thing it slips away beneath the tables.

'Mustafa! Mustafa! Your friend's moustache has escaped. If I catch it can we call it all square? It's a good moustache,' I scream.

He looks into my eyes with horror and begins babbling, then slowly shifts his body from the chair and crouches down in the corner against the wall.

'You'll get blood all over your coat hiding down there.'

'Please, please . . .' he whispers.

Frankie the sorcerer leans over him. 'Listen you turd, from now on you do exactly as I say, otherwise I destroy your mind . . .'

'Please, please . . .'

'You owe me. Tomorrow, when this spell wears off you go home to mummy and be good. Or else.' Frankie seems to have grown upwards until he almost touches the ceiling and is staring down at me like Rasputin. 'You coming Tommy, or what?'

But echoing voices and laughter are now trapped inside my skull and are making my eardrums vibrate almost unbearably. And overawed by Frankie's height, I'm creeping away bent double alongside him. Beneath my feet the carpets are three-dimensional and I have to balance along the top of the multi-coloured maze very carefully to avoid stumbling and falling into the abyss.

'Come on!' booms Frankie. 'You look like fucking Rumpelstiltskin.'

Outside, soft darkness caresses the skin and golden light falling from tiny shop windows bursts into rainbow clusters over the cobbles. High above, the deep blue night is flashing in starry waves which sweep across the sky from the black domed skyline and suddenly I become aware of overwhelming love which pulsates from the earth, up through the body and into my chest. The sensation is fantastic and tears begin to run from my eyes, burning tracks down my cheeks, turning to icicles on my chin and falling off to shatter tinkling onto the warm granite.

There seems to be no beginning or end to anything: the ground on which I stand, the buildings, the sky, the people, the colours, smells and sounds are all one, inextricably linked by energy, by a mind, an intelligence which makes everything what it is, and I see nothing but perfection. Everything is glowing, not reflecting light from other separate sources, but glowing from within, inhabited by a life force of its own which passes from one body of matter to another. This is Brama's world.

'You all right?' asks Frankie, and his voice carries light – the sound glows. As he moves he merges in and out of his surroundings receiving and giving energy, changing colour like a chameleon. Around us, night strollers project vivid energy from their eyes as they merge, disappear and rematerialise and I feel my body pulsating, disintegrating and reforming as I pass through this incredible channel in the universe. Now I'm in a restaurant, now in a tiny shop full of scintillating but transparent brassware among which human spirits dwell. Now inside a dazzling and voluptuous humming time machine and outside the world becomes bigger and smaller and faster and slower, stretching into infinity in all directions. The breath of God is upon me.

'Put your head in you prick!' sings Frankie behind me as he reappears. The freezing tears on my cheeks are horizontal now, flying like diamonds into the past . . .

'Seeds of ecstasy paving the way along the wheel of life.'

'What's up with you?' he laughs.

And back out into the stars, through a blinding portal of light and spirits staring, up, up, up, and out into space, stars above and stars below. Love and peace, man, and an eternity of exploding galaxies and nebulae and breathtaking, unbelievably dazzling beauty, and infinity is mine . . .

'Take it easy, man, it's a long way down.'

'God is love. Where there's love there's no illusion. Believe me. I know.'

But slowly I am solidifying, coming back, thinking again, being someone, and suddenly I'm aware that I'm standing on the parapet of the Gulhane roof being watched by dozens of stoned freaks. Frankie is sitting among them smoking a nargile.

I float back to him.

'You back with us yet? Or are you still flying?'

'Nice one, man,' my mouth says. Then I remember Terry waiting for me back at the Adana Hotel. 'Have you got the bottle?'

'Here.' He passes it to me. Empty. Or maybe just about enough for a trip. 'You've been standing on that wall for two hours.' His voice is metallic now, and I can feel myself coming up again. Everyone's glowing, looking beautiful, especially the girls who have electric hair. One of them gestures to me to sit down, to join her and her friends smoking hashish. And suddenly I'm there, the universe is in my mouth, crackling with insolence.

'Hello, I'm Jane, this is Philadelphia, this is Martine, Georges, Antioch and Babylon, Paulio and Leonardio da Vincio. We are all flowery powery and Love and Peacio. After you smoke this you can fuck all of us one at a time, in a golden chain of orifices and narrow misters and misses, one after the other or not as you feel inclined because we are Children of the Earth and we don't care.'

'Basically I need love satisfaction, yeh, ejaculation and sublime stickiness lubricate the ovaries with potency and dream babies for future coolness of the progeny and . . . well . . . am I casting swine before pearls, or are these the devils of mankind to be evicted from the coffers of the Church?'

'Jesus was cool, man.'

'Jesus was very hot, hotter than a Madras whore's arsehole, ah ha ah ha ah ha ah ha ah ha . . .'

Something is trying to clamp the back of my head, like one half of a vice. Slowly I turn to look at Jane and Philadelphia and Martine and Georges and Antioch and Babylon and Paulio and Leonardio da Vincio and note with incredulity that they are all defying gravity and are stuck firmly to the wall by their arses, their heads pointing horizontally to the stars. I too am stuck to the wall by my back by some incredible magnetism and cannot tear myself away.

'Jesus, this is powerful,' I gasp. The only way is to roll, over and over and over until I come to a door in the wall, beyond which is a strange staircase leading sideways instead of going up and down. But as I squeeze through this door the magnetism sucks me in with such force that I'm slammed up against the far wall beyond the last step and knocked breathless. I have to find the generator and turn it off, stop the magnetism, otherwise we're all trapped.

Frankie comes jumping along the sideways stairs and stands horizontally on the wall to which I'm pinned. I gaze out over him. 'How the fuck do you do that?'

'Do what?'

'Stick to this wall by your feet.'

He's laughing. 'Are you all right? I think you're cracking up.'

'I'm fine.'

'Well, try and stay that way because we've got to get out of here at first light.'

'None of us have any choice unless we can find the generator and switch it off.'

'What generator?'

'The electro-magnetic generator. Can't you feel it?' But I'm coming back again, and sit up and look about. The world is upright again. Frankie's straightness has brought me down, dragged my head back to the Gulhane. He still looks very strange under the neon light but I can handle it. 'How d'you plan on getting out then?' I croak through a desert-dry throat.

'I don't know about you but I'm flying out. I had the fare from the till last night.'

Nice one, Frankie – talk about look after number one. 'What about me? Didn't you take enough to cover two tickets?'

'There wasn't that much in there. Mahmud clears it out every hour or so. Anyway, two of us'd draw too much attention, especially with you looking like Ali Baba.'

'Well, fuck you. I come all the way back here to get you out and you do this. Nice one.'

'I told you not to come back. I had it all sussed.'

'I can't believe you.'

'Well, maybe you should have thought about it before having it away to Germany with that little scrubber. That's when all the problems started, when you decided to be Mister Knight in Shining fucking Armour. All you wanted was to shag her anyway. I know where your head's at, Spitz.'

'Being at the feet of the Master's done you a lot of good then – Jai sat chit ananda. Where's the brotherly love?'

'As it happens it did. It made me realise what a bunch of tossers they all are. This is it sunshine. Make the best of it and look after numero uno, because no one else is going to do it for you. So get your head together and get out of here before Mustafa realises what's happened.' He walks away, leaving me in a sea of confusion, wondering what to do next, wishing the acid would wear off.

I sit there for a while feeling it wash in and out of my brain, but the main thrust has lost its potency and now I'm slowly but surely coming down just as the sun comes up and light begins to creep through the windows and the trap door to the roof through which I've fallen. I get up off the floor and make my way, aching all over, to the Adana Hotel.

When I get there Terry's just up, showered and damp. 'You all right?' she asks.

'Sort of.' Coming down from acid's a bit like coming down from speed – grey and depressing. Depressing in a big way if you start thinking too much. 'I got Frankie out, and he's probably on a plane right now, and I've got to get out too, because we've stirred up a hornets' nest. The longer I hang about the more chance there is of me getting captured, and I don't fancy that very much right now.'

'So what are you going to do?'

'Well, leave . . .'

Terry's brain ticks over. 'Did you see Karen?'

'I was out of it.'

'I expect she's still with that bloke. Where are you going?'

'I don't know. I can't get my head around it at the moment.'

I'm feeling increasingly unsettled, and deep inside the fear's rumbling about again. I hope it doesn't surface.

'I'll come with you. I've got money.'

The money would be useful, though I've got enough of my own to see me back home if I'm careful, but if I'm honest, I just don't fancy Terry. I mean, I wouldn't mind a one-off if I was in a better frame of mind, but that's as far as it goes. And she's so sweet I don't want to bring her down by being honest. Anyway, she's only using me while her friend's off elsewhere. 'It's too dodgy. If they find you with me you'll probably get dragged in too. It's bad enough as it is. I mean, you've already been seen with me so if I were you I'd get out quick, take off out of Istanbul. Go and grab your mate Karen by the scruff of the neck and take her off to Greece – there's plenty of Germans there.'

'She won't come until she's good and ready. But if you and I went together, well, I'd feel a lot safer. Karen'll be all right.'

'No. It's not worth the risk. I like you too much. We're going to have to split, maybe meet up somewhere else.'

She gets the message. 'Okay. I'll go back and speak to Karen. Can I meet you somewhere later today?'

'I don't know. It depends on what happens. I might just leave as soon as you're gone.'

'Okay. I'll be at the Gulhane until tomorrow morning,' she says, shaking her hair. She puts on her shoes and departs.

Now I'm alone again. And very strung out.

Shit! My bag's at the Gulhane. What was I thinking of? Somebody's bound to have nicked it, or at least the money.

So it's a doom-laden walk back, and sure enough when I get there the money's gone. Passport still there but money gone.

And Terry's diverted her attention to some French freak. 'Tommy . . . I thought you were going . . . me and Jean-Yves are thinking about going down to Antalya together.'

So I've blown it. Never look a gift horse in the mouth as they say.

On the way back I get a real big scary whoosh of terror from my guts which brings me out in an icy sweat. And I'm still flashing back on the trip. Brinking on panic again, I'm so wrapped up in myself that I almost lose my way, shoving people aside as I try to find somewhere recognisable. Karachi all over again, but unstoned.

There seems to be a devil in my brain which keeps telling me I've done some irreparable damage which is causing these malfunctions. Worse is the realisation of just how close insanity is . . . a split second and I don't recognise anything. I don't know my name or where I come from and I have to look at my passport photograph for reassurance, and when that fails to work I start to hear a sound like a jet airliner carrying a cargo of pure panic round and round inside my head, and I run.

And run.

Out of Istanbul and on to the road to Tekirdag and the Greek border.

A lorry stops and picks me up, and the driver's face is almost too grotesque to look at, but I manage to cope and by nightfall I'm in a little town of dark shadows and vicious dogs. Almost instantly another lorry stops and takes me to a town just a few miles from Greece. A local motorist takes pity and offers me a lift to the border. I'm overcome by the kindness but all the while still fighting to keep myself together. The fear is gushing in and out now and I feel exhausted by the effort required to stay sane and I'm on the verge of giving up but I want to be somewhere I feel safe before I let go, somewhere no one's going to call the police or lock me up. It seems an age ago now that I craved this and went to a lonely beach to find it, and thought I had found it, but now I know I found nothing but my own emptiness. Never look for the truth in case you find it. I curse my stupidity, my foolhardiness, and wish to God I was normal again, unravaged by this purity of vision which keeps freaking me out. I have no choice but to go on now and live or collapse into madness.

And the fear leaves me again . . .

The Turkish border is cool. Two guards just watch as I walk past. One hisses 'Hashish – you got hashish?' And they both laugh.

Look at me. Crossing the border at midnight, on foot, dressed like this, carrying a small shoulder bag, wild-eyed and paranoid. No wonder they can tell. It's just as well I'm getting out now, before my time runs out. Like Afghanistan. Om om om . . . no. Stop! All that stuff's too scary – it just pushes me to the brink again.

A weird floodlit bridge carpetted with squashed frogs and large beetles. The others are croaking, whistling, honking, whirring and bleeping in their thousands down below in the darkness beneath the bridge. In the distance glows the Greek border post.

'You got drugs?'

'No, of course not.'

'Why "of course not"? You been in Turkey . . .'

'That's why. Anyway, drugs no good.' Big smile, but the fear's coming on again. Hope they don't keep me too long.

The officer in charge then has a feel around my crutch. 'Okay, you good boy Johnny. You go.' And I walk out into the Greek night air.

EIGHT

'And from there?'

I'm talking to an Indian consultant in St Pancras Hospital, having been referred there by my own doctor. 'I hitched home in three days.'

'But surely that's over 2,000 miles?'

'Non-stop. One lift after another.'

'Without any money.'

'People were amazing – they fed me.'

'How about the English Channel? How did you get across without any money?'

'By asking around the lorries – they go over as a unit.'

'I see. And you had these feelings of terror all the way back?'

'On and off.'

'Describe them again to me.'

'As I say, they start without warning or cause – at least, I can't see anything obvious that triggers them – coming up from here' I indicate my upper stomach area, 'and sort of spreading into my mind. That's when it gets worse.' I don't want to mention panic because I've been brought up to believe that panic is something to which only miserable weaklings succumb.

'And it makes you panic?'

'Not panic really, but frightened, yeh . . .'

'Hm hm . . .'

'I break out in a cold sweat. And need to get to a lavatory fast.'

'Whereupon you pass watery foul-smelling faeces.'

'Yes.'

'Were you taking drugs before all this started?'

'I started taking drugs – amphetamines – when I was about 16 or 17.'

'But you didn't smoke hashish until last year, when you first went to Istanbul.'

'A bit of weed when I was about seventeen, but only once or twice and it never worked.'

'And you smoked it excessively from then on. After Istanbul.'

'I suppose so. But it didn't seem a problem until Karachi. That's when I had the first memory slip – you know, when I lose my identity, when I forget who I am or where I am.'

'And you are still getting them?'

'I can feel them coming on. It's weird. It's almost as if I can deliberately trigger them just by thinking about it. That's when the panic sets in. The fear, I mean.' Even thinking about it is causing a ripple inside right now, and I couldn't be in a safer place.

'How do you feel now?'

'Not too bad. A bit shaky.'

He writes something in a notebook, sits back in his chair and takes a long look at me. 'I'll try to put this into layman's terms. You are suffering from a psychosis caused by a combination of factors: one – drug abuse; two – an unbalanced diet; three – travel shock; four – excessive fatigue build-up; and five, well, how does one put this – you have perhaps been a bit too careless in your quest for self-discovery. It is not something one should take light-heartedly. Nowadays it is fashionable to speak of such things, but few are those who discover anything beyond their own weakness. Which is a start I suppose.' He smiles. 'And of course you have Giardia, a debilitating affliction which we will clear up for you. You'll have to stay in for a week.'

Giardia: a tiny worm in the gut.

'How long will it take to get over the . . . psychosis, you call it?'

He toys with his pen for a few seconds. 'I think if we are positive and regard it as personal development rather than psychosis, and eat well, build yourself up again – you say you were very fit once – I think it will be sooner rather than later. You are young and strong and have everything on your side.'

Nice words, but I don't know if I can cope. One minute I'm feeling fine and taking girls out, showing off about my exploits, the next I've switched over into a moody paranoid bastard. I've been back three weeks now, living at home with my mother and father, but it's getting them down too and I think I might have to get a flat somewhere so that I don't have to worry about them as well. Somehow or other I have to get to the bottom of all this. I need to find answers to all the Brama stuff which is plaguing my mind. Or maybe I don't. He said there weren't any answers, but how can I let all this mind-blowing stuff just sit around unresolved in my head? Somewhere there must be a key to it all.

'This guru I told you about, the one I came across in Karachi, is there any way . . . do you know anyone who . . . thinks like this? I mean, I need to talk to someone who can help me sort it out in my head.' It's difficult getting across to a straight person, especially a doctor, exactly what I mean. 'Something's happened to me that I can't explain. Before I went away I was full of confidence, arrogance even; now I'm not sure about anything. I mean, people don't worry me – it's life itself. It's so big, but it seems to amount to nothing.'

'You told me you went travelling abroad to "find yourself". I think perhaps that you have found a little more than you can at present cope with. The man Jesus said, and please forgive me for using his phrase, that often the passing of wisdom is like "casting pearls before swine". He meant to say that we are often blind to reality when it is handed to us on a plate. We do not have the necessary background to comprehend.'

He's trying to say I'm ignorant.

And Brama used those words.

He continues: 'Worse, we even misconstrue the wisdom which is being passed on, often to the detriment of ourselves or others.

Misunderstood information can be far more dangerous than a foreign language of which we cannot understand one word. As a doctor I am only too aware of this. For example, how would it be if us doctors went around telling our patients that the most lethal disease known to man is influenza? There would be a terrible panic every winter. Instead, we say, "Don't worry, it's only flu", and they go away happy. In your case you have wrenched open the Book of Wisdom, forced it open somewhere in the middle, and have misconstrued what you have read.'

Exactly. So how do I undo – or defuse – this information that's now lodged firmly in my brain? This exhausting energy that keeps kicking in when I'm at low ebb.

'I think time will sort it out,' he adds.

Or I could start at the beginning of the book.

But finding the beginning's the problem. At least I'll have seven days of being waited-on hand and foot to think about it. 'I think you're right, doctor. Thanks for sparing me the time.' He nods and smiles benignly and I leave.

I'm in a ward with just one other person, although there are six beds, and I feel safe. My companion is here after being caught up in the war in Biafra when a riverboat became stranded in the middle of the West African jungle for six weeks while the locals butchered each other. Apart from going mad, he's contracted something called Bilharzia and pisses blood faster than his body can manufacture it. So I'm in good company.

After the blood-collecting nurse has done her thing – jabbed a needle painfully into our finger tips and smeared the results onto slides – we joke about the agony of the pricks for a bit, usually with her, drink tea or orange squash, then read or slide into silent contemplation. This is when I attempt to get to grips with my head, during daylight hours when life is going on all around.

Third day. Comfortable and secure, surrounded by nurses and doctors. I'm going to put myself into that state of memory-slip to see if I can operate within it without the fear, just like I did once for ten minutes, 8,000 miles away in Karachi. Okay, here goes, just go for it, straight in.

Fear rushes in from the stomach, the central nervous system. It seems to have been triggered by a message from the brain, an automatic alarm system which goes off just before its own shut-down, and I want to open my eyes, get up, make a noise, charge around, do *anything* that will kick-start it back into motion. For an instant the surge of terror is almost uncontrollable, but I hang on, trying to control this reaction because I know I'm safe, despite frightening suggestions from the brain that I might stay in the memory slip state for ever and be lost in the darkness of insanity.

But suddenly I'm there again. Easy. Now there's no fear. The brain is at minimum tickover, keeping the body alive and alert.

And I don't know who I am.

The odd thing is, I know I'm in hospital. I also know that I know the guy sleeping in the next bed and that I understand things around me.

I know that I know.

It's not at all like everything's completely unfamiliar – it's just that I've lost my identity, the image I've unconsciously built since being born, the image that shapes and colours everything I think and do. I am aware of this. Is this what Brama meant when he said I would lose my mind?

And I've been resisting this moment all my life.

A beautiful, wonderful female comes in, a nurse, a smiling nurse. 'Hello, Tommy,' she says, 'how are you today?'

'Tommy, is that my name?' I whisper. Speaking is difficult, difficult but possible.

She looks suddenly slightly concerned but tries to hide it. 'Yes. Tommy. Tommy Spitz. And I've come to take your blood pressure.' She is radiating light, without doubt an angel.

'You're an angel, did you know that?'

'Oh, I know. Everyone says that. Now sit up please.'

'Really you are, and I love you.'

'Don't be silly.' She straps on the pressure tester and starts pumping as we stare at each other, her beautiful eyes gazing into mine as the golden glow about her pulsates slowly . . .

Those lips, now slightly apart, and I want to kiss them, touch tongues . . .

I want to shag her.

And I'm back. The brain's working again. Tommy Spitz is back and my angel has fled. Instead nurse Owen is sitting there, as plain as ever, the dream over.

'Are you feeling all right?' she asks.

* * *

The pub's packed, just what I didn't want. I've been out of hospital for over a week now and thought it about time I went out to face up to what I'd left behind. Eighteen months have passed since I last saw any of the boys and I'm wondering what sort of welcome I'm going to get. If I'm honest, I don't really know why I'm doing this, but the urge was there and here I am.

Granger, the tall ugly one with the knock-out punch is there as usual, pouring pints of beer down his throat in time with his equally ugly brother, Bobby. None of the others are there yet, the time being not long after six. As I walk in Granger sees me – as does everyone else in the bar, this being a back-street local.

'Tommy! I heard you was back. D'you want a drink?'

I look about and everyone else looks away, gets on with their drinking.

'Cheers.' Even the choice of drink is difficult because it's been so long now, and I don't know what effect it's going to have on me, so I go back to square one. 'I'll have a light and bitter.'

Bobby looks me up and down. 'So where you been all this time?'

Behind me Granger's ordering the drink.

'All over Europe and the Middle East. As far as India. Well, Pakistan. Cheers.' I take the light and bitter from Granger and swallow a mouthful. Weird.

'Pakistan?' sneers Bobby. 'What d'you want to go there for?'

I shrug, not knowing quite what to say, but feel confident. My mind switches back to the big-bearded guy in Karachi who sorted out the post office counter clerk. He'd eat these two for breakfast. So could I come to that. And the Afghanis . . . 'Don't know really . . . just sort of ended up there.'

'How can you end up in Pakistan?' He roars with laughter. 'You'll

263

be telling me you've been shagging Pakis next, you dirty bastard.'

I used to hang out with these people, and I know he's only joking but I'm not in the mood. 'No Bobby, I won't be telling you anything because you're a tosser.'

As expected, Granger sides with me against his brother. 'Yeh, leave it out Bob, what's the matter with you? We ain't seen the bloke for nearly two years and you're already having a go at him.'

'I'm not having a go at him.'

I'm being relegated to third party here – they're waiting for a show of weakness from me so that they can reform as a unit of force. Until then they're ambivalent. So what's new? I could be in any dodgy little backstreet dive anywhere in the world. The only difference is that here I can't play the foreigner. And Love and Peace? I don't know, it might work. But tell the truth, I don't feel very loving right now. I'm all for peace, but these two are already on a war footing and I've only been here six minutes.

Granger's clothes haven't changed much either: still dressed in Mod Tonik and sporting a cheap striped Terylene tie – he looks like a reject from some dated East End movie.

My mind flashes back to the last meeting we had in this very same pub – nothing's changed but me. And life here is very disturbing. The guy at the end of the bar is a small time bookie, but everyone looks up to him because he's 'shrewd' – despite systematically ripping them off – and here he stands lording it, taking free whiskies from his victims. Behind him is old Bert, a vacuous prick living in the past, revered as a 'diamond geezer' for being able to sing a few boring London songs and recall tales of misery and cockney stoicism in the face of adversity. At the next table sit John and Maurice, affectionately Jonjo and Mo, a couple of small-time thieves looked up to because they shout the odd drink on the house when they've pulled-off a job. And just inside the door stands Jimmy the One who survives on the reputation of having *almost* killed someone with a single blow. Then there's Smithy, the court jester, who makes people laugh with his sharp observation and piss-taking – a two-faced sneak with an aptitude for causing trouble.

Do I really want to know these people?

'D'you know what it is?' asks Bobby suddenly, examining his glass of beer.

'About two thirds of a pint of light and bitter?'

He ignores this. 'No. It's you. You've gone away and come back all la-di-da. You used to have a lovely cockney accent, but now you've come back speaking all above your station.'

'Above it.'

'Yeh.' He's getting a bit lairy now. I recognise the symptoms: his eyes have narrowed, his head's come down defensively into his right shoulder, and the pitch of his voice has risen an octave.

With Bobby, at times like this, you attack or retreat. But I can't make up my mind. The thing is, I really don't care. 'Now what, then?' I say.

But I'm astonished at the reaction – Bobby and his brother back down unreservedly. They even look scared.

'We didn't mean no offence, Tommy,' says Bobby, 'Drink up. What you going to have?'

But I decline and leave.

Now the word's gone around that I'm back with a screw loose and everyone I meet on the street's humouring me, looking at me with that quizzical scared expression that says, 'You don't mind if I stand back a few paces do you?'

Well, to be quite honest, man, I don't. In fact there's no need to worry any more because my head's moved on. You're not part of my life any more.

I'm going to move to another, nicer part of London – Blackheath, Bayswater or Pimlico, somewhere like that – where the residents don't mind too much if you're a bit weird, although I suppose I should really stop wearing these clothes I had made in Karachi, it's getting far too cold as winter creeps in.

I hate this country.

My new local, the Three Tuns, is a good place to be, always packed with beautiful people, painters and poets, musicians, rich drunkards, poor drunkards, wits and hippies, girls with long eyelashes, pouty lips and feather boas. Everyone's spoilt for choice. There's no need to snake in on someone and mesmerise them, because everyone shags. It's just a question of who, where and when, and it's cool to be unfussed about it. Last night Annie, the night before Judith. Two nights before that the fabled Nicola, but I came the moment our mouths met when I realised she really meant it. The unobtainable Nicola, lusted after by everyone, and I blew it. And I bumped into Sandy again, an old girlfriend I'd always been too blocked or awkward or just too young and inexperienced to cope with, and we finally did it – and keep doing it whenever we meet, like we're making up for lost time. I've a picture in my mind of her sitting astride me, little breasts bobbing up and down, her cheeks flushed, looking down, saying breathlessly, 'I'm different now, you know. I'm into PR.'

'Yeh? What's PR?'

And at last I feel that I'm being welcomed back.

Welcomed back by strangers.

Then one day I'm sitting at a side table in the Tuns with Sandy, and Frankie walks through the door with a groovy chick on his heels.

'Frankie!' I shout, despite my reservations about Istanbul. It's just good to see an old mate again, someone you've been through the mill with, someone who knows the way you tick. And he looks good, fits in with the scene with his long hair and Afghan coat, his silk scarf and red satin pants. He spots me and pushes his way through the crowd clustered around the bar, followed by the chick.

'Tommy!' He's as cool as ever. 'I heard you were hanging out up here. You getting them in then? Oh, this is Angela.'

'Hello, Angela. Very nice too. This is Sandy.' Angela's tall and beautiful, a model if ever I saw one. But far too classy for Frankie.

'Hi, it's a pleasure.' she says in an accent that's definitely not common or garden, and I wonder where Frankie's found her.

They grab two seats and Frankie buys a round. Angela likes Campari and soda.

And for a while we drink and talk about ourselves and each other and John and Yoko's arrest and *Hair!* and the Vietnam war demonstrations and Nixon being elected, and eventually it gets round to what we're doing for money. Sandy talks about public relations and her boss for a while – I know he's shagging her by the way she talks about him, but it doesn't matter because we're just good friends – and Angie tells us she's a photographic model: apparently she's in the current issue of *Harper's Bazaar*.

'Anyway, the point is,' says Frankie, 'what are you up to right now?'

'Writing articles for magazines,' I answer, a bit too slowly. The fact is I'm on the dole, and sharing Sandy's bed-sit, because selling articles to magazines is nowhere near as easy as I'd dreamed.

'Are you making enough at it?'

''Course not,' says Angela, 'don't be silly. No one ever does, freelance.'

Feeling the inferiority coming on I quickly point out that I only do it part-time, as a gap-filler until something else comes along, meanwhile I'm researching Eastern philosophy in every spare moment I can find.

'You're not still into that, are you?' laughs Frankie. 'You should have met Guru Maharaj-ji. He'd have put you off for life. Listen, apart from all that bollocks, d'you want a job?'

Here we go again. Another one of Frankie's scams coming up. 'Like what?'

'Do you want a job or not?'

'Well, yeh.'

'Right, I've got this contract shifting and storing stage props. All it needs is a bit of muscle, a driving licence, and half an ounce of common sense. Pound an hour.'

'When do I start?'

Later, while Angela and Sandy are holding each other's hands in the lavatory, I ask Frankie where he found his new girlfriend.

'Perks of the job mate.'

'Nice. I'll have some of that if there's any more where she came from. I could do with a bit of Lady Ponsonby-Smythe right now.'

Frankie looks pleased with himself. 'She's the only one I'm afraid old chap – keep it under your hat but she's engaged to the geezer I've got the contract with.'

'You sly bastard.'

'I couldn't believe my luck. I mean he's not top drawer like her – just come up through the undergrowth like the rest of us – but he's worked hard for a living and made a few bob, which is where she comes in. But does she shag or what! You wouldn't believe what she's into – like everything, know what I mean? I can't keep her off me.'

Two days later I'm waiting in a café in Aldwych where I'm due to meet Frankie's main man, the guy who runs the outfit, one Keith Bull. According to Frankie we have to load a van with lighting equipment and run it along to a warehouse off the Mile End Road. Once there I'll be shown what to do next.

And all in all I'm beginning to feel much happier with my lot. The problems I've been having with the psychosis as the doctor calls it have largely cleared up, although on the odd day, usually if I'm feeling a bit low after a bout of over-indulgence, I might feel a tremor in my gut which temporarily unnerves me. But I feel that getting the chance to face up to it in hospital really did help to put the thing behind me. And the stomach problem? Well, that's gone. At least, the microscopic worms that caused it have been removed.

But the appearance of Keith Bull does little to help.

I'm sitting there drinking my coffee when in he walks. And would you believe it but it's Michael Mouse! Like mine, his hair is longer now, and he may have put on a bit of weight, but it's definitely him. He looks about, our eyes lock and he strolls over.

'Tommy Spitz?'

I stand up and we shake hands. 'Keith, nice to meet you.' But he doesn't seem to recognise me and we begin to chat about the weather and the job. He seems fair enough, relaxed, a man of the world. He describes the way the business works, how he sub-contracts to Frankie who pays me, and so on, but I can't help thinking about him all those months ago, screaming as I kicked his ribs and head. At least he's unscarred but for a slight blemish beneath his left eye. He goes on to explain that punctuality is the main thing when dealing with the clients, but when I'm at the warehouse I can please myself when I come and go providing it suits Frankie.

'Anyway,' he says, 'in between carting contracts about, when we'll be working together a lot of the time, I'll be popping into the warehouse every so often to see how you're getting on, so if you've got any problems you'll have plenty of opportunity to let me know. The secret to all this stuff's teamwork and reliability. It's how I made my name.'

Sure enough, a few days later he turns up at the warehouse while I'm crashed-out on one of the prop sofas we have in store. I'm fast asleep, snoring, my feet resting on the back of a papier maché Egyptian temple lion, after a heavy night dope-smoking with a few friends.

It's the laughter that wakes me, the laughter of a male and female, and when I jump up, standing before me are Keith and Angela, arm in arm.

'Bloody hell, I must've dropped off . . .'

'Don't worry about it. We all have late nights. How's it going Tommy? I hear you've caught up with the Royal's backlog.'

'Yeh, yeh . . . we brought the last load in yesterday. The old man was well pleased.'

'I got the contract by promising we could do it, well done. You'd better ask Frankie for a rise.' He laughs.

But I hate being talked down to, like I'm a worker and they're the bosses. Yeh, I know in theory they are, but I'm just doing this to save money to clear off again. And Frankie's my mate. Keith's just Michael Mouse who had his head kicked once. And Frankie's shagging his bird, the one who's standing there smiling nicely at me right now.

'Oh, I'm sorry,' he adds, 'this is Angela, my fiancée, we're getting married next March.'

I stand up and shake her hand. 'Congratulations.' She looks gorgeous in her black and white Mary Quant, all legs, white lipstick and false eyelashes, but Frankie tells me in detail what she gets up to behind her future husband's back.

She doesn't let on that we've met, and after a quick look around at the props the two leave.

About a week later as I'm locking up to go home, Keith's racing-green Mini-Cooper S swerves to a stop outside and he leans over and waves. I walk over to the car.

'Keith! What brings you here?'

'Jump in. D'you fancy a pint?'

'Sure, why not. You'll have to front it because I'm skint.'

'No prob. Get in.'

We drive down through dark Wapping streets to the Prospect of Whitby and install ourselves by the window overlooking the Thames, and begin to talk. I'm wondering where it's all leading because something's a bit out of place, but all he wants to know about is Afghanistan and Pakistan, the people, the customs, the dangers, the other travellers and the religion, and he listens while I ramble on a bit too casually, interrupting only to ask more questions. He's particularly interested in the guru, Brama, and I describe the two encounters with the man.

Deep in thought he sits back, then turns to look at the murky darkness outside over the river. A tug boat hoots in the distance.

'So it's all an illusion is it?' he asks.

'Looking at it like that it has to be.'

He turns back to face me. 'D'you really believe that?'

I think about it for a few seconds, for the dramatic effect if nothing else. 'Yeh. I have to say I do. Nothing's permanent, is it – even the scientists have proved that. And time's only relative. So everything has to be an illusion. Now you see it, now you don't.'

'The funny thing is,' he says suddenly, 'I was going to kill you once.'

He's sussed me.

'Yeh, I really was. I found out everything about you, and even planned how to do it. D'you know who I am?'

'Keith Bull.'

'Who else?'

I shrug. 'Tell me. At least let me know before I die.'

He laughs half-heartedly. 'Do you remember one night about a year and a half ago, May 1967, in the Crown and Anchor?'

'Should I?' I'm bracing myself now, ready for that glass he's holding.

'Do you remember giving some bloke a bad kicking, you and your mate Waller, in someone's front garden after you left the pub?'

I look mystified for a bit, then allow the dawn of realisation to creep across my face. 'Fuck! Was that you?'

'That was me.'

'Shit.'

A long silence as we stare at each other. Finally he speaks again. 'Since I've got to know you Tommy, I think you're all right – you're nothing like the person I had the bad luck to meet that night. All this feeling of revenge I've been sitting on, waiting for you to come back, has gone. There's no way I could have a go at you now. But I couldn't believe it when I walked into that café and saw you sitting there.' He managed a bitter laugh.

'Weird.' But I knew it was all bullshit: if he really wanted revenge he would have had me there and then. No, he was trying to come to terms with his self-respect after discovering that he was still too scared to fight – after kidding himself for eighteen months that he would get his own back. He'd survived on that.

It's a good thing he doesn't know about Frankie and Angela . . .

'Listen,' he says suddenly, 'I've got to go see someone. Here's a tenner . . .' he drops the note on the table, 'have a drink on me and get a cab home. I'll see you later.' And he ups and leaves. Just like that.

Poor old Michael Mouse. I can hear his Mini roar away in the distance.

Poor old Michael Mouse. Some people's lives are shit . . .

Next day I'm sweeping up in the warehouse when Frankie strides in. 'Best put that broom down – work ends here.'

'Yeh? Why's that?'

'It's Keith, that's why – he's gone and topped hisself. Well, don't stand there like a prat with your mouth open . . . we'll have to sort out how we're going to get paid . . .'

'Paid? What do you mean he's topped hisself?'

'He caught me giving Angie one last night and threw hisself off the top of the flats, silly bastard. He owes me five hundred pounds . . .'